By Lynsay Sands

Vampires Like It Hot
Twice Bitten
Immortally Yours
Immortal Unchained
Immortal Nights
Runaway Vampire
About a Vampire
The Immortal Who Loved Me
Vampire Most Wanted
One Lucky Vampire
Immortal Ever After
The Lady Is a Vamp
Under a Vampire Moon
The Reluctant Vampire
Hungry For You
Born to Bite
The Renegade Hunter
The Immortal Hunter
The Rogue Hunter
Vampire, Interrupted
Vampires Are Forever
The Accidental Vampire
Bite Me if You Can
A Bite to Remember
Tall, Dark & Hungry
Single White Vampire
Love Bites
A Quick Bite

The Highlander's Promise
Surrender to the Highlander
Falling for the Highlander
The Highlander Takes a Bride
To Marry a Scottish Laird
An English Bride in Scotland
The Husband Hunt
The Heiress
The Countess
The Hellion and the Highlander
Taming the Highland Bride
Devil of the Highlands

The Loving Daylights

VAMPIRES LIKE IT HOT

LYNSAY SANDS

VAMPIRES LIKE IT HOT

AN ARGENEAU NOVEL

AVONBOOKS

An Imprint of HarperCollins*Publishers*

This is a work of fiction. Names, characters, places, and incidents are products of the author's imagination or are used fictitiously and are not to be construed as real. Any resemblance to actual events, locales, organizations, or persons, living or dead, is entirely coincidental.

 For information, address HarperCollins Publishers, 195 Broadway, New York, NY 10007.

First Avon Books mass market printing: October 2018
First Avon Books hardcover printing: September 2018

Print Edition ISBN: 978-0-06-285516-9
Digital Edition ISBN: 978-0-06-285514-5

FIRST EDITION

18 19 20 21 22 LSC 10 9 8 7 6 5 4 3 2 1

VAMPIRES LIKE IT HOT

Prologue

"It's hot, huh?"

Raffaele grimaced at his cousin Zanipolo's comment and glanced down the length of his reclining body again to ensure he was still fully in the shade of the umbrella. He was, but it didn't seem to make much difference when it came to the early-morning heat. Damn, it *was* hot. Humid too, and that was worse. He'd lived more than two thousand years and yet had never traveled to a place where the humidity was 88 percent as it was here in Punta Cana. That was a choice. Raffaele disliked feeling sticky for no reason. Sweating due to hard labor was one thing, but being coated with dampness when just standing still was not pleasant to his mind.

Sighing, he leaned back on the lounge chair and squinted unhappily around the sun-drenched beach. They'd flown in that morning, landing at 5 A.M. After settling into their room at the resort, Zani had insisted on coming out for a swim before the sun rose and they retired to sleep the day away. Raffaele had agreed to accompany him, but had got out of the ocean first and, feeling zapped by the heat and humidity already in evidence at that early hour, had lain down on a lounge chair on the beach for a nap. He'd told Zanipolo to wake him when he was ready to return to their room.

Zani hadn't woken him. Instead, Raffaele had woken up on his own three hours later . . . by which time the beach was filling with people and the sun was high in the sky. Now he was stuck here until nightfall unless he wanted to expose himself to the damaging rays of the sun and have to dig deep into their stash of blood to repair that damage, which he didn't want to do. Getting more blood wasn't like ordering a margarita here on the beach, especially in the Dominican Republic. It got complicated in countries like this, so why cause all that trouble when he was perfectly safe and could avoid the necessity simply by staying where he was?

Mind you, it meant their cousin Santo was left alone up in their room. The thought made Raffaele glance back toward the resort's buildings. Santo was the reason they were on this trip. Not that he'd wanted to come. They were here at the insistence of Lucian Argeneau, the head of the North American Council. While they were Europeans and shouldn't really fall under his purview, the man had pull pretty much everywhere. He was also a relative by marriage now. Sort of.

Raffaele frowned briefly over the complexity of Lucian Argeneau's relationship to his family, and then shrugged it away in favor of worrying about his cousin Santo . . . and he *was* worried about him. Santo Notte was quiet and grim by nature, but had been even grimmer than usual the last fourteen months since their "adventures" in Venezuela. The poor bastard had been one of the hunters kidnapped near the end of the ordeal, and he'd basically been tortured by the madman Dr. Dressler. Physically, Santo had recovered quickly once they'd rescued him and the other Enforcers who had been taken, but psychologically . . .

Raffaele's mouth tightened grimly. Everyone had been upset when Dr. Dressler had avoided capture and fled Venezuela, but Santo had taken it worse than most. His determination to find the scientist who had put him through such torture verged on obsession. It was all he thought about anymore.

The way Raffaele saw it, Dressler wouldn't make it to the Council for judgment if Santo was the one to find him. He would have the man's head. Which was fine, really. There was a Kill-on-Sight order on Dressler. The man was just too dangerous to both mortal and immortal alike to risk losing him again . . . if they ever found him.

Unfortunately, after more than a year of fruitless searching, there had been no sign of Dressler, and Santo wasn't taking it well. He was angry, frustrated, and even more withdrawn than he had been before the torture. His nightmares weren't helping, Raffaele was sure. While Santo had always had them, they were more frequent now and, if the screams that woke him—and everyone else—from sleep were anything to judge by, more violent. Worse than all of that, though, while Santo insisted on helping the hunters search for Dressler, he had begun to ignore the orders Mortimer gave and started rushing into rogue nests without caution or care. He was taking risks that put not only his own life in danger, but the lives of the hunters who worked with him.

That wasn't acceptable behavior, and Raffaele hadn't been surprised when Lucian Argeneau and their uncle Julius had got together and decided Santo needed some counseling. They basically forced him to talk to Gregory Hewitt, an immortal psychologist who was also married to Lucian's niece, Lissianna Argeneau. Raffaele hadn't been terribly surprised when the man didn't get far with him. Santo had never been much of a talker. After three sessions, Greg had suggested Santo be forced to take a break and see if that helped.

Of course, Santo hadn't wanted to take this break. In fact, he'd at first refused, and announced that he intended to continue his hunt for Dressler with, or without, the Enforcers. Only Julius and Lucian threatening to approach the Council about performing a 3-on-1 to erase the unpleasant memories had made him give in. Once they had his reluctant agreement, Raffaele and Zani had been enlisted to accompany him. They were supposed to keep an eye on him, and make sure that he relaxed. If they didn't see some improvement in him over this enforced holiday, Santo would be in for another round of counseling on their return. If that failed, a 3-on-1 was inevitable.

A 3-on-1 was a procedure where three immortals merged together and wiped away the memories of a fourth individual, and Raffaele was a bit torn on the issue. On one hand, a 3-on-1 might be the best thing for his cousin. The man had a score of bad memories to remove. Dressler was not the first to torture him. On the other hand, it was a risky business, with all sorts of possible drawbacks, including leaving the immortal in question a drooling idiot, which was why it had been outlawed unless condoned by the Council. On the other hand, dead was no better, and if it worked and gave Santo some peace and the ability to sleep without night terrors that left him screaming and thrashing . . . well, maybe it was for the best.

Sighing, Raffaele turned away from the buildings and relaxed on the recliner again. By his estimation, Santo should be asleep by now in their room, and no doubt shrieking his head off as he struggled with the nightmares that plagued him. In truth, the beach, hot as it was, would probably be more restful . . . if he could actually risk falling asleep here now that the sun was up.

"Drink, *señor*?"

Raffaele glanced at the waiter who now stood at the end of his lounge chair. The man was bent at the waist to peer at him under the thatched umbrella.

"No . . . Thank you." The last part was almost a sigh. It was only nine thirty in the morning, for God's sake, far too early for alcohol. Not that he bothered with alcohol, but mortals did and even for them it must surely be too early? But this was the third time he'd had to say "no thank you," and by his reckoning, he'd have to say it again in about fifteen minutes either to the same eager waiter, or to another one of the men in orange shorts and shirts carrying trays around the beach.

"He'll have water," Zanipolo announced. "And a margarita. The same for me."

When Raffaele scowled at him, Zanipolo shrugged. "You need to stay hydrated."

"Right, 'cause liquor hydrates so well," Raffaele said dryly.

"No, but it will look to others like you're relaxed and fun and ready to party, rather than the grumpy old bastard you are," Zanipolo said lightly.

Raffaele grunted at that, and then demanded irritably, "Tell me again why you didn't wake me up when you got out of the water so we could return to our room to sleep?"

"We'll never find life mates hiding out in the hotel room all day long," Zanipolo pointed out. "This is where we need to be to catch one."

"Right. Here on the beach in the Dominican Republic . . . in *May*, for God's sake," he said with disgust, and then muttered, "I can't believe I let you take charge of making arrangements for this trip. What was wrong with Italy? Or anywhere it wouldn't be so hot and humid?"

"We've spent our entire lives avoiding the sun and places like this," Zanipolo said with exaggerated patience, probably because it was the tenth time he'd had to say it since they'd landed. "Instead, we search clubs and other nightspots for our life mates. But Christian found his life mate at a resort like this." He paused and raised his eyebrows, as if that were a significant point, and then continued, "Maybe we've been looking in the wrong spots. Maybe one of these sunny spots we've always avoided is where we will actually find our life mates."

Raffaele heaved a sigh, shook his head, and leaned back on the lounge chair. While Zanipolo's suggestion had made sense back in Canada, where it was cooler, now that they were here, Raffaele didn't see how they could catch anything in this place . . . other than heatstroke. Unable to risk the sun, they couldn't swim, couldn't play volleyball, and couldn't participate in anything else that might allow them to actually interact with females. All they could do was lie there on the loungers in the relative safety of the umbrella's shade and wait for night so they could actually move. By that time, he'd no doubt be stiff from the damned hard lounge chair and too exhausted to catch anything but some z's.

"Take a nap," Zanipolo suggested.

"I can't," Raffaele muttered grumpily.

"Why?"

"The sun moves," he pointed out with exasperation. "It could move enough that I'm no longer in the shade and I'd get burned. I need to stay awake to guard against that."

"I'll tell you if you need to move," Zanipolo assured him.

"Like you told me you were done swimming?" Raffaele asked grimly.

"You told me to wake you when I was *ready* to return to our room, not when I was done swimming," Zanipolo said firmly, and then grinned. "I am not yet ready to go in."

Raffaele grimaced with irritation and closed his eyes. The little pipsqueak was right. He *had* said that—a stupid oversight on his part. Next time, he'd have to be more careful in his choice of words.

"Did you notice the marks on that girl when she walked past us?" Zanipolo asked suddenly.

Sighing, Raffaele opened his eyes and glanced around. Despite the early hour, there were at least fifty females in the near vicinity, and while more than half of them were over forty, they were still just girls to an immortal who had seen as many centuries as he had. "Which girl? What marks?"

"The blonde in the yellow bikini," Zanipolo said, pointing.

Raffaele followed his gesture to a young woman in a large crowd of people in their mid-twenties. They were gathered in a circle between the rows of lounge chairs just a little to the right of them, chatting and laughing. Raffaele's gaze slid over her. She had a killer figure, but he didn't see anything unusual. "Okay. What marks?"

"Her neck."

Raffaele raised his gaze, pausing on the marks in question.

"What do you think?" Zanipolo asked after a moment of silence.

"I think we're sharing the resort with a vampire," Raffaele said solemnly, and was vaguely aware of the other man turning to peer at him with surprise. He usually didn't use that term to refer to one of their kind. None of them did. It was an insult in their eyes. Vampires were dead and soulless creatures who crawled out of their graves to feed on mortals. Raffaele and his kind were immortals, all very much alive, all still retaining their souls, and nowadays they stuck to bagged blood. However, he was cranky and felt like insulting the rogue immortal who was breaking their laws, so *vampire* it was.

"Most mortals would call *us* vampires," Zanipolo pointed out with amusement.

"Yes," Raffaele agreed, watching as the woman laughed and then started to turn away from the group. "But we aren't biters."

"Well, except in a pinch," Zanipolo pointed out, and then glanced back to the blonde as she headed toward the buildings. Pursing his lips thoughtfully, he added, "Maybe her biter wasn't a rogue immortal, but a good one in a pinch."

"Yeah. And maybe Frosty the Snowman will visit us here," Raffaele said, his gaze narrowing as it moved to the others in the group.

"Such cynicism," Zanipolo admonished.

"Not cynicism," he assured him. "Take a closer look at her friends, but not the necks."

As Zanipolo followed his suggestion, Raffaele slid his own gaze over the group again. Each individual had similar marks . . . two holes, about the same distance apart give or take a millimeter or so. But the others didn't have them on the neck. One bore the mark on the inner curve of the elbow, another the wrist, another the ankle. One fellow even had them on his inner thigh, quite visible below the tight Speedo swimsuit he wore.

Eyes narrowed, Raffaele quickly scanned the other sunbathers around them, before adding, "And that group on our left."

"A nest," Zanipolo breathed with dismay as he noted the marks on the group of four, seated three lounge chairs over from them.

"That's what it looks like to me," Raffaele said quietly.

"What do we do?" Zanipolo asked with a frown.

Raffaele drew his gaze away from the group and let it slide to the ocean as he shrugged. "You've got your cell phone. Call Lucian or Mortimer. They'll know who runs the Rogue Hunters here in the Dominican Republic and can give them a heads-up."

"If there even are Rogue Hunters here," Zanipolo said with concern. "Is this part of the purview of the South American Council?"

Raffaele was silent for a moment and then said, "Whether it is or not, Lucian will know what to do."

"Yeah," Zanipolo muttered, and reached for the cell phone lying on his towel between the chairs. "I'll call it in."

One

"Looky, looky, beautiful señorita. You like? *Sí?* You buy? Very cheap."

Jess forced a smile even as she shook her head at the stall owner walking along beside her. The man was moving backward next to her, matching her slow stride and running one hand over the many colorful wraps hanging along the front of his shop.

"But look! Is beautiful for you. Cheapy cheapy too," he protested, somehow managing to sound hurt at her lack of interest.

Jess merely shook her head again, and then moved more quickly to get away from him. Much to her relief, the man dropped away to approach someone else, his good cheer returning to his voice as he called out, "Looky, looky, beautiful señorita. Very cheap. You like? You buy?"

Jess didn't bother glancing around to see who he had approached now. She already knew that any female tourist, whether she was aged eight or eighty, fifty pounds or five hundred, was a beautiful señorita. The vendors didn't discriminate here. They were also incredibly aggressive. Jess found that a bit distressing. She didn't like attention being drawn to herself and didn't like constantly having to say no to people. It was one thing she would not miss when they headed home . . . that and the humidity. Dear God, every time she stepped out of her hotel room it was like stepping into a sauna. Not that the hotel room was much better. It was cooler, but just as wet, so that everything in it was wet too—her clothes, the bedsheets, the towels, herself. She hadn't felt dry since arriving and was sure she was going to start growing mold on her body somewhere before they left.

"I don't see our bus, but perhaps it's farther down the street," Jess said to her cousin now, glancing at the open area ahead. The gates between the vendors' stalls and the road had been wide open when they'd arrived, but were half-closed now, leaving enough room for people to walk out but not for vehicles to get through.

When Allison didn't immediately respond, Jess added, "What do you think?" She glanced around, only to stop dead when she didn't find her cousin behind her as she had been since leaving the boat.

"Allison?" She turned to peer over the mass of bodies moving toward her. A good eighty to a hundred people had been on the trip to the Seaquarium. A large boat altered to look like a pirate's ship had picked them up at the dock here and taken them out to the Seaquarium, where they'd "swum" with stingrays and sharks.

Eager to get back to land, Allison had rushed Jess off the boat at the head of the group to file back up the beach to the vending stalls. Most of their hundred shipmates were now moving toward her, a wave of people in swimsuits, some with cover-ups, some carrying bags, and most of them still wet from snorkeling at the coral reef after the Seaquarium. They moved around her like a wave around a boulder when the tide came in, all headed for the half-closed gate and the vehicles waiting beyond.

"Allie?" Jess said a little louder, not seeing her and unsure when she'd lost her.

"If you're looking for your blonde friend, she stopped to talk to one of those dangerous-looking pirates," an elderly lady in a black bathing suit and cover-up said helpfully, tipping her head up to see her from under the large straw hat she wore.

"One of the dangerous-looking pirates? You mean the performers?" Jess asked with confusion. They'd arrived onshore to a "surprise" performance by men and women dressed as pirates. They had put on a show of fighting and dancing in a circle, performing some tricks and tumbling that hadn't been half-bad. Certainly, they had been better than the dance show the crew had performed on the boat. Still, Jess wouldn't have called them dangerous looking . . . a little dashing, perhaps, but not dangerous.

"No. Not them. One of the ones who came to mix and mingle with the crowd after the performers' show ended," the old woman explained.

"Oh," Jess murmured, glancing past the woman toward the stalls and stores again. Hot, tired, suffering sore feet, and basically sick of listening to Allison's whining, she'd agreed easily when the other girl had insisted they start back to the bus before the show had ended. It was hard to imagine she'd then just suddenly decided to stop to chat up one of the men in costume. Although her cousin did tend to find "dangerous-looking" men attractive, she thought on a sigh. For Allison, well-muscled men in tight leather pants were like cream to a cat. Throw in some tattoos and a clean-shaven head and he became catnip.

Jess thanked the elderly lady, and then started back toward the stalls, her eyes scanning the people moving her way. She couldn't see Allison. For that matter, she couldn't see any dangerous-looking pirates. At least not in the immediate throng surrounding her, but then she noted small clusters of people moving in the opposite direction and back toward the dock. They were mostly twosomes consisting of someone, male or female, in a pirate's costume and a member of the opposite sex in beach clothes, but there were a few trios as well. Jess quickly scanned them, breathing a little sigh of relief when she spotted Allison's pale blond hair. She'd had it cornrowed by a strolling vendor on the beach the day before and the red and teal beads threaded through it were quite distinctive.

Allison was walking back toward the boat they'd just left, clinging to the arm of a good-looking pirate with dark hair and swarthy skin. Jess's eyebrows rose as she took in his clothes. While the costumes the earlier performers had worn had been good, they'd still obviously been costumes. In comparison, this man's outfit looked almost authentic . . . or perhaps it was just his confidence and swagger that made him look like he could have stepped out of a Renaissance version of *GQ* if they'd published a "Bad Boys of the Sea" issue. In a billowing white shirt, dark pants, a bloodred sash around his waist, brown leather boots, and a large tricorn captain's hat also in weathered brown leather with metal rivets along the rim, he looked every inch a pirate captain. Jess had to admit that she understood how he'd caught Allison's eye. He did cut quite a dashing figure. Still, just moments ago Allison had been whining about the boat ride, having sand up her crack, and being seasick, exhausted, and eager to return to the resort. This was a rather sudden about-face, even by her flighty standards.

For one moment, Jess considered just returning to the bus as planned and waiting there for her cousin to join her. After all, the bus wouldn't leave until they were all on it, and if Allison dawdled too long, the bus driver would no doubt go fetch her back himself. But she had promised Krista—her cousin, and Allison's younger sister—that she'd keep the woman out of trouble during this trip and Jess took her promises seriously.

Muttering under her breath, she started resignedly forward, weaving her way through the happily exhausted crowd, to follow the couple. Her resignation turned to irritation after a moment, though. Jess had expected the man to lead Allison back to the stalls and try to sell her a trinket. That was what most of the people here had seemed to be about.

Instead, the man was following several other couples back toward the boat they'd just disembarked. Allison, who was supposedly exhausted and seasick, was going willingly, even eagerly, gazing up at him wide-eyed and hanging off him like a leech.

"Allison!" Jess shouted, moving a little more quickly through the shifting sand. Much to her relief, Allison paused. The other woman even glanced back, albeit with confusion, as if she'd forgotten all about her and hadn't a clue why she'd be shouting her name with such irritation.

"The bus?" Jess called with exasperation, continuing forward. "Come on!"

Allison hesitated, but then her attention returned to the man she was walking with as he said something. Nodding, Allison turned suddenly to hurry back to Jess.

"What are you thinking walking off like that without—?" She paused with surprise when Allison latched on to her arm and began to drag her back toward the pirate, who had continued to walk.

"We're going to feed the sharks and Vasco says you can come too," Allison said, urging her along.

"What? Hang on," Jess muttered, dragging her feet. "I thought you were tired and hot and seasick and—"

"Oh, that was just to make Krista miserable. I feel fine," Allison assured her.

"What?" Jess immediately dug her feet into the sand, resisting her pull. She had suspected that was the case all along, but hearing her admit it outright was rather shocking.

"You heard me," Allison said with unconcern and a complete lack of shame as she tugged a little harder. "She's had things entirely too much her way this trip and I wanted her to feel bad."

"Of course she's had things her way. *It's her wedding trip*," Jess said with disbelief. "This trip is all about her and Pat."

"This last year *everything* has been about her," Allison muttered with irritation. "Ever since they announced their engagement it's been gifts and congratulations for Krista and Pat, showers for Krista, a stag and doe for them, and then all this planning and fuss. What about me?" she asked plaintively. "I wanted them to have the wedding in the spring when the weather was better here, but no, they had to have it at the end of May when it's the off-season, hot as hell, twice as humid, and there are no hunks to play with. Would it have hurt her to have it in February or March?"

"A lot of their friends are students, or newly graduated. They had classes still in February and March. Besides, it was cheaper for them to come here in May. The high season is expensive," Jess said with a frown. "And Pat and Krista wanted to marry a year to the day after he proposed."

"Yeah, well, *I* want to have some fun," Allison said grimly. "Now hurry up or they'll leave without us."

"Let them," Jess growled. "The bus is waiting, and can't leave until everyone is on board. We have to go."

"No. You go wait on that hot airless bus if you want, but I'm going with Vasco."

"Oh, for God's sake, Allison," Jess muttered, trying to draw her to a halt. "You cannot seriously intend to make an entire busload of people wait hours for you to—"

"Look," Allison interrupted impatiently, waving toward the groupings of people moving toward the boat. "Several other members of our group are going to the ship. The bus'll have to wait for them too. Would you rather wait on a hot airless bus, or go with the others to feed sharks?"

Jess peered toward the people Allison was gesturing to and frowned as she recognized several people from their bus among them, including the couple who had sat in the seat in front of them. The bus *would* have to wait, she realized, and recalling how humid and uncomfortably hot it had been on the way out even with the warm breeze coming in the open windows, Jess could imagine how unbearable it would be sitting still in the heat. It would be a damned oven.

"Well?" Allison said impatiently.

"Yes, fine," Jess muttered, allowing her cousin to drag her toward the dock and the waiting boat. But as she did, Jess promised herself that she would never again get roped into even traveling with Allison, let alone taking responsibility for keeping the other woman out of trouble. It was an impossible task and not something she normally would have agreed to, except that it had been Krista who made the request. When Krista had asked her to share a room with her older sister and "keep her in line," Jess had found it impossible to say no. She knew how difficult Allison could be. In truth, Jess suspected Krista would have preferred someone else to be her maid of honor, but faced with the hell Allison would make of her life if she didn't give her that honor, and no doubt under pressure from their father, she'd bowed to the inevitable and asked her to stand up for her.

Allison, of course, had taken it as her due, even while complaining unendingly about what a bother it was. Honestly, the woman was enough to drive a person mad with frustration. She was never ready for anything on time. They had nearly missed their flight here thanks to her lollygagging. If Jess hadn't grabbed her arm and dragged her along as she'd raced through the airport, they would still be back home in Montana, reading about the wedding on Facebook.

If that weren't enough, Allison had piddled about so much on their second day here, dragging out breakfast, and then insisting on going for a swim before getting ready, that they'd nearly missed the wedding as well, and she was the maid of honor! Talk about how to stress out a bride on her wedding day. As the maid of honor, Allison was supposed to help and support the bride. Instead, she'd had poor Krista in tears with her nonsense.

It wasn't just that, though; Allison was contrary as hell. The whole wedding party had flown here for two weeks and all the younger members of the party had been mostly hanging out together whether it was relaxing at the beach, hitting the disco, or eating dinner. But it never failed that if everyone else wanted Mexican, Allison wanted Italian. If everyone wanted to go to a concert on the beach, she wanted to go to a club in town. Even today, she'd wanted to go ziplining rather than the Seaquarium and had argued strenuously for her preferred pastime, stressing everyone out.

Spoiled rotten by an overindulgent father who felt guilty about the divorce that had left him a single parent, Allison was far too used to getting her own way, and made life unpleasant for anyone who didn't immediately fall in with her plans. That being the case, everyone usually simply gave in to her rather than risk her wrath, but this trip, no one seemed willing to indulge her wants and demands. This trip was about the bride and groom, Krista and Pat. Whatever they wanted, everyone else had agreed with, which had done nothing but infuriate Allison, who disliked not getting her way over her younger sister. She'd made life as miserable as she could for anyone she could with her constant complaints about the resort, the heat, etc., and since Jess was her roommate for this trip, that meant it was most often her who got to listen.

"Never again," she promised herself grimly as she followed Allison past the large barge that had been made to look like a pirate ship, and to a slightly smaller sloop that actually could have *been* a pirate ship. Like the crew's costumes that looked so authentic, so did this ship, and Jess felt a shiver of trepidation as she followed Allison up the gangplank.

"Ah. You convinced your friend to join us."

Jess had been peering at the masts, sails, and the skull and crossbones flag as she stepped on board, but shifted her attention quickly to the pirate Allison had called Vasco, as he approached. The man was simply gorgeous, she acknowledged as her gaze slid over his wide smile and beautiful green eyes. He was also incredibly big, she noted, as he slid between her and Allison and draped a heavy arm around each of them.

"And so pretty too," he declared, beaming down at Jess as he urged them through the people milling around the ship's deck. "I am the luckiest of men tonight."

Jess smiled a little stiffly at the comment. He made it sound like they were going to be having a threesome, and that wasn't anything she was interested in signing up for. He was a good-looking guy, but she didn't know him from Adam. She did know Allison, though. Her cousin was a pain in the ass and the very last person she would consider having a threesome with. Not that she was the threesome type anyway, but that wasn't the point.

"Everyone's on board, Capitan."

Jess glanced around at that announcement, her eyes widening slightly as she found herself staring at a Johnny Depp wannabe. The guy had the same mustache, goatee, and dreadlocks kept out of his face by the same dirty beige bandanna that Depp sported as the character Captain Jack Sparrow. He even wore the same type costume: dark brown pantaloons, dirty white top, and a dark brown vest. The only thing missing was the captain's hat.

"Good, tell the men to cast off," Vasco said, his expression stern and his tone all business. His smile and charm were back in place when he glanced from Jess to Allison, though. Like a mask, she thought as he said, "It breaks me heart, lasses, but I've work to do now. You're welcome to join me at the helm while I steer us out, though."

"Oh, yes," Allison said eagerly, still clinging to his arm and accompanying him toward the stairs to an upper deck at the back of the ship where a large wooden steering wheel waited.

Jess was slower to follow, her gaze sliding around the large ship and the people on it. The crew were all moving to perform their individual tasks, leaving the visitors they'd brought on board to look around and chat among themselves. Jess recognized four or five young people from their wedding group, as well as several other people from their hotel who had traveled out with them on the same bus, but Krista and Pat weren't among them. She wasn't terribly surprised. Even if Krista had been interested in this jaunt to feed the sharks, that interest would have died the minute she saw that Allison planned to go. Jess couldn't blame her. She just hoped it didn't mean the couple was sitting in the hot bus waiting for them. Hopefully, she and Pat had caught a taxi back to the hotel, where they could enjoy a massage on the beach, or a swim or something.

"Lass?"

Jess glanced toward Vasco at his call. He had stopped walking and was peering back at her with raised eyebrows.

"Are you coming?" he asked, seeming completely oblivious to the way Allison hung off his arm and stared up at his chiseled face with adoring eyes. "There's a nice breeze at the helm once we're moving."

It was the promise of a breeze that decided it for her. Jess really couldn't bear this stifling heat and humidity. Nodding, she joined them and allowed Vasco to take her elbow to usher her up the steps to the upper deck, which she thought might be called the quarterdeck, although she wasn't sure. Jess was no sailor.

"Now, you two lovelies just stand here by me and look pretty. It'll keep you out of the way while we men work," Vasco said cheerfully as he led them to the helm.

Jess's mouth tightened at the comment. Good Lord, could he sound any more sexist? Just barely managing to refrain from rolling her eyes, she ignored his suggestion and moved to the side of the ship to peer down at the dock below as members of the crew pulled in the gangplank. Her gaze slid to the beach then and she noted that it was nearly empty of people now. The only ones remaining were the stall workers who were closing up shop. It seemed theirs had been the last tour of the day to the Seaquarium, which made her glance instinctively at her wrist. Jess grimaced as her naked wrist reminded her that she wasn't wearing her watch. It wasn't waterproof, and she hadn't wanted to risk taking it off and possibly losing it, or having it stolen at the Seaquarium.

She shifted her gaze to the sky to find the sun's position, and her eyes widened slightly as she noted how low it was. The sun had nearly reached the horizon. They'd been out at the Seaquarium for much longer than she'd realized and the daylight would soon be gone. The sun had seemed to set about ten or fifteen minutes before seven the two nights they'd been here so far, so she guessed it was probably around or just after 6 P.M. now. That explained the grumbling in her stomach, she supposed, and thought that the members of their group that hadn't come on the shark feed would be impatient to get back and have their dinner.

Jess glanced toward the beach again, but this time noticed that she could see the road from the ship . . . and their bus was leaving. On the one hand, she was relieved everyone wouldn't be left sitting there waiting for them, but now she had to worry about how they were going to get back to the resort. Would the bus return for those who had been lured on this trip to feed the sharks? If not, she supposed they'd just have to hire a taxi.

Jess's next thought was to wonder if there would be snacks offered on the boat ride out. There had been both snacks and drinks on the trip out to the Seaquarium, but that had been hours ago now. It had been included in the fee for the tour.

That thought made her wonder about the fee for this little jaunt. Surely it wasn't free? Glancing around, she caught Allison's eye and waved her over. Her cousin hesitated, peering toward Vasco before reluctantly moving over to join her.

"What?" Allison asked irritably.

"What is the fare for this tour?" Jess asked, ignoring her surliness. It wasn't like it was new.

Allison shrugged with disinterest. "Vasco didn't mention a fare. He just asked if I wanted to go with them to feed the sharks."

"Well, maybe you should ask," Jess suggested with exasperation. "Nothing in life is free, Allison, and if it's too damned expensive, I'll want off."

"Fine," she snapped, and stomped back to Vasco. Jess noted that her attitude changed the moment she got close to the man, though, and watched with disgust as Allison simpered and mewled at him. Honestly, she'd never thought much of her cousin, but this trip was making her positively loathe the woman. Not only would Jess not be traveling with her again, but she was starting to think she might want to avoid any future family gatherings the woman attended. Jess didn't know how Krista had put up with her for so long without killing her, or at least cutting out her nasty tongue. She didn't think she would have managed to avoid doing one or the other if Allison was her sister.

A warm breeze and the crackle and snap of the sails distracted Jess then and she glanced around to see that they'd moved away from the dock and were heading out to deeper water. It was too late to get off now. She'd have to pay the fare whether she liked it or not. Jess just hoped the price wasn't too steep.

"Rogue immortals?" Santo echoed the words as if he'd never heard them before. "Here?"

Raffaele nodded solemnly. It was after 6 P.M., and the sun had finally got so low in the sky that returning to the hotel had been more feasible. They'd returned to find Santo up and dressed and preparing to come find them. After explaining where they'd been, Raffaele had quickly told him about their discovery on the beach.

"What immortal would be stupid enough to live here in this hellish heat?" Santo asked.

"Apparently, one who knows you can feed indiscriminately and not be taken to task for it," Raffaele said, and when Santo raised his eyebrows, he explained, "Zani called Lucian first thing this morning about it. He said he'd contact the local Enforcers and have them contact us, but we haven't heard anything yet. It's looking like they can't be bothered about it."

"Maybe I should call Lucian again," Zanipolo suggested. "See what news he has."

"That or we could just leave it up to the locals to deal with," Raffaele said, nodding slightly toward Santo. They were supposed to be ensuring their cousin relaxed, after all, not getting him involved in another hunt.

"It could be Dressler," Santo said suddenly, his face tight. "He likes warm-weather places."

"There were too many people bitten for it to be one man," Raffaele said, his voice soothing.

"Yeah," Zanipolo agreed. "We saw dozens of mortals with bite marks out there on the beach today."

Santo's eyebrows rose. "And none of them are wondering about it? About where they're all getting the bite marks?"

"They all have it in their heads that it's a couple of insect bites close together," Raffaele said in a dry voice. He'd started reading the minds of the passing sunbathers with bites to find out why they weren't all freaking out. "But it is definitely more than one immortal feeding on the guests."

"Dressler could have turned minions," Santo argued at once. "He's had a year to do it. In that time, he could have turned dozens of them, and I wouldn't put it past the bastard to create his own army."

Raffaele frowned. That was a possibility he hadn't considered. Good Lord, Dressler creating an army of immortals. It was a scary thought, and one he suspected the man would enjoy. Dressler was just the sort of megalomaniac who would love to have an army of flunkies at his beck and call.

"I'll call Lucian and see what he's heard," Zanipolo decided, and headed for the bedroom, pulling his phone out of the beach bag he'd dragged down to the shore with them.

Raffaele watched him go and then glanced worriedly toward Santo. They were supposed to see that he relaxed this trip. Finding themselves in the midst of a nest of rogue immortals was not relaxing.

"He must be here at the resort," Santo said suddenly. "He's living here and turned the staff."

Raffaele raised his eyebrows with surprise. "The resort staff?"

Santo nodded and pointed out, "They'd have access to the rooms. They could creep in while the guests were sleeping, or hell, while they were awake, and simply take control of them."

Raffaele shook his head at once. "I haven't encountered any immortals on staff."

"We only got here at 5 A.M.," Santo pointed out. "Other than the man who checked us in, there was no one around, and then you two headed straight down to the beach for a swim. The only staff you've encountered are day workers. The immortals wouldn't work the day shift. They'd work nights."

Unfortunately, Raffaele couldn't argue with that logic.

"Lucian isn't picking up. I got his voice mail," Zanipolo announced, returning from the bedroom. "I left a message."

Raffaele nodded and then caught Santo's arm as he headed for the door. "Where are you going?"

"To see if there are immortals on staff," Santo said grimly, trying to tug his arm free, but Raffaele held fast.

"Just wait a damned minute for us to get changed and we'll go with you," he said, his voice short. "We can have a quick look around and then hit one of the restaurants so Zani can have dinner, and we'll check out the staff there too. But a look is all we're doing," he added firmly. "We're on vacation, remember? You're supposed to be relaxing. So, we'll see if we spot any immortals on staff and pass that info on to the immortal Enforcers when they show up, but that's all. Got it?"

When Santo scowled at him without responding, Raffaele added, "I really don't want you to have to go through a 3-on-1, *cugino*, and you know Julius and Lucian will insist on one if we don't help you get past what happened to you on the island. We need to concentrate on that, not on yet more rogues."

Santo closed his eyes, his body slumping slightly as he nodded in acquiescence.

Relieved, Raffaele released his arm and patted his shoulder as he moved past him. "We'll be quick about changing."

Two

Jess slid out of the tiny ship's bathroom, and then hesitated in the narrow hall, not eager to return above deck. Apparently "feed the sharks" was Punta Cana–speak for *party.* At least, that was the only thing she could think. They'd been sailing for a good hour now without stopping, and the sun had set. It didn't seem likely to her that they'd "feed the sharks" in the dark. After all, why bother if they couldn't see them eating?

Aside from that, the moment the sun had disappeared there had been a distinct change in the crew. Music had been turned on, and was now pounding from speakers all over the ship. Then clothes had started to disappear. Every single male crewmember had stripped off their shirts, vests, and jackets and were now running around in just their pantaloons. The female members of the crew weren't even wearing that. They'd stripped down to bikinis that were sexy enough to heat up the ship without the glare of the sun to aid it.

Vasco was the only one who hadn't stripped. He still wore the same outfit he had when Allison had dragged her to him, but his personality had definitely changed, although she couldn't exactly pinpoint how. He hadn't seemed tense before, so it wasn't exactly that he seemed more relaxed. And the man was still charming, but there was an added something to his attitude. Perhaps a touch of anticipation, combined with a sly smile that she'd caught at times, as if he was secretly amused at something he knew and they didn't.

Jess found it a bit disconcerting, and was reluctant to return to the helm. Especially since Vasco planned to show them the captain's cabin when she did. At least, that was what he'd said as she'd slipped away to find the bathroom he'd given her directions to. "I'll have my first mate, Cristoval, take over the wheel when you return and will show you and your cousin my cabin."

There hadn't been anything suggestive in his words or tone, but the hungry way he'd looked her over as he'd said it had made her leery.

A startled half cry that was quickly cut off caught her ear and Jess peered along the hall in the direction it had come from. It had sounded like a cry of pain, and it had come from the back of the ship. The opposite direction to the one she needed to take to return to the deck. That in itself was reason enough for Jess to decide she should check it out and make sure everything was okay. After all, someone might have had an accident and need help. Right?

Jess moved along the hall, looking through the doors she passed. Every single one was open. Through each one she saw a small bed built into the wall and other furnishings. Every room she passed was presently unoccupied. The hall ended at a doorway without a door. It opened into a large room that appeared to run from one side of the ship to the other. It was also a good fifteen or twenty feet deep.

Pausing in the entry, Jess peered curiously around, noting the cupboards and the two long wooden tables, each with benches on either side. It was obviously where the crew ate, she thought, and believing it to be empty, started to turn to leave, but stopped when she spotted a couple several feet away along the wall. One of the men from the wedding party and one of the female crew stood about ten feet away from her. Well, he was actually sagging against the wall, held up by the woman kneeling before him. She was pressing him against the wall with a hand at his stomach. Her other hand was wrapped around the base of his penis before it disappeared into her mouth.

Jess wasn't a Peeping Tom. Normally, she would have averted her eyes and retreated quickly to give them their privacy . . . if that was what you could call going down on someone in a public room. However, this time Jess didn't retreat. She was held transfixed, her attention caught by the sight of the bright red blood dripping from the woman's chin and splashing onto the wooden floor.

Horror rising within her, Jess lifted her gaze to the man's face. She didn't know him. He was a guest of the groom's, but she'd been introduced to everyone and thought his name was Tyler. He'd seemed a nice enough guy, friendly and cheerful, but right now he was staring down at the woman with his mouth open on a silent scream of horror and pain.

"Mmm, good."

Jess jerked her gaze down to the woman at that, and found she'd released Tyler's poor abused and bleeding member and was peering at her with a wide smile on her bloody face . . . a smile that revealed two long and pointy, bloodstained fangs.

"I bet you're tasty too," the woman added, smacking her lips obscenely. "Too bad you're Vasco's dinner tonight. Maybe another time, hmm?"

"Jessica!"

Jess turned her head sharply at that call, and peered up the hall to where Allison now stood scowling at her from the bottom of the steps leading up to the main deck.

"Come on," her cousin said with irritation. "Vasco won't show me his cabin without you. He sent me to fetch you while he waits for his first mate, Cristo."

"Run along, little one," the creature with Tyler said with amusement. "You shouldn't keep Vasco waiting. He has a temper. Besides, he's not like me. He'll make sure you enjoy it. I promise."

When Jess turned to peer at the woman, the crewmember's gaze became concentrated and she added, "Now go to Vasco and give him a big kiss. Tell him it's from Ildaria."

Jess found herself turning and leaving the room, her only thought that she should go to Vasco.

"What were you doing?" Allison asked with annoyance as Jess approached. "I thought you had to go to the bathroom? It's up here, not back there."

"I have to go to Vasco," Jess said, continuing past her.

"No shit, I just said that," Allison snapped with irritation, hustling to keep up with her. "Hang on. Wait for me. I found him. He's mine. Remember that and clear out the first chance you get or I'll make your life miserable."

Jess didn't respond; she was already mounting the steps to the main deck. She was vaguely aware that Allison was nattering at her the whole way across the ship to the steps to the upper deck where the helm was, but nothing her cousin was saying was piercing the bubble Jess was now in. All she was really aware of was that she had to go to Vasco, kiss him, and tell him it was from Ildaria.

"Ah! There you are. I was beginning to worry." Vasco grinned at them as they stepped onto the quarterdeck. Gesturing for the tall, bare-chested pirate next to him to take the wheel, the captain stepped away from it and watched them approach. His eyebrows rose as he took in Jess's expression, though, and he murmured, "What do we have here? Have you been exploring where you shouldn't have?"

Jess didn't respond. She didn't stop either until she was directly in front of him, and then she reached up on tiptoe, slid her hand around his neck, and tugged, whispering, "From Ildaria."

Amusement curved Vasco's lips, but he lowered his head willingly for Jess to press her mouth to his. She had only intended to give him a quick peck, but the moment their lips touched, a strange, almost electric charge went through Jess and she gasped in surprise. She was vaguely aware of Allison's outraged howl, and the startled sound Vasco made, but then his mouth pressed more firmly on hers and his tongue thrust between her lips to fill her, and she was lost to a sudden and violent passion that swept through her like a tidal wave.

It was like nothing Jess had ever experienced. She was no innocent, but this was the first time she'd lost herself so completely in a simple kiss that she forgot where she was and just who she was kissing.

"*What the hell!* Jesus, Jess! I just told you he was mine! Get off of him! Get off! Get off! Get off!"

Those orders rang out in concert with the blows Allison was showering on Jessica's back and shoulders. Gasping in startled pain at a well-placed blow to her kidney, Jess tore her mouth from Vasco's and blinked with confusion as she realized that she was presently clinging to the pirate captain like a koala up a tree. His hat was gone, dislodged by her fingers, which were presently buried in his hair, still tugging in demand, and her legs were wrapped around his hips so tightly that their groins were pressed firmly together.

Shocked, Jess was about to scramble down off the man when Allison grabbed her arm and yanked hard, cussing her out the entire time for her betrayal. Jess would have fallen backward and probably would have landed headfirst if Vasco hadn't tightened his arms and saved her. Turning away from the still-shrieking Allison, he set her down gently, and then swung back to give her cousin a narrow-eyed glare. That was all. He just glared at her in a concentrated way and she settled down at once.

Apparently satisfied by her submissive behavior, he turned back to Jess and his expression changed at once. A smile eased onto his face, and he ran one finger lightly down her cheek, murmuring, "Ildaria obviously knows what I like. You are a delicious little bundle. You've actually managed to reawaken my passions. I think I might even fuck you while I feed."

Jess barely heard the words; she was too distracted by the feel of his fingers caressing her cheek and the way her body shivered in response. But when his hand fell away, she glanced nervously toward Allison to see how she was reacting to the captain's attention to her. Jess expected her cousin to be glaring daggers at her at the very least, but Allison was still and blank-faced.

"Really?" the first mate, Cristoval, said, drawing her attention back to the two men. "You haven't done that in centuries, Vasco."

"No, I haven't," Vasco agreed thoughtfully, a frown tugging at his lips as he peered at Jess.

"Have you tried to read her?" Cristoval asked.

Jess blinked in confusion at the question, but Vasco apparently understood. Straightening, he nodded slowly. "I cannot read her, but am a little fired up just now and still controlling her cousin. I will try again once I get her to my cabin. My passions should have cooled a bit by then."

Jess frowned. Her passion was cooling quickly now that she was no longer touching the man and his words were finally making their way through the clearing mist. It was raising questions in her. What did he mean he was still controlling her cousin? And had he really said he planned to fuck her while he fed? Was that why he wanted to "show them his cabin"? He planned to feed on her there? Feed like the woman Ildaria was doing to Tyler? To her mind, that made the cabin the very last place Jess wanted to go. She glanced to Allison, hoping to signal her that the cabin was a no-go and enlist her aid in avoiding it, but her cousin was still standing silent and blank-faced.

"Come."

Jess glanced around with alarm when he took her arm and started to lead her away from the helm, saying, "You've got the wheel, Cristo. Let me know when we reach international waters."

"Aye-aye, Capitan," the first mate responded, but then asked, "Have you any orders regarding Ildaria?"

Vasco stopped abruptly, his hold bringing Jess to a halt as well. She tried to tug her arm free then, but his fingers were like a vise around her upper arm. Not painfully tight, just firm.

"Ildaria?" Vasco asked now, not even seeming to notice that she was trying to get free of his hold.

Cristo nodded. "I can read the señorita, and she caught Ildaria with one of the guests . . . starting the festivities early again."

As Vasco frowned and glanced around at the night surrounding them, Cristo said, "The wind is good now that we're around the point, but there was little when we first set out. We can't be more than six or seven miles out yet," he finished meaningfully.

It was a meaning that completely escaped Jess. She had no idea what the distance they'd traveled had to do with anything. The woman, Ildaria, had been chewing on Tyler's penis like it was a pickle. And she'd had fangs! That memory had her peering anxiously toward Allison again, but while her cousin had followed them when they'd started to leave, and stopped when they'd stopped, she was now simply standing there, still looking blank-faced. She wasn't going to be any help at all in getting out of this situation.

A violent curse drew Jess's wary gaze to Vasco, and she watched nervously as he ran his free hand agitatedly through his hair. Letting his hand drop, he shook his head. "I will put the women in my cabin and then deal with Ildaria. Just let me know when we are in international waters."

Jess almost sighed her relief at the words. If Vasco left them alone in his cabin it would give her a chance to try to bring Allison around. It would also give her a bit of time to think of a way out of this mess, she thought, and then noted the concentrated way Cristo was peering at her. Afraid he was reading her thoughts, she shut them down at once.

The moment she did, a small smile tugged at the corner of his mouth, and then he glanced back to Vasco and offered, "I could get Gascon to take the helm, and deal with Ildaria for you myself. That way you need not leave the women alone."

Jess started to tense up with alarm, but Vasco shook his head and said, "I am the captain. It is my responsibility. You warned Ildaria the first time. I will warn her this last time. I want to be sure she understands the consequences if she disobeys orders again."

"Sí, Capitan," Cristo said solemnly, and then asked, "Did you want to leave the troublesome one with me?"

Much to her relief, Vasco again shook his head. "If—" he began, and then paused, his mouth hanging open briefly as he stared down at Jess.

"Jessica," Cristo said gently. "Her name is Jessica."

"Jessica," Vasco said the name softly, and smiled at her.

"Her full name is Jessica Anne Stewart," Cristo added, apparently plucking the information out of thin air. Unless Allison had told him her name at some point, Jess thought with a frown as Cristo added, "And I am quite sure she is your mate, Vasco. I am hearing your thoughts."

Vasco glanced at him sharply. "You are?"

"*Sí.* You are thinking what with Jessica being your life mate, you will need all of your strength for the marathon of sex the two of you will no doubt enjoy, so you will need the blonde to feed on." Smiling, he added, "Good thinking."

Vasco grinned back. "I like to plan ahead."

"*Sí.* It is why you make a good capitan," Cristo said on a laugh, and then waved them away. "Go tend to Ildaria, and then enjoy your life mate. I will see to the rest of this voyage, and the next several as necessary until you can crawl out from between her legs."

"Sí." Turning sharply, Vasco urged Jess to the steps.

She went willingly, but only because she was about to be escorted to his cabin and then he was going to leave, at least for a while, and she needed some alone time to figure out what the hell was going on. A lot of what the two men had said had gone right over her head. What did they mean she was his life mate? And what did the distance they were from shore have to do with anything? It was bad of Ildaria to attack Tyler six or seven miles from shore, but what? It would be okay farther out? Really? And what was that bit about Vasco's reading her? She wasn't a billboard.

Jess didn't know. Hell, even the stuff she thought she did understand didn't make much sense to her. For instance, she got the parts about needing strength for marathon sex, and the suggestion that Vasco might not "crawl out from between her legs" for a while . . . but just how long was this marathon sex? Apparently, really long, she thought as she recalled Cristo was offering to handle the "next several trips." That was alarming. Mostly because the idea of marathon sex with the big, handsome captain was exciting the hell out of her despite the fact that he was crude and a vampire and apparently planned to feed on her cousin as Ildaria had been feeding on Tyler. Well, not exactly the same way, of course. Allison didn't have a penis . . . that she knew of. Her cousin could be a dickhead at times, though, so who could say?

Grimacing, Jess glanced back to see that, yes, her cousin was still following them, and her expression was still as blank as Jess's mind had been after Ildaria had ordered her to go to Vasco and kiss him. Since she doubted Allison would want to be anyone's dinner, Jess supposed her cousin was under some kind of compulsion like the one that had sent her marching out to kiss Vasco. She figured that was some kind of vampire trick, taking control of her mind, or somehow sublimating her will, so that she did what she was told. She didn't appear to be under control anymore. At least she was able to think now, and could drag her feet and tug at his hold on her arm as she wished, she noted as she tried both options.

Allison, however, was another matter, Jess thought. She was quite sure Vasco was controlling her cousin right that minute. Because there was no way the Allison she knew could manage to remain silent this long. And certainly, obeying anyone was not her strong suit. Vasco was definitely controlling Allison.

Mouth tightening, Jess turned her gaze forward again, and glanced around at the groups of people spaced around the deck. For one mad moment, she considered shrieking at them to flee for their lives, they were among vampires. She might even have done it despite the fact that they'd probably not believe her and think her nuts, but then she noticed that the majority of the tourists on board all had the same blank expressions on their faces that Allison wore. Apparently, she was the only one left with her awareness.

Lucky me, Jess thought unhappily, almost wishing she was still being controlled and could just go along with Vasco's plans. As much as she would like to claim the man was completely abhorrent and she wanted nothing more than to get off this ship and away from him, Vasco was gorgeous! He was also one hell of a kisser. Parts of her were still humming from their first encounter . . . and would be happy to experience more.

Not good, Jess thought grimly. She needed to rein in her body's urges, or she feared she could very easily be seduced into having crazy good monkey sex with the bloodsucking vampire pirate captain . . . and probably end up a vampire herself!

That possibility went a long way toward silencing her body's humming. Jess was not interested in becoming the bride of Dracula. She liked her soul. She wanted to keep it. Which meant she needed to figure out a way to get herself out of this mess, and rescue the others while she was at it.

"Here we are. My cabin."

Jess blinked her thoughts away and peered around as they entered the room he'd led her to. She got an impression of a large room done in soothing earth tones and then her gaze landed on the huge bed against the opposite wall. When her mind immediately began to fill with images of their bodies entwined on that bed, Jess closed her eyes against it, trying to regain control of her poor hormone-hijacked brain.

"You, my lovely, can wait right here."

Forcing her eyes open, she saw with relief that he was steering her toward a desk in a corner of the room.

Halfway there, though, he stopped, and glanced around, muttering, "Or perhaps the bed."

"I think we should go above deck again," Jess said anxiously, afraid to go anywhere near the bed with this man. She might drag him onto it herself and that so would not be heroic. Or even decent, really. Nice girls didn't bang vampires, she was sure.

"Above deck?" Vasco asked with surprise.

"Well, you've shown us your cabin now," she pointed out. "And really, we should be reaching the spot where we feed the sharks soon, don't you think?"

"Oh," Vasco said nonplussed, and then a smile pulled at his lips and he cupped her face with both his hands. "You do not understand yet. How sweet."

Jess grimaced, unimpressed at being thought an idiot. "You're not even going to pretend anymore that there are sharks, huh?"

Eyebrows rising slightly, he grinned. "So you *do* know?"

"That there are no sharks and that this 'feed the sharks' thing is just a way to bait tourists and lure them onto your ship?" she suggested dryly.

"That is one way to put it," he agreed.

"There's another way?" Jess asked dubiously.

Vasco shrugged. "Some people would say *we* are the sharks," he pointed out, and then opened his mouth so that she could watch as two of his seemingly normal canine teeth shifted and dropped down to form fangs.

Eyes widening with horror, Jess backed away until she came up against the desk. Pausing then, she lifted her chin determinedly. "I won't willingly have sex with you. You'll have to rape me."

"Rape?" Vasco had started to crowd forward, but her words brought him up short and he stared down at her with dismay.

"Yes, rape. And I'll fight," Jess lied firmly, quite sure she wouldn't fight at all. He was so close she could feel the heat of his body, and she was struggling not to lean into it. Jess very much feared that all it would take was one kiss for her to be climbing him like a monkey going up a tree after bananas.

"Oh, lass," he said finally, shaking his head. "I'd never rape ye. I've not forced a woman to my bed in all my five hundred years and I'd surely not start with you." He had relaxed his stance, and eased forward just enough that their bodies were brushing against each other. Now he ran his knuckles lightly down her cheek, and asked, "Do ye know why?"

Jess just shook her head. She had no idea why. She also had no idea what she could do or say to get her and Allison out of this mess. She found it incredibly difficult to think with him caressing her cheek as he was, and the way his body was pressing into hers wasn't helping any either. She knew that her body's response to him under these circumstances was utterly ridiculous, but it *was* responding. Apparently, her body didn't give a fig that he was a vampire about to bite her and suck her dry . . . so long as he was touching her while he did it.

"Because you are me life mate," he said solemnly, as if that explained everything, and then he smiled crookedly and added, "That's why I find ye irresistible, and why ye find me so damnably attractive too. We are both helpless in the face of life mate passion."

Life mates. Jess turned the words over in her mind. She had no idea what it even meant. Sure, she knew what she and the rest of the world thought of when you said *life mate*—a partner in life, a mate, and so on. But he said it with such reverence she suspected it meant something entirely different, or at least more, to him.

"Your skin is so soft and you smell so good," Vasco murmured now, and she refocused on him to see that his gaze was now fixed on her lips. Even as she noted that, he glanced briefly to the door, but then his eyes returned to her mouth as if drawn by some sort of magnet, and he muttered, "Ildaria can wait," before lowering his head and kissing her.

Jess tried to resist. Truly she did. He was a vampire, for God's sake, and a pirate captain vampire at that, a vampirate, with a ship full of vampires under him who planned to bite and probably kill every nonvampire on this ship and throw their bodies to the sharks afterward. That knowledge terrified and repulsed her, but damn, he was an amazing kisser. That was the last even half-sensible thought Jess had before she groaned and gave in to the passion he brought to roaring life within her.

The next few moments were a blur of sexual frenzy as Jess tried to get as close to and touch as much of him as she could. Apparently, he felt the same way, because Jess felt him tug her T-shirt up, and half expected him to break their kiss to pull it up over her head and remove it. Instead, she heard the tearing sound as he ripped it apart from hem to neckline. Much to their mutual frustration, it still left her swimsuit top in the way . . . briefly. Jess added that last thought as Vasco grasped the top between the cups and simply jerked, tearing it off.

Warm evening air washed over her skin. Jess sighed at the ethereal caress, and then groaned as his hands kneaded her eager flesh briefly, before he broke their kiss to peer down at her with wonder.

"I felt it," he told her with amazement.

"What?" she asked with confusion, and then gasped and clutched at his shoulders as he caught her nipple between thumb and finger and tweaked and then rolled it.

"That," he groaned, bending to press a kiss to her forehead. "I am feeling your pleasure. The shared pleasure life mates enjoy."

"Oh," Jess murmured, a little nonplussed. She had been quite enjoying herself until he'd started to talk, but now she was remembering the business about vampires. As well as Tyler's chewed-up tchotchke, and the—Her thoughts ended on a startled gasp as he scooped her up in his arms.

Clutching at his shoulders, Jess glanced around, alarmed to see that he was carrying her to the bed. Oh, that couldn't be good, she decided as she recalled the conversation on deck about marathon sex with her while he fed on Allison. How the hell did he think that would work? Was he planning to do both at the same time?

An image came to mind of his laying her on the end of the bed, and then standing there thrusting into her as he sucked on—also standing—Allison's neck. Jess gave her head a shake. That so wasn't going to happen. In fact, none of it was happening. Though it pained her to even consider it, she wasn't having sex with him. And he wasn't biting Allison. Or her.

"Vasco," she began tentatively, searching her mind for a way out of this. "Perhaps we should . . ." Unfortunately, her mind didn't suddenly fill the blank for her mouth.

"Celebrate our finding each other," he suggested.

"Yes!" Jess grasped eagerly at the suggestion, thinking champagne, a party, a chance to escape.

"We will, my sweet," Vasco assured her, crawling onto the bed and settling to sit cross-legged with her in his lap. "I am going to fuck you until you bleed," he proclaimed as if it was a good thing. "And then I will lick away every drop of blood and fuck you again."

"Oh . . . my," she said weakly. Wasn't that a pretty picture?

"I want you naked."

Jess blinked at that announcement and then grabbed frantically for her shorts as he began to drag them off. Too slow. They were flying through the air before she could get her hand anywhere near her waistline to stop him. Damn, he was fast, she thought with dismay, and then gasped in surprise as he slid a hand between her legs and pressed against her, through her black bikini bottoms.

"My God, I am the luckiest of men. You are beautiful," he said, his voice deepening and the arm at her back lifting, raising her breasts nearer to his mouth.

"Oh," Jess breathed, her eyes widening at the sweet words, and her legs shifting restlessly as his hand began to move, caressing her through the cloth. Dammit! She couldn't catch a break here. How was a girl supposed to resist when—?

"You have nice big jugs. I just want to gnaw on them."

Okay, that was a break. Calling her babies "jugs" totally wrecked the mood and vanquished to hell this pesky excitement and need he kept bringing about in her, Jess decided. The threat of his gnawing on them didn't help much either, she thought, and opened her eyes, intending to push him away. Instead, she was just in time to see his head lower and his mouth close over one eager breast. At least it was all perky, the nipple hard and looking pretty eager to her as half of her breast disappeared into his mouth.

Jess's eyes widened and then closed on a moan of despair as he began to suck at the sensitive flesh. But when his tongue rasped across the tender nipple, she groaned and opened her eyes so that she could see to thread her fingers through his long . . . really greasy hair, she noticed, and the desire to clasp his head to her chest fell away along with some of her passion.

Before Jess could grab ahold of the brief clearing of her thoughts and use it, Vasco nipped at her nipple, sending a new wave of excitement through her.

"Oh, God! This is so not fair!" Jess cried, clutching at his shoulders and squirming violently in his lap as his hand rubbed between her legs, sending wave after wave of increasing pleasure roaring through her trembling body and silencing her head again. Jess was so caught up in the need screaming through her body, and the promise of his easing it, that she hardly noticed when he shifted to sit on his haunches.

She did notice when he lifted her and then set her down to straddle his thighs on the bed, though, because he had to remove his hand from between her legs to do it. But his mouth continued its work at her breast, and his hand soon returned between her legs. He was just tugging the scrap of her bathing suit bottoms aside to touch her without it in the way when shouting suddenly erupted in the room and something slammed into them from the side.

Allison, Jess realized as she was knocked off Vasco's lap and sent tumbling to the floor. Apparently, Vasco couldn't control Allison and ravish her at the same time. Her cousin had come out of her blank state to turn into a woman raging with, of all things, jealousy. It seemed obvious; Allison still hadn't cottoned on to what was going on here and that they were on a ship full of vampires. She didn't even appear to realize that she'd been being controlled earlier. She was just ranting on about how Vasco was hers, and Jess was a slut for trying to steal him from her.

Vasco didn't seem to take well to Allison's calling her a slut. At least, that was the point that he got over his surprise and growled at the woman. Seriously, he growled like an animal, and then narrowed his gaze in the general area of Allison's forehead and she suddenly went silent and still, all expression slipping off her face and leaving it blank.

The moment she did, Vasco leapt off the bed and hurried to Jess's side.

"Are you all right?" he asked, helping her to her feet.

"Yes," Jess said, forcing a smile as she tugged together the sides of her torn T-shirt to try to cover her breasts as she became aware of her lack of clothing.

"Do not hide them from me," he admonished, brushing her hands away from the cloth. "I like your jugs."

Jess winced at the words. Honestly, the man would be perfect if he could just keep his mouth shut. Well, and if he weren't a bloodsucking vampire who wanted to fuck her until she bled and then lick it up. And the pirate thing maybe wasn't a plus. Was that like his *job*? Really? Jess wondered, and then realized she actually didn't know much about him at all, other than that he was her sexual kryptonite, and he talked like a combination of a pirate and a . . . well, honestly, she didn't know what. She heard a lot of different influences in his voice and words. There was a hint of a Spanish accent, but some English too, and something else Jess didn't recognize. There were also some salty words and phrases to his speech, but some antique terms as well.

Sighing, Vasco slid his arms around her waist and leaned his chin on her head, saying, "I suppose we cannot do anything with the lass here."

Yes! Jess cried silently. She could stop trying to fight him off. Okay, she hadn't really tried hard. But in her defense, he had some serious skills, and some powerful mojo working for him.

"Damn," Vasco breathed. "One more minute and I'd have had my whore pipe in your tuzzy-muzzy too."

"My what?" she asked, pulling back to stare at him with disbelief. "What does that even mean?"

"I was just about to slide you onto my cock and have you riding St. George," he explained.

Vasco then turned to scowl at Allison, totally missing the way Jess grimaced and rolled her eyes at his description. Honestly, if he could just *not talk* she would be forever grateful.

"Unfortunately," Vasco continued, "I cannot maintain control of yer friend there while giving you a good seeing-to. Ye excite me too much."

Jess's eyebrows rose at that. Other than returning his kisses, she hadn't done a damned thing that could have been described as exciting him. She certainly hadn't caressed or even touched him other than to hold on for dear life as he ravished her. That realization actually made her feel a little better. At least she hadn't been an active participant in her ruination, and ruin it would be if she became the girlfriend of a vampire pirate who sailed around the high seas feeding on her fellow mortals.

Unfortunately, that looked like where this was headed, Jess acknowledged. She wasn't seeing a way out here. She apparently had the self-control of a gnat. All the man had to do was touch her and she melted like butter in the skillet. This was bad.

"Well," Vasco said on a sigh. "I suppose I had best remove yer cousin and take her above for Cristo to look after."

Jess frowned, unsure whether that was a good thing or not. It would keep Allison from being fed on by Vasco, but what about Cristo? Would he—?

"And then I will deal with Ildaria before I return to you," Vasco said, eyeing her solemnly as he reminded her, "It was my original plan before you distracted me with your tuzzy-muzzy and jugs, and it was a good one. It is better if I handle her first. Then I can grope for trout in your river again without worrying about anything I left undone."

"Grope for . . . ?" Jess echoed with bewilderment.

Vasco grinned at her confusion. "I will show you when I return," he promised with a wink, and then slapped her behind and released her to walk to the door. He opened it, and then paused to peer back at her and suddenly smiled. "You are pretty as a picture."

Jess was just softening at the compliment when he added, "But I want you naked in bed when I get back. I plan to fuck you for four days straight at least and in every hole. Clothes will just get in the way."

Jess groaned and dropped her face into her hands with despair. The man had no couth at all. How could someone she found so damned repugnant intellectually make her body burn and weep for his attention?

How could she find a vampire sexy? He drank blood! Feeding off mortals like they were little better than cows. He was a monster, and she found his kisses and caresses irresistible? What was wrong with her? she wondered, and shame immediately claimed Jess. Fortunately, she was saved from suffering it for too long when the sound of the door closing reached her ears.

Lifting her head abruptly, Jess saw that Vasco had left, and sagged with relief before turning toward the bed. "Allison, we have to . . ."

Her words trailed off into silence. Allison was gone.

Three

Jess tied a knot in the end of the strip of cloth she'd ripped from the bedsheet and considered her handiwork grimly. During a fevered search of the room after Vasco left, she'd found an inflatable life jacket in an armoire next to the bed. The presence of the life jacket had rather surprised her. It was the last thing she'd expected to find on a pirate ship full of vampires, but then who said vampires had to know how to swim? Even vampire pirates?

At any rate, the life jacket was uninflated, folded neatly, and packaged in a square bag made of very thick but clear plastic. It was about the size of a ream of paper, but much lighter, and it had a small handle on the top. Jess had threaded the strip of cloth through the handle and now had some really ugly neckwear. On the other hand, she was hoping her efforts would keep the packaged life vest out of her way while she climbed out of the ship. She was also hoping it would prevent her accidentally dropping and losing it as she jumped into the ocean.

That was her plan. Jess had thought long and hard about what to do . . . well, really, she'd thought short and hard about it. Time wasn't exactly her friend at the moment. But anyway, she'd decided that escape was her only option here. She had to get off this ship before Vasco returned and she ended up in bed with him, and probably, eventually, a dead, soulless, bloodsucking pirate. Her very soul was at stake here.

Aside from that, Jess was really the only hope any of the other tourists on this ship had. She hoped to get off the ship, swim to shore, get help, and send them out to the ship to save everyone else.

It was possible her plan would fail miserably, of course. She might drown, be eaten by a shark, a whale, or a giant squid. Or she might get to shore and be locked up as completely insane when she started babbling about vampire pirates and such. She might also make it to shore, get help, and get back to the ship only to find that the tourists had all been slaughtered in her absence and fed to the sharks. But Jess was hoping her absence would save them. She was hoping that when Vasco discovered she was missing, he would set out to search for her and leave the tourists alone for as long as it took for her to get them help. Because hopefully he would stay away from the room long enough that she'd be able to get a good distance away before he noticed her absence.

There was a lot of hoping in this plan, Jess acknowledged grimly, and walked to the porthole she was going to try to leave the ship through. She'd decided that slipping out of the room and trying to jump over the side of the ship wouldn't work. There were too many crewmembers who might see her jump, and they'd just fish her out and lock her in the cabin. She needed to escape without being seen and hopefully have enough time between her jumping and their realizing she'd jumped ship that they couldn't find her easily and fish her out. The porthole was her best bet. If it *was* a porthole. Jess wasn't sure. It was rectangular rather than round, although the corners were rounded. It was bigger than the other portholes in the room that were actually round, but it was still quite snug, and if she got out at all, it would be a tight squeeze.

Sighing, Jess stepped up on the captain's chair that she'd set before the porthole and quickly unsnapped the four locks on the window and swung it open. She took the time to stick out her head and look around, to be sure no one would be able to see her leaving. Not spotting anyone hanging over the side of the ship looking her way, she pulled her head back in, and then slid one arm out instead. Her head followed, and then she eased the inflatable life jacket out to dangle from her neck before she tried to squeeze her other arm out. It was a tight fit, and Jess was pretty sure she scraped a good deal of skin off her left arm forcing it through, but eventually she had it out and was standing on the chair with her head and shoulders out of the porthole. Her breasts came next, but they weren't too much trouble. They were a good size, but more malleable than arm bones were, and she was able to squeeze and pull them out. Once that was done, Jess just had to get the rest of her out. Mouth tightening, she placed her hands flat on the wood hull on either side of the window and began to push.

Yeah, getting out was easier said than done, she soon learned, and wondered if this was how babies felt during birth. It seemed to take forever, was painful, and Jess felt like she was skinning herself alive, but she finally managed to force enough of herself out of the hole that gravity took over and dragged the rest of her out. Fortunately, Jess had the good sense to push herself away from the ship and grab ahold of her neckwear as she tumbled out. It saved her hitting her head on the ship hull, and losing her life jacket.

Jess hit the water hard, and almost gasped as she was enveloped by the cold liquid, but managed at the last minute to remember to keep her mouth shut. She sank a lot deeper than she'd expected, and was gasping for breath when she resurfaced, but immediately turned in the choppy waves, looking for the ship. The boat was moving much more quickly than she'd realized, Jess acknowledged as she saw that it was already several boat lengths away. No one had heard the splash of her entering the water and was peering back at her pointing and shouting the alarm, but then she hadn't expected there to be. The reggae music that had been playing since sunset would have covered any sound she'd made.

Sighing her relief, Jess did her best to tread water with one hand while unsnapping the flap on the bag holding the inflatable life jacket with the other. It was trickier than she'd expected in the choppy water, and she went under once or twice for a brief moment, but eventually managed to get it open and get the life jacket out. Fortunately, it wasn't one of those newfangled ones that inflated as soon as water hit it. She was able to get it on, and get it buckled in place without problem, and then pulled the lanyard to make it inflate once it was in place.

That task done, Jess turned in the water, searching for land. Her heart sank when she saw how far away the lights of shore were. Six or seven miles hadn't sounded that far when Cristo and Vasco had mentioned the number. She'd run marathons that long for charity and managed it. But six or seven miles certainly looked a good distance at sea. Of course, some time had passed since Cristo had guessed at how far out they were and, judging by how rough the water was, the wind had definitely picked up. She might be seven or eight miles out now. Maybe even nine.

Well, Jess thought, far away or not, she had no choice unless she wanted to wait around for Vasco to discover that she was missing, search the ship for her, and then turn around to come look for her and carry her off to be his vampire bride.

"No thanks," Jess muttered, and struck out for shore.

She'd read once that the average person could swim about three miles per hour. She was not an average swimmer. Jess figured she had a good four-hour swim ahead of her. Maybe even five . . . plenty of time for a shark to find and dine on her.

"Well, that was a waste of time," Zanipolo grumbled, dropping into a chair at the table the maître d' had led them to.

Raffaele waited until the server had handed them each a menu and left before saying, "I would not say it was a waste of time. We at least now know the rogues are not on staff here."

"Then where are they?" Santo asked grimly.

Raffaele shook his head. He had no idea, but he was quite certain they weren't at this resort. They'd walked over every inch of the place, including the kitchens, and every room marked Employees Only, as well as the other restaurants. Although they hadn't stopped to order anything at any of those restaurants; they'd merely entered, given the staff a quick once-over, and left once certain that there were no immortals on staff. This was the last restaurant and the last spot they'd had left to look.

"You are ready to order, *señors*?"

All three men turned to peer blankly at the waiter who had approached their table, but it was Raffaele who recovered first and shook his head. Opening his menu, he murmured, "No, sorry. We'll need a minute."

"*Sí.* Of course. I will return," the man said, smiling brightly.

Santo shifted with agitation as the waiter moved away, and then asked, "How many people did you see with bites?"

"A good forty or fifty throughout the day," Raffaele guessed. Once they'd noticed the first two groups with bite marks on them, they'd started examining everyone who had come down to the beach. At least those who had got close enough for them to look over.

"And they were all young," Zanipolo said suddenly and, when Raffaele glanced at him with surprise, added, "Didn't you notice? They were all in their early twenties." He pursed his lips briefly, and then added, "They were all fit and attractive too."

"Or maybe we didn't see anyone older or unfit with bite marks because they are sensible enough not to go to the beach wearing little more than tiny triangles of cloth connected by bits of floss," Raffaele said dryly.

Zanipolo grinned at his comment. "Careful, *cugino*, your age is showing."

"Were the—?" Santo began, and then paused to scowl at their waiter as he approached again. "Not yet. We will signal you when we are ready," he said, waving him away.

"*Sí.* Of course, *señor.*"

The waiter's smile was a little strained this time, Raffaele noticed, but turned his attention to Santo as the man asked, "Were the bite marks not all on the neck?"

Raffaele shook his head. "Some were, but most were on the arms, wrists, legs, ankles, and even thighs."

"Odd," Santo said with a frown.

"Smart, more like," Raffaele countered. "Fifty people with bite marks on their necks would definitely draw more attention than a rogue would want. Bite marks in different spots on several individuals could pass as bug bites of some kind, and that's what most of them thought they were. At least in the case of the people I bothered to read."

"Did you learn anything else from the people you read?" Santo asked at once.

Raffaele eyed him briefly. He didn't really want Santo getting too invested in this matter. The trip was supposed to be so he'd relax, after all. However, curiosity soon got to him, and he reluctantly asked, "Like what?"

Santo shrugged discontentedly. "Anything. Trips or tours they might all have in common?"

"You mean like maybe a nest of immortals run the local ziplining place and they feed on each customer as part of their payment?" Zanipolo suggested.

"*Sì.* Like that," Santo said at once.

Raffaele shook his head slowly, and admitted, "I did not think to search for that kind of information."

"Maybe we should," Zanipolo said solemnly, and then added, "That group at the table in the corner behind you were one of the ones where everyone seemed to have a bite."

Raffaele glanced over his shoulder at the table in question. They looked a little different dressed than they had on the beach in almost nothing, but he recognized them anyway.

"The group has been on a lot of tours," Santo said, focusing on one member after another with narrowed eyes. "A monkey safari, a catamaran trip, an island tour, the Seaquarium, shark feeding, ziplining, scuba diving . . ."

"Those are all day tours," Raffaele pointed out. "Immortals are more likely to run night tours of some kind."

"Maybe not," Zanipolo argued when Santo sat back in his seat with a cluck of irritation. "What do they care if they're out in the day if they're rogues who feed freely off of every mortal who passes through? I mean, we saw a lot of people with bite marks, Raff, and that was just here at this resort, and it was only the ones dressed scantily enough for us to see the marks. If this all comes down to a local tour, and there are tourists at every resort with these marks . . ." He arched his eyebrows. "That's a lot of people bitten."

"A hell of a lot of people bitten," Raffaele muttered, frowning at the thought. This could be a lot bigger nest than they'd considered.

"*Señors*, I apologize to interrupt."

All three men turned to eye their waiter as he stopped at their table again. He was still smiling, but it was a cross between a pained smile and one of apology as he said, "But if you wish to order, you must do so now. The kitchen is closing."

Raffaele raised his eyebrows at this news and glanced at his watch, surprised to see how late it was. They'd been searching the resort for much longer than he'd thought. It was almost ten o'clock. Lifting his head, he glanced to Zanipolo in question. "Well?"

Zanipolo took a quick glance through his menu, but then let it slip closed and shook his head as he got to his feet. "If the kitchen is closing, the restaurant is too. I don't want to keep these guys past their shift. We can go down to the waterside pub-style restaurant. They're open until two or something, and had a burger on their menu I wanted to try anyway."

"Oh, no, *señors, por favor.* You are welcome to order. We do not mind the staying late," their waiter protested, glancing from them to the maître d' with alarm. It seemed obvious he feared getting in trouble.

Smiling faintly, Raffaele reached into his pocket and retrieved a couple of bills as he stood. He slipped the tip to the man as he shook his hand, and then said loudly enough for the maître d' to hear, "We aren't feeling like Italian tonight, after all. Maybe another time. Sorry for the trouble. Have a good evening."

"Gracias," the waiter said sincerely. *"Por favor.* You must come back. Anytime. I will be happy to serve you."

Raffaele nodded and ushered Santo and Zanipolo out. The three of them were silent as they made their way across the resort toward the beach and the restaurant there. It was a much more relaxed restaurant, a bar as much as a food place, and had a band playing when they entered.

"This is more my style," Zanipolo said cheerfully as they took their seats and accepted the menus offered them.

"It reminds me of the restaurant where we played in St. Lucia," Santo said, his voice a deep rumble.

"Yeah," Raffaele agreed with a smile, glancing around at the high, round wooden tables and the barstool chairs. They'd asked for the deck, and had been led straight to a table along the rail. It overlooked the dark beach and the water beyond.

A beautiful view, Raffaele decided, and it truly was. The night was so clear and the ocean so calm inside the reef that the moon and stars were reflected on the water's surface as if it were a mirror. Shaking his head, he murmured, "You can see for miles."

"Yeah, but I was talking about the food," Zanipolo said with amusement. "Look, they have chicken fingers, and fish and chips."

"I thought you wanted a burger?" Santo said, sounding amused.

"*Sì*, but look at all the options," Zanipolo said.

Raffaele didn't look. He was busy squinting out at the ocean.

"What's got your attention, *cugino*?" Zanipolo asked suddenly.

Raffaele frowned. "I think there's something floating out there."

"What? A boat?" Zanipolo asked, turning to peer out at the water now too.

"No. Not a boat," he said with certainty.

"Madre de Dio," Zanipolo gasped suddenly. "It looks like a floater."

Raffaele's mouth tightened at the word. That was exactly what he'd feared it was—a dead body floating in the water. Someone who had fallen off a cruise ship, or simply been dragged out by the currents and was now being floated gently back in, he thought, and then stiffened as an arm came up out of the water and then slid back in as the other arm rose and did the same.

"Is that—? They're swimming! They're alive!" Zanipolo exclaimed with excitement.

"Not for long," Santo predicted grimly, and then pointed out, "Whoever they are, they're beyond the reef that protects the swimmers on the beach, and I'm quite sure that's a shark fin I see off to the right out there."

Raffaele didn't comment. He was already on his feet and leaping over the railing surrounding the deck. He hit the soft sand below with a jolt and took off running, shedding his clothes as he went. By the time he reached the water, Raffaele had torn off his T-shirt, kicked off his shoes, and undone his pants. He paused at the shoreline long enough to push them off, and then raced into the cool water, his gaze measuring the distance between the shark fin and the swimmer. By his guess, it would be close, but he should reach the swimmer before the shark did . . . hopefully.

Jess managed another couple of strokes before she had to pause again and return to simply floating along in the water. She knew she should probably turn over and look around to be sure she was still moving toward shore and hadn't somehow drifted off course, but she was so tired she couldn't make herself do it. She'd just float for a bit more first, she decided, her eyes drooping closed.

Jess was exhausted. The waves had helped, carrying her along as she kicked her feet, but she'd had to battle them to keep from being taken off course. She was hoping to reach shore near the resort where they were staying. She had no money, and all she was wearing was her bikini bottoms and the torn T-shirt, which she'd knotted between her breasts in an attempt to make it more decent. Jess would really rather not stroll up on shore at the hedonist's resort she'd heard was up the beach from theirs in one direction, or the private nudist's resort in the other. Her resort, where her family was, and where her room waited with her clothes in the closet, and her money in the safe, was her aim.

Fortunately, her battle with the waves had ended when she reached the protected bay. The wind had died abruptly, the waves disappearing, and swimming had become much easier. Unfortunately, Jess had been exhausted by then, and now faced a different battle. Her arms felt leaden, as did her legs, and she was struggling to keep from falling asleep and drifting back out to sea.

Sighing wearily, Jess forced her eyes open and stared up at the starry sky as she dragged one arm out of the water, swung it up over her head, and plunged it down to push through the cool liquid and propel herself along. Her second arm had followed in the same action before she realized she'd stopped kicking her feet again.

"Idiot," she muttered, fluttering her feet in the water. It was really the best she could do at the moment.

A splashing sound behind her caught Jess's ear and she stilled briefly to listen. It was a sound she'd heard several times since entering the calm of the bay. There were fish here. They jumped. Still, she decided she'd put it off long enough and should roll over and check to see that she was still heading for what she thought was her resort. Letting her legs drop, she straightened in the water, turned, and then shrieked in surprised horror when she saw the shape moving toward her through the water. It was so close it was nearly on top of her, and for one second she thought it was a whale, or a huge shark rising up out of the water, and then she realized it was a human doing the butterfly swim stroke. She'd just happened to turn as they were in the push phase, their head and arms out of the water.

Apparently, realizing how close they were, the swimmer stopped abruptly and treaded water in front of her, but didn't say anything. He simply stared at her through the darkness, his eyes seeming to glow. A trick of the light, she supposed.

"I thought you were a shark or something," Jess said finally, so exhausted her words came out slurred.

"No," he growled the word, and then added, "There *was* a shark when I headed out. Fortunately, he lost interest before he got too close to you and turned back the way he came."

Tilting her head, Jess eyed him silently. The man had an Italian accent so was obviously a guest at one of the resorts and not a native. She was trying to figure out if he was joking with that shark bit when he asked, "How did you end up out here, *cara*?"

Startled at his using what she was quite sure was an Italian endearment, Jess hesitated to answer.

"You are wearing a life jacket," he added, and this time she noticed the accent as he asked, "Did you fall off a boat or cruise ship?"

Jess shook her head wearily. "I jumped."

"Jumped?" he echoed a bit sharply.

Jess nodded, and then craned her head to try to get a look at the shoreline beyond him. The waves had carried her into the bay, but the water had been much calmer from there and, recognizing the area, Jess had pinpointed where she thought her resort was and had swam in that direction, crossing the large bay at an angle meant to get her there. She wanted to know if she'd succeeded or not.

"Why?"

"Vampires," Jess muttered distractedly as she surveyed the buildings directly ahead of her onshore, which, incidentally, still looked a long way away to her. The good news was, she was quite sure the lights belonged to her resort, which was made up of one large, sprawling main building and six long, narrower buildings. The large building was where the reception lobby, the spa, several small stores, the resort clinic, and several of the restaurants were situated. The rectangular buildings were four stories high and held the hotel rooms. From what she could see, the building shapes and colors were the same as her resort. Dear God, had she actually done something right tonight?

Realizing that the man had gone silent, Jess shifted her attention back to him. She couldn't really make out features, and was pretty sure she was imagining the glowing eyes. That combination made her wonder if he was even really there. Maybe she was having exhaustion-induced hallucinations. Was that a thing?

"Did you say vampires?" the man asked, his voice at least an octave deeper than the last time he spoke.

That was when Jess recalled her decision to keep mention of vampires out of her explanation. She'd debated the matter thoroughly in her head as she swam. On the one hand, not mentioning vampires meant that the authorities would be wholly unprepared for what they would encounter when they chased down and boarded the ship. On the other hand, mentioning vampires would probably get her labeled a crackpot, and leave the other tourists without any chance of rescue at all. However, leaving out the mention of vampires, and perhaps just hinting at the ship's crew being strange, and uncommonly strong, and suggesting the officers take crosses might be enough to ensure they went to help and were also on their toes.

"No," Jess lied. "I . . ." She was too tired to come up with a lie to cover her error, and really, staying there, treading water, was just sapping more of her energy. "I need to get to shore," she said politely. "Can you move, please?"

Rather than move aside, the man moved closer and then just stared at her and treaded water.

Jess bore that for what felt like forever and then shifted impatiently in the water. She was about to snap at him to get out of the way when a tension she hadn't realized was there left his shoulders, and he said, "Turn around and relax."

"Why?" she asked warily.

"Because I'm going to tow you to shore. You're too exhausted to make it on your own. You'll fall asleep and drift back out to sea," he added gently. "Let me help you."

"Thank you," Jess breathed, and immediately rolled on her back in the water. She'd barely done so when she felt a tug on her life jacket and then began to glide backward through the water at a steady, rather impressive speed. She'd be onshore in no time at this rate, Jess thought just before she lost consciousness.

"It's a woman."

"Who is she?"

"She's wearing a life jacket."

"What happened?"

"How did she end up in the water?"

Raffaele shook his head at the rapid-fire questions shot at him by Zanipolo and Santo as he carried the woman out of the water. Rather than answer, he merely said, "Bring my clothes, please," and walked past them, heading for the resort buildings.

The men had already gathered his clothes for him on the way down, so merely fell into step on either side of him as he walked.

"Is she alive?" Zanipolo asked with a frown, leaning slightly in front of Raffaele to look at the woman in his arms as they walked.

"Yes," Raffaele said quietly. "I think she has just fainted from her exhaustion."

"Are you taking her to the resort clinic?" Santo asked as they reached the rows of lounge chairs at the head of the beach.

"No. I want to look her over myself first," Raffaele said solemnly.

"Why?" Santo asked at once.

"Two reasons," Raffaele responded as they made their way out of the rows of chairs and reached the concrete paths leading to the various resort buildings. Much to his relief the paths were pretty much deserted at this hour with most people already in bed, or situated in the bar enjoying the entertainment. There were only one or two guests making their way to their rooms and they paid them no attention.

"What is the first reason?" Santo asked as they approached the paths around the pools.

"I want to look her over for bites," Raffaele admitted.

"Bites?" Zanipolo asked with interest. "What makes you think she might have been bitten?"

"Because when I asked her if she'd fallen off a boat or cruise ship, she said no, she jumped, and when I asked why, she said—" he glanced around to be sure no one was near enough to hear, and then lowered his voice anyway as he finished with "'—vampires.'"

"Bingo," Zanipolo said with grim satisfaction as they got past the pools and approached their building. "She'll be able to tell us where the vampire nest is and how they operate. It's got to be some kind of dinner cruise or something. Or it could be a day cruise. She could have had to swim a long way." He frowned over that briefly as they reached their building and walked along the open hall to the stairs, and then asked, "What is the second reason you want to examine her before we take her to the resort clinic?"

"When I got to her she was beyond exhausted," Raffaele said as they started up the stairs. "Her words were slurred and she could hardly keep her eyes open. I thought it would be easier all around if I read her mind to see what had happened, and took control of her to drag her in."

"And?" Santo prodded as they exited the stairs at their floor and started along the hall to their room.

Raffaele was silent for a minute, having trouble accepting what he was about to say himself, but when they reached the door to their suite and Santo pulled out his key card to unlock the door, Raffaele swallowed and said in almost a whisper, "I couldn't read her."

Santo had got the door unlocked and started to open it before Raffaele spoke, but now he stiffened and turned sharply to peer at him with amazement. "What?"

Raffaele merely nodded.

"Score!" Zanipolo shouted gleefully. "Didn't I tell you? I told you! Didn't I? Hot resorts are the way to go to find our mates! I so *told* you that!"

"Yes, you did," Raffaele admitted with amusement as Santo pushed the door open for him to carry his life mate into the room.

"And he'll remind you of that every day for the rest of his life," Santo said dryly as he let the door close, locked it, and then hit the light switch, turning on the overhead light.

"*Sì*, I will," Zanipolo agreed gleefully, moving to Raffaele's side to peer down at the woman he held. Eyeing her almost reverently now, he whispered, "*Cugino*, your life mate is very pretty."

"Yes, she is," Raffaele agreed solemnly, his gaze sliding over her as well. Her lips were full and looked soft, her nose straight, and while they were closed now, he knew her eyes were large and lovely, and an eggshell blue. Her hair, of course, was wet, but appeared to be a dark brown.

"What is her name?" Santo asked, moving closer to look her over as well.

Raffaele stiffened at the question. "I don't know her name," he admitted.

"You didn't ask her?" Santo asked with surprise.

Raffaele shook his head.

"Are you kidding me?" Zanipolo asked with disbelief. "You finally meet your mate and you did not even ask her name?"

Raffaele opened his mouth to respond, but was forestalled when the woman in his arms suddenly began to shriek and thrash wildly about.

Four

Jess had been dreaming that Vasco had caught up to her, pulled her from the ocean, and was carrying her to his cabin to ravish her and turn her into his vampire whore when voices pierced her dreams and dragged her from sleep. The first words that she heard clearly as she reached consciousness were, “Are you kidding me? You finally meet your mate and you did not even ask her name?”

Blinking her eyes open, she’d found herself staring up at three heads bent over her, their faces in shadow. Jess had been sure it was Vasco, Cristo, and Ildaria. And then she’d become aware of liquid dripping on her from one of them and—positive it was Tyler’s blood dripping from Ildaria’s gruesome, blood-covered face—well, it had been pure instinct to shriek in horror and fury and begin to struggle.

“It’s okay. You’re safe now. We’ll protect you.”

The words were a litany Jess suspected had been repeated many times, but she didn’t really hear them and grasp their meaning until the three heads broke apart and the one carrying her rushed to set her down on something and then backed away. It was only then that she was able to see the faces of the three people in the room with her. The light was now overhead rather than behind their faces and Jess recognized that there wasn't a Vasco, Cristo, or Ildaria among them. In fact, it was three strangers. All male and one of them soaking wet.

It had been water dripping on her face, Jess realized, and she reached up to run her finger over the wet spot. She then pulled it away to peer at what she'd collected on her fingertip just to be sure. Yes, clear liquid, not blood.

Sighing, Jess slumped wearily back on what she now saw was a couch and surveyed the three men eyeing her warily from the other side of the coffee table. They were all attractive, each in a different way. The one on the left had black mid-length hair that looked a little shaggy, as if he were trying to grow it out. He also wore a black T-shirt and black jeans. His body was made up of lean muscle, leaving him tall and lanky.

The one in the middle, on the other hand, was bald as a cue ball and carrying some serious mass. He definitely worked out. He also apparently liked jewelry, Jess decided as she noted that every one of his fingers seemed to sport a thick silver ring.

Her gaze shifted to the last man, the one on the right, and she blinked as she peered at him. He had short, dark hair that was soaking wet and slicked back from his face. But she noted that almost distractedly, because her attention seemed to be taken up with trying to look over every inch of his body. The man was standing there in only a pair of body-hugging black briefs . . . and what a body to hug. He was more muscular than the lean one, but not as Hulk-ish as the big one. In truth, with nice, muscular shoulders, narrowing down to an eight- or ten-pack stomach, he was just perfect, and then there was the package the briefs were hugging . . . which was growing, Jess realized, and knew she should politely avert her eyes, but just couldn't seem to. Instead, she stared with fascination, her exhausted mind for some reason recalling the story of Pinocchio.

"Right. Shall we talk now, or would you two like to put on some clothes first so I can stop feeling like a perv?"

The lean guy was the one who asked that question, and his tone of pained amusement managed to drag Jess's attention away from the amazing Penisocchio. The moment her weary gaze landed on him, the lean guy gestured vaguely to her chest while averting his eyes. Jess glanced down and then squawked in dismay and scrambled to cover herself when she saw that her torn T-shirt had come undone and her life jacket had shifted, leaving one breast to play peekaboo. It was presently flashing them its nipple.

"I will fetch you both towels," the big guy said solemnly as she reached under the life jacket, caught at the damp cloth of the torn T-shirt, and dragged it over the exposed breast. He then slipped through the open double doors behind him into the bedroom off this sitting area. The main bathroom was off the bedroom, which Jess knew because this room was an exact duplicate of the one she shared with—

"Allison!" she cried, sitting up with alarm. Glancing from Lean Guy to Penisocchio almost frantically, she said, "You need to call the authorities. We have to help Allison. And the others," she added with a frown, wondering if Tyler even could be helped. She wasn't sure; he might be a vampire now but the others might still be all right. Vasco would have discovered she was missing by now and be searching for her. Surely, he would have the crew concentrate on that rather than feasting on the tourists. Wouldn't he?

"Who is Vasco?" the lean one asked.

Jess jerked her head up sharply, her gaze narrowing suspiciously at the question. She hadn't told them about Vasco. How did he know the name?

"You mentioned the name Vasco as well as Cristo and Ildaria while you were unconscious. You must have been having nightmares," Lean Guy explained as if she'd asked the question aloud.

"Oh," Jess breathed, and relaxed. She *had* been dreaming about Vasco and the pirate ship just before she woke up. She just hadn't known she talked in her sleep, Jess thought, her gaze shifting to the big guy when he returned to the room with two towels.

"Thank you," she murmured, taking the towel he offered to her before giving the other to Penisocchio. For a moment, Jess just sat staring at the towel, her mind slow to tell her what to do with it, and then movement drew her gaze to Penisocchio as he quickly scrubbed it over his damp hair. When he then started to run it over his arms and chest, Jess peered down at herself and frowned at the bulky life jacket she wore.

She'd have to take the vest off to dry herself, Jess supposed wearily, and forced herself to stand. Her legs were shaky, but they held her up and she turned her back to the men to concentrate on removing the life jacket. Her arms felt incredibly heavy when she lifted them, and her fingers were trembling and clumsy, making the task more difficult, but Jess managed to unbuckle and remove the bulky life jacket. She immediately let it drop to the floor with a little sigh. It was a great relief to get it off. She'd fastened it tightly to ensure she didn't slip out of it while battling the waves, but after hours of it rubbing her skin raw, Jess almost would rather have slid out of the darned thing.

Shifting her attention to her ruined T-shirt, Jess pulled the ends together, and retied the knot between her breasts. She then made a hasty effort at drying her arms and legs before giving it up as too much work and simply wrapping the towel around herself sarong-style. Feeling a little more put together, Jess then turned to face the men again.

Penisocchio, she noted, had been busy while her back was turned. He'd finished drying himself, doing a much more thorough job than her, she was sure, and now had the towel wrapped around his waist. He'd also donned a tight white T-shirt, although Lean Guy still held a pair of jeans dangling from one hand. Jess supposed these were the clothes he'd been wearing before jumping in the water to save her and that he didn't want to pull the jeans on over damp briefs. Whatever the case, there would be no more watching the bulge in his briefs grow, Jess realized, and felt a keen disappointment that made her frown.

Good Lord, she was all about the sex tonight, wasn't she? Jess asked herself with disgust. First it was a fight to not become a vampirate's bloodsucking whore, and now she was entirely too interested in Penisocchio's package. What on earth was the matter with her?

"We should introduce ourselves," Lean Guy said, his tone abrupt. When Jess turned her gaze to him, he pointed to Penisocchio and said, "That's Raffaele."

"Raffaele," Jess murmured, managing a smile of greeting. It was a much nicer name than Penisocchio. Shorter too.

"This big guy is Santo."

Jess shifted her attention to the bald man now as he offered her a nod of greeting, his face solemn. Following his example, she didn't smile but offered a polite nod in return.

"I'm Zanipolo," Lean Guy finished, and before she could react at all to the unusual name, he raised his eyebrows and asked, "And you are?"

"Jess," she said quietly, and then bent to pick up the life vest she'd discarded. Clasping the bulky vest to her chest, she hesitated, and then asked, "May I use your bathroom?"

"Of course," Raffaele said at once.

"Thanks." Jess managed a smile and made her way on shaky feet to the small hallway between the sitting area and the suite's entrance. As expected, there was a door on the right that led to into a full, but compact, bathroom. It was the same in the suite she and Allison shared.

Worry assailed her at the thought of her cousin. She really needed to get help for Allison and the others. As annoying as her cousin was, she couldn't just leave her to the vampires. After she finished in the bathroom, she'd thank Raffaele and the other two men for their assistance, and then leave and head to reception to make them call in the local police.

Raffaele watched Jess disappear into the bathroom and then turned and strode quickly into the bedroom and straight to his suitcase.

"Are you sure you cannot read her thoughts?" Santo asked, following him with Zanipolo on his heels.

"Yes. I tried again when we got back here," Raffaele admitted, digging out a pair of clean dry briefs, and then he jerked his head up and eyed his cousins with concern. "Can you two read her?"

When both men nodded, he sagged with relief and then headed for the much larger, ensuite bathroom off the bedroom. The fact that he couldn't read her while the other two could meant she was definitely his life mate and that she wasn't just crazy. Those were the only two reasons an immortal couldn't read a mortal.

Raffaele whipped off the towel he'd fastened around his waist as he entered the bathroom. He paused in the middle of the room, tossed the towel across the end of the tub, and turned back to see his cousins had followed. Raising his eyebrows, he asked, "So what happened to her? What was the boat she was on? Who were Vasco, Cristo, and Ildaria? How big a nest are we dealing with?"

When Santo glanced to Zanipolo, leaving him to explain, the younger man grimaced. “She was in the ocean a long time and spent most of it battling high waves that were tossing her around a bit,” he began carefully. “As a result, she is exhausted to the point that her thoughts are sluggish and a bit scattered.”

“How long was she out there?” Raffaele asked with a frown as he switched his wet briefs for the dry ones.

“Hours,” Zanipolo said, handing him the jeans he’d collected off the beach and brought back for him. “Since shortly after sunset, I think.”

Raffaele frowned at this news as he dragged on his pants. The sun had set before seven and it was ten thirty now. Jess had been in the water for nearly four hours. That was a long time to be struggling with waves and trying to swim to shore. It was no wonder she had lost consciousness by the time he got her out of the water. In fact, he was surprised she was already up and about. She was recovering quickly. It suggested a strong constitution, he thought as he did up his jeans.

Straightening then, Raffaele raised his eyebrows. “So? What else did you learn? Who are this Vasco, Cristo, and Ildaria you mentioned? I presume you read those names from her memory?” he added. Despite what Zani had said, Jess hadn’t mentioned the name. Before Zani could respond, he asked, “What was the ship she escaped? Some kind of dinner tour?” Even as the words left his lips, Raffaele suspected that couldn’t be the case. She was wearing swimsuit bottoms, and a torn T-shirt, not exactly dinner attire, even if that dinner was on a boat.

“It was a pirate ship.”

Raffaele stiffened, his eyes widening with disbelief. “What?”

Zanipolo shrugged helplessly. “That’s what I got from her memory. She was on a pirate ship with vampires, and Vasco, Cristo, and Ildaria were some of the crew.”

“Vampirates,” Santo growled.

“Vampirates?” Raffaele echoed with amazement.

“Her name for them in her head when she thinks of them,” Zanipolo explained. “But appropriate from the few memories I saw,” he assured him, and then added dryly, “She appears to have a penchant for nicknames. For instance, until I told her your proper name, she was thinking of you as Penisocchio."

"What?" Raffaele gasped with shock.

Zanipolo nodded. "That's why I told her your name was Raffaele when I did. I was finding it difficult not to burst out laughing every time she thought the name," he explained, and then taunted, "But again, the nickname was appropriate."

Raffaele closed his eyes briefly. He didn't need to ask why Zanipolo thought the nickname appropriate. The minute he'd set Jess down on the couch and stepped back to look her over in her skimpy outfit he'd started to develop an erection. Her gaze sliding over his body hadn't helped the situation much either. Just recalling it made him start to harden again. Mouth tightening, he opened his eyes, and raised his eyebrows.

Zanipolo grimaced. "Like I said, her thoughts are a bit scattered, but from what I could sort out, it looked like they went to the Seaquarium—"

"Some of the people on the beach had gone there. What is it?" Raffaele asked.

"You didn't even *look* at the pamphlets I gave you, did you?" Zanipolo asked with disgust.

"I looked at some, but there were a lot of pamphlets," Raffaele said defensively.

"Well, you can look up what it is later, because that's not the important part. It's when the boat that took them to the Seaquarium got back that matters. That's when the pirates, or vampirates as she thinks of them, approached the returning guests. They lured a bunch of them to their sloop with some story of feeding the sharks, including her cousin Allison. Allison in turn dragged Jess along."

"But they weren't feeding finned sharks," Raffaele guessed grimly.

Zanipolo shook his head. "Jess apparently happened on one of the rogues starting early on a guest." He grimaced with distaste at the memory. "It was pretty bad."

"Gruesome," Santo added.

"Yeah." Zanipolo shook his head as if trying to shake the memory away, and then continued. "The rogue she interrupted was Ildaria. She took control of Jess and sent her to kiss someone named Vasco, who I think was the ship's captain, so maybe the head rogue."

"Kiss him?" Raffaele asked with a start, his mouth turning down at this news.

"That's what I got," Zanipolo said apologetically. "But like I said, it all gets a bit scattered once she walked in on the rogue chewing on some guy named Tyler. She was kind of traumatized at seeing that. Hell, I was traumatized seeing it secondhand."

"Yes." Santo nodded. "Very traumatizing."

Raffaele's mouth tightened, but he nodded. "Okay, so the rogue sent her to kiss the captain and then what?"

Zanipolo shifted, looking reluctant to continue, but then sighed and said, "It got a bit heated, and then the cousin attacked them, I think."

"Yes," Santo agreed.

"And then the captain took both women down to his cabin."

Raffaele stiffened, alarm coursing down his back. "Did he bite her?"

"No," Zanipolo said at once. "No, I don't think he did that."

Raffaele's eyes narrowed. "Did he rape her?"

"No," Santo assured him.

"She escaped before things went that far," Zanipolo added.

"That far?" Raffaele echoed. "How far did things go?"

Zanipolo hesitated, and then glanced to Santo. The bigger man was opening his mouth to answer that question when the sound of a door closing had all of them glancing toward the sitting room.

"Jess must be out of the bathroom," Raffaele muttered, and led the other two men back out to the sitting room, only to find it empty.

"She's gone," Zanipolo said with surprise, staring at the open bathroom door.

It was Santo who spotted the note on the coffee table and picked it up. Moving to his side, Raffaele looked down at it. It was on the resort notepad that had been sitting on one of the end tables earlier with a pen with the resort's logo lying next to it. He had noticed it when they first arrived. Apparently, not finding them in the sitting room when she'd finished in the bathroom, Jess had decided to leave rather than wait to find out where they'd gone. She'd left a nice thank-you note, though, he thought as he read it.

Hey, guys!

Thank you for all your help.

I have to go have the front desk call the authorities to help my friends.

I'll return your towel as soon as I can.

Thanks again,

Jess

"If she tells anyone there are vampires out there—" Santo began in a concerned rumble that died when Raffaele cursed and hurried for the door.

Clutching the still-damp life vest with one hand, and the front of the towel with her other to be sure it didn't slip apart, Jess hurried to the stairs and jogged lightly down them. She thought she heard a door close as she turned the first bend and started down the next flight, but didn't slow or stop to see if it might be Raffaele or one of the other men looking for her. She didn't have time to explain things to them. That was why she'd simply scribbled a note and left when she stepped out of the bathroom to find the sitting room empty. She'd known they'd want her to tell them how she'd wound up floating around in the ocean, and that was a long conversation, and one Jess wasn't even sure she should have . . . with anyone. They'd think she was nuts.

The thought made Jess frown. She still wasn't sure what she was going to say to the authorities to get them to call in the coast guard and go after the pirate ship, but was hoping something would come to mind before she reached the hotel lobby.

The sound of feet pounding down the stairs above her made her heart jump suddenly. Intellectually, Jess knew it was probably one of the men, or all of them, simply looking to help her. But her body responded with the panic of a rabbit being chased by a fox, and despite the fact that every muscle in her body was still weak and rubbery from her marathon swim, Jess broke into a run as she reached the bottom of the stairs.

There were two routes to the hotel lobby. The inner path alongside the system of pools that filled the center of the resort, and the outer path that ran between the buildings and the tropical forest that surrounded three sides of the resort. Jess chose the outer route. It was a sloping path the staff used to push carts and luggage carriers down and was longer, but the inner path finished with a set of a good thirty steps leading up to the lobby. Jess just didn't think she had the strength and energy needed to manage the steps.

She was halfway up the sloping lane and breathing heavily when Jess realized she could no longer hear the pounding of feet behind her. Whoever had been on the stairs hadn't come this way, she realized with relief, and allowed herself to slow, but only a little. It was dark on the path and she was a woman alone in a world that apparently had more dangers than she'd ever imagined, so she continued at a fast jog. But the rush of adrenaline that had sent her running out of the stairwell in the first place was quickly draining away, leaving her weak, shaky, and feeling like she was on the verge of hyperventilating. The combination forced her to slow to a walk. Even so, Jess was gasping for breath when she rounded the curve at the top of the hill and bumped into someone.

"Sorry," she wheezed, pressing a hand to the stitch that had developed in her side. Jess was so exhausted that she didn't even look up to see who she'd bumped into, but simply stepped to the side. The front entrance of the lobby was just steps away now. She could make it.

"Wait. Jess?"

A hand caught her arm as she continued forward, and Jess paused and swung back, her eyes widening as she recognized Raffaele in the lights from the porte cochere where vehicles picked up and dropped off hotel guests. It must have been him on the stairs, and he'd obviously taken the shorter, inner path and beat her up here.

"Oh, hi," Jess puffed weakly, her gaze drifting toward the hotel entry. Noting the bus parked in front of the doors, she frowned slightly. It was late for a tour to be returning, she thought as she watched the people file off the bus. All were laughing and chattering as they disembarked.

"Jess?" Raffaele said again.

"Hmm?" she murmured, her gaze narrowing on the growing group ahead, gathering in front of the lobby doors. A couple of the people looked familiar.

"I know you want to call the authorities and get help for your friend."

"Allison," Jess breathed as she spotted her cousin in the group.

"Yes, for your friend Allison," he agreed, but Jess wasn't listening anymore.

She tugged her arm free, dropped the life jacket she'd been clutching since leaving the room, and rushed forward, calling, "Allison!"

Her cousin turned to glance her way at the call, but so did the others and Jess's eyes widened as she recognized Tyler and several other people from the pirate ship. Dear God, they were all here and all alive and well, she thought, almost faint with relief.

"Jessica!" Allison snapped when Jess reached her and tried to give her a relieved hug. "Get off me! God, it's bad enough you left me to go on the shark-feeding tour alone, don't—"

"What?" Jess asked with shock, stepping back to stare at her.

"You heard me." Allison scowled at her briefly, but then a smile suddenly plucked at her lips and she added with satisfaction, "Your loss in the end. We had a blast. Didn't we, Tyler?"

Tyler had been standing back, waiting for Allison while everyone else slowly moved through the hotel doors and into the lobby in small, laughing, and chattering groups, but now he stepped forward and smiled at Jess. "She's right. It was a great time. You should have come."

Jess gaped at the pair of them, unable to believe what she was hearing.

"Vasco will be pleased to learn you are alive and well, little dove."

Jess froze at that voice with its strange accent, and then turned warily to see Cristo stepping down from the bus.

"He was crushed when he found you missing," Cristo said, his expression and tone reprimanding. "We searched the ship from top to bottom three times before he would admit you must have jumped overboard rather than be with him. By then, we were sure you must have drowned." Eyes narrowing, he said, "The waters were rough and we were far out to sea—how did you survive and make it ashore?"

Jess glanced instinctively down at her hand, but she was no longer clutching the life jacket.

"Ah," Cristo said with understanding. "Clever lady. You stole a life jacket and escaped through the porthole."

Jess jerked her head up sharply at the words. He'd obviously read her mind, which reminded her that these creatures could do things humans couldn't. Like control them.

"Aye, we can," Cristo said with a smile. "And now I think you should get on the bus. The tourists are all off, and Vasco will be pleased to have you back. He is looking forward to enjoying your . . . company," he said with a suggestive wink.

Jess didn't want to get on the bus, and she tried not to, but she was no longer in control. Cristo was. Only it felt different than when Ildaria had taken control of her. Then, Jess hadn't really realized she'd been under someone's control until after. Her only thought had been that she must go to Vasco and kiss him, as if her thoughts were not her own. Now, her thoughts were her own, and it was her body betraying her and moving toward the bus against her will.

"I think not." Those words were spoken in a cold, hard voice as a hand closed around Jess's upper arm, drawing her to a halt.

Turning her head, Jess peered at Raffaele with surprise, relief, and concern. She hadn't realized he'd followed her to her cousin, and she was grateful for the intervention, but also worried that Cristo would just take control of him too.

"I believe this is yours." Raffaele shoved the lost life jacket at the pirate even as he drew Jess back so that she stood a step behind and to the side of him. "I suggest you take it and go, or you'll force me to do something in front of all these witnesses that we may both regret."

Cristo didn't take the life jacket at first. Instead, his eyes narrowed on Raffaele and then widened with something like realization, or perhaps recognition. She saw the pirate's hand reach instinctively to his side as if to grab a sword, but the scabbard that hung there was empty. Apparently, he'd left his weapon on the ship rather than risk trouble from mortals for carrying it around.

Cristo's mouth tightened briefly, and then his gaze slid to Jess before moving beyond her and narrowing again.

Jess glanced over her shoulder with curiosity, her eyebrows rising when she saw Santo and Zanipolo pushing their way through the crowd in the lobby, trying to get to the doors and, presumably, out to them.

A curse from Cristo drew her gaze around in time to see the look of regret he cast her way.

"I fear this is one of those situations where discretion is the better part of valor, little dove," he said, beginning to back toward the bus. "But we will meet again. Vasco will see to that."

Raffaele released Jess's arm and started after the pirate, but she caught his hand to stop him. He paused at once and glanced back with surprise.

Jess merely stared at him at first, too surprised by the tingle of awareness that shot through her fingers to speak. She lowered her gaze to their clasped hands with confusion. She hadn't experienced that same awareness when he'd grabbed her arm, she thought. But their skin hadn't touched then; his hand had closed around the sleeve of her T-shirt.

Raffaele gave a tug on his hand, trying to free himself, and Jess instinctively tightened her grip. Lifting her head, she said, "Let him go. He can . . . do things," she finished lamely, and then added, "I wouldn't want you hurt."

Raffaele's expression softened at her words. He covered her hand with his own, sending more tingles up her arm, and then squeezed gently, before removing her hold.

"It is fine," he assured her, and then turned to start forward again, only to pause almost at once.

Jess glanced around to see that while they had been distracted, Cristo had returned to the bus. She let out a relieved breath as she watched it pull away. They were safe. For now, she thought grimly, recalling Cristo's promise that they would meet again. He'd said Vasco would see to that, and remembering the passion that had exploded between them on the ship, Jess had no doubt Cristo was right. Vasco would come for her.

The thought was a terrifying one. The man was a big scary vampire, but all he had to do was touch her and she went up in flames. She had managed to override the desire he stirred in her and escape him once, but wasn't at all sure she could again. She needed to get away from there. She needed to check out, head straight for the airport, and catch the first available flight out of Punta Cana. Jess didn't even care where it was going. She could catch a connecting flight home to Montana from nearly anywhere, but she desperately needed to leave Punta Cana as soon as humanly possible.

With that thought dominating her mind, Jess glanced around a bit wildly for Allison and frowned when she saw that her cousin was gone. Every last member of the returning party was now inside the lobby, heading for the exit at the back, and the steps down to the short path around the pools. It left only her and Raffaele under the lighted porte cochere. And Santo and Zanipolo, Jess saw as the two men finally pushed through the hotel doors and hurried toward them.

Quite sure that Allison would head back to their room, Jess turned to Raffaele and forced a smile. "I need to speak to my cousin. But thank you again. For everything."

Not waiting for a response, Jess then turned and hurried back the way she'd come. She could have taken the shorter route this time and tried to catch up with Allison; but while going down stairs was always easier than going up, she wasn't sure her rubbery legs could manage them. Jess had no desire to take a tumble down the stairs and end up dead, or stuck in a hospital here where Vasco might find her and tempt her to join the dark side.

Grimacing, Jess rolled her eyes at her own thoughts. Join the dark side? Seriously? Could she get any more drama queen-ish? But it did speak to what was happening. Vasco was a huge temptation. Well . . . when he could manage to keep his mouth shut he was, she added on a sigh. However, if she gave in to the temptation he offered, and he turned her into a vampire . . . The thought of sleeping in a coffin made her shudder. As for biting people and drinking their blood? Well, that was just gross.

"Not gonna happen," Jess muttered to herself as she rounded the corner and started down the slope toward the buildings holding the hotel rooms.

Raffaele watched Jess hurry away, torn between chasing after her and waiting for Santo and Zanipolo to reach him. In the end, he waited for the men. The pirate had left. Jess should be safe . . . for now at least. But he needed to talk to Santo and Zanipolo and come up with a plan to keep her that way. He hadn't missed Cristo's last words to her. They'd sounded like a threat to him. The man seemed sure that this Vasco fellow would pursue her, and he probably would. Even rogues weren't foolish enough to leave mortals running around with the knowledge of their existence in their heads. The pirates would want to wipe the memory of the whole incident from her mind.

"That guy was one of the vampirates from the ship Jess was on," Zanipolo said as he and Santo reached him.

"Yes," Raffaele said grimly. "And now that they know Jess survived her dunk in the ocean, they'll be back. We're going to have to keep her safe."

"Hmm." Zanipolo nodded. "Did you see the people who came off the bus? At least half of them had visible bites on them. Some had more than one."

"And the others no doubt have them where they aren't easily seen," Raffaele said, running a hand through his hair.

"They think they were feeding the sharks," Santo said in a deep rumble full of disgust.

"They were," Raffaele assured him. "Just not the kind with fins and gills."

Santo grunted in agreement, and turned to Zanipolo. "Has Lucian returned your call yet?"

"No. I'll call him again," Zanipolo said, pulling out his phone and scrolling through his contacts.

"What will you do about Jess?" Santo asked.

"Keep her safe," Raffaele said at once.

Santo nodded and then they both glanced to Zani as he muttered under his breath and put his phone away.

"No answer," he explained. "I'll try again in half an hour and leave a message if he doesn't answer then."

Nodding, Raffaele turned to start following the path Jess had taken just moments ago.

"So, are we heading back to the restaurant?" Zanipolo asked as they rounded the building. "I still haven't had my dinner."

"You and Santo can go there if you like. I need to go talk to Jess, convince her that she needs protection, and assure her that we can be that protection."

Zanipolo nodded, and then pointed out, "She probably hasn't eaten either. Do you want us to pick her up something when we head back?"

"That's a good idea. Thank you."

Zanipolo nodded. "You can text us her order and her room number after you ask her what she wants."

Raffaele stopped walking.

"What's wrong?" Zanipolo asked.

"I don't know her room number," Raffaele admitted with alarm. He peered from one man to the other. "Did either of you read it from her mind?"

Both men shook their heads, and Raffaele was just starting to panic when Zanipolo said, "We can go to reception and have them look up her room number."

"Right," Raffaele said with relief.

"Except we do not know her last name," Santo pointed out quietly. "Once she told us her name was Jess, I didn't trouble to read her mind for the rest of her name." Turning to Zanipolo, he asked, "Did you?"

Zanipolo grimaced and shook his head apologetically.

Cursing, Raffaele closed his eyes briefly and then shook his head and started walking again. "We're going to have to search this entire resort again to find out her room number. We're going to have to go door-to-door."

"Or we could go to the restaurant first," Zanipolo suggested, and then pointed out, "She has to be starved after expending all that energy in the ocean, not to mention everything else that has happened to her today. The beachside restaurant is the only one still open. She'll have to go there if she wants food."

Raffaele's mouth tightened briefly with irritation at the suggestion. It was obvious the man was just trying to find an excuse to be able to eat. But then he forced himself to be patient. Zanipolo wasn't yet a hundred years old. He still ate food, and he'd been without it for quite a while. The man must be starved, he realized. Besides, they weren't on a job. Finding Jess was really his problem, and not something the other two men need trouble themselves with, yet neither of them were protesting being tasked with the chore. Zanipolo just wanted some food to sustain him for the effort. He could hardly begrudge him that.

"You two go down to the restaurant and see if she shows up while you're there, and I'll start the door-to-door search," he suggested. "Perhaps I'll get lucky and find someone who knows her and can give me her room number before you guys get done."

"Or you could ask her," Santo said suddenly.

When Raffaele glanced at him sharply, the big man nodded to the path ahead. Raffaele turned to scan the area. His eyebrows rose and relief coursed through him when he saw Jess sitting on a bench across the footpath from where Buildings 1 and 2 met.

"Thank God," Zanipolo muttered. A sentiment Raffaele silently echoed as he hurried forward, determined to get to the woman before she disappeared again.

Five

Shifting impatiently on the bench, Jess glanced toward Building 2 and then along the path between it and Building 1, but there was still no light coming from their room, or sign of her cousin on the path. Allison appeared to be taking her time about returning to their room.

Jess sat back with a disgruntled sigh. She needed to get into their room. She had to put some clothes on, pack, call the airport to see what the first available flight out of Punta Cana was. And find out if she could somehow switch her ticket or, if not, figure out if she could afford the new one, she thought grimly. Fortunately, the room was already paid for. They'd had to prepay months ago. Having to buy a new plane ticket would be a problem, though. She would have to put it on her credit card, and work extra shifts at the bar, or get a third job, to pay for it once she got home.

Sighing, Jess glanced toward Building 2 and then to the path between the buildings again. There was still no sign of Allison.

Muttering impatiently under her breath, Jess leaned her head back to peer up at the stars. She planned to try to convince her cousin to leave with her, but didn't think she was likely to succeed. As far as she could tell, Allison had absolutely no memory of what had really taken place on the pirate ship. She and Tyler, and everyone else from the bus, seemed to be convinced they'd had a grand time.

Jess shook her head with amazement. Several groups of people from the bus had passed her while she sat here waiting for Allison, and everyone had been laughing and talking about what a great time the shark feeding tour had been, and how they should tell so-and-so to go on it. But Jess had seen the bite marks on several of them, and she distinctly remembered Tyler's horrified and pain-filled expression as Ildaria had chewed on his family jewels. She *knew* he hadn't had a good time. He, however, didn't.

Lowering her chin, Jess rubbed her forehead unhappily. Part of her wanted to tell them all what had really occurred, but she was sure they'd think she was crazy. They all had a different memory of events. Besides, it seemed the pirates were smart vampires. They didn't kill their victims, which might have drawn attention to their existence. Instead, they just snacked on the tourists they lured aboard ship, and then returned them safe and sound and even with happy memories of the trip. What would she achieve by changing that? Did she really want them to be as afraid and freaked out as she was? Where was the value in that? As far as she could tell, they were all probably safe enough now that they were back. She doubted any of them would suffer a second encounter with the pirates, unless they went back to the pirate ship on their own because they thought they'd had such fun. Jess didn't think the pirates would come back looking for a second round themselves, though. At least not with the others. If the pirates had wanted more from them, they could have simply kept them. No, Jess was pretty sure she was the only one who had to worry about the vampirates coming for her.

She gave her head a shake, finding it hard to believe she was even thinking that. Jess had never imagined that would be a concern in her life. That she'd have to worry about vampirates coming for her. It hardly seemed possible. She could still hardly believe there *were* vampires, or even pirates.

"Maybe I'm crazy and hallucinated it all," she muttered.

"Jess?"

Stiffening, she jerked her head up and stared at the man approaching through the shadows. Jess breathed out a sigh of relief when he got close enough that the light from the lamppost behind the bench she sat on reached his face.

"Raffaele," she said, managing a shaky smile. "Hi."

"Hello," he responded, pausing in front of her. Glancing around with a frown, he asked, "What are you doing out here?"

"Waiting for Allison to come to our room so I can get in," she admitted, and then added ruefully, "Apparently, I lost my room key today. Along with everything else I had in my waist belt."

Raffaele's eyebrows rose slightly. "What is a waist belt?"

"Oh." Jess smiled faintly. "It's a small nylon sack, kind of like a big wallet, that you wear strapped around your waist. You keep your valuables in it," she explained. "Money, ID, room key, stuff like that."

"And you lost it in the water?" he asked with concern.

Jess frowned. She'd had it when she'd boarded the pirate ship, but not when she'd left it. She was quite sure about that. It would have caught on the porthole when she'd pushed herself through it. Besides, Jess couldn't remember it being there when Vasco had pulled her shorts off during their wrestling session on his bed. The only thing she could think was that she'd lost it during their first session on deck when Ildaria had sent her out to kiss him and Jess had found she'd climbed the man like a telephone pole. It must have somehow got dislodged then, along with Vasco's hat, she decided.

"Jess?" Raffaele queried.

"Sorry," she muttered, forcing a smile. "I was thinking. But no, I didn't lose it in the water. I'm pretty sure I lost it on the pirate ship."

"The pirate ship?" he asked with interest.

Jess glanced to him with surprise and then realized she hadn't yet told him anything about her adventures. Probably a good thing, she decided. He'd seen everyone get off the bus happy and chatty, and would hardly believe her version of events anyway. She was having trouble believing it herself.

"It doesn't matter," she said finally, and glanced past him to Santo and Zanipolo as the two men joined them at the bench and took up position on either side of Raffaele.

Before she could offer a greeting to the men, Raffaele asked, "Did you have anything of value in the waist belt?"

"Well, my key card to our room was in it. That's why I'm sitting here waiting for Allison," she pointed out. "As for anything of value—"

"What is it?" Raffaele asked when she stopped abruptly, her eyes going wide with alarm.

"My iPhone and driver's license were in it," she breathed shakily.

"You took your iPhone and driver's license with you on your outing?" Raffaele asked with surprise.

"Yes," Jess moaned, closing her eyes. "My iPhone is my camera, of course I took it. I wanted pictures of the sharks and stingrays and our swimming with them," she explained, and silently mourned the loss of those pictures. All of her pictures from this trip were on it—the wedding, the wedding dinner, their excursions so far—and she'd lost all of them.

"I understand the phone," Zanipolo said. "But your driver's license?"

"Oh," Jess sighed, and waved a hand vaguely. "Allison insisted I bring my driver's license. She said she'd heard that you had to have photo ID if you wanted to rent anything on these excursions. She thought there might be Jet-Skis or Seabobs to try at the Seaquarium, and if there was, she wanted to rent one."

"And her wanting to rent one meant *you* had to bring *your* ID?" Santo asked heavily, sounding like he didn't like her cousin. She didn't know how that could be, though; as far as she knew they hadn't even met. Of course, they were in the same resort and might have had a brief encounter in passing. With Allison, a brief encounter in passing could be enough to cause animosity in the kindest person.

"Both of our driver's licenses were in the waist belt," she admitted unhappily. "That way we could both rent a Seabob. Unfortunately, I lost hers as well as mine, and she is so going to kill me for it."

A moment of silence passed and then Raffaele cleared his throat and asked, "So these vampires have your room key?"

"Vampires?" she squeaked, peering at him with wide eyes.

"That is what you called them when we were in the water," he reminded her.

"Oh, right." She stared at him wide-eyed, suddenly understanding why these men were following her around. They thought she was off her nut because of the vampire thing. Clearing her throat, she forced a laugh. "Yeah. Vampires. Ha ha. That was a joke," she lied anxiously, not wanting him to think her crazy, and then she stiffened as his question filtered through her mind. The vampires had her room key.

Vasco had her room key.

For a moment, panic assailed her, but then Jess realized that was okay. The room keys didn't list the room number on them, so it wasn't like he could use it to find her here. Unfortunately, he also had her iPhone and driver's license, which meant he had tons of info about her, including her home address. But surely, he wouldn't sail all the way to Montana to hunt her down? Well, no, he couldn't. Montana was hundreds of miles from the ocean. No one could sail there. She supposed he could fly, but what would he do about his coffin?

Speaking of coffins, where had those been? Vampires slept in coffins; the ship was full of vampires. Where did they keep their coffins? Jess pursed her lips as she considered the question. She hadn't seen one in Vasco's cabin. But maybe they kept the coffins down in the hull of the ship where the tourists wouldn't find them.

That made sense, Jess decided. But wherever it was, he wouldn't fly to Montana to hunt her down without his coffin just in the hopes of a good lay. That would be crazy, she assured herself.

"We were heading down to the restaurant on the beach to get some food," Zanipolo blurted suddenly. "Did you want to join us?"

Jess glanced to the man, tempted to say yes. Now that he'd mentioned food, she was starving . . . and had been for a while, she realized. She'd been suffering hunger pangs for hours, even while she was in the water, but had been too distracted with other issues to pay it any attention. Now that he'd brought it to her awareness with his invitation, however, she was tempted. But . . .

"No," she said on a sigh, her eyes shifting to Building 2 and then the path again. "Thank you, but I have to wait for Allison."

"I think she would be here already if she was returning directly to the room," Raffaele pointed out gently.

"But where else would she go?" Jess asked with frustration. She'd kind of come to that conclusion herself, but had no idea where else her cousin could have gone.

"Maybe she went down to the restaurant," Zanipolo suggested. "There's a band playing tonight, and she and the others were probably hungry after their tour. They might have headed there after getting off the bus."

Jess perked up at the suggestion. That actually made sense, especially since none of them had had supper. At least, she hadn't seen anything that might suggest the vampirates planned to feed them after feeding off of them. The blood loss might even add to their hunger, she thought. And her not having any money on her wouldn't be an issue. The resort was all-inclusive; all she had to do was give her room number.

"Yes, I think I will join you, then," Jess said, standing up, only to hesitate as she glanced down at her outfit. A towel over a ripped T-shirt and bikini bottoms was hardly acceptable attire for a restaurant. On top of that, the rest of her was probably a sight too. She wasn't wearing a bit of makeup, which Jess didn't mind so much, but she also didn't have a brush and her hair had dried au naturel. It was probably a mess.

Sighing, she dropped back onto the bench. "You'd better go without me. I'm not dressed for a restaurant. They'd throw me out."

Zanipolo immediately started to protest, but Raffaele said, "I have a better idea."

Jess peered at him curiously, actually hoping he had a solution, because she was really hungry.

"Among the three of us, we must have something that you can wear," Raffaele assured her. "We'll go to our room and see if we can find you something. If we can, we can all go down to the restaurant. If we cannot, then Zanipolo and Santo can go themselves, look for Allison, and bring you back food."

"Or," Zanipolo countered, "you two can go to our room and see if we have anything for Jess to wear, and Santo and I can go down to the restaurant and wait for you," he said brightly.

"He is very hungry," Santo said solemnly.

Jess saw guilt flash across Raffaele's face, and then he nodded. "Yes. Go. You've been waiting for your supper for long enough."

Zanipolo grinned, but then said, "Call us if you can't find anything for her to wear and we'll bring back food right away. I'll even order mine to go so Jess doesn't have to wait."

"Thank you, that's very kind," Jess said sincerely.

"Yes, it is," Raffaele agreed. "Thank you, Zani. Now, go on. I'll call you in a few minutes and let you know if we are coming or not."

The two men started away, but then Santo stopped and peered back, his gaze sliding over Jess as she stood up. "One of my dress shirts is robin's egg blue like your eyes."

Jess raised her eyebrows and said uncertainly, "Okay."

"I have seen women wearing what looks like overlarge shirts as dresses," he explained quietly. "My blue dress shirt should be long enough on you to make a dress. It will be too large in the arms, but you can roll up the sleeves, and wear a belt, and the color would suit you. You may wear it."

"Oh, I see," Jess said, a wide smile claiming her lips. "Thank you."

"What?" Zanipolo howled, turning on the large man. "*Robin's egg* blue? Seriously? You never say more than one or two words at a time, three at most on the rare occasion, and the first time you speak more than that it's about women's fashion? Really?" He shook his head. "Damn, big guy!"

"Shut up," Santo said mildly, taking the smaller man's arm and turning him away. "Walk."

Jess grinned as she watched the pair continue along the path, Zanipolo taunting the big man, and Santo strutting along, ignoring him. It made her think of a cartoon she'd once seen where a large bulldog was walking along ignoring a much littler dog who was yipping and hopping excitedly around him.

"Shall we?" Raffaele asked, and Jess glanced around to see him gesturing toward the buildings in front of them.

"Oh, yes. Sorry," she said, moving onto the path that ran along the buildings. "You're in Building 2, right?" She'd been a bit stressed when she'd rushed out earlier and wasn't sure.

"Yes. And you?"

"Two as well," she murmured. "But we're on the fourth floor. You were three?"

He smiled faintly. "Yes."

Jess nodded, and then searched her mind for something else to say. She didn't know why, but she was suddenly nervous around the man. Not about her safety. They'd had her in their room while she was unconscious, and then once she'd woken up and hadn't done anything to harm her. In fact, the man had saved her life. Still, now that it was just him, she was very aware that they were alone, and that she found him attractive, and really, she hadn't been making very good decisions today when it came to attraction—

"You have had enough exercise today, I think."

Jess blinked her thoughts away and glanced around to see that they were standing in front of the elevator in Building 2 and he was pushing the call button. Obviously, the comment had been to explain why they weren't using the stairs. Smiling faintly, she murmured, "Thank you. You're right." Grimacing, she added, "I'm sure I'll feel it tomorrow."

"A good massage should help with that," Raffaele said, ushering her onto the elevator when the doors opened.

"Yeah, too bad I won't be here tomorrow to book one in the spa," she said on a sigh.

"What?" Raffaele glanced at her sharply. "You have plans for tomorrow?"

Jess hesitated, and then admitted, "Actually, I was thinking it would be better if I leave Punta Cana and go home. I was hoping Allison would return, and I could get into our room, pack up, call to see what time the next flight is, and leave."

"I see," Raffaele said slowly, but then fell silent, his expression conflicted. She got the feeling that he didn't want her to go, but thought it might be for the best.

Which was probably just wishful thinking on her part, Jess decided. At least the part about his not wanting her to go. They'd just met, after all, and other than his being kind and helping her, had shared little interaction. She hadn't even really explained what had happened to her today, and how she had ended up jumping off a ship.

No, there was no reason he should care whether she stayed or left. But then there was no reason she should regret having to go, and yet Jess was sorry she couldn't stay and get to know him better. Raffaele was an attractive man. He was also kind and helpful, and made her feel safe for some reason. Plus, he wasn't a pirate or a vampire, was very polite, and hadn't once said anything crude or—

A ding sounded, announcing their arrival at the third floor, and Jess gave up her thoughts and stepped off the elevator when the doors opened. When Raffaele followed and took her elbow to usher her along the hall, Jess experienced the same tingling sensation rushing along her skin as she had when she'd grabbed his hand to stop him from pursuing Cristo.

"It's too late for any flights this evening," Raffaele said suddenly, his voice slightly husky.

"Oh," Jess murmured, distracted by the sensations she was experiencing.

"The airport is probably closed for the night," he added, pausing at the door to what she presumed was the suite he shared with Santo and Zanipolo. Raffaele released her arm then to retrieve his key card, and Jess started to breathe again, realizing only then that she'd been holding her breath as she focused on his effect on her.

She glanced at the number on the door as he unlocked it, and was surprised to see that this suite was the one directly below the one she and Allison shared. Small world, she thought, and cleared her throat to say, "Then I'll have to see if I can catch a flight out in the morning."

First thing in the morning, Jess added silently. She knew she wouldn't get a lick of sleep tonight. She'd lie awake in bed, jumping at every creak and sound because Vasco had her key card, and while it didn't reveal a room number, he also had her driver's license, with her name on it. Not that he'd needed that, she thought with a frown as she recalled Cristo telling Vasco her full name. All the man had to do was control whoever was working reception and make them tell him her room number. Yeah, it was going to be a long night.

Actually, Jess wasn't sure she'd sleep well once she got home either, now that she knew Vasco had her home address. Chances were he wouldn't follow her to Montana, but what if he did? Maybe she should go to a hotel when she landed, get some sleep, and then start looking for an apartment or something. The very thought made her frown. She really didn't want to sell the house she'd inherited from her parents, but knew she wouldn't feel safe there anymore.

"Jess?"

Dragging herself from her thoughts, she glanced up to see that Raffaele had the door unlocked and was standing to the side, holding it open as he waited for her to enter.

"Sorry," she muttered, slipping quickly past him into the room.

"The shirt Santo mentioned is hanging in the closet in the bedroom," Raffaele said as he followed her in. "Go take a look and I'll see if I can find something for you to use as a belt."

Nodding, Jess led the way through the sitting area and into the bedroom. She headed straight for the closet, while Raffaele moved to the dresser and began to riffle through the drawers.

Jess found the shirt right away. It was the only blue dress shirt in the closet. As Santo had said, it was a lovely robin's egg blue. Pulling it out, Jess eyed it with interest, noting that it was a very soft, thin linen that would feel amazing on.

"I might have to improvise something."

Jess glanced around at that comment to see that Raffaele had given up on finding anything in the dresser and was now staring at the suitcase that stood next to it. The suitcase had a dark blue luggage strap around it. Eyebrows rising, she walked over to join him and peered at the strap. It was custom-made, with "Property of R. Notte" stamped on it in black. "That might work. And it's even blue."

"Yes, but I suspect it will be too large," he said, his brow furrowing.

Jess shrugged. "Most luggage straps can be adjusted from something like forty-one inches to eighty-something. That one probably does too."

"Much too big, then," he said with a sigh.

"Not if I wrap it around my waist twice," she pointed out.

Raffaele's eyebrows rose at that, and then he grinned and murmured, "Clever lady."

Jess stiffened at the words. It was what Cristo had said to her in front of the lobby. And it brought the pirate and Vasco, and everything that had passed between them, immediately to mind.

"Jess? Is something troubling you?" Raffaele asked, reaching out to take her free hand gently in his.

She sucked in a breath at the shock of awareness that again tingled its way up her arm from where his skin touched hers, and then just shook her head and stared at their entangled fingers. As she did, he used his hold on her hand to turn her arm slightly so that he could get a better look at the scrape by her elbow. Frowning, he ran a finger lightly alongside the injury. The action sent another tingle through Jess, one that made her shiver and close her eyes.

"I originally intended to take you to see the resort physician, but—"

"The resort physician?" Jess's eyes widened with surprise.

Raffaele nodded solemnly. "You should really be examined by a doctor to be sure your injuries will not be an issue."

Jess smiled faintly at his concern. She thought it was sweet, but shook her head. "I'm fine. I don't have any injuries."

Raffaele arched an eyebrow and then returned his gaze to her arm.

"Well, a couple of scrapes, maybe," she muttered with chagrin. "But nothing serious."

"You also have scrapes on your stomach and hips," he said quietly, "and they are very large and appeared deeper than this one."

Jess glanced to him sharply. "When did you see my stomach and hips?"

"I carried you up here from the beach," he reminded her gently. "The life jacket only partially covered your stomach, and didn't do anything to hide your hips."

"Oh," Jess muttered, aware that she was blushing. She could feel the heat in her cheeks. Irritated at herself for it, she handed him Santo's shirt, and then turned away from him and opened the towel so she could get a look at herself. She'd been so eager to cover up that she hadn't had the chance to check the scrapes on her stomach and hips before wrapping the towel around herself earlier. Now she peered down at her stomach, and then her hips, and winced as she saw where she'd been skinned while forcing herself through the porthole. Jess had known it was happening at the time, but was surprised at how big they all were. None of them appeared too terribly deep, but they were deep enough, and the one on her stomach was a monster, stretching across her entire stomach from side to side.

Still, while they weren't pretty, they weren't life-threatening either,

Jess decided, and closed the towel over herself again before turning back to face Raffaele. "I'm fine. Really. They'll heal quickly."

"Infection is a real danger in the tropics," Raffaele informed her quietly.

Jess was frowning at that when he cleared his throat and asked, "Do you have any other wounds anywhere?"

"Probably," she admitted with a grimace. "Some bruises at least, maybe other stuff."

"What kind of stuff? Where?" Raffaele asked at once.

"My back for one," she admitted, recalling Allison attacking her while she kissed Vasco. "I got hit in the kidney pretty hard. It probably bruised."

"May I see?" he asked with concern.

Jess hesitated, but then sighed and turned her back to him again and opened her towel. This time, though, she let it drop just below the waist of her bikini bottoms and glanced over her shoulder. "Is there a bruise?"

"Hmm, yes," Raffaele murmured, and she felt his fingers gently probing the area, making her shiver as more tingles raced through her. "You have a couple of bruises back here actually."

"Yeah, aside from getting punched, I got knocked around a bit," Jess admitted, turning to face him so that he'd stop touching her. "Allison—Well, it doesn't matter. I just took a tumble off a raised surface," she muttered, unwilling to discuss how she'd been bounced from a bed by her cousin who was jealous of the crazy-sexy vampirate who had been ravishing her.

"You have a bruise here too," he said with concern.

Jess glanced down with a start when he ran one finger lightly across the curve of her breast where the edge of the knotted T-shirt didn't cover it. The action reminded her at once that she hadn't wrapped the towel around herself again, but it seemed a bit late for that. Besides, between the ripped T-shirt and the bikini bottoms, she supposed she was wearing more than she wore on the beach. Of course, she didn't usually have people touching her this way in her swimsuit, Jess thought, and glanced down at the bruise he was examining. She was quite sure it was a result of her forcing herself through the porthole. Before she could say as much, however, she noted the way her nipple was pebbling and pressing against the cloth of the T-shirt in response to Raffaele gently probing just the curve of her breast. It seemed a ridiculous response to her. It wasn't like he'd actually caressed the nipple that was sticking its head up for attention. But her body obviously wanted him too.

Dear God, Jess thought with dismay, was she just going to respond like this to every man who touched her now? She'd never been like this before. Maybe her hormones were out of whack. Perhaps a trip to the clinic was a good idea.

Stepping back, Jess closed the towel, and then reached out to take the blue shirt from him. Heading for the bathroom with it, she muttered, "I'll be right back."

"Of course," Raffaele said. "I'll call Zanipolo and tell him we'll be down soon and he needn't order the food to go."

Jess merely nodded, and closed the bathroom door. Spotting the hook on the back of the door, she hung the hanger there and then quickly stripped off her T-shirt. Dropping it on the floor, she considered her damp bikini bottoms, but then left them on. She had no underwear. Wet bikini bottoms were better than nothing, Jess decided, and removed the shirt from the hanger to pull it on over her head. It was big enough for her to get into it that way, and much easier than undoing and redoing the buttons.

Of course, the sleeves were too long. She would definitely have to roll them up, but it did reach two-thirds of the way down her upper legs.

"How is it?" Raffaele asked through the door, and Jess tugged one sleeve up to open the door.

"Good, I think. Or it will be once I put the luggage strap on," she assured him.

Raffaele held it up at once.

Jess reached for it, but paused when the sleeve flapped around like a flipper.

"Allow me," Raffaele said with amusement. Resting the luggage strap over his shoulder, he set to work on the sleeves, quickly rolling up first one, and then the other. Jess stood completely still while he worked, her nose twitching as his scent wafted around her. He smelled quite nice, she noted. Delicious even, and she realized that she hadn't really noticed how Vasco smelled. Just that his hair was greasy. She shifted her gaze to Raffaele's bent head and noted that his hair was dry now, and a lovely silky-looking black that wasn't greasy.

"There we go," Raffaele said, straightening as he finished with his efforts.

"Thank you," Jess said softly.

"Now the belt," he announced, and removed it from his shoulder to wrap it around her waist twice, explaining as he did, "I adjusted it to the size I thought might work, but—Oh, look, it's perfect."

Jess glanced down with relief when he finished and stepped back. She'd felt odd having him wrapping the belt around her waist. He'd had to bend forward slightly to do it, his head nearly on her shoulder and his arms going around her waist and back, and it had made her stomach jump and quiver a bit. Now, she took a couple of deep breaths to settle herself and turned to peer at her reflection in the vanity mirror that ran the length of the counter that held the double sinks.

Jess considered her reflection with surprise. Actually, it didn't look half-bad. Belting it had raised it an inch or so, but it wasn't too too short.

"Nice," she decided, and then lifted her gaze and groaned as she saw her face and hair.

Raffaele chuckled at her expression. "My hairbrush is the brown one. Feel free to use it. I'll wait for you in the sitting room."

Jess didn't bother to close the door behind him. She was dressed. Or as dressed as she could be at that moment. It felt a little odd to be without a bra. She hadn't gone braless since she was eleven or twelve. But the shirt was big and blousy enough that you couldn't really tell, so she picked up Raffaele's brush and began to run it through her hair. That felt odd too. Not the brush itself, but that she was using *his* brush. She had no idea why. It wasn't like it was his toothbrush or something, but it still felt strange and somewhat intimate when she finished and saw the long chestnut-brown hairs caught in the brush along with his shorter, black ones. Jess stared at it briefly, and then quickly pulled all of the hair from the bristles before setting it down.

Jess bent to toss the ball of hair into the little garbage can under the sink and then straightened to look at herself again. Her hair looked much better. A quick brushing had done a world of good and her hair now fell around her face in soft waves.

Her attention shifted to her face. She was a little pale and had dark smudges under her eyes. The result of exhaustion, Jess supposed. And probably dehydration caused by too much sun and too little water. Not having eaten since lunch probably didn't help either, she guessed. A little concealer to remove the dark shadows, and a touch of blush to add color would have done wonders, but she didn't have either.

Shrugging, Jess pinched her cheeks and bit her lips to draw out some natural color and then turned to leave the room, telling herself that food would help.

Six

Raffaele wiped away a circle of the condensation filming the sliding glass doors and shook his head. The entire room had a film of moisture on it and had since they'd arrived—the walls, the floor, the tabletops—and every item of cloth felt limp and damp, from the sheets to the clothes they'd hung in the closet. It was like the room was crying. He'd never seen anything like it, and hoped never to again. Even at this hour it was crazy hot and humid.

Having cleared a spot on the glass door, Raffaele peered out at the night and thought about what Jess had said. She wanted to leave, and the hell of it was, he couldn't tell her not to go. Not only did he not have the right, but if he talked her into staying and something happened, like the rogues getting their hands on her again . . . Well, he'd never forgive himself. It seemed to him it might be better to let her leave. The question then became, did he follow her at once, or wait until this trip was done to follow her? Because follow her he would. She was his life mate. He fully intended on wooing, seducing, and claiming her.

Raffaele's instinct was to follow her at once, get on the same damned plane, hell, even take the same taxi from the resort to the airport. He'd waited too long for her not to want to follow her like a dog following a nice juicy steak on a string. However, he was here to help Santo, and didn't feel he could leave right away.

"Well, this is the best I can do, so we may as well head down now."

Raffaele turned and smiled when he saw her. She looked lovely to him, but then she had before she'd brushed her hair and done whatever she had to put color into her cheeks.

"You look perfect," he assured her, starting across the room.

Jess snorted rudely at the claim and turned to lead the way to the door. "Yeah, sure, and you've got vision probl—Ah!"

Raffaele reached out quickly and caught her arm as she slipped on the wet floor and nearly fell.

"Thanks," Jess breathed once she'd regained her balance and he'd released her arm. She took a couple of deep breaths as if to steady herself and then smiled weakly, and said, "This doesn't mean you can go telling your friends that I've fallen for you."

Raffaele chuckled at her teasing, but said, "Actually, they are my cousins, not my friends. Well, friends and cousins, I suppose."

"Really? Cousins?" she asked with surprise as he escorted her to the door.

"Yes, really," he assured her, keeping a firm grip on her elbow in case of another slip. Raffaele had donned his shoes while waiting for her, but she was barefoot and that, combined with the slippery condensation, was dangerous.

Fortunately, Santo's shirt acted as a buffer between his hand and her arm. The tingle of excitement and awareness from where he gripped her was more muted this time, and that was for the best. He knew Jess had experienced it too; he'd heard her heart rate pick up and the way she caught her breath the previous times it had happened. Her body was definitely responding to his. Unfortunately, Raffaele was thinking they should avoid any physical exchange until she was safely back in Montana and he had followed. Raffaele suspected it would be hard to let her go otherwise, and he wanted her to be safe. Her leaving was the best way to ascertain that.

"But you all look so different," Jess said, drawing him from his thoughts as they stepped out into the hall.

Raffaele glanced to her with surprise as they started to walk. "Do you think so? Most people think we are similar in looks."

"Hmm." She considered that as he ushered her toward the elevator. "I guess you all have similar eyes, but . . ." She shrugged. "I'll have to take a closer look once we're at the restaurant."

Raffaele nodded and pressed the call button for the elevator. "I shall look forward to your decision."

"Where are you guys from?" Jess asked now.

"Italy," he answered promptly, and then added, "Although we flew here from Canada. We were visiting family there."

"Ah," she murmured. The elevator doors opened, and they stepped inside. As the door closed again, she asked, "Are you here for a wedding?"

"Vacation," Raffaele said, and smiled with amusement at her dubious expression.

"Whose idea was it to come here? At this time of year?" she asked, her tone suggesting that whoever it was couldn't be very bright.

"Zanipolo's," he admitted with amusement. "I gave him a hard time about it when we first arrived, but now I think I was wrong and this was the perfect spot to vacation."

"Why?" she asked with obvious surprise.

Because you are here, Raffaele thought, but merely shrugged, and said, "I presume you are here for a wedding?"

Jess hesitated, seeming reluctant to move the conversation along without getting an answer to her question, but when the elevator stopped and the doors opened, she nodded and said, "Yes," before leading the way out.

"Family or friend?" Raffaele asked as they started walking in the direction of the beach.

"Both," she said at once. "My cousin Krista, who is also a friend as your cousins are to you."

"And Allison is your cousin too?"

Jess nodded.

"But not a friend?" Raffaele guessed, recalling the woman's treatment of Jess earlier.

Jess's mouth twitched, and then she sighed and shook her head. "I don't think Allison *has* friends. She is Krista's older sister and . . . a bit difficult," she finished in what he suspected was a vast understatement. While he couldn't read Jess, he *had* been able to read Allison when Jess had rushed to embrace her, and he'd found little of merit in the woman's mind. It had been filled with *I* and *me* and sly cruelty.

"So, why did Krista choose to marry here?" Raffaele asked, changing the subject.

"She always wanted a destination wedding," Jess explained. "And years ago decided it would take place in Punta Cana."

"But could she not have held it at a better time of year?" he asked. "When it wasn't so hot, for instance."

Jess chuckled and shook her head. "The wedding was a year to the day from when Pat proposed."

"Ah." Raffaele nodded with understanding. "She is sentimental."

"Yes, although when someone told her how hot and humid it could get this time of year, she did briefly consider changing the date. But it would have meant a lot of people couldn't attend."

"Because?" he asked.

"Because most of her friends and cousins are still in university or college and couldn't take ten days to attend a wedding during classes."

"Ah, yes." He nodded again.

"And," Jess added, "because off-season means great deals. The price during the busy season would have been at least double what we paid to be here now. That would have meant that at least half of the people who are here wouldn't have been able to afford to attend. Including me."

"I knew it!" Raffaele said with disgust. "Zani had us vacation here because it was cheap."

Jess chuckled. "I'm not buying your supposed outrage for a minute, buddy. You told me in the elevator not five minutes ago that this was the perfect spot to vacation in."

"Yes, I did," he admitted, enjoying her amusement. "But do not ever tell Zanipolo I said so. He will become unbearably smug and say 'I told you so' at least twenty times a day for the next three centuries if you tell him I did."

She raised her eyebrows at the obvious exaggeration, and then pursed her lips. "I don't know. It seems to me that he deserves to know that you are pleased with the trip." Jess clucked her tongue a couple times and then waggled her eyebrows up and down. "What will you give me if I keep my mouth shut?"

"Blackmail?" Raffaele asked with delight, knowing she was teasing.

"Hey, I'm a starving student, buddy," she said with a shrug. "I'll take what I can get."

"Hmm." He nodded, his mouth twitching with amusement, and then offered, "How about if I buy you dinner, then?"

She snorted at the suggestion. "This place is all-inclusive, my friend. You won't have to pay a thing."

"True," he agreed solemnly. Raffaele then pursed his lips, and followed it up with some clucking in imitation of her, before asking, "Well, what would you have of me, then?"

Jess opened her mouth to answer, and then paused as they rounded the building they'd been walking by, and they heard music from the restaurant ahead. A slow smile claimed her lips then, and she announced gleefully, "A dance!"

"Done," he said at once, unable to tear his gaze away from her happy face. She was absolutely stunning when she smiled like that, and he couldn't wait to claim that dance . . . at least until he recalled his intention to keep his distance from her until they were back in North America. Holding her in his arms on the dance floor, her body pressed to his, didn't seem likely to help him with that.

"Do you see them?" Jess asked moments later as they entered the busy bar/restaurant.

Raffaele narrowed his gaze and peered around the dim interior, and then shook his head. "They are probably out on the deck overlooking the beach. That is where we were when we spotted you in the water."

"Really?" Jess asked with surprise as he took her arm to usher her through the crowd.

"Really," he assured her, and then said, "Aha!" as he spotted Santo.

"You see them?" she asked, craning her head to try to see over the crowd.

The tables were all full and people had resorted to standing in small groups, drinks in hand. It looked to him as if everyone from the bus was here. Although he didn't see Allison, he noted as he nodded in response to her question.

"Where are they?" Jess asked as he urged her through the crowd.

"On the deck, and at the exact same table we were at when we spotted you and the shark in the water."

"There wasn't really a shark!" she protested on a laugh.

"There was," he assured her as they reached the deck and made their way to where Santo and Zanipolo waited at a table full of food. "Ask Santo. He was the one who spotted it first."

"Who spotted what first?" Zanipolo asked, catching the tail end of the conversation as they reached the table.

"The shark," Jess said, settling in the seat Raffaele pulled out for her. "There wasn't really a shark, was there?"

"Sì," Santo assured her.

"Yeah," Zanipolo agreed as Raffaele took the seat between him and Jess. "Santo saw it just seconds after Raffaele pointed you out to us. We thought for sure you were a goner, but it lost interest about ten or twenty feet away from you and just turned around and swam the other way."

"Damn," she breathed, looking horrified.

Raffaele reached out to clasp her hand and squeeze it, and then glanced from Santo to Zanipolo. "No Allison?"

Both men shook their heads, and then Santo said, "She obviously went elsewhere."

"Hmm," Raffaele murmured and, noting the frown on Jess's face, pointed out, "If she hasn't returned to your room by the time you finish eating, we can go to the reception desk and get another key."

"But where *is* she?" Jess asked with a frown.

"She was walking away with some fellow as we tried to get through the crowd in the lobby to reach you two," Zanipolo announced. "They looked pretty chummy. Maybe she went to his room."

"Tyler?" Jess asked, her eyes going wide. "Tall guy? Blond hair, green T-shirt?"

"Yes," Santo said with a nod.

"Oh, they'd never—Well, I don't know him. He might if he doesn't know her, but Allison positively loathes all of Pat's friends. She'd never . . . Nuh-uh." She shook her head firmly.

"Then perhaps they have gone to a club in town," Zanipolo suggested.

Jess appeared to consider that, and then sighed and turned her attention to the food on the table. Her expression immediately transformed into one of amazement. "What's all this?"

"I wasn't sure what you'd like so I ordered two of several different dishes," Zanipolo said with a grin. "Eat up. There's plenty of everything."

Raffaele surveyed the various plates on the table, not recognizing much of it. But then he hadn't eaten in centuries and while he had, on occasion, kept Zanipolo company as he ate, he'd never troubled himself to pay much attention to what his cousin was eating. Mostly, he'd spent his time trying to avoid showing his distaste of the smells assailing him, and calculating how long it would be before Zanipolo finished and he could escape those smells. The scent of food had often turned his stomach over the past couple of centuries. He didn't know why. It hadn't bothered him before that, but . . .

Shrugging the concern away, Raffaele took a tentative sniff of the various scents wafting up from the dishes spread out before them, and raised his eyebrows. This food wasn't turning his stomach. In fact, some of the smells filling his nose were rather interesting, Raffaele thought as he watched Jess pull a plate with little misshapen light brown logs, thin, pale yellow sticks, and a very tiny bowl of some kind of thick pinkish/red liquid with seeds in it toward her. She picked up one of the logs, dipped it in the small bowl of syrupy liquid, took a bite, and moaned with pleasure.

"What's that?" Raffaele asked with interest, unable to tear his gaze away from the expression of ecstasy on her face.

"Chicken fingers with sweet Thai chili sauce," she said on a little sigh. And then dipped the log again and leaned toward him, holding it out. "Here, try it."

Raffaele didn't have to be asked twice. It smelled scrumptious. Leaning forward, he took a bite and then abruptly sat up straight in his seat, his eyes widening incredulously. Sweet and heat exploded in his mouth together first and were followed by the spice in the breading and the unmistakable flavor of chicken as he chewed.

"Good, huh?" Jess asked with a grin.

Nodding, he swallowed the food and then glanced around to catch the eye of a passing waitress. When he did, he smiled at the woman. She smiled in return and immediately made her way to their table.

"What do you want to drink, Jess?" Raffaele asked, turning to her in question when the waitress reached them.

"A glass of the house wine would be nice," she said, offering the waitress a smile.

"Sí." The woman nodded and then glanced to Raffaele in question.

"Water is fine for me," he murmured, not wanting to partake of alcohol, but unsure what else would be good. He didn't normally drink even water. The blood he consumed generally took care of nutrients as well as hydration. But he also didn't normally eat food either, and this food was tasty, but spicy and a bit salty. Raffaele suspected he'd need a drink or two to help wash it down.

"Do you want half?"

Raffaele glanced to Jess at her question, and saw that she had shifted the plate between them so that he could share. He smiled, but knew it was probably a little wry. As much as he liked the chicken fingers, and would be happy to partake of them, he'd quite enjoyed her feeding it to him as well. However, it appeared he would have to forego that pleasure now. A good thing, Raffaele assured himself. He'd barely refrained from licking or nipping her fingers the last time she'd held the food out. He didn't trust himself not to do it the next time if the log was shorter and her fingers closer.

"Eat up," Jess suggested, nudging the plate a little closer to him.

"Thank you," he said, picking up one of the chicken fingers and dipping it himself.

"Did you get any gravy for the fries?"

Raffaele glanced to Jess when she asked that question and noted the way she was peering over the items on the table. There were so many small bowls on the table he thought there must be gravy, but Zanipolo shook his head.

"No, I wasn't sure if it would be any good," he admitted.

"It is," she assured him. "It's real gravy, not the packaged stuff." Reaching for a red bottle, she shrugged and added, "But ketchup will do."

"Not if they have real gravy," Zanipolo said at once. "Most places have the packaged stuff that tastes like . . ."

"Packaged stuff," Jess suggested with amusement when he seemed at a loss as to how to describe the fake stuff.

Chuckling, Zanipolo nodded and stood up. "I'll go ask the waitress to—Oh." He dropped back into his seat. "No need. She's coming with our drinks already."

Raffaele glanced around to see that Zanipolo was right; the waitress was returning with three drinks.

Zanipolo thanked the waitress when she set them down by each of them and then asked for three orders of gravy.

"We thought we heard a band playing as we approached," Jess commented, glancing around as the waitress left.

"There was a band when we were here earlier," he assured her, glancing toward the slightly raised stage where the band had been situated.

"They were still playing when we got here," Zanipolo said. "They stopped to take a break, literally, just before you two came in."

"Ah. That explains it," Raffaele said, nodding.

"They sounded pretty good," Jess commented.

"They are," Zanipolo said. "Not as good as the NCs, of course. But good."

"Who are the NCs?" Jess asked with curiosity before taking a drink of her wine.

"Our band," Zanipolo told her with a grin.

Jess stilled, her eyes widening. "Band? You guys are in a band?"

Raffaele narrowed his eyes on her. She didn't seem pleased at the news. In fact, she appeared disappointed.

"Yes, a rock band. You don't like music?" Zanipolo asked, obviously noting her reaction too.

"Oh. Yes. I like music," she said quickly.

"So why the attitude about our being in a band?" Zanipolo asked, and Raffaele knew it was purely for his benefit. His cousin would already know the answer. He could read her thoughts.

"Oh, no!" she said with dismay. "I'm sorry. I didn't mean to—"

"You obviously don't think much of musicians," Santo interrupted gently.

Jess met the bald man's gaze, hesitated briefly, and then sighed and shrugged. "I'm sorry. It's not musicians per se. It's just you guys seemed so nice, and . . . I guess it's stereotyping, but I tend to think of guys in bands as being interested only in the whole sex, drugs, and rock 'n' roll thing." She grimaced. "You know, groupies and partying and stuff."

Raffaele smiled. Her words told him that Jess was definitely not a groupie type. One of those women who chased band members, just because they *were* a band member. And he liked that. Raffaele had experienced enough of that to last a lifetime. As had the others. It was rather annoying actually, because the women weren't really seeing them at all, just an ideal in their head, and it was that ideal they were chasing.

Of course, if he were young and still interested in sex, he'd probably love it, Raffaele acknowledged. Women throwing themselves at him, willing to sleep with him at the drop of a hat . . . What young horny guy wouldn't love that? However, Raffaele had lost his interest in sex centuries ago, as had Santo. And Christian and Gia, the other members of their band, were already mated. That left Zanipolo to enjoy whatever groupies their band attracted, something he didn't seem to mind at all.

"We don't party," Santo said, the words a rumble of sound. "We have day jobs."

"And we don't do drugs," Raffaele assured her. That wasn't even a possibility for them. Their bodies would remove the drugs, as well as any alcohol, before the substances had a chance to work on them. It was why he'd ordered water rather than wine like Jess.

"We do have sex, though," Zanipolo said cheerfully, and then added, "Well, at least I do. Christian and Gia—the other members of our band," he explained to Jess, "they're both mated and not interested in groupies. And Santo and Raff are just plain not interested. In fact, Raff finds them pathetic. He says those women would sleep with anyone with a guitar given half the chance."

"He's probably right," Jess said, turning to give Raffaele a small smile as she picked up her glass again for another sip. She was obviously glad he wasn't into groupies.

Zanipolo shrugged. "Maybe. But it's not like I want to marry the women. I'm a healthy, young, unmated im—man," he finished, catching his slip before he said *immortal*. "Who am I to refuse if a pretty woman wants to sleep with me? Besides, with the rest of the band all shunning the girls, I make out like a bandit," Zanipolo admitted, flashing Jess a toothy grin when his words drew her gaze back to him.

"So, you do go in for groupies," she said dryly, setting her glass back.

"Definitely," he assured her without shame. "But I'm still a nice guy. I don't break hearts or make promises I don't intend to keep, and I do not get into drugs or partying. Like Santo said, we all have day jobs."

"Hmm." Jess considered that briefly and then asked, "So what are your day jobs?"

"We work for Notte Construction," Raffaele answered for all of them. "It's a family business."

"So you're construction workers?" she asked with interest, and then smiled crookedly and said, "I should have guessed."

Her gaze was sliding over his shoulders and chest with appreciation as she said that and Raffaele felt his body tighten in response.

"Why should you have guessed that?" Santo asked with interest.

Much to Raffaele's relief, Jess tore her gaze away and turned to the other man to shrug and say, "Because you're all in great shape."

"Ah." Santo nodded as if that made sense, when really none of them were actual laborers who slung hammers and such.

Jess opened her mouth, as if she was going to ask another question, but then frowned slightly as she noted that Santo hadn't pulled a plate in front of him. "Aren't you going to eat anything?"

Santo shook his head. "Indigestion."

"Oh. I'm sorry to hear that," she said sincerely. "I have some Tums in my room. After we finish eating I'll go get a replacement key and fetch them for you."

Santo looked startled at the offer and then shook his head. "Thank you, no. I'll be fine."

"It's no problem," she assured him. "In fact, you can keep the whole bottle. I'm leaving tomorrow anyway, so I won't need them."

"You are leaving?" Santo asked with surprise.

"Yes," Jess said. "I would have left tonight, but I guess there wouldn't be any flights out this late. Or at least none I'd be likely to get to in time."

"No. There would not be," Santo agreed and, apparently having read that Raffaele was fine with her leaving, turned to offer her a smile. But Jess was no longer looking his way. Something had drawn her attention to the beach off the deck. Raffaele saw her frown, and followed her gaze to see what held her attention, but there was nothing there as far as he could tell.

"You'll have to give us your address in Montana in case we are able to get your waist belt back."

Raffaele glanced to Zanipolo with surprise at that comment, but his cousin was biting into his burger and not looking his way. It didn't matter; a quick glimpse of his thoughts told him that the younger immortal was trying to get her to give them her address verbally so he wouldn't have to explain how he found her when he followed her to Montana.

"Get my waist belt back?" Jess asked with surprise, finally turning from the beach.

Zanipolo nodded, and then swallowed and said, "I'm quite sure we'll be going to the Seaquarium after you leave. We can check out the shark feeding tour afterward and see if your waist belt is in their lost and found."

Raffaele noted the way Jess stiffened, and felt himself tense up in response as her eyes narrowed on Zanipolo. Her voice was suspicious as she asked, "How did you know I left it on the shark boat?"

Zanipolo had been about to bite into his burger again, but paused and lowered it to eye Jess briefly, before saying, "You said earlier that you left it on the pirate ship. The people in the lobby were talking about the pirates who took them to feed the sharks after the Seaquarium. I just assumed it was the same ship. Was it not?"

"Oh." Jess relaxed and smiled crookedly. "Yes. Yes, it was."

Raffaele felt his body relax at the save, and then concern claimed Jess's expression and she said, "But I don't recommend the shark feeding tour. You should avoid that at all costs. In fact, I think you should skip the Seaquarium too." Becoming agitated, she added, "Just stay away from that area altogether. All right?"

Raffaele nodded solemnly. It wasn't a hard promise to make. They had been told to leave the rogues to the local hunters anyway.

"Promise," she insisted. "Promise you'll stay away from any pirates and pirate ships you see."

"Oh, look, the band's coming back," Santo said, and Raffaele glanced to him, noting the way he was looking at Jess. He had the concentrated look that suggested he was doing something to her thoughts. He wasn't sure what, however, until Jess suddenly relaxed beside him and turned to peer at the band members returning to the stage at the end of the deck.

"How nice. Dinner music," she said, sounding completely relaxed. Santo must have slipped in and soothed her mind, Raffaele realized, and wasn't sure if he was glad or not. He didn't want Jess upset, but he was starting to dislike the other men slipping in and out of her head as he knew they were doing. She was his woman, his life mate, and they had no business messing about in her thoughts.

"Humph, that's gratitude for you," Zanipolo muttered, and Raffaele looked at him just as he turned a concentrated gaze toward the stage. Zani focused on the band members briefly, and they began to play a slow ballad for their first song.

"Zani," Raffaele growled in warning as his cousin then turned his attention to Jess. He gave up scowling at him to glance at her in question, though, when she placed a hand on his arm.

"I think you owe me a dance," she said chirpily when he met her gaze.

Raffaele stared at her blankly. Zanipolo hadn't had enough time to take control of her mind and make her say that. The request was all Jess, he realized, and supposed he shouldn't be surprised. She'd made him promise her a dance in exchange for her silence on appreciating Zani's choice of the resort for their vacation as they'd approached the restaurant. He just hadn't expected to have to carry through on the promise. He'd thought the whole exchange just teasing banter. But it seemed she was going to make him keep his promise.

"If you owe her a dance, you should really *give it* to her," Zanipolo said earnestly. But Raffaele didn't miss the emphasis on "give it." The bastard knew exactly how dancing with Jess would affect him, and that it was why he'd hoped the promise was a joke of sorts.

Opening his eyes, he glared at his cousin briefly, and then glanced to the side with a start when Jess stood up and took his hand, sending a shock wave of sensation through him. "Come on. Before the song ends."

Casting one last scowl at his cousin, Raffaele reluctantly stood and followed Jess to the small empty space that made up the dance floor.

Seven

When Jess led Raffaele to the center of the dance floor and turned to face him, he didn't pull her close as she expected. Instead, he held her in a proper dance stance, with his left hand at her right hip, and his right hand lifting her left until their entwined fingers were at about shoulder level. He also left a good eight inches or so of space between their bodies as he started to move, leading her with the hand at her hip and his hold on her hand.

Jess followed his lead wide-eyed, rather amazed that she *could* follow. She had never danced "properly." Most of her experience came from high school dances when she was younger, and dancing at bars or nightclubs once she was in university, and most of that was fast dancing. When it came to slow dancing in those environments, it had always come down to the guy just putting his arms around her waist, and her resting her arms across his shoulders while the pair of them leaned into each other as they shuffled around, or at least swayed back and forth until the music ended.

Jess had seen older couples dance like this, though. With this proper hold and the distance between them. Still, it felt odd and even awkward doing it. Not that Raffaele wasn't a good dancer; he was. He was leading her with his hands, a little pressure on her hip, or by pulling her hand one way or the other. She found following him easy. But Jess didn't know where to look. He was taller than her, his chest directly in front of her face, but she didn't want to tip her head and look at his face; she was afraid she'd just blush and feel foolish. In the end, she turned her head to the side and stared at the other couples on the dance floor, and then out at the dark beach when they slowly turned and it came into view.

The night was shades of black out there beyond the deck lights, a world of shadows. Most were stationary—the huts and lounge chairs and beach umbrellas that were all still out. But some of the shadows were moving as couples drifted down to the beach for privacy, she noted. And then her eyes landed on one dark shape among all the others and Jess felt fear leap in her chest. It was a man, which was no surprise; there were a dozen or so of them on the beach, most with a partner, but some alone. This one, though, cut a rather distinctive figure, and then a second figure joined him.

"Jess?"

Turning her head reluctantly, she peered up at Raffaele in question.

"Are you all right?" he asked. "You stopped moving . . . and you've gone pale," he added with a frown.

Jess hesitated, and then turned to peer out at the beach again, searching for the two men she'd thought she'd seen the first time, but they were gone. Did that mean Vasco and Cristo had never been there? Or that they had been there and had slipped away? Because that was who she thought she'd spotted down there on the beach. There was just no way to mistake Vasco's hat, and she was quite sure the second figure had been Cristo.

"What did you see?"

Jess turned to find him searching the beach now, his narrowed eyes scanning the dark shadows and people. When he turned back to her, there was grim concern on his face.

"What did you see?" he repeated, his voice hard this time.

Jess opened her mouth to answer, but suddenly couldn't remember what she'd seen. Frowning with confusion, she looked out toward the beach again and then shook her head. "It was nothing." Sighing, she turned back to him and forced a smile. "I think I'd like to sit down now."

"Of course." Maintaining his hold on her hand, Raffaele wrapped his arm around her and ushered her back through the dancing couples to the table. Jess didn't miss the irony in the fact that he held her closer to walk her to their table than he had while they were dancing. She also didn't miss her body's response to being so close. But then they were at the table and he was releasing her and pulling out her chair.

"Is everything all right?" Santo asked, eyeing the two of them.

Jess forced a smile. "Of course. I'm just hungry," she assured him, and then reached for her wine, surprised to find the glass empty. She hadn't realized she'd drank it all.

"I'll order you another," Raffaele murmured, turning to search for their waitress.

Jess opened her mouth to ask him to order her an iced tea instead, but he'd already caught the waitress's attention and was gesturing to her glass. Shrugging, she let the order stand. Two glasses wouldn't hurt her, she thought as she glanced over the food on the table. There was still a lot of it there. Oddly enough, though, her appetite was gone. But the gravy was there now, she noted, and since Zanipolo had only ordered it because of her, she felt she had to eat at least some of it, and so pulled one of the bowls closer to dip the fries in.

"So," Zanipolo said after a moment, "you know we work for our family's construction company. What do you do?"

"Oh." Jess smiled faintly, and then paused to thank their waitress as she arrived and set a glass of wine next to her. Once the woman had left, she said, "I have two part-time jobs."

"Two?" Raffaele asked with interest as she dipped a fry in the gravy and popped it into her mouth.

Jess nodded as she chewed and swallowed, and then took a drink of her wine before explaining, "I'm still a student, which kind of messes with the hours I can work, but my employers work around my classes."

"What do you study?" Raffaele asked as she picked up another fry and repeated the dipping and eating.

Jess swallowed and picked up her glass again, but merely held it as she answered, "Well, originally my major was psychology and I planned to be a clinical psychologist. But now I have a double major, psychology and history. I've decided to teach history instead."

"Why the switch?" Raffaele asked with interest. "Didn't you like psychology?"

"Oh, yes. I enjoyed it a great deal," Jess assured him, and then admitted with wry amusement, "And I was very good at it. My test scores were always in the top percentile, often even one hundred percent, and I got my master's." Pausing, she grimaced slightly and then added, "But books are wholly different than reality, and my part-time jobs helped convince me I might do better in a different field."

Raffaele raised his eyebrows with curiosity. "And what are your part-time jobs?"

"I work part-time at a counseling center where I . . . well, I counsel," she said with amusement.

"And the other job?" Zanipolo asked.

"I sling drinks at a local bar . . ." she said wryly, and then lifted her glass and grinned at them before downing the rest of her drink.

"Another?" Raffaele asked attentively when she set the empty glass down.

"Yes, please. But iced tea this time. Two is my limit for alcohol. I get wonky after that."

Nodding, Raffaele turned to search for their waitress, and found himself staring at the woman's bosom. She'd apparently approached to see if they needed anything and now stood next to him.

"You want something, *sí*?" the woman asked brightly as Raffaele jerked his eyes to her face.

"Sí," he said at once, offering an apologetic smile. Raising his voice a little to be heard over the murmur of the crowd, he added, "My lady friend would like an iced tea, *por favor*."

"One Island Iced Tea," she said with a smile. "Anything else?"

"No, that's it, *gracias*."

She nodded cheerfully and hurried away, and Raffaele turned back to the table as Zanipolo commented. "So, Jess, counseling and bartending. As jobs go, I don't think you could choose two more polar opposites."

"Not really," Jess said with a grin, and assured them, "In truth, bartending is really just more counseling, but with people who are liquored up and more honest and forthcoming with their issues."

Raffaele smiled faintly, but thought it was a shame they couldn't do that with Santo—get him liquored up so he'd relax and discuss his issues. A grunt from Santo drew his attention to the fact that his bald cousin was staring at him, narrow-eyed. He'd probably heard his thoughts, Raffaele realized, and grimaced, but quickly turned his attention back to Jess as Zanipolo asked with amusement, "And counseling people, both sober and drunk, convinced you that you shouldn't counsel people?"

"Basically, yes," Jess admitted with a crooked smile. "I find it hard to separate myself emotionally from what I'm hearing. From their pain," she explained, her expression growing solemn. "A clinical psychologist needs to remain objective to help their patient. I couldn't do that."

"It must have been hard when you came to that conclusion. I mean, all that time wasted on one degree, only to have to switch to another," Raffaele said solemnly.

"Not really," Jess said, her smile returning. "I got a lot out of it."

Raffaele tilted his head, his confusion, he knew, plain on his face. It made her smile widen.

"In truth, I took psychology mostly so I could figure out how to fix myself," Jess admitted now, and then said more seriously, "I think that's probably why most psychologists get into it."

"Fix what?" Raffaele asked with surprise. "You seem perfectly fine to me."

"Well, sure. *Now.*" Jess added the word in a tone as dry as dirt. She then explained, "Counseling is pretty much free on campus, and the professors are happy to muck about in your head if you're a psych major and they like you. I've had loads of counseling over the years. But I went through a nightmare childhood. *All* the abuses: physical, sexual, *and* mental."

Raffaele frowned. "Your parents—"

"No." Jess shook her head and explained, "My birth father died before I was born, and my birth mom when I was two. After that I was in the foster care system. That's where the abuse happened. By the time my parents adopted me at age eight, I was one damaged kid," she admitted, her gaze perusing the other dishes on the table.

"These are good," Zani said, sliding a plate of breaded something-or-other toward her. "I'm not sure what they are, and they're a bit spicy, but bursting with flavor."

As Raffaele watched her select one of the breaded nuggets, he said, "But things got better for you once you were adopted." The words were a hopeful suggestion. The thought of this beautiful, vibrant woman being abused as an innocent child was extremely distressing to him, and he wished he'd been in her life earlier, and able to protect her.

Jess paused with the breaded treat in hand to smile wryly and say, "Oh, yes, but for a long time, I couldn't escape what had happened. It was stuck in my head like a rut in the road. Even when I slept, the abusers visited me in my dreams. So, of course, I became one angry, hurting, and suicidal teen." She shrugged. "I knew there had to be something better, a happier way to live. So I took psychology hoping to heal myself and find it."

"And did you?" Santo asked, his voice a deep rumble. "Have you escaped your past? Or do your abusers still visit your dreams?"

Raffaele glanced at his cousin solemnly, knowing it wasn't idle curiosity that made him ask that. Santo was obviously interested in healing. Perhaps a 3-on-1 could be avoided, after all.

Jess considered his question seriously. "I haven't escaped it, per se. You just can't *escape* the past, or erase it like it was never there. It happened. But I learned to accept it, and even appreciate it."

"Appreciate it?" Santo asked sharply, his disbelief evident.

Jess smiled wryly. "Yeah, I know. Sounds crazy, right? But I really did luck out with my adoptive parents, and with them came a really awesome family full of wonderful grandparents, aunts, uncles, and cousins. Well, not counting Allison," she added dryly, and then continued. "I might never have had them if my life had taken a different path. And," she added, "I've learned to like myself. To value how strong I am, a strength I gained from surviving so much."

"And you don't think you could have been strong without the abuses put upon you in your past?" Santo asked.

Jess shrugged. "Maybe. But probably not." Tilting her head, she asked, "Have you ever heard the saying 'Strong winds, strong tree'?"

Santo shook his head.

"Well, my father—the one who adopted me," she added, "he was a horticulturalist. He worked for the government doing Lord knows what. I know he had to visit a lot of government parks and lands. But anyway, he taught me that strong winds make strong trees, because the winds force the tree to send out a deeper root system to withstand those winds. Of course, having a deeper and larger root system helps the tree in other ways, in getting water in a drought and so on. So that adversity while the tree was young and growing makes it stronger later . . . if you see what I mean?"

Santo nodded.

"Well, I really think that's true of humans too," she said solemnly. "I mean, I've counseled a lot of people since starting work at the clinic, and what I've found is that the ones who had it rough when younger tend to bounce back better when life kicks them in the teeth as an adult, which you know happens to everyone. We lose the people we love, we're robbed, we find ourselves on a pirate ship full of . . . er . . . bad guys," she finished in a mutter.

Grimacing, she continued, "Anyway, in my opinion, people who experienced adversity earlier in their life tend to withstand and come back from that kind of stuff better as an adult than people who didn't have adversity while young. In fact, people who were protected and cosseted while young often don't seem to have learned the coping skills needed to handle stressors as an adult, and they're the ones more likely to completely fall apart when adversity does hit them."

Expression turning solemn, she added, "I'd rather be a strong tree than one that will topple over under the first big wind. And I am. I appreciate that."

"And the dreams that haunted you?" Santo asked, his body tense.

Jess met his gaze, and something about her expression made Raffaele think she knew she was looking at another of the walking wounded, someone with a troubled and painful past that still haunted him.

"Once I accepted my past and decided I probably wouldn't be me without that past . . . it seemed to lose a lot of its power over me," she said slowly. "A lot of my anger slipped away, and a lot of . . ." Jess frowned, and then said, "When it's happening, you start to feel like you must have deserved or caused the abuse . . . which is really just a kind of self-defense mechanism. You think, well, if I just hadn't angered him, he wouldn't have hit me. I should walk more quietly, clean better, do whatever better, and he won't hit me again. Or if I hadn't worn that skirt he wouldn't have raped me. Or if I hadn't walked down that road, or hadn't gone to that party . . ." She paused and shrugged. "But that's just your mind trying desperately to figure out why it was you and not someone else, so that it can find a way to prevent it happening again. Because to acknowledge that it was them and not you, and that you could encounter that kind of abuse or torture again *no matter what you do* . . . well, that's scary as hell. And, *I* think, the nightmares are your mind struggling to come to terms, not only with what happened, but with the knowledge it could happen again." Shrugging mildly, she added, "But that's just what I think."

"And why do you think that?" Santo asked.

"Because when I decided I liked myself, and accepted my past as a part of me, that made me the way I am, and acknowledged that bad things probably would happen again no matter my choices, but that I would survive them as I had everything else . . ." She shrugged. "The nightmares stopped coming. It wasn't overnight, but it didn't take ages either."

She waved the breaded treat around briefly, and added with a wry smile, "At least those nightmares about my childhood. I still have nightmares on occasion, but they're just your standard type nightmare: being lost or trapped, falling or drowning, being naked in public, flunking a test, that sort of thing. And that's how it went for me. Doesn't guarantee it will go that way for others."

Raffaele watched Santo consider that for a moment, and then glanced to Jess and said, "You said you didn't think you were a good counselor, and yet you still counsel?"

"Well, perhaps it's not so much that I'm not a good counselor, as that counseling wasn't necessarily healthy for me since I empathized too much with my clients."

"And yet you still do it," Raffaele said quietly.

"I need to eat," she said with a shrug. "And working at the clinic pays well. Besides, I don't really counsel anymore. Mostly I'm on intake. I interview new clients, and decide which of our counselors would best suit them. Apparently, I have a knack for that. So, I'll probably do it until I finish my history degree, and then teacher's college."

Sitting back, she shook her head. "Boy, I sure turned into a Chatty Kathy, didn't I?" she said almost apologetically, and then shook her head again and admitted, "Wine tends to loosen my tongue. I should probably eat more to soak it up." With that, she finally popped the breaded treat into her mouth and began to chew.

The change in her was almost immediate and somewhat alarming. Her eyes widened with dismay, her mouth stopped moving, and then she flushed bright red and began to search the table almost desperately for something. Raffaele wasn't sure what was happening, or what she was looking for. He was about to ask when the waitress arrived with her iced tea. Jess didn't even wait for the woman to set it down, but snatched it from her hand with a gasped *"Gracias"* as she raised it to her mouth. She gulped down the contents of that glass like there was a fire in her stomach she needed to douse.

Or a fire in her mouth, Raffaele corrected when Zani offered an apologetic, "I did warn you it was spicy."

Jess lowered her nearly empty glass to glare at the man.

"*Sí*, spicy," their waitress said brightly. "There are ghost peppers in the . . . how you say? Breading?" She didn't wait for a response, but moved a bowl of creamy dip toward Jess. "The sour cream, she helps, *sí*? Try."

Jess didn't hesitate. She pulled the bowl toward herself, grabbed a spoon, and began to scoop up the thick dip and transfer it to her mouth like it was soup. After a couple of spoonfuls and much swishing it around in her mouth, she sighed and sagged in her seat. Apparently, the fire was out. Or at least the worst of it was, he guessed when she then reached for her iced tea.

"Better, *sí*?" the waitress asked with a sympathetic smile as she watched her gulp down the last of her drink.

Jess started to nod as she took the glass away from her mouth, but then paused and moved her tongue around the inside of her mouth as she now stared at her empty glass, a frown slowly claiming her lips.

"What's wrong?" Raffaele asked with concern.

"This isn't iced tea," she said with dismay, glancing from him to the waitress.

"It should be. I ordered you iced tea," he assured her, and glanced to the waitress in question.

"*Sí.* Is the iced tea. The Island Iced Tea," the woman said brightly.

"Island Iced Tea?" Jess asked slowly, and then her eyes narrowed. "*Long* Island Iced Tea?"

"Sí." She nodded happily. "Té helado Long Island. I'll get you another."

"No! I didn't want the first," Jess cried at once, but the waitress was already bustling away to fetch another drink. Shaking her head, Jess set the empty glass down with a groan. "Oh, God."

"What's wrong?" Raffaele repeated, frowning now as well.

"What's wrong?" she echoed with disbelief. "I already had two glasses of wine. That's why I asked for iced tea. I didn't want to get pickled."

"But she says it *was* iced tea," Raffaele pointed out with confusion.

When Jess scowled at him, Zani put in, "I told you we don't drink. But Raff and Santo don't even hang around with people who drink. He has no idea what a Long Island Iced Tea is."

Jess nodded grimly, and then turned to Raffaele to explain. "A Long Island Iced Tea is pretty much pure alcohol. Vodka, rum, gin, tequila, triple sec, and a bit of sour mix over ice with literally a splash of cola for color. In the States, it's pretty much like two, or three or sometimes even four, drinks in one. But from the size of the glass, the skimpy use of ice in it, and the way they're so liberal with the booze here at the resort, this one was probably more like five or six drinks in one." Closing her eyes, she shook her head and sighed. "I should have recognized at once that it wasn't iced tea, but my taste buds were traumatized at first. It was only after the dip soothed them a bit that I even realized there was something off about the tea."

"Oh." Raffaele glanced at the empty glass and then back to her face.

Her color was still high, but now he wasn't sure if that was from the heat of the ghost peppers in the breading, or from the alcohol.

Sighing, Jess pushed her chair back from the table, saying, "Guess I'd better go see about that new room key and find my bed before the alcohol reaches my system. Thank you for the company, guys. And for all your help," she added as she got to her feet. Pausing then, she glanced to Santo and smiled. "Especially the loan of your shirt. I'll bring it down here to you as soon as I can get into my room and change."

Raffaele had got up when she did and now took her arm to steady her when she swayed. "I'll walk you up to the lobby," he announced solemnly, and wasn't surprised when Santo and Zanipolo decided to accompany them.

"I can't believe I messed up with that drink order," Raffaele said grimly several minutes later as he watched Jess talk to the man at the resort's registration desk. It was a long walk from the beach restaurant to the lobby in the main building and her gait had grown more and more unsteady as they'd traversed the distance. Her speech had also started to be affected, so that she was slurring the occasional word.

"You didn't mess up, the waitress did," Zanipolo said soothingly. "Although, to be fair to her, it was loud in the restaurant, and most people probably don't drink alcohol-free drinks at night here."

Still feeling responsible, Raffaele grunted at that, and then muttered, "I can't believe one drink could be this effective so quickly."

"Well, she had two glasses of wine before the iced tea, and as she said, that one Long Island Iced Tea is probably the equivalent of five or six drinks the way they mix their drinks here," Zanipolo said wryly. "I've noticed the bartenders are all pretty liberal with the booze. They seem to think drunk guests are happy guests." He pursed his lips then and added, "It is a shame, though. She was really opening up and revealing a lot about herself before that happened. But the Long Island Iced Tea thing kind of brought a quick end to all that."

"Hmm," Raffaele muttered, and then heaved a sigh that released a good deal of his tension. Zanipolo was right. Jess had revealed a lot about herself in the restaurant, and all of it had just made him like her more. She'd obviously had a very tough childhood, and yet didn't lay some sob story on them. Instead, she saw it as a positive, a strength even, and used it as such. He admired her for that. It kind of made him look at some experiences in his own past a little differently, as shaping tools rather than just bad experiences. It made him wonder what Santo had come away with from the conversation, and he glanced to his cousin and friend. But Santo's face was often hard to read, and it was now as well.

Thinking he'd talk with Santo a little later and do a little probing to see how he was doing then, Raffaele turned his thoughts back to Jess and suddenly asked what he'd been wondering about since the dance they'd shared. "What did she see when we were on the dance floor?"

"I don't know," Zanipolo admitted, watching Jess too, but his expression was troubled now.

"She had a blank spot," Santo announced, running one hand over his bald head with worry.

Raffaele stiffened and glanced to his cousins with concern. "Like someone erased her memory of what she saw?" he asked sharply.

"That would be my guess," Santo admitted grimly.

"Mine too," Zanipolo admitted.

"Then it was probably those pirates," Raffaele said, turning his concerned gaze back to Jess.

"Probably," Santo agreed.

"I feel ridiculous calling them pirates. They're just damned rogues," Zanipolo pointed out with irritation.

"But we can't risk slipping up and calling them that in front of Jess," Raffaele pointed out.

"True," Zanipolo muttered with a sigh, and then shook his head. "Pirates, for God's sake. The guy on the bus was even dressed as one, and so were the ones in Jess's memories."

"It's for the tourists, probably lures them in in droves," Raffaele pointed out grimly, and then shook his head and said, "I don't get why they brought them back."

"The tourists?" Santo asked.

Raffaele nodded. "Most rogues turn, kill, or torture their victims. They don't just feed on them and send them home, or back to their hotel, like these guys did."

"It *is* unusual," Santo agreed thoughtfully.

"The one on the bus said—"

"Phew! For a minute there I didn't think he was going to give me a new key card."

Raffaele snapped his mouth shut mid-sentence and turned at those words from Jess as she approached them. Raising his eyebrows, he asked, "He was difficult?"

"I'll say," she said with a snort. "He kept saying I needed ID or Allison to verify I was me, that I could be anyone. And then he just suddenly changed his tune and couldn't get me the card quickly enough. Guess he was tired of me begging," she said cheerfully.

Raffaele turned to Santo and Zanipolo in question, but both men shook their heads. Neither of them had controlled the man at the desk and made him give Jess a new key. Mouth tightening, Raffaele peered around the lobby and then out the front windows and back, looking for any sign of the pirates. But he didn't see the man he'd encountered by the bus, or anyone else who looked like a pirate.

"Wow! That Long Island Iced Tea is kicking my butt," Jess said now, regaining his attention to see that she'd placed a hand on the back of the sofa next to them to steady herself. "It's really starting to hit now. I should probably get back to my room while I can still walk straight."

"We'll escort you," Raffaele said quietly, taking her arm, but urging her toward the front door of the lobby, rather than the door overlooking the steps. He didn't trust her to be able to negotiate the steps in her state.

"So, you really think it is a good idea to let her stay in her room tonight?" Zanipolo asked as they made their way out of the building and walked under the porte cochere.

"Oh, I'm good," Jess assured him. "It doesn't matter if the vampirates have my original key card—it doesn't have the room number on it. Besides, I probably won't sleep anyway. I have to pack and make phone calls and stuff."

When Zanipolo continued to look at him, Raffaele merely shook his head. He had no intention of leaving Jess by herself. He would help her pack her things, gather what she needed, and then try to convince her to come back to their room to wait until dawn. If that didn't work, he'd stand guard outside the door to her room if necessary. He fully intended on sticking to her like glue until he had her safely on a plane out of Punta Cana.

"God, this place is *sooo* hot," Jess complained suddenly, tugging fretfully at the collar of her borrowed shirt/dress as they started around the corner of the building and headed down the slanted path.

Raffaele grunted an agreement. The heat and humidity here were a bit extreme this time of year.

"We shoulda gone the other way," Jess said now. "Then we coulda jumped in the pool on the way back and could could off." Frowning, she shook her head. "Could could off. Could . . . *cool* . . . off," she enunciated slowly and carefully, and then relaxed and grinned. "That's it."

Raffaele eyed her with concern. He had no idea how long it usually took for the effects of alcohol to hit a mortal, but he was guessing it had only been twenty minutes or so since she'd downed the iced tea. Of course, she'd had two glasses of wine before that. Still, he was quite sure her inebriation was going to get worse.

Jess suddenly pulled on the hold he had on her arm. She wasn't trying to break free of him, he saw with relief. She was simply starting to weave a good deal on the downward slope.

"I think we should ger our swimsuits and gofer aswim," she slurred now, tugging again at the collar of Santo's shirt, and then stopping and tipping her head down to try to see to undo the top buttons.

"Let me help you," Raffaele said patiently.

"Oh, tank you," Jess muttered, lifting her head to beam at him. "You're so nice. And cute too. You're a cuuuutie. And you don' have greasy hair. That's nice."

Raffaele had no idea what the hell she was talking about with the greasy hair business, but he liked hearing she thought him cute. Still, he didn't fiddle with her buttons, but instead simply scooped her up and began to hurry along the path, moving at a speed his people generally didn't use in the open where they might be seen. He needed to get her to her room and have her help him gather everything before the full impact of the alcohol hit and she was unable to help. He had no idea what she'd brought with her, and didn't want her forgetting something important.

"Oh." Jess peered around wide-eyed when they reached the building and he began running up the stairs. "You're fast."

Raffaele grunted in response. What could he say?

"Which room are you in?" he asked as he hurried out of the stairwell and started up the hall with Santo and Zanipolo on his heels.

"Room 406," she answered and then grinned. "Right above yours."

"Yes," Raffaele agreed with surprise.

"Jeez, it's like it was fate," Zanipolo said with wonder behind them.

Raffaele ignored him. As they neared the room, he asked, "Do you have your new key card?"

"Oh." She looked concerned for a minute and then noticed it in her hand and held it up triumphantly. "Yes."

"Good. Run it over the security pad," he suggested as he stopped, and Jess did as instructed. She even managed to do it right the first time.

The moment the green light flashed and a click sounded, Santo reached past them to open the door.

"Thanks," Raffaele muttered as he carried Jess inside.

"Is Allison here?" Jess asked, craning her head to look toward the bedroom as Raffaele carried her into the sitting room.

Pausing, he hesitated, and then turned to carry her into the bedroom. His gaze slid over the two double beds in the room and then to the open bathroom door. "No. Sorry."

"Thass okay, she'd just be all bitchy and mean anyway. She's a mean *mean* meanie," Jess told him solemnly.

"Yes, she is," Zanipolo agreed with amusement from behind them as Raffaele set Jess on her feet. "But you're adorable."

Ignoring him, Raffaele clasped Jess by the upper arms until she turned her attention to him and then asked, "Do you remember the combination to your room safe?"

"Oh. Yes." She nodded. "It's 2–2–2–2 'cause there are two of us and Allison couldn't remember anything else."

"Okay," he said with amusement. "Well, then, why don't you go get your passport and stuff out of the safe, change your clothes, and then pack your bags. We'll wait for you in the sitting room. Okay?"

"Okay," she said agreeably, and staggered to the closet where the room safes were situated in this resort.

Raffaele watched her for a minute as she began to punch numbers, and then turned and moved out to the sitting room.

"Wow," Zanipolo murmured as he followed him into the sitting room. "That iced tea is hitting her hard. She really doesn't hold her liquor well." When Raffaele glanced at him with a questioning frown, he shrugged and pointed out, "She only had two glasses of wine and the Long Island. The girls who follow the band could handle twice that easy and just be relaxed."

"The women who follow the band drink like fish," Raffaele said dryly. "No doubt they have a higher tolerance."

"Yeah, but Jess works in a bar," Zanipolo pointed out. "You'd think she'd have a higher tolerance too."

"Why? Because she absorbs the alcohol through osmosis while pouring drinks for customers?" he asked sarcastically, a little miffed at what he saw as criticism of his mate. He liked that Jess had a lower tolerance. It proved she hadn't used alcohol as a crutch to help her get beyond the tragedies of her past.

Zanipolo opened his mouth to respond, and then his eyes slid past him and widened incredulously before he said, "I think I just saw someone go over the balcony rail."

Raffaele started to turn to look, but then froze as Jess screamed from the next room. Cursing, he turned toward the double doors just as she shrieked again. Leaving Santo and Zanipolo to deal with the Peeping Tom on the balcony, he hurried in to the bedroom.

Eight

Jess leaned against the balcony railing and sighed. A cool breeze was brushing across her face and naked shoulders and playing with the hem of her strapless dress, flapping it lightly around her legs almost in time to the music drifting up from the restaurant on the beach. Smiling, she lifted her face to the night sky, simply enjoying the breeze and the scent of tropical flowers drifting to her.

"Jess?"

She glanced over her shoulder, and it seemed perfectly natural for Raffaele to be there. Jess offered him a smile and then turned to peer out over the lights of the resort and the beach and water beyond.

"It's beautiful, isn't it," she said softly as his hands settled on her shoulders.

"Beautiful," he agreed, letting his hands slide off her shoulders and down her arms. "Perfect."

"Perfect," she agreed as he pressed a kiss to the spot where his hand had been a moment ago.

Jess closed her eyes and tilted her head slightly as his lips traveled toward her neck, trailing kisses along the way.

"I've waited forever for a night like this," he whispered, brushing her hair aside so that his lips could travel up her neck to her ear. "For you."

"For me," she almost moaned breathlessly as he nibbled her ear, and then his hand came around to clasp her chin and he turned her head up and back so that he could kiss her. Jess sighed as his mouth covered hers, and then slid her hand up and back to encircle his neck as they kissed, her mouth clinging to his and her body arching and pressing back against him.

When his hand dropped from her chin to glide lightly down into the valley between her breasts, Jess gasped into his mouth, her back arching harder, offering herself to him.

"I want you," he growled against her mouth.

"Yes," Jess moaned, reaching her free hand back to clasp his hip and pull him closer as both of his hands covered her breasts. When he began to knead the soft globes through the light cotton of her dress, Jess groaned and thrust her bottom backward, rubbing herself against the hardness she could feel growing there.

"Jesus, Jess," Raffaele groaned, one hand dropping down to slide between her legs.

"Raffaele," she gasped, clutching at his arm. "Please."

Covering her mouth again, he kissed her deeply, his tongue invading and exploring as his hand slid under the skirt of her dress to creep up to her panties. Easing them aside, he slid his fingers across her damp skin, his mouth catching her startled gasp of pleasure as she jerked and shuddered in his arms. But then he broke their kiss to growl, "Spread your legs a little."

Jess obeyed at once, easing her stance, giving him more room, and then cried out as his fingers slid between her folds, and found the nub of her excitement.

"So wet," he groaned, beginning to run his fingers around that nub in circles.

"Please," Jess gasped, her fingers clutching at his hip almost desperately.

"Please what, my love? Tell me what you want." His voice was a deep rumble she could feel in her very core, and Jess shook her head, unable to give voice to what she needed. Instead, she released her hold on his arm and reached back to search for the hardness behind her. Finding the bulge in his dress pants, she squeezed gently and then rubbed her hand over it.

Raffaele stiffened and groaned, and then suddenly removed the hand at her breast. She never felt him undo her dress, but when it suddenly fell away, Jess was left standing in high heels and white lace panties, and then he spun her around, caught her by the waist, and lifted her to sit on the railing so that he could feast on her breasts.

Groaning, Jess caught his head in her hands, her fingers curling in his short soft hair and holding on as he laved and suckled at first one breast and then the other, until Jess shook her head helplessly and cried, "Raffaele, please," again.

Growling, he urged her legs around his hips and scooped her off the railing to carry her to the built-in, cushioned bed-sized bench seat against one wall of the balcony. Kneeling in front of it, he set her to sit on the end, and then urged her to lie back with one hand on her chest. Jess fell back, and bit her lip as she watched him tug her panties off.

Meeting her gaze, Raffaele watched her face as he ran his hands up the insides of her legs, urging them wider open. One hand stopped halfway up, but the other continued and found her core again and Jess gasped, her back arching and legs trying instinctively to close as he began to caress her.

"What do you want?" Raffaele asked again as he caressed her.

"You," she gasped breathlessly, grabbing at the cushion to try to ground herself, and then a startled scream slid from her lips when he bent and replaced his hand with his mouth. Jess stared up at the night sky overhead, a long ululating sound slipping from her lips as he devoured her, his mouth doing things she'd never experienced, and pulling pleasure she hadn't known possible from her body as he paid attention to every inch of her sensitive skin there. When her release came, it was so fast and hard Jess lost it for a minute. Her body was quaking and convulsing, her head thrashing, and her breath coming in sobbing gasps, and then he slid into her, hard and swollen and filling her to capacity, and her orgasm began all over again.

Crying his name, Jess sat up abruptly and clutched at his shoulders as he thrust into her, holding on for dear life until he thrust one last time and threw his head back with a roar of pleasure.

Shifting sleepily, Jess reached instinctively for Raffaele, but found the built-in lounge mattress empty beside her. Frowning, she opened her eyes to bright sunlight, and quickly closed them again on a groan as her head began to pound. God, she felt like complete and utter crap! She must have overdone the drinking last night, but . . .

Jess stilled suddenly and opened her eyes again, doing so slowly this time to allow her eyes to adjust to the bright daylight, and then sighed as she saw that she wasn't out on the balcony, but on the pull-out couch in the sitting room. She glanced down at the blue shirt she still wore, and then turned her head and spotted Raffaele shifting sleepily in the overstuffed chair next to the couch, and turned her head unhappily away. She was in Room 306, the suite Raffaele shared with Santo and Zanipolo.

It had all been a dream. That lovely, hot episode on the balcony had just been a damned wet dream. It seemed her sudden spate of horniness had followed her into sleep. Sighing, she closed her eyes as the memory of what had really happened last night moved across her mind and she recalled that everything was gone.

The alcohol had really started to affect Jess by the time they'd reached her room and she'd had to enter the combination to the safe three times to get the damned thing open . . . then it was only to find all of her belongings gone. Allison's things had still been there, but Jess's passport, wallet, and even her return ticket for the flight home were gone. She'd shrieked in dismay and horror when she'd made that discovery, and then shrieked again as she noted that all her clothes, and even her suitcase, had been removed from the closet as well.

Not only could she not fly out today, but Jess didn't have a single stitch of clothing other than the borrowed shirt she still wore.

Well, she supposed she had the torn T-shirt and the bikini, Jess thought on a sigh. Yay.

It had to be Vasco, of course . . . or Cristo, or one of his other vampirates. It just had to be connected to him. If it had been a straight-out theft, Allison's things would have been taken as well, and Jess's clothes would have been left behind. It wasn't like they were designer or anything. Allison had more expensive clothes that she'd badgered her father into buying her, but Jess bought hers at Walmart, for Pete's sake.

No, it was Vasco. He was trying to prevent her leaving. Although she had no idea how he knew of her plan to flee.

Jess barely had that thought when she recalled Cristo telling Vasco her name without her mentioning it, and his asking Vasco if he had tried to read her. That must be another vampire trick they had. Besides controlling people, they must be able to read their minds, she thought. And Cristo must have read her plans to fly out today from her mind when he'd tried to force her onto the bus. He'd taken that news back to Vasco, and they'd set out to make sure it didn't happen.

Dear God, they had her trapped here! At least temporarily, Jess added with a frown. Surely, she could get a replacement passport from the American embassy here? Was there an American embassy in Punta Cana? God, she hoped it wasn't in some other city in the Dominican like Puerto Plata or somewhere else way far away. She didn't have any damned money to get to Puerto Plata, or any other Dominican city, really. Or for a flight home now that her credit cards were gone. She'd have to borrow that, as well as clothes and . . . She had no idea what she'd have to do to get a replacement passport.

But whatever it was, she'd do it, Jess thought grimly. She wasn't letting Vasco force her into being his vampirate bitch, or whatever he was after. He'd pissed her off now.

Opening her eyes, Jess turned her head and peered at Raffaele again. His eyes were closed. It looked like he'd fallen back to sleep, if he'd ever even woken up fully. It left her free to examine his face. He really was attractive. At least, he was to her. She supposed he didn't have classical good looks, but there was just something about him that appealed to her. And he had an amazing body. He'd carried her around like she weighed nothing last night, both on the way to the room she shared with Allison, and then again when he'd carried her back here to the suite he shared with Santo and Zanipolo. Jess had been a bit hysterical at the time over her things being stolen, and she suspected she'd been babbling about vampire pirates and not wanting to be a vampire bitch when he rushed into the bedroom after she screamed. But he'd been incredibly sweet and soothing and had simply scooped her up and carried her out of the room.

He'd brought her straight here, set her in the chair while he opened the pull-out couch, which was already made. He'd then set her on it, tucked her in, and had promised that she was safe, and he would make sure it stayed that way as Santo and Zanipolo had finally caught up to them.

"It was the pirates!" Zanipolo had blurted, rushing into the room. "They had a small motorboat down on the beach. By the time we got there—"

That was all Jess could remember . . . except she was pretty sure Santo had suddenly turned to look at her then. But that was it, so she must have passed out at that point . . . and fallen into some pretty steamy dreams, Jess recalled, biting her lip. All of them had starred Raffaele, and all had included some pretty rockin' sex in a variety of places and positions. The balcony had just been the last of the lot, and a tamer one than most of the others. She supposed she'd been wearying as morning approached.

A loud snore sounded from behind the closed double doors to the bedroom. It was followed by a much quieter snore, and then they both repeated one after the other. Santo and Zanipolo were obviously sleeping well, she thought dryly. But then they didn't have some crazy, sexy, murderous vampirate wreaking havoc in their life and stealing everything they possessed in an effort to force them into being their bitch.

Well, not murderous, she supposed. As far as Jess could tell everyone who had been on the ship had returned to the resort safe and sound . . . just probably a pint or two lower in blood. Still . . . she just wanted her life back the way it was before Allison had dragged her onto that damned boat. She wanted her passport and everything else back. And she wanted *not* to know there were vampires out there, sailing the high seas and biting people.

But she couldn't have that, Jess told herself firmly. So, it was better to deal with reality and do what she could. She would have to find out where the nearest embassy was and see about getting a temporary passport. Fortunately, she'd scanned and emailed herself her passport pages as a precaution before the trip. That should make getting a replacement a lot easier. She hoped. But even then, her problems weren't over. Sure, she could probably borrow money from one of her aunts and uncles for a ticket home, but they'd wonder why she wanted to leave early, so she supposed she'd have to come up with an excuse for that. But even once she got home, her troubles weren't over. She'd have to replace all her ID, all her credit and bank cards, her health card, driver's license . . .

The list seemed endless, and it would be expensive, and time-consuming, and the whole time she'd be worried about Vasco showing up at her door, because he had her address. It would be easier if she could just get her stuff back from him.

Jess contemplated that briefly. Could she get it back? He probably had it on the ship. Probably in his cabin and she knew where that was. If she could slip on board while he was gone, say, while they were all out luring tourists back to the ship . . .

That idea had some merit to it, Jess thought suddenly. It might work. She just needed to come up with a plan to stay hidden near the dock until she saw the vampirates disembark to mix among the returning tourists. But first she needed to get rid of her headache so her thinking was a little sharper. She needed a foolproof plan if she was going to do this. Jess hadn't escaped the ship, just to turn around and get caught sneaking back onto it.

Opening her eyes once more, Jess turned her head toward Raffaele again. Much to her relief, he appeared to be sleeping pretty soundly. Jess didn't think she could face him this morning. He couldn't know about her dreams, of course, but she was afraid she'd blush and stammer like an idiot if she had to deal with him before she at least had a coffee and cleared her head.

And maybe a stern internal lecture about this sudden horn-dog streak she had going on, Jess thought with a grimace as she pushed the sheet aside, and got quietly out of the pull-out bed. She hesitated then, every instinct in her demanding she make the bed and put it away, back to its original station as a couch. That was what a good guest would do, but Jess was afraid of waking Raffaele. She debated the issue briefly, and then merely tugged the sheet back into place, and then did the same with the blanket she'd apparently kicked aside. She'd straightened and was surveying her handiwork when Jess spotted the key card on the end table next to the couch.

It had to be hers. Probably. She couldn't be sure. They all looked the same, but she'd just got a new key card and it might be it. Or it might be Raffaele's key card to this room. She hesitated briefly, and then blew her breath out and took it. She'd try it and see. If it didn't work for her room, she'd bring it back, let herself in, leave it where she found it, and tiptoe back out.

Jess managed to leave without waking Raffaele. Breathing a sigh of relief once she'd eased the door silently closed, she turned and hurried along the open hall to the stairs. The whole way back to the suite she shared with Allison, Jess was half hoping her cousin wouldn't be there. With the way her head was pounding, she could really do without Allison's bitchiness this morning, Jess thought as she reached the door to their suite and quickly ran the key card over the security panel.

It unlocked without issue, and Jess opened the door and stepped inside, her eyes scanning the empty sitting room, and then sliding to peer through the open bathroom door before she let the door ease closed. Not wanting to wake Allison if she was there, Jess closed it as quietly as she had the door to the men's suite, and then pretty much tiptoed farther inside until she could see through the open doors to the bedroom. It was empty, and both beds still made. It looked like Allison hadn't even slept there.

Jess relaxed a little, but then noticed that the bathroom door was closed and hesitated. But there was nothing for it. She had to check the bathroom too. Crossing the room, she opened the door to darkness, and automatically flipped the switch on the wall. Light exploded into the room, making her wince, but it revealed for sure that Allison wasn't there. Not that she'd imagined her cousin was sitting there in the dark.

Jess started to back out of the room, but paused as her gaze landed on the shower. She always showered before and after going swimming, but she hadn't got the chance to last night. Having one before she put on Allison's clean clothes would certainly be nice. Nodding, she crossed the room, stripping off Santo's shirt as she went. Jess almost let the shirt drop to the floor, but aware that it wasn't hers to treat so shabbily, she laid it over the end of the tub instead, and then opened the shower door and reached in to turn on the taps. The water came out ice cold, of course, and she knew from the first two mornings they'd been here that it would be slow to warm, so Jess left the bathroom, pulling the door closed as she went. There was no need to add more humidity to the rest of the suite, she thought dryly as she crossed to the closet.

Both trifold doors were still open from her visit last night, and Jess surveyed the clothes still in the closet as she approached. Even with all of her clothing missing, the closet was three-quarters full. Allison was one of those overpackers. In a serious way. She probably wouldn't even miss anything Jess took, but she didn't want to borrow anything expensive. Allison wasn't above insisting Jess replace rather than return anything she borrowed.

Jess was about to start shifting hangers to go through what was available when she realized that not only had she left the closet doors open last night, she'd left the door to the safe built into the middle of the back wall of the closet wide open as well.

Nice, she thought with self-disgust. *Let's get Allison's stuff stolen too.* Shaking her head, Jess reached for the safe door, intending to close it, but then thought better of it. She should really check and make sure nothing of hers had been left behind. It was pretty obvious that her wallet was gone, but her passport was thin; maybe it had slipped under Allison's stuff and they'd missed it. With that hope in mind, Jess stepped between the hanging clothes to check out the items remaining in the safe, and that was where she was when she heard someone say, "Sounds like she's in the shower, Capitan."

Freezing, Jess turned her head sharply to look into the bedroom, but there was no one there yet. The voice had come from the sitting room, drawing nearer with each word. Panic racing through her, Jess stepped to the left, behind the hanging clothes on that side, her mind scrambling for a way to save herself.

"It would appear so." There was no mistaking Vasco's voice. "And I'm thinking I should join her."

Jess closed her eyes, just barely restraining a groan. He was about to find out she wasn't in there, and then they'd search the room.

"Do you think that's wise?"

Her eyes popped open, and she listened breathlessly.

"I'm just thinking," Cristo continued after a pause, "that maybe it would be better to wait until you get her to the ship to start anything. You're not likely to want to stop once you start, and—"

"Aye-aye, ye're right. Better to wait until we're back at the ship," Vasco said with obvious disappointment. "I guess we might as well take a seat, then. Women take forever at these things."

There was a grunt of what she assumed was agreement and then silence.

Jess slowly let out the breath she'd been holding, afraid to make any kind of a sound to let the men know she wasn't in the shower, and then bit her lip and tried to think what to do. She had to get out of there, obviously, but couldn't leave through the suite door with the men in the sitting room. That left the sliding glass doors to the balcony, but there were two problems with that. One, she wasn't sure she could get to them without being seen by someone in the sitting room. It depended on what seats the men had chosen. If they'd chosen to sit at the small table by the window she'd be okay, but if they were seated on the couch she'd be seen. The other problem was what did she do once she was on the balcony? This was the fourth floor and that made it a long way to the ground.

Although, she thought suddenly, the suite Raffaele, Santo, and Zanipolo shared was right below this one. Maybe she could climb over the railing and lower herself to their balcony.

Jess grimaced at the very thought. She so hated heights. On top of that, she really wasn't very athletic. She spent most of her time studying or counseling. The only exercise she really got was slinging drinks at the bar.

The murmur of voices from the sitting room made up Jess's mind for her. She didn't really have a choice. She had to at least try to escape. Swallowing, Jess eased slowly out through the clothes, wincing and stilling when one of the hangers let out a small screech as it scraped along the metal rod. She listened desperately for anyone coming to check out what the sound was, but when the murmurs continued from the next room, she decided the small sound hadn't been heard and eased all the way out, her gaze locked on the open doors to the sitting area as she did.

Jess nearly sobbed with relief when the couch came into view and she saw that it was empty. They'd sat by the window. She could slip out unseen, Jess thought, and started to do that, but then realized she was only wearing her bikini bottoms. Pausing, she glanced swiftly over the clothes available, chose the dark blue sundress with white flowers because she knew it was older, and then eased it carefully from the hanger.

Afraid of bumping the hangers and sending them screeching along the rod, Jess didn't take the time to put it on now. She simply clasped it in her hand and tiptoed to the sliding glass doors. She unlocked it slowly and cautiously, wincing at the snick of sound it made. But when the voices continued from the next room, she eased the door open along its track, moving it at a snail's pace to avoid any sound or sudden change in air pressure that might alert the men. It seemed to take forever, but eventually she had it wide enough to slip through. Jess didn't bother to close it, but turned to peer nervously toward the sliding glass doors off the sitting room.

If the men were seated at the table as she suspected, they would see her the minute she stepped away from the door. She had to move quickly during this next part, Jess thought, and glanced toward the balcony railing, only to stiffen with shock. It wasn't a railing at all. Well, it was, but only a half railing on top of a two-foot-high half wall. Why hadn't she noticed that? How the hell was she supposed to climb down that?

Jess closed her eyes and just managed to bite back a moan. This so wasn't good. She was going to kill herself in the attempt. But she didn't have a lot of choices here. It was try, or just surrender to Vasco.

Mouth tightening, Jess opened her eyes, slung Allison's dress around her neck and raced for the rail. She had reached it, stepped on the half wall, and slung first one leg and then the other over the rail before she heard a sliding door open and salty curses. Uttering a salty curse of her own, Jess grasped the rails tightly and stepped backward, letting herself fall. Her hands slid down the metal rails with a squeal, but stopped abruptly at the half wall, jerking her to a halt.

Biting back a scream of pain as the metal dug into her hands, Jess glanced desperately down, her heart sinking when she saw that the two feet of half wall wasn't all the wall there was. Two feet only reached the top of her balcony floor, then there was the thickness of the balcony itself and apparently more wall at the top of the third-floor balcony. At least, that was what it looked like to her, because she was hanging from the top of her half wall, but the wall stretched down to just above her waist. She could barely see the edge of Raffaele's balcony, and didn't think she'd be able to swing herself anywhere.

"Hang on, lovey. I'm coming!"

Jess jerked her head up just in time to snatch her hand off the railing as Vasco appeared above her and made to close his fingers over hers. That had been instinct, and a stupid one, she realized, squawking in alarm as her body swung out so that she hung sideways to the balcony, dangling from one hand that was starting to slip. She was almost glad when Vasco slapped his hand over that one instead, and tightened his grip.

"I've got ye, love. Ye'll be all right," he assured her, managing a smile that didn't hide a real concern. Turning his head, he bellowed, "Cristo! Get over here and hold her hand while I climb over to get her."

Jess closed her eyes and debated what to do as awareness slid through her body at his touch. Should she try to make the balcony below? Or wait to be rescued and taken away by Vasco? Hanging there from one arm that felt like it was being dislocated, while her body hummed in response to just their hands touching . . . well, his saving her actually didn't seem *that* horrible. After all, Vasco wasn't so bad—a bath, shampoo, and a muzzle would even make him amazing . . . Except for the whole biting thing.

"Here, I'm going to take my hand away and you slap yours on. Don't let her go," Vasco ordered.

"Just pull her up by her hand, Vasco," Cristo suggested.

"I'll not risk dislocating her arm or something jerking her up by her wrist," Vasco growled.

Jess was just telling herself that was very thoughtful of him, when he added, "I can hardly give her a good rogering if she's got broken bones."

"Dear God," Jess muttered, and lifted her head, intending to swing her lower body toward the balcony below and let go when he let go. But she was too late; her eyes were only half-raised to him when his hand was gone and another immediately closed around hers in its place.

"Trying to escape again, I see, little dove," Cristo said by way of greeting when her eyes met his through the rails.

"Nah," Vasco said for her. "I'm her life mate. No one can resist their life mate. She's just playing hard to get to prove she's not a doxy," he continued good-naturedly as he straightened and stepped up on the half wall. Peering over the rail at her, he paused to add, "You're adding a little spice to the rum, love, and I like spiced rum."

His gaze shifted to her bare breasts then and Vasco licked his lips and then sighed and shook his head. "Damn, I do like them jugs, lovey. Can't wait to suck on them and grope for trout in your river again," he muttered, and slung one leg over the rail before stopping again to look at her some more.

Jess gaped at him, her eyes wide as she noted the silver gathering in his beautiful green eyes as he looked down at her.

"Yer pretty as a picture hanging stretched out there, lass," he said with a gusty sigh. "I'm thinking when we get back to the ship I might tie ye down stretched out like and just look on ye a bit 'ere I give you a good quiffing."

Jess was trying to figure out what a quiffing was when he suddenly laughed and slapped his knee. "Who am I kidding, love? My whore pipe's already so hard for ye the first time'll most likely be a flyer."

Jess just gaped as he swung his second leg over to stand on the half wall on the same side of the railing as her. It was like the man spoke a whole other language. She hadn't a clue what he was saying he was going to do with her, but suspected she should be glad of that. Turning her gaze back to Cristo, she eyed his hand on hers.

"Don't do it, little dove," he said softly. "There's no coming back from death and there's no need. The capitan'll treat you like royalty if ye let 'em. Yer his life mate. You'll be happy together and you'll get used to feeding on mortals."

Those words made up Jess's mind for her. He'd just verified what she'd feared. Taking her for a lover wasn't enough; the pirate planned to turn her into a vampire too. Crazy passionate sex was one thing, but becoming a dead soulless vampire who fed on other mortals? Not bloody likely. Swinging her other hand back up, she gouged Cristo's hand with her nails, scoring deep.

Caught by surprise by the viciousness of the attack, Cristo's grasp slackened and Jess pushed with her free hand, managing to pull free. For one exhilarating and terrifying moment, she was dropping, and then her wrist was caught, and she screamed as her body jerked, her weight wrenching painfully on her arm.

"Damn me, lass, that was close," Vasco growled, and she glanced up to see that he was kneeling on the thin lip of the half wall, clutching the rail with one hand and her with the other. When he began to pull her upward, she closed her eyes and moaned in despair.

Nine

Raffaele smacked his lips together and grimaced at the dryness and horrible taste in his mouth. Both were sure signs he'd been sleeping with his mouth open, and probably snoring, he thought, opening his eyes, and then he frowned with confusion as he noted that he was in the sitting room. In a chair actually, he realized.

His gaze slid over the pull-out couch and he wondered why he hadn't slept there rather than the chair, and then his memory returned and he sat up abruptly.

Jess.

She'd been sleeping on the couch and he'd taken the chair to guard her, but she wasn't there now. He was just starting to jump to his feet when a squawk on the balcony caught his ear. Turning, he peered out and was momentarily frozen in place as he stared at the legs kicking in the air at the far end of the balcony. They were a woman's legs, long and shapely, and easily recognizable mostly because of the bikini bottoms at the top of them.

"Jess," he hissed, and rushed to the French doors to the bedroom, shouting at Santo and Zanipolo as he thrust them open and continued to the sliding doors leading to the balcony from there. Raffaele had no idea if the men woke up, and didn't have the time to check; he simply unlocked and dragged the sliding door open and then rushed out to grab Jess just as she started to rise out of sight. Catching her beneath the knees, he started to lean out, but heard a deep voice growl, "Stand up, Cristo, and I'll pass her to you."

Mouth tightening, Raffaele tightened his grip on Jess's legs and yanked, hard. He heard Jess's startled cry, and then a deep voice cursed, and Jess's upper body fell back. Moving quickly, Raffaele released one leg, and got that hand under the base of her spine as she dropped. He then tugged her toward him as he stumbled back from the railing. Holding her close, he watched the owner of the voice he'd heard tumble past them, heading for the ground below.

Jess flinched in his arms as they heard the thud when the pirate hit the ground three stories down, but Raffaele didn't look to see how the rogue immortal had faired. Instead, he turned and carried Jess into the suite.

"Lock the door," he growled to Santo and Zanipolo, who were up, but only just stumbling toward the door, pulling their pants on as they went. Raffaele then carried Jess to the sitting room and sat on the pull-out bed with her in his lap. The moment he did, she crossed her arms and turned to bury her face in his chest.

Mouth compressed, Raffaele held her tight, one hand patting her back soothingly. He'd come so close to losing her, he needed the time to calm himself, but after a moment, he eased her back to look her over.

Raffaele's mouth tightened when he saw that she had a few new scrapes and bruises on her cheek, and what he could see of her chest. From scraping against the wall when he'd pulled her down and toward him, he supposed. She also had bruising starting on her one wrist, he noted. But all in all, she'd made out relatively well, he thought, just before she turned toward him and pressed close, trying to hide herself.

"It's all right," he said, his voice a growl of sound. Now that his concern for her well-being had been eased, he was very aware that she was sitting there in his arms wearing nothing but the damned bikini bottoms.

Sighing, Raffaele tried to pretend she wasn't nearly naked, and his life mate, and said, "Tell me what happened. How did you end up hanging in front of the balcony? Did they come in and steal you from the bed and try to drag you upstairs?"

It sounded ridiculous, but he couldn't imagine any other way she could have ended up out there.

Jess shook her head, and then, her voice soft and almost embarrassed, she admitted, "I went up to shower and change."

"To your *room*?" he asked with dismay as Santo and Zanipolo came out to the sitting room, both fully dressed now.

Jess nodded.

"By yourself?" he asked with disbelief, his voice raising. "Why didn't you wake me? I would have gone with you."

"You were sleeping, and you've already done so much, and I just wanted to . . ." She paused and shook her head helplessly, and then said, "But they came in and . . . I tried to climb down, but it was too far and I lost Allison's dress and he wanted to tie me up and quiff river trout," she ended on a moan, and buried her face against his chest again.

"She means grope for trout in her river," Santo explained quietly.

"He also mentioned quiffing," Zanipolo added. "She's confused the two."

"Dear God," Raffaele breathed, his arms tightening protectively around Jess. He hadn't heard those terms in years . . . like hundreds of years. Shakespeare had used "groping for trout in a peculiar river" to mean infidelity, but the young lords of the day had quite got a kick out of the term and it had quickly come to be a euphemism for other things back then. The pirate had been telling her he was going to stimulate her digitally, before quiffing her, which was slang around the same time for sex. The bastard wanted to tie his life mate up and rape her and was terrorizing her by telling her ahead of time exactly what he meant to do.

Sighing, he peered down at Jess. All he could see was her back. She was still huddled against his chest . . . like a child seeking protection from monsters, he thought sympathetically. This must be terrifying for her.

"She's huddling against you because she has no clothes on," Zanipolo told him with exasperation.

"We should go buy her some," Santo said.

"Good idea," Zanipolo said, heading for the door.

Raffaele was opening his mouth, intending to protest that they had to stay, Jess needed protecting, but then Jess mumbled against his chest, "Oh, God, thank you so much. Just something cheap, a resort T-shirt, shorts, and flip-flops are fine. I promise I'll pay you back the first chance I get."

Raffaele closed his mouth. The woman was sitting here in bikini bottoms, the only item of clothing she had to her name at the moment. At least here in Punta Cana.

"We might be a while," Zanipolo said, stopping at the door.

When Raffaele glanced to him with surprise, the man waggled his eyebrows up and down, and then dropped his eyes to Jess and back up to his face, obviously trying to convey some kind of message. It didn't take much effort for Raffaele to sort out what the man was suggesting. Shaking his head, he waved the men out, and then just sat there for a minute, unsure what to do while they waited.

"Would you like me to get you a shirt while you wait?" he asked finally, and then said, "Oh, wait, you said you were going to shower, did you get to do that?"

"No," Jess sighed against his chest, her breath ruffling the short hairs there and sending a shiver of awareness through him. Now that his shock and worry for her well-being were easing a bit, his body was having the expected response to holding her nearly naked in his lap.

Time to change that, he decided grimly. If he didn't, his determination to refrain from the physical side of life mates until they were both safely back in North America would fall by the wayside. Standing abruptly, he carried her into the bathroom and set her down on the side of the large whirlpool tub. He then straightened and grabbed a towel.

"Would you rather have a shower or bath?" Raffaele asked, keeping his face averted as he handed her the towel. "I'm sure you have time for a bath if you want one. Zanipolo is a slow shopper at the best of times, but when shopping for someone else he can agonize forever."

"Maybe I'll take a bath, then," Jess decided on a sigh as she accepted the towel and wrapped it quickly around herself, sarong-style. "It might ease my shoulder. I think I pulled something. Or Vasco pulled something when I got free of Cristo and he caught me mid-fall."

Raffaele hesitated, and then moved closer and looked her over. "Which shoulder?"

"This one." She gestured to her left shoulder.

Raffaele probed the shoulder gently, taking her arm and raising and lowering it as he felt around the joint. "How bad is the pain?"

"Not bad," Jess assured him. "Just a little tender."

Raffaele nodded and released her arm. "I was afraid it might be dislocated, but it doesn't seem to be. There's a little swelling, though. You're probably right and a muscle got pulled. A nice long soak might do it a lot of good. But I'll call down to reception and have them send up some ice and ibuprofen."

"Thank you," Jess said solemnly.

"You're welcome." Raffaele smiled faintly, and then moved to set the plug in the tub and start the taps. Straightening, he then headed for the door, saying, "I'll be out in the sitting room. Take your time, and shout if you have any problems."

Raffaele heard her murmured, "Thank you," over the sound of rushing water as he pulled the door closed. He paused then and leaned back against the door with a sigh. Damn, it had been hard leaving her in there alone when all he wanted to do was strip off her bikini bottoms and . . .

Yeah, not good to think too much about what he wanted to do, Raffaele told himself grimly. *Go call reception and get her ice and ibuprofen. And order her some breakfast.* She was probably hungry. He was. A sensation he hadn't experienced in millennia. It was most uncomfortable.

Jess watched the door close, and then peered at the bottles on the side of the tub. Spotting one that said *bubble bath* on it, she grabbed and opened it to take a whiff. When the scent of tropical flowers wafted from the bottle, she nodded and upended the contents into the tub. Setting the bottle back, she then stood up and had to grab her towel as it started to unravel. She tucked it back in place, with a grimace that only grew when she caught a glimpse of herself in the mirror.

Obviously, she should have looked at herself before sneaking out of the men's suite earlier that day to return to the one she shared with Allison.

She was wearing a towel, had a serious case of bedhead, and her face had tearstains from her upset last night. This was how she'd made her way through the halls to her room, and how she'd looked when Vasco had been trying to drag her back onto the balcony. Honestly, she didn't know why he'd bothered, looking as she did.

Making a face, Jess reached under the towel to tug down her bikini bottoms and then stepped out of them and moved to the sink to turn on the taps. She wasn't wearing them for another twenty-four-hour period without washing them first. Jess stuck them under the water, frowning as she noted that they were getting a bit frayed. It looked like the material had got caught on the sides of the porthole as she'd squeezed herself through it. There were some runs on both sides, and the material around the elastic trim was pulling away from the seams.

Sighing, Jess grabbed the bottle of liquid body wash, squirted some on, and set to work scrubbing the material together. Before this trip, she had never really considered fashion very important. Clothes had always just been a necessity, but not something that defined a person. However, her wardrobe at the moment seemed to define her perfectly: lacking, worn, and not her own. That was her and her life at the moment, lacking nearly everything she had brought with her, tired and worn out from being hunted by the pirates, and with nothing of her own . . . well, except for her bikini bottoms. The shirtdress she'd worn last night and the towel she was wearing now were borrowed. It was enough to make her rethink her position. Clothes were crazy important, and not having them was frustrating and embarrassing and basically a pain.

Really, Vasco wasn't playing fair taking all her clothes like that. She still would have been stuck here if he'd just taken her passport and wallet with all her ID and bank cards, but at least she wouldn't be running around in a towel and bikini bottoms that were starting to fray a bit from constant wear and tear. If the man ever did get ahold of her, she'd have an earful for him on the subject. Not to mention other things, like what he'd said that morning on the balcony.

"Playing hard to get," Jess muttered to herself with disgust. Seriously, was that what he thought she was doing? And what was that bit about not being able to resist a life mate and her being his? Actually, that comment had been a bit frightening to her; mostly because she did seem to find it hard to resist him . . . at least when he was touching and kissing her and not talking.

On the other hand, she seemed to have a similar response to Raffaele. Well, somewhat anyway. He'd never kissed or touched her that way, but judging by her physical response when he took her arm or hand or simply probed her bruises and such, she thought she might. The dreams had been pretty hot. Unfortunately, not as hot as Vasco's real kisses had been. Those had been mind-blowing. Literally. The moment their lips had met, Jess had been lost in a whirl of passion, oblivious to everything but her need and her desire for it to be slaked.

But, surely, she could have that with someone else, Jess thought desperately. Someone who didn't go around biting people and sucking their blood? Someone kind and sweet, like Raffaele, would be good. But he didn't seem to be interested in her that way. He was always a complete gentleman with her, taking her elbow to escort her around, dancing with that space between them, and never so much as trying to kiss her.

Jess rinsed out her bikini bottoms, wrung them out, and hung them over the towel rack to dry. She then walked over to the tub, turned off the taps, dropped her towel, and stepped in. A small sigh slid from her lips as she settled in the warm water. It felt like the first time her muscles had unclenched since the pirate ship the day before . . . and she needed it.

Raffaele closed his eyes, concentrating on listening, but didn't hear a sound, not even a light splash. Opening his eyes, he peered at the bathroom door and tapped the fingers of one hand against his leg as he debated whether he should knock on the door. Jess had been in there for quite a while. She might have fallen asleep in the tub and be in danger of drowning. But he'd suggested she take a long soak, so she might just be relaxing in there. He pondered the thought for a minute, imagining it in his mind. Jess lying naked in the tub, the warm water caressing her body, lapping around her breasts . . .

Licking his lips, Raffaele peered down at the doorknob, his hand moving toward it. He should really make sure Jess was okay, he thought, and then stilled as a light splash sounded through the door. She wasn't asleep and in danger of drowning; she was just relaxing in the warm water . . . naked and wet. His fingers continued to the metal doorknob and were just closing around it when he heard the door open in the other room and the murmur of Santo's voice and then a laugh from Zanipolo.

Snatching his hand back, Raffaele turned and hurried into the sitting room, thinking his cousins had just saved him from making what probably would have been a big mistake.

"Oh, hey, you're awake," Zanipolo said with surprise when Raffaele entered the room as he was setting three large bags on the dining table by the sliding glass doors.

"Of course I am," Raffaele said, his eyebrows rising. "Why would I not be?"

Zanipolo shrugged. "I was thinking that maybe while we were out shopping, you might want to seal the deal with Jess."

Raffaele arched his eyebrows at his chosen terminology and shook his head. "I am leaving it until she is safely back home and I can join her there."

"Yeah." Zanipolo drew out the word with a frown. "But that was when she was leaving right away. Now that she's stuck here, I'm thinking you might want to speed up your game a bit."

Raffaele shook his head. "She's still leaving. If we can't get her a replacement passport and a flight out today, I'll call Julius and see if he can send a company plane for her. They can take her home. I'll accompany her for the flight, and control the customs and immigration people so there are no issues with her reentering the country without a passport, and then fly right back to finish out our vacation before returning to the States and starting to woo her."

"Yeah, I thought of that and called Julius while we had breakfast," Zanipolo informed him solemnly, and then shook his head. "The earliest they can possibly get a plane out here is the day after tomorrow and that's only if there are no delays on the flights they have booked. It might even be the day after that."

Raffaele frowned at this news. Notte Construction had two private planes, but they were used for both the business and to transport family members around the world as well. They were always busy, and always booked well ahead of time. The only way he could have got them to change the schedule was if it was an emergency. This wouldn't be considered urgent. Jess was safe for now, and a two- or three-day wait for the plane was actually pretty good, but he'd been hoping to get lucky and get one out here right away. Two or three days meant forty-eight to seventy-two hours that Vasco could use to try to take Jess again. But it looked like there was nothing he could do about that.

Straightening his shoulders, he said grimly, "Then we'll just have to hope the embassy can get her a replacement passport quickly and we can get her on a flight out of here directly afterward."

"Do you really want to pin your hopes of a future with Jess on the possibility that the government will work quickly?" Zanipolo asked dubiously. "Governments aren't known for doing anything quickly . . . except perhaps going after taxes."

Raffaele scowled at the truth of those words.

"Look," Zanipolo said, sitting down at the table and eyeing him with concern, "I know you wanted to wait until after this trip to start to woo Jess, and I applaud your self-control, but I really think you need to show her the pleasure you can experience together now, just in case."

"Just in case what?" Raffaele asked, eyes narrowing.

"In case Vasco does get her," Zanipolo said quietly.

"He's not going to get his hands on her," Raffaele said with a scowl at the very thought.

"But if he does," Zanipolo said insistently, "and if he does it before you seal the deal with her, you could very well lose her."

"Don't be ridiculous," Raffaele said with irritation. "She's my life mate."

"Unfortunately, she is his too," Santo said quietly.

Raffaele rounded on him with shock and roared, "*What?*"

"It's true," Zanipolo assured him apologetically. "Vasco's desires have been reawakened and he felt her pleasure."

Raffaele's head jerked back in shock and he stared at his cousin with dismay before asking in a bare whisper, "He gave her pleasure?"

"They're possible life mates too, Raff," Santo said solemnly, as if that said everything, and it did. The passion between Jess and Vasco would be as strong as it was between him and her.

"But she likes you," Zanipolo said now, and Raff peered at him blankly.

"What?"

"She *likes* you," Zanipolo repeated. "She doesn't really like Vasco. The passion is there, but she doesn't want it to be. He's too crude for her with his talk about trout and jugs. And she's horrified at his being a vampirate. And he has greasy hair. Those things along with the horror she was experiencing helped her fight the passion, and luck gave her the opportunity to escape before he could consummate their passion."

"But she might not be so lucky a second time," Santo pointed out in a rumble.

"And you know once she experiences the full life mate passion with him . . ." Zanipolo shook his head, not bothering to say more. But he didn't have to. If Jess experienced the passion life mates enjoyed with Vasco without knowing she could also have it with him, she might very well overlook the things she didn't like. Greasy hair could be washed. She could insist he alter his speech around her and he would. Any immortal would for a life mate. He might even give up his ship and being rogue for her, and just the promise of that combined with the life mate passion would most likely make her agree to be his mate.

Raff sank down onto the nearest chair and stared at his cousins briefly before asking, "Why didn't you tell me this before?"

"Because I figured you'd do the whole fair thing," Zanipolo admitted quietly.

"Fair thing?" he asked with bewilderment.

"You'd feel you had to tell her about immortals, and explain everything before you tried wooing her," he said dryly.

"Yes," he admitted, because that was the right thing to do.

"It won't work here, Raff. What she saw Ildaria do to Tyler . . ." He shook his head. "If I weren't one myself and didn't know Ildaria was breaking our laws, I'd think we were monsters too."

Raffaele scowled, but said, "I'm sure if I explain things properly, she'll understand and—"

"Read my mind," Zanipolo interrupted with exasperation.

"What? Why?" Raffaele asked with surprise.

"Because explaining it will not have the same impact as seeing what Jess saw. I'm thinking of what I saw in her mind. Of exactly what she saw. Read my mind so you can see it for yourself, and then tell me again that explaining will help anything."

Raffaele's mouth tightened, but he slid into the other man's mind and then stilled at the visuals coming at him.

"Dear God," he whispered, quickly withdrawing from Zanipolo's mind.

"Yeah." Zani nodded. "Explaining is not going to cut it if you do not have some kind of hook in her first. You need to seduce her, show her life mate passion, show her that you are perfect for each other, and then, maybe after a couple months of ravishing her, once she is good and hooked on the sex, you can explain about what we are and whatnot. But, *cugino*, if you tell her you're an immortal like Vasco right now, she will be running away screaming from you too."

Raffaele nodded silently, seeing the wisdom behind the suggestion. After what she'd seen Ildaria do, Jess was not going to be willing to hear anything he had to say if he admitted to being an immortal too. He needed to do some serious wooing here. Not just seducing, but everything and anything he could do to make her feel safe and secure with him. She needed to trust him fully before he revealed what he was to her, or he would lose her.

For a moment, Raffaele debated what to do first. Seduce her? Or get her to the American embassy and seduce her after that? After all, surely they wouldn't be able to get her a passport the same day? They'd have to check to be sure she was who she claimed to be. Wouldn't they? And that would give him at least one night to seduce her. Wouldn't it? Raffaele didn't know. He had no idea how long it would take her to get a replacement passport or a flight out, and that was a problem. If he took her to the embassy first, he risked her leaving before he could seduce her.

"We have a kind of plan that will allow you to do both—seduce her and get her to the U.S. embassy," Zanipolo said suddenly, obviously reading his thoughts.

Raffaele merely raised an eyebrow in question at the news, not at all surprised that the man had been reading his thoughts.

"We asked about the embassy. It's in Arroyo Hondo, a section of Santo Domingo. That's about a three-and-a-half-hour drive from here," Zanipolo informed him. "But the office closes at four thirty."

Raffaele glanced at the wall clock. It was just before nine o'clock now. That gave them seven and a half hours until it closed. Plenty of time to get her there.

"Not if we work it right," Zanipolo assured him as if he'd spoken the thoughts aloud. "Say she's another hour in the tub and then dressing and stuff. Then we take her to breakfast."

"I was going to order room service," he said with a frown.

"Even better," Zanipolo said with a grin. "I asked about room service breakfast while we were in the restaurant and they said it usually takes a good hour for breakfast to be delivered in the morning, or even more depending on when you order it."

"That's one hour down," he said quietly.

"Right, so you eat here and then we take a taxi into town to a car rental place to rent a car for the drive. Another hour if we're lucky."

"That still leaves five and half hours to get there before it closes," he said with a sigh.

"We have to stop for lunch," Zanipolo pointed out. "And probably for a bathroom break." He shrugged. "We get there just after it closes, and then rent a suite at a nearby hotel. She's away from here, safe from Vasco, and will be able to go to the embassy the next morning. She'll relax, you'll relax, and bada boom bada bing! Life mate sex, fireworks, an orchestra plays 'Ah, Sweet Mystery of Life' and you—"

"What?" Raffaele interrupted with disbelief.

"He watched *Young Frankenstein* again the night before we flew out," Santo said dryly.

Raffaele just shook his head, not sure what the hell he was talking about.

"Never mind," Zanipolo said with a laugh. "Point is, you'll get to both take her where she wants to go, and seduce her."

"Hmm," Raffaele murmured, admitting to himself that it was a good plan.

Jess stared silently at her toes sticking out of the bubbles and tried to relax, but her mind was spinning with worries and questions. Vasco, pirates, and vampires were only a part of them and they fell in the worries department rather than the questions area. After all, she knew that Vasco was a pirate captain and a vampire. She also knew he thought she was his life mate, whatever that was, and that he was determined to get her into his bed. So . . . worry, not questions. The questions all came in with Raffaele and his cousins.

Jess let her feet sink into the warm, sudsy bathwater and leaned her head back as she considered the three cousins. They'd dragged her from the ocean, well, Raffaele had, and had brought her here to their room, and . . . basically they'd been taking care of, and saving, her again and again since. Raffaele had saved her from being taken by Cristo when the pirate had taken control of her and would have forced her on the bus, he'd carried her back down here when she had her hysterics about her passport and such missing, and he'd grabbed her legs and dragged her down to his balcony when Vasco had nearly caught her.

Thinking of that made her remember the terrible thud of the pirate captain hitting the ground four stories below the balcony and Jess found herself wondering if he was all right. Frowning, she gave her head a shake. Of course he was all right, he was a vampire. A fall couldn't kill him. Besides, she shouldn't even be worrying about that. She should be wondering how to escape or, alternately, kill the monster.

That thought definitely caused conflict in Jess. She couldn't kill Vasco. To be honest, she didn't even want to. He hadn't hurt her. In fact, he'd given her great pleasure . . . when he wasn't talking. And, in truth, she wasn't really afraid of him. Ildaria? Yes, she was definitely afraid of her. And she was even afraid of Cristo. When it came to Vasco, though, she was more afraid of herself and what he made her feel . . . the temptation he presented.

"All right, you've lost your mind," she told herself grimly. "He's a threat to your very life and soul."

Is he? part of her mind asked. Surely he wouldn't turn her without her agreeing? Besides, everyone who went on that boat seemed to have returned perfectly fine. Well, except maybe for being a quart or so lower on blood, she supposed. Maybe she would have too . . . after experiencing the best sex of her life. And you know it would have been good. Just the foreplay was mind-blowing.

"The man is a *vampire*. A bloodsucking fiend," she reminded herself firmly.

But a hell of a kisser, the little voice in her head countered, and Jess groaned and slid down in the tub, allowing the water to cover her head briefly. She sat up again a moment later, but her thoughts were no clearer on the subject. The part of her that was able to reason knew she should be afraid of the man and do everything possible to escape this power he had over her. But another part, mostly her lady parts, she suspected, wasn't so sure.

Unable to resolve the issue, Jess pushed it away and turned her thoughts to the questions she had, which mostly had to do with Raffaele. The man had saved her three times, four if you included his picking her up and carrying her down here when she'd had her fit of hysterics on finding all of her things missing. He'd rescued her, and offered her rest and respite in his hotel room, and hadn't asked for a thing in return.

Jess almost would have been happier had he tried to seduce her while she was distressed. At least then she'd have understood his motivations, but he'd been a complete gentleman. Why was he taking up his vacation helping her?

She understood, or thought she understood, why his cousins were helping. Santo and Zanipolo were obviously helping him, not really her, but why was Raffaele doing it? And why the hell hadn't he kissed her yet? If he did, and it was even close to the passion Vasco had shown her, she might at least have something to help her fight the temptation the pirate presented.

And how sad was that? she thought grimly. Vasco was a soulless vampire who lured unsuspecting tourists onto his ship to feed off of, and that wasn't enough to keep her from lusting after him. But as ashamed as she was to admit it, part of her panic when he'd caught her hand while she was trying to escape had been a result of the awareness that had shot through her the moment his skin made contact with hers.

She'd felt that same awareness, though, when Raffaele had wrapped his arms around her legs to prevent her being dragged upward by Vasco. For one moment, before he'd tugged her free, Jess had felt pulled in two directions. Not by the men, so much as her own desires. Which was why she had questions about Raffaele. Why was he helping her? Had he felt the same pull of attraction? Was he just resisting it? If so, why? Was he, maybe, married? Or did he have a serious girlfriend or fiancée?

Jess scowled. The thought of Raffaele already being taken was a depressing one, but did it really matter? she asked herself. After all, it wasn't like they were going to have the opportunity to have a relationship. Maybe if she didn't have to get out of there, find the embassy, and fly home to stay safe from Vasco, things would have been different. They could have had a vacation romance or something if he was single, but as things stood, staying wasn't an option.

Still, if he could give her the same passion Vasco had inspired in her, resisting the pirate would be easier. But since the man showed no interest in that, she just had to get the heck away from the resort and to the embassy as quickly as she could.

With that thought in mind, Jess sat up and glanced over the small bottles with the hotel logo on them. Spotting the one that said *shampoo*, she grabbed and opened it. She'd lollygagged long enough in the bath. It was time to get moving.

Ten

Jess finished brushing her hair, and then pulled on her damp bikini bottoms with a grimace. They weren't dry, of course, but wouldn't have been even if she'd let them sit for hours. The humidity would have prevented it.

Hopefully she wouldn't have to wear them much longer. In fact, Zanipolo and Santo may have already brought back a T-shirt and shorts or something for her to wear. The thought was enough to encourage her to move a little quicker. Jess grabbed a fresh towel and wrapped it around herself sarong-style as she headed for the door.

"Ah, perfect timing," Raffaele said as she joined him in the sitting room. "Zanipolo and Santo just delivered your clothes."

"Oh," she said with relief and then her eyes widened as she spotted the bags on the coffee table. Moving toward them, she asked, "Which bag is for me?"

"All of them."

"What?" She glanced to him with surprise.

"Zanipolo likes to shop," Raffaele said with a shrug and wry smile, but Jess frowned.

"That was kind, but I'm pretty sure I can't afford all of this," she muttered, moving to the bags. Jess had browsed through the boutique stores here, and knew the prices were crazy expensive. Looking through the bags didn't reassure her any. The two men hadn't just picked her up a T-shirt and shorts, they'd bought her dresses, and swimsuits, and a couple pairs of shorts as well as several T-shirts. They'd also thought to get her panties and bras, which were amazingly the right size, as well as sandals, both the high-heeled strappy kind, and flat walking sandals. No flip-flops. Glancing to Raffaele, she shook her head. "I can't accept this. I mean, I'll take a T-shirt and a pair of panties and shorts, as well as the flat sandals, but we'll just have to take everything else back, and I'll pay you back for what I do use when—"

"You don't have to take anything back, and no one expects you to pay for these clothes, Jess," he interrupted solemnly. "They're a gift."

She shook her head firmly. "You guys have already done enough for me. I—"

"You might need the extra clothes," he interrupted.

"No," she assured him. "The shorts and T-shirt are good enough to go to the embassy with, get a replacement passport, and then fly home."

"Zanipolo and Santo asked about the embassy," he announced, as if just recalling it. "They were told it's in Arroyo Hondo. I guess that's in Santo Domingo." He shrugged, and then added, "So, after you dress and we eat, the plan is to take one of the hotel buses into town and rent a car to drive there. I gather it'll take a couple hours."

Jess stared at him wide-eyed. She'd assumed there would be an embassy in Punta Cana. Foolish, she supposed. They could hardly have an embassy in every small town or city of every foreign country. But she could hardly believe that the men were willing to drive her there. She wanted to refuse the offer, and insist they continue with their vacation and forget about her. Unfortunately, that wasn't really an option. She was a starving student still. She might be able to borrow money from the family members who were here, but paying them back would be a problem. Not impossible, but another burden added on top of the extra costs she already had. Replacing her passport wouldn't be free, and the clothes she'd lost were a write-off, and then there was her purse and all her credit cards that—Crap! she thought suddenly. She couldn't buy a plane ticket without her credit cards. Dear God, it didn't matter if she went to the embassy and got a passport, Vasco had made sure she couldn't leave.

"Jess?" Raffaele said with concern, moving a little closer. "Are you all right? You've gone pale. What's the matter?"

"I just—" She shook her head and sighed. "I need to dress. I'll feel better once I'm dressed."

"Of course," he said gently, and picked up the three bags for her. He then led the way back to the bathroom.

Jess followed silently, her mind whirling in a sort of panic, but when he set the bags down on the bathroom counter and turned to leave the room, she asked, "Why are you guys helping me like this?"

Raffaele paused and turned back with surprise. For a moment, he just stared at her, and she got the feeling he was debating what to say, but finally he simply said, "Because you need help."

"That's it?" she asked, a frown pulling at her lips.

Raffaele shrugged. "That and . . . well, if my sister were in a situation like this I would hope someone would help her too."

"Your sister," she murmured with disappointment. It didn't seem to her to be a good thing that she was making him think of his sister. Not when her attraction to him was anything but brotherly. It seemed he must not be experiencing that attraction as she was. How depressing. Although that explained why he wasn't trying to kiss her, she supposed, and wondered if he was gay. Jess would have liked to believe that was the case for her pride's sake, but wasn't egotistical enough for that. Just because he wasn't interested didn't make him gay.

"I'll let you dress," Raffaele said softly, and slid from the room, pulling the door closed quietly behind him.

Sighing, Jess glanced at the bags, but then crossed the room to sit on the side of the raised tiled floor around the tub. She needed money to leave Punta Cana, a lot of money by her estimation. She also needed a good excuse to borrow that money. Her adopted family was pretty amazing for the most part, and they would no doubt be happy to help her if she gave them a good excuse for leaving. But if she told them she was fleeing a pirate captain, who was also a vampire who had designs on her body and not her blood, they'd help her onto a plane, for sure. They'd even accompany her home, and then check her into the nearest mental hospital when that plane landed.

Groaning, she rubbed her face wearily and then stood to sort through the bags of clothes. She'd rather hoped price tags on the items of clothing would help her select the least expensive ones, but those had been removed. She settled for a pair of panties, dark blue shorts, and a light blue T-shirt with a tropical scene and "Punta Cana" written on it. She was skipping a bra in the interest of saving money.

Once dressed in the chosen attire, Jess peered at herself in the mirror. She looked okay. While she wasn't used to going braless, you couldn't really tell she wasn't wearing one. At least, she didn't think so as she peered critically at her reflection. The design on the T-shirt helped, she supposed.

Shrugging, Jess turned and headed for the door. She'd have breakfast, which at least was already paid for, and then she'd consider the best plan of action. Hopefully, once she'd eaten she'd think up a good excuse to give one of her uncles for needing to borrow money and leave early.

"What are those?"

Raffaele glanced up with a start at that question, and paused as he took in Jess. She looked incredibly young and carefree in the T-shirt and shorts she'd donned. At least on first impression. If you looked too closely at the forced smile and the strain around her eyes, the carefree part dropped away, though.

"Pamphlets?" she asked when he remained silent.

"Oh." Glancing down, he peered at the pamphlets he'd been going through. After her protest about the clothes, he'd known she'd protest the expense of their renting a car and driving her to Santo Domingo too. The pamphlets had been his answer. He'd decided he'd claim they'd planned to take a trip to Santo Domingo anyway on this vacation and so it was no problem to take her along.

Raffaele had gone through the selection Zanipolo had given him to peruse and actually found several attractions in Santo Domingo that his cousin had apparently been interested in. One was an eleven-hour tour of the "historic" city of Santo Domingo. Seven hours of which were just getting there and back from Punta Cana. He'd shaken his head at that, and then spotted a pamphlet on a place called Parque Los Tres Ojos, which translated to the Three Eyes National Park. It had a group of interconnected caves that were supposed to be beautiful and worth a visit. And then there was the Columbus Lighthouse where Christopher Columbus's remains were supposed to be. Apparently, the lighthouse was both something of a museum and mausoleum to the man.

"Parque Los Tres Ojos?" Jess murmured, mangling the words somewhat.

Raffaele raised his gaze to find she'd crossed the room to stand next to him. He handed the pamphlets to her with a faint smile. "Yes. It's one of the places we planned to see in Santo Domingo. There are a couple of them," he added, and she peered at him with surprise.

"You planned to go to Santo Domingo anyway?" she asked, sounding almost hopeful.

"Sure," Raffaele said with a shrug, and suspected he wasn't even lying. He had no doubt Zanipolo would have dragged them to Santo Domingo to see it, and not on one of the buses where the sun would have poured in the windows on them. He would have insisted on renting a private car, preferably one with air-conditioning and windows with SPF protection.

"So, it wouldn't be taking you out of your way to go to Santo Domingo," she murmured, shuffling through the pamphlets.

"Not at all," he assured her. "We will take you to the embassy and see that taken care of, and then go check into a hotel. I am not sure if you will be able to get a passport right away, or if it will take a day or two. You are welcome to stay with us and join us on the tours if that is the case. We planned to stay for a couple of days."

"Thank you," Jess murmured, her expression thoughtful.

Raffaele watched her for a moment, wondering what she was thinking. She appeared to have agreed to traveling to Santo Domingo with them, but was thinking pretty hard. He suspected there was something he hadn't considered, but wasn't sure what that was.

"I ordered breakfast," he announced, hoping to draw her from her thoughts.

Jess glanced up from the pamphlets and smiled. "Breakfast sounds good. But we didn't have to eat here. We could have gone down to the restaurant now that I have clothes."

"Zanipolo and Santo said the lineup was pretty bad to get into the restaurant," he told her, which was true. The boys had mentioned that before leaving. "They said there was no one in line when they got there, but by the time they finished eating and were leaving, there was a line that stretched outside and along the entire back of the building in both directions."

"Oh." Jess glanced to the clock on the wall and grimaced. "Yeah. The lineup gets pretty brutal by this hour. At least it has since we got here."

Raffaele nodded, and then stood and moved to the small coffee machine on the counter just inside the living room area. "Would you like coffee?"

"Oh, yeah, that sounds great," she murmured, and moved to join him. They worked together, Jess unwrapping two cups and gathering powdered cream and sugar while he read the instructions on the small one-cup coffee machine and then opened and inserted one of the enclosed sacks of coffee.

"So where did the boys go?" she asked as the machine started to hum and brown water began to drip into the first cup.

"They went down to sit by the pool for a bit," he murmured, not bothering to mention that they'd be under the biggest umbrella they could find. "We're to join them after we break our fast."

"Break our fast?" Jess echoed with surprise.

Hearing the words from her made Raffaele realize that he'd used the antiquated term for breakfast. Shrugging, he turned back to the coffee machine and slid the first cup out. He handed it to her and then began to prepare the machine to make the second cup and said, "English is my second language. Sometimes I get terminology wrong. I suppose I should have said 'after we breakfast,' or 'eat our breakfast'?"

"Either one," she said with a faint smile as she added the powdered milk and a packet of sugar to her coffee. Her smile widened then and she added, "I keep forgetting you're from Italy. Your accent isn't really Italian. It's . . ."

When she paused and frowned, apparently unable to place his accent, he explained, "We moved around quite a bit when I was younger. I've lived many places over the years. My accent is probably a hodgepodge of different influences."

"Ah," she murmured, nodding her head. "That explains it."

Raffaele relaxed a bit then and retrieved his cup of coffee from the machine. He then fixed it the same way she had, adding a pouch of the powdered milk, and a sachet of sugar. That wasn't from preference. He didn't know what his preference would be. Raffaele had never had coffee. By the time it had become the world's beverage of choice, Raffaele had lost interest in food and drink. He wasn't sure he'd like it. In fact, he wasn't sure he should drink it. He'd heard the caffeine could have a deleterious effect on immortals. He'd only made himself one because she'd grabbed the cups and fixings for two and had seemed to expect him to have one as well.

"Shall we sit at the table while we wait for our food?" he asked, picking up his cup.

"Sure." Jess led the way.

Once at the table, Raffaele moved quickly around her and pulled the chair out for her.

"Thank you," Jess said softly as she settled in the seat.

"You are welcome," he murmured in response, and moved to the seat opposite.

"So," she said once he'd settled in his seat. "You have a sister?"

Raffaele blinked in surprise at the question, and then recalled saying he'd wish someone would help his sister if she were in her position. Nodding, he admitted, "Yes. Several of them actually, and a couple of brothers too."

"Older or younger?" she asked with interest.

"All younger. I'm the oldest child," he admitted, and then to keep her from asking questions he couldn't answer, like how many years were between him and his siblings and such, he said, "I know you are adopted, but did they have, or adopt, other children, or are you their only—?"

"Only child," she said softly. "Mom couldn't have children."

"Why did they not adopt others?" Raffaele asked with curiosity.

"Probably because I was so much trouble," she said with a faint smile.

"I am sure that is not true," he said quietly.

Her smile widened, but she said, "My parents loved me, and considered me worth the effort they put in, but I *was* a troubled kid, and did keep them busy."

"You talk about them in the past tense," he pointed out. "I take it they are no longer with us?"

Jess shook her head. "You know that cruise ship that sank several years ago?"

Raffaele narrowed his eyes. "An Italian cruise ship?"

Jess nodded. "They were on it. From what I was able to piece together, they'd had a busy day and were both tired, but Dad always had a walk in the evening after supper. He escorted Mom back to their cabin before leaving for his walk, and she was resting when the ship hit the rock that sank it. She never got out of the cabin. Dad tried to get to her to get her out, but had a heart attack. Some guests got him off the ship, but he had a second heart attack two days later and this time died."

"I am sorry," Raffaele said sincerely, and noted her eyes going glassy with tears.

Blinking them away, she turned to peer out the window next to the table and cleared her throat before saying softly, "So am I. They were really good people."

Raffaele nodded, but some part of his mind acknowledged that it would make the choice to become immortal easier for her. She wouldn't have to consider abandoning the relationship she had with parents who had saved her from the foster care system.

Realizing what he was thinking, and recognizing how selfish it was, Raffaele lowered his head briefly. The loss of people who had cared for, loved, and helped her heal from what had been a nightmare early childhood . . . well, it must have been a crushing blow and all he could think was how it might benefit him.

"I am sorry," he repeated quietly, and raised his head, adding, "From the little you've said about them, they sound to have been wonderful people."

"They were," she acknowledged. "And I was lucky as can be to have them in my life for the seventeen years I had them. I honestly don't know where I'd be if they hadn't taken me in and cared for me." Grimacing, she added, "Probably not a good place. Definitely not where I am now."

Raffaele smiled crookedly. After everything that had happened to her, Jess still managed to see the bright side of things. Even when it came to the loss of the first really good people she'd had in her life.

"Fortunately, I had my aunts and uncles. They really closed ranks around me. I'm invited to every holiday and birthday party from both my mom's side, and my father's." She laughed slightly. "In truth, it can be a bit of a pain sometimes."

"How?" he asked with surprise.

"Well, one year, I attended four Christmas dinners in two days, plus a Christmas breakfast." She grimaced and shook her head, before saying, "But it was good too. It helped me keep from moping around weeping at the loss of my parents, and not having them on special days."

She fell silent, and Raffaele eyed her for a moment before commenting, "You are very honest about yourself."

Jess glanced up, her eyes wide with surprise, and then smiled wryly and shrugged. "I don't see a reason not to be." She paused briefly, seeming to gather her thoughts, and then said, "A lot of people present a mask to the world. They lie about, or hide, their past, and even about things they like and don't like in the present. I know it's an effort to fit in and be liked, but that just seems stupid to me. Because when you do that, you aren't making people like you at all. They don't even know the real you. Isn't it better to be honest and find friends who *really* like you for yourself than to have to pretend to be something you aren't, and do things you don't like just to have people around you?"

She fell briefly silent and Raffaele was about to agree with her when she suddenly shrugged and said, "Anyway, while I don't hide my past, I'm not usually quite as forthcoming as I was last night. At least, not on first meeting people. I guess the stress and long swim had me a little punchy with exhaustion." Grimacing, Jess added, "I'd like to blame it on too much drink, but since I did all my talking before the Long Island Iced Tea, and hadn't had enough wine before that for it to affect me, I don't really know what got into me."

"Exhaustion and stress can affect people oddly," Raffaele said gently.

"Besides, it was a blessing in a way. I think you may have helped my cousin Santo with what you revealed and said."

"Hmm." Jess nodded. "He seems . . ."

"Troubled?" Raffaele suggested when she hesitated.

"Yes," she agreed on a sigh, apparently relieved she hadn't had to say the word herself.

Raffaele hesitated, but then admitted, "He suffered some serious trauma in his past, and a more recent trauma that has churned it all up. He's struggling with it."

"I'm sorry to hear that," Jess said quietly.

Raffaele nodded acknowledgment and then said, "Actually, he is the reason we are here. The family was growing concerned and Zani and I were enlisted to try to help him get past it. Or at least relax and forget about it for a while. It was beginning to consume him."

Jess smiled faintly. "And how's that working out?"

"Actually, he hasn't mentioned his experience once since we found you," Raffaele told her solemnly, and realized it was true. Dressler was the first thing Santo's mind had jumped to when they'd spotted the bites on the resort guests. But he hadn't brought the man's name up once since Jess had told them about the pirates. That might be a good sign. Perhaps they just needed to keep him distracted.

"Well, I hope he's able to put it behind him," she said sincerely.

"But you don't think he will?" Raffaele guessed.

"I don't know. I'm not a psychologist," she reminded him solemnly, but then added, "But from what I have seen so far in life and while working at the clinic, it works differently for everyone. Some people work through their issues on their own without counseling, others need counseling and get it, and then there are those who need it and don't go for it, but just push it down, push it down, push it down, never realizing that while they're pretending it never happened, it's affecting every part of their life and every decision they make." She shrugged. "But as I said, I'm not a psychologist, and I don't know Santo well enough to tell you which he'll be."

"Right." Raffaele breathed the word on a sigh. He didn't know which kind Santo would be either. The man had never gone for counseling about the torture he'd gone through several centuries ago, but then there hadn't been psychologists back then. He hadn't been very receptive to Greg more recently, though, from what he could tell. On the other hand, he'd been very interested in what Jess had to say about trauma and how she'd handled it. Maybe he would be more open to talking to Greg when they returned.

"So, your family is close?"

Raffaele glanced up at her question and then smiled wryly. "We're Italian," he said with a shrug. "Always in each other's business, so yes, very close."

"And big?" she guessed.

Raffaele nodded. "Very big. Lots of aunts and uncles, and even more cousins . . . and we're all as thick as thieves." Grimacing, he added, "Well, many of us are anyway. Some live far enough away that we don't see them often, but when we do it is as if we saw them just yesterday."

"Are your parents still alive?"

"*Sì.* Yes. Very much alive and interested in everything I do," he said dryly. "In fact, I'm rather surprised that they have not called to check on me yet," he murmured, and frowned as he realized that was true. His mother usually called every other day at least, but he hadn't heard from her since arriving in Punta Cana, other than her response to his text that they'd arrived safely. "Although they are probably getting reports from Uncle Julius or his wife, Aunt Marguerite," he decided aloud.

"And who are Uncle Julius and Aunt Marguerite?" she asked with interest. "Zani's or Santo's parents?"

"No, they are my cousin Christian's parents," he explained, and then, realizing she had no idea who that was, explained, "He's the fiddler in our band."

"I thought your band was rock?" she said with confusion.

"It is. He plays hard rock songs on his fiddle. He's quite good," Raffaele added when she appeared blank-faced.

"Okay," she said dubiously. "But he isn't here, so why would your aunt and uncle have any news to report to your parents?"

"Ah. Well, because I called my uncle to see if he could help with your situation," he admitted solemnly. When Jess raised her eyebrows at this news, he added, "I thought if we had trouble getting your passport we could return you to Canada on one of the company planes."

Her eyes widened incredulously. "Wow. That's so sweet," she breathed with wonder, but then shook her head and pointed out, "It really is kind of you to even think of that, but I'd still need a passport to get back into the country. Unless you planned to have the pilot fly low and let me parachute out before they reached the airport." Her comment was teasing, but there was an undertone of wistfulness to her voice that made him suspect she wished she could do that.

"Do you know how to skydive?" he asked with curiosity.

Jess grinned and nodded. "I always wanted to try it, so Mom bought me lessons for my eighteenth birthday. She even went with me. We had a blast," she added with a reminiscent smile. "And we went skydiving three or four times every summer after that until they died."

"Your father didn't join you?" Raffaele asked with interest.

Jess smiled faintly and shook her head. "Dad was a rock. They both were," she added quickly, "but different kinds. Dad was a big, solid rock, planted firmly in the mud. He was support and strength and steady. Not a risk taker," she added dryly, and then grinning, she added, "But Mom was a different kind of rock, a bright, sparkly one tumbling down the hill and skipping across the riverbed. She was strong too, but she was a risk taker."

"And which did you take after?" Raffaele asked with a smile, suspecting he already knew the answer.

"A little of both, I think," she said slowly. "I have a strong sensible streak, and a calm exterior, which is why I got stuck babysitting Allison."

Her grimace as she said that made him chuckle softly.

"But," she added, "I will take risks at times."

"Like jumping off a pirate ship into an ocean full of sharks," he suggested.

Jess nodded. "And trusting my well-being to three complete strangers who could have been just as bad as the pirates I'd escaped."

Raffaele's eyebrows flew up at the words. It hadn't occurred to him that she might have some fears and concerns about him and his cousins, but they *were* strangers to her. In fact, he suspected if she hadn't been hysterical, and drunk, she would not have stayed here in the room with them last night. She probably would have insisted on going to the room of one of her other relatives here at the resort rather than risk trusting strangers in a strange land, he thought with a frown. The thought made him reach out to clasp her hands where they lay on the table. "I promise you are safe with us, Jess. Neither I, nor my cousins, would ever do you harm."

"I believe you," she said softly, but her eyes were on their entwined hands.

His own gaze moved to them as his desire to reassure her gave way to an awareness of the sensations popping to life where their skin touched. Little frissons and a warm tingling had already enwrapped his hand and were now coursing up his arm to race through his body like an intravenous drug. It was bringing the blood rushing to the surface of his skin, making his muscles tighten with anticipation, increasing his heart rate and blood pressure, and his breathing was becoming faster and more shallow. His body was like an engine that had been turned on and was now revving, waiting for him to take his foot off the break. Raffaele almost retrieved his hand and sat back to allow the moment to pass. He'd intended not to start the physical relationship with Jess until they were away from Punta Cana and the worries and responsibilities both had here.

But then he recalled what Zani and Santo had said. Jess could be a life mate to the pirate captain too. He had given her a taste of the pleasure that could be had between life mates. Jess, however, didn't care for the man and between that and her fear because he was a "vampire" had managed to fight her natural attraction to him and escape his clutches. But if the rogue pirate got his hands on her again . . .

Raffaele tightened his fingers gently and leaned forward as he drew her hand toward him.

Jess stared at their entwined hands, noting his darker skin against her still-pale flesh despite the sun she'd gotten since arriving in Punta Cana. Her skin was positively sparking under his. That was what it felt like anyway. It was the same thing she'd experienced with him before, and with Vasco. It was what gave her hope that she could still experience that crazy heady passion she'd experienced with the vampire pirate. But with someone else. Probably not Raffaele, though, she admitted on a small sigh. He always pulled back at this point, and she fully expected him to do it again now, so was surprised when, instead, he began to draw her hands across the small table and leaned forward in his seat.

Raising her gaze from their hands, she peered at his face and simply stared. She'd thought his eyes a brown so dark they looked black, with flecks of a blue so pale they seemed silver in the dark pool of his irises. But now his pupils were dilated, she saw. A sign of attraction Jess recalled from one of her classes as she stared at the large black holes and the silver rimming them. It was as if the flecks had coalesced in the smaller space left by the dilating pupils, shrouding the darker eye color. They almost seemed to glow in the sunlight coming in the window, she thought with wonder, and then glanced down with a start at their hands again. He had drawn her fingers to his mouth and was now pressing a kiss to her knuckles in an old-world gesture she'd read about but never seen.

Even as Jess thought that, his tongue slid out and ran between two of her fingers. The action left her mind blank, but not her body. It stiffened, every muscle and even her nipples tensing, even as something in her core softened like warmed butter and began to melt, sending liquid heat pouring downward. She wasn't aware that her mouth had dropped slightly open until he suddenly raised his head and leaned across the table to claim her lips with his.

It started with a sweet brush of his soft mouth across hers that had an almost electrifying effect, and then it exploded into heat and passion. His tongue was filling her mouth, his lips slanting hungrily over hers and stealing her ability to think of anything but the need suddenly shuddering through her in mounting and overwhelming waves.

Jess was aware of his hands reaching for her, but still wasn't sure how she ended up lying diagonally across the table, while he remained seated. But the position allowed his mouth to devour hers while his hands roamed freely over her body. He caressed her breasts through the thin T-shirt, kneading and massaging the eager flesh, and rubbing over her erect nipples, teasing them to a pebble-like state that was almost painful before moving down to cup her between the legs.

Jess cried out when his fingers pressed firmly there, rubbing eagerly over the cloth of her shorts and the panties barring his way as his tongue thrust in and out of her mouth. When he suddenly stood, she clutched at his upper arms, her upper body coming upright as he urged her legs around until she was sitting on the edge of the table in front of him.

She moaned with distress when he broke their kiss, and then gasped with surprise as her T-shirt briefly covered her face, but then it was gone, flying through the air. Raffaele paused briefly then, his gaze eating up what he'd revealed. There was no surprise on his face that she wasn't wearing a bra, but then he'd probably felt the absence of one when he'd been caressing her through the T-shirt, she supposed, and then let her thoughts drift away as he kissed her again. Jess responded eagerly to his mouth on hers, kissing him fervently back, and then his hands slid up her stomach and claimed her breasts without the cloth in the way.

Jess gasped and jumped slightly on the tabletop at the contact, and then arched into the caress, her response to his kisses becoming more violent and demanding as he kneaded the eager flesh and teased the hard nipples. This time when he broke their kiss, she didn't moan in protest. Instead, she leaned back and arched her chest upward, offering herself to him as he lowered his head to catch one excited nipple between his lips and began to lash and suckle it.

Moaning, Jess raised one hand to clasp his neck, and lowered her head to kiss the top of his as she murmured encouragement. She noted absently that his hair was clean and sweet-smelling and then one of his hands slid between her legs and began to rub her again and she let her head fall back on an excited cry, her bottom lifting up off the table and her legs spreading wider to allow him to step between them as he caressed her. Small tremors began coursing through her body. She was almost vibrating with excitement, some part of her mind acknowledged, and then Raffaele urged her to lie back on the table and released the breast he'd been suckling, to straighten and tug her shorts and panties off.

Jess sat up the moment they were off and was pulling his head back for another kiss before he'd even finished tossing them aside. Raffaele responded to the demand, his mouth claiming hers in a searing kiss, and then his hand was between her legs again and she cried out into his mouth as his fingers plundered her excited flesh, finding the center of her excitement and circling it firmly. Jess's body responded eagerly, her hips shifting to meet the touch and her legs closing around his legs.

Desperate to end this sweet torture, Jess reached for the button of Raffaele's jeans and managed to quickly unsnap and unzip them. She didn't bother pushing them off. Instead, she ran one hand blindly along the cotton briefs underneath, and then slid her hand in to find and clasp the erection waiting there.

Dear God, he felt as hard as rock, she noted as her hand slid over him. And while he wasn't a foot long or anything crazy like that, the man had some serious girth going there. Her fingers wouldn't meet when she closed her hand around him and slid it along his hardness.

Distracted as she was by what she'd found, Jess wasn't sure what Raffaele did then to cause the response she suddenly had. It was as if a second wave of pleasure was riding right next to the waves she was already enjoying. Before she could worry overmuch about that, Raffaele tried to urge her hand away. But Jess resisted and instead drew his erection closer, directing him to where she wanted. Getting the message, he stopped caressing her at once, but he also broke their kiss and pulled back to peer at her.

"Are you sure?" he asked, his body as stiff as a rod.

Jess didn't even stop to think. She was trembling with need, her body dripping with desire. It knew what it wanted. She nodded abruptly and tugged his head back down to reclaim his lips. Much to her relief, even as he bent his head to kiss her, he clasped her hips, and when his tongue thrust into her mouth, he also thrust himself into her body. It was a double whammy that had her crying out into his mouth as her body closed around him, legs wrapping around his hips, arms around his neck, her lips sucking desperately as he withdrew and then thrust back into her.

Jess's brain winked out then, able only to handle the mounting pleasure coursing through her and unable to process much else. She was vaguely aware of his shifting and that he was suddenly sitting in his straight-backed chair with her facing him in his lap, his hands urging her to ride him, and then one of his hands slid between them to begin to touch her again and Jess screamed as that barely started caress pushed her over the edge. Her release hit her with the violence of a tsunami so that she was hardly aware of Raffaele's shout joining her own before darkness rushed in to wipe out her awareness.

It took Jess a moment to get her bearings when she woke up. At first, she had no idea where she was or how she'd got there except that she was sitting up slumped against something rather than lying down. She also didn't seem to have the strength to move. Her body was still quivering like a harp string after it's been plucked. That thought gave her pause. Still quivering? Oh. Right. She and Raffaele had—

Jess opened her eyes. They were seated at the dining table in the living room of the men's suite. Well, Raffaele was seated at the table; she was still on his lap, facing him, her body slumped against his chest, her head resting—and mouth drooling—on his shoulder.

Grimacing, she closed her mouth and then her eyes to take stock. So, okay, she'd just had the best mind-blowing, earthshaking sex of her life. That was good, right? So, Vasco shouldn't be such a temptation again if he got his hands on her. That made life a little less scary. Knowing she had this to turn to, she should be able to resist the lure of the vampire pirate and avoid becoming his soulless vampire/pirate bride, roaming the high seas, feeding on poor unsuspecting tourists.

Definitely good, Jess decided, and then gave her head a little shake. She was no shrinking violet. She'd dated in high school and university, and had sex with a handful of different boyfriends along the way. She considered herself experienced, and she'd thought at least two of her lovers in the past had been superskilled, but she had never before enjoyed sex so hot and passionate that it had left her a mindless, quivering mass near the end, and then unconscious once it was over. Good Lord! What was that? First Vasco had made her a mindless twit, and now Raffaele had just blown her mind entirely. Was it the men? Or did she have a tumor or something that was causing a release of hormones that would make sex with any man seem like the be-all and end-all?

Jess frowned at the thought. If just Vasco or Raffaele had affected her like this, that would have been one thing. But having two of them causing this reaction in her so close together was suspect. She might have a serious health issue here.

"Jess?" That murmur by her ear was accompanied by his hand sliding slowly up her back.

The caress made her groan as her body reacted eagerly to the touch. Jess was quite sure that, if it could, her skin would pull itself from her body and wrap itself around him like a blanket. Honestly, his touch was leaving a tingling path in its wake, she noted as his hand paused and started back down the way it had come in what was probably supposed to be a soothing caress, but was just exciting the hell out of her.

Hoping to end the caress, Jess raised her head and sat up. Big mistake, she realized at once. Not only did Raffaele immediately focus on her breasts now in front of his face within licking distance, but her lower body shifting on his reminded her of what they'd been doing when she'd passed out. He was still inside her, and while he'd apparently deflated and slid partway out after finding his satisfaction, he was now swelling again . . . and pushing back up into her as he did. Groaning, Jess closed her eyes and bit her lower lip as she fought not to shift on top of him again to encourage the growth happening.

"Jess."

His voice was almost a growl this time, and she opened her eyes just in time to see his mouth close over one already hardening nipple.

"Oh, God," Jess breathed, and then moaned as his mouth sent excitement whipping through her body once more. And then his hand slid between them again and he began to caress her. That was all he did, suckle her breast and caress her. Jess moved in response to his touch, her hips shifting, but she wasn't riding him. She was chasing the pleasure he offered as he urged her to lean her upper body back against the table and bent over her, his mouth and tongue toying with first one nipple, and then licking their way to the other as his fingers danced over the damp eager flesh above where they were joined.

Her second orgasm came so hard and fast Jess almost bit her tongue in her surprise and then she screamed and thrashed on his lap briefly before welcoming the soothing embrace of the darkness that followed.

It was knocking at the door that woke Raffaele. Blinking his eyes open, he lifted his head abruptly and stared at Jess. While she still rested in his lap, her legs hanging limply on either side of his, she had fainted and fallen back, her upper body resting on the table, her face in repose and her breasts on display. She was beautiful, a feast to the eyes, and he couldn't resist taking in his fill.

"Room service."

The words pushed through his fascination and he glanced toward the door with a frown and then began to move. Slipping his arms around Jess, he stood and then grimaced when his body responded to the movement. He was still inside of her, and had to lift her off of his again-growing cock, and then shift her and scoop her up into his arms before carrying her quickly to the bedroom. Raffaele laid her gently on the bed and covered her, then hurried back out of the room, pulling the door quietly closed behind him. He then put himself back in his pants and did them up as he hurried to the door.

The knocking hadn't come again after the shout, so Raffaele wasn't surprised when he opened the door to nothing. Stepping out into the open landing, he peered in the direction of the elevators and spotted the worker wheeling the cart back up the hall. Raffaele called out and the man glanced back, smiled, and then turned the cart to head back.

"Sorry. We'd fallen asleep," Raffaele murmured when the man reached him.

"Ah," the waiter said wisely, and then wheeled the cart into the room when Raffaele held it open for him.

Raffaele let the door slide closed and then followed the man across the living room.

The waiter wheeled the cart up to the table by the windows, but then retrieved a cleaning cloth and a spray bottle of cleaning fluid from the cabinet of the cart.

"Everything is always wet this time of year," the man commented as he moved to the table.

Raffaele started to nod, but then stilled as he noted the dry spots on the table. One was definitely an ass print, he thought, and noted handprints as well before it all disappeared under a mist of cleaning fluid. Deciding it was probably a good thing Jess wasn't awake and out here right now, Raffaele left the man to it and moved to the tray to look over the many covered plates, the coffee carafe, a small pitcher of orange juice, and a smaller one of cream. It looked to him as if everything was there.

The sound of voices woke Jess. Opening her eyes, she peered around at the bedroom with two double beds in it, confused at first as to how she'd got there. The last thing she remembered doing was—

Oh, Jess thought, recalling exactly what she'd last been doing. Or what she and Raffaele had been doing, she supposed as memories rushed through her. They left her both stunned and turned on all over again. Dear God, the man had some serious mojo going for him. She'd thought Vasco hot, but Raffaele had sent her up in flames. The pleasure she'd experienced had been off the charts and literally mind-blowing. This was the first time Jess had ever been so overwhelmed by pleasure that she'd actually fainted. She hadn't even known that was a thing, but had fainted both times after finding her release. As alarming as that was, it was also addictive. Her body was humming and wanting again just from the memory of what they'd done. If Raffaele were there with her now, she'd be reaching for him.

Male laughter drew her attention to the door, and Jess sat up and glanced around. Her clothes weren't there, which meant they were probably still on the floor where they'd landed when Raffaele had tugged them off of her. Out there where the men were, no doubt giving Raffaele's cousins a clear idea of what they'd been doing while the two men had lounged around the pool.

Yeah, that wasn't embarrassing at all, she thought, and then rolled her eyes at herself. She was a grown-up. They were all grown-ups. Sex was a grown-up thing, she lectured herself as she slid out of the bed and walked quickly to the open closet to grab one of the hotel robes. It was a waffled white affair with gold trimming. Not especially soft or comfy, she decided as she pulled it on. But that probably kept guests from stealing them.

Jess started to tie the belt around her waist, but then paused. Now that she was standing upright, she was aware of the dampness between her legs. In fact, it was starting to run down one inner thigh. Grimacing, she turned and headed into the bathroom.

A quick shower was in order here before she had to face Raffaele's cousins, she decided. *Quick* was the key word. Jess didn't linger under the water. She got in, cleaned herself up, and got out. She was just as quick about drying herself off, but found herself considering the bags of clothes as she did. She briefly contemplated grabbing and putting on a fresh pair of shorts, underwear, and a top, but then shook her head. She wasn't wasting the money on another outfit. There was nothing wrong with the clothes she'd had on earlier. She hadn't worn them long enough for them to even be dirty. She just had to fetch them.

Back in the robe, she tied it up this time, ran a brush through her damp hair, and headed through the bedroom. She paused at the doors to the living room, though, her head tilting as she noted that the men's voices appeared to be growing fainter as if they were moving away. She listened briefly until the sound of the suite door closing reached her ears, and then opened the bedroom door and stuck her head out to see Raffaele turning to face her.

"Oh! You're up," he said with a surprised smile as he moved back toward her.

Relaxing now that she saw they were alone, Jess nodded and stepped into the living room, her gaze shifting around the floor in search of her clothes. Spotting her T-shirt in a little heap near the couch, she moved toward it, saying, "Yes. Did your cousins head back to the pool?"

"Cousins?" Raffaele asked with confusion, and then said, "Oh, you thought—No, that was room service, delivering our breakfast."

Jess straightened with her T-shirt in hand and stuffed it in one of her robe's large pockets as she glanced toward the table. She'd forgotten that he'd said he'd ordered breakfast. Now she recalled, and gaped at the various covered plates on the table. That explained why the waiter had been in the room so long. There were at least half a dozen large covered plates, but several smaller ones as well. There were also two white thermos carafes, cream and sugar, a variety of jams, butter, and what looked like little containers of peanut butter on an uncovered plate.

"Are your cousins joining us?" she asked and, spotting her shorts and underwear in a knotted ball next to the table, moved quickly to scoop them up. She stuffed them in the robe's other pocket as Raffaele moved to join her.

"No. It's just the two of us," Raffaele said, pulling out her chair for her.

"Thank you." Jess settled in the chair and smiled crookedly as she watched him walk around to sit down. Most of her friends would have thought his manners were old-fashioned, but her father used to do little things like this for her mother. Holding her chair, getting the door for her, carrying things for her, letting her order first in restaurants . . . Jess had dated a lot of guys who didn't bother with such niceties, but she liked that Raffaele did it. It made her feel special somehow.

"What?" Raffaele asked suddenly when he caught her expression.

"Nothing," she said at once, and turned her attention to the table crowded with plates and cups. It must have taken the waiter forever to transfer the items from the cart to the table, and Jess found herself hoping that Raffaele had tipped him. The resort was all-inclusive, but Jess still tipped. Not extravagantly. She was still a student, after all, but she did tip here and there as she could for good service. She knew a lot of guests at the resort didn't do that, precisely because it was all-inclusive. But with one of her jobs being a part-time booze jockey in a bar, Jess knew how hard the service industry could be. The majority of customers were okay, some were even great, but some could be demanding pricks, and others ungrateful assholes. Unfortunately, it only took one asshole to wreck your whole day. So, she tried to be patient and kind and always tipped to balance the scales.

"It smells good," Raffaele said as he began removing the silver covers.

"Yes, but there seems to be an awful lot of food here," Jess commented.

"I was not sure what you would like, so ordered a variety," he explained.

Jess just shook her head and started to help remove lids as she said, "You know room service isn't included in the all-inclusive thing, right? Your meals in the restaurants are free, but room service costs extra."

"Yes," Raffaele said with unconcern as he set the last cover aside.

Shrugging to herself, Jess peered at the selection. Her eyes widened as they slid over pancakes, bacon, sausage, omelets, and hash browns.

"I hope there's something you like," Raffaele said when she simply stared at the offerings.

"There is," she assured him. "Several somethings I like, in fact."

"Good." He relaxed a bit and peered over the food too. But when he noticed her glancing toward the carafes on the table, he said, "Orange juice and coffee."

"Wonderful," Jess said on a sigh, reaching for the coffee first. She poured for herself and then for him, and then set the carafe aside and doctored her coffee with cream and sugar, vaguely aware that Raffaele followed suit.

Both hungry, they ate in silence at first, but as Jess started to feel full, she found herself glancing toward Raffaele with curiosity and then suddenly blurted, "Are you married?"

She didn't know where the question came from. She hadn't really thought it out. The words had simply tumbled from her lips. It had been one of the possible explanations she'd given herself earlier for why he hadn't hit on her. Apparently, now that he had, and it had gone so far so fast, she'd worried about it. Raffaele stiffened and then raised shocked eyes to her face.

"No," he said firmly. "I'd hardly make love to you if I was already mated."

Jess blinked at the term *make love*. They barely knew each other, so calling it lovemaking was a bit of a stretch, but it certainly sounded better than some of the other terms he could have used. Offering him an apologetic smile, she said, "I didn't really think you were."

"But you wanted to be sure," he suggested dryly.

Jess shrugged. "Some people wouldn't care, but . . ."

"You do," he said quietly, and set his fork and knife down to meet her gaze and assure her. "I have no wife, no girlfriend, no mate of any kind. I am completely free of entanglement except now for you. I would never be unfaithful to a mate."

Jess relaxed and nodded, but asked, "Recent breakup?"

His eyebrows rose at the question, and he shook his head, but then narrowed his gaze and asked, "What about you? Husband, boyfriend, recent breakup?"

Jess shook her head. "My messed-up hours don't leave much time for dating. I work the bar most weekends when everyone else is on their dates, have classes in the late morning and afternoons, and the gig at the clinic sometimes in the afternoon and sometimes in the evening. So, unless the guy wants to do things between nine at night and 4 A.M. on weekdays, or after the bar closes on the weekend . . ." She shrugged. "It makes dating hard."

"I imagine it does," he murmured, and then asked, "Between nine at night and 4 A.M.?"

Jess wrinkled her nose. "The counseling center closes at nine, and I've always been a night owl." She shrugged. "Probably to do with my childhood in the foster homes, lying awake at night listening for footsteps or shouting and such. Now it's just habit after years of training, I think. I don't usually fall asleep before three or four in the morning most nights, so I schedule my classes for afternoons, or later in the morning if they aren't available after lunch."

"Perfect," he said with a smile.

Jess raised her eyebrows. "Why is that perfect?"

Raffaele blinked, and then shook his head. "Sorry. I just meant . . . I'm a night owl too."

"Really?" she asked with surprise. "I'd think it would be hard to be a night owl as a construction worker."

"I don't actually work in construction," he explained. "I work for the family construction company, but I'm actually an architect."

"Oh," she said with surprise, and then smiled wryly. "I guess that'll teach me to assume things."

They both fell briefly silent again, and Jess picked at the food remaining on her plate, and then asked, "Do you suppose there are any American banks in Santo Domingo?"

It had occurred to her that if there was a branch of her bank here in the Dominican, she might be able to withdraw money from her account once she had a passport to prove her identity. Maybe. Hopefully.

"I do not know," Raffaele admitted, his solemn gaze moving slowly over her. "If you have need of money, I—"

"No," Jess said quickly, shutting him down. She was not taking money from the man, and she was paying him back for whatever clothes she used. She'd rather try to sneak onto Vasco's ship and get her stuff back than take money from Raffaele or his cousins. Borrowing from her family was one thing, but . . . Well, the truth is, she couldn't move herself to actually borrow from them either. That had always been a thing with her. She hated asking anyone for anything. Probably because she was afraid of rejection or some damned thing. She didn't know. It was just the way things were. She would rather do things on her own than depend on anyone.

Realizing how silent the room had gone, she glanced toward Raffaele and then shifted uncomfortably when she noted the way he was watching her.

"You have issues with money," he said quietly.

Jess shrugged. "My parents did all right, but they weren't exactly the Rockefellers. And school is expensive . . . as I found out after they died," she added under her breath. It seemed Raffaele had incredible hearing, however, and caught her words.

"Did your parents not—" he began with a frown, and she cut him off.

"My parents were wonderful, hard-working people. I was their only heir and got everything. Unfortunately, it was kind of a mixed bag. My parents had been paying for my education up until then. Whenever I asked if it was too expensive and suggested I should quit for a while and work to pay my own way later, they insisted everything was fine, that they'd put away for this. What they didn't tell me was that they had put away what they'd expected to need for three or four years of college. My going further and changing majors, however, meant they'd dug deep into their retirement savings. Apparently, they felt they could sell the house later, buy somewhere smaller, and sink the extra money back into their retirement."

"I see," he murmured.

Jess shrugged. "I got the house, the little bit left of their retirement fund, and the insurance. What was left in the retirement fund was just enough to pay to have my parents' bodies shipped back home and have nice funerals for them. The insurance was the true blessing. It was just enough for me to finish my schooling."

"And yet you work two jobs," he pointed out with a small frown.

"Of course. Well, I have to eat," she said with amusement. "And pay taxes on my parents' house, as well as water, phone bills, internet, etc."

"The insurance wasn't enough to cover that?" he asked with surprise.

"Did I not mention school is expensive?" she asked with amusement.

Raffaele was silent for a minute and then asked, "You were unwilling to sell your parents' house to ease the situation?"

Jess glanced down at her plate, and pushed a bit of egg around with her fork before saying, "It's foolish, I know. My life would be a lot easier if I did, but . . ." Grimacing, she raised her head, and admitted, "I'm not ready to let it go yet. And I may never be. It's all I have left of them, and where I spent the best and happiest part of my life so far. I'd like to keep it and hopefully someday raise my own children there."

"You would like to have children, then?"

She glanced at him with surprise. "Well, sure I do. And hopefully I will."

"Why hopefully?" he asked with interest.

Jess shrugged and sat back in her seat. "Well, I'm twenty-seven now. By the time I get my degree, establish a career, and then find a man . . . I'll be lucky if my ovaries haven't shriveled up and fallen off. At least that's what Aunt Zita tells me," she added with amusement.

"Is she related to Allison?" Raffaele asked with interest.

Jess burst out laughing and nodded. "She's Allison's mother, and the two are as charming as each other."

"Hmm. The apple never falls far from the tree, and it seems every family has at least one apple tree," he said dryly.

Jess grinned and nodded in agreement.

"Well . . ." He stood and began to stack plates. "I suppose I should shift this all out to the hallway and call down for someone to collect it."

Nodding, Jess stood and helped, gathering the plates closest to her and stacking them as he was doing. Shifting the collection of dishes to one hand, she then picked up one of the carafes with the other and led the way to the door.

"Wait, let me get the do—Oh, I—"

Jess glanced back and chuckled as she saw the exasperated expression on his face as he peered down at his full hands. Shaking her head, she caught the carafe between her inner arm and chest, and used her now-free hand to open the door.

"After you," she said lightly.

"Drink jockey, did you say?" he asked with amusement as he stepped out into the hall to set his dishes and carafe down.

"Booze jockey," she corrected, passing him the items she held when he straightened and reached for them.

"Booze jockey," he murmured, turning to set the dishes down.

It was when he bent that she saw them. Across the children's play area next to their building, standing in the shade from the awning of the not-yet-open pizza restaurant on the edge of the resort property. Vasco and Cristo. Just standing there, watching them.

"I think—Jess?" Raffaele cut himself off to ask as he straightened and saw her face. Clasping her upper arms, he peered at her with concern and then turned to glance over his shoulder. She knew he'd seen them when he stiffened and whipped back around.

The next thing Jess knew she was back in the hotel room and the door was closed. It happened crazy fast. That or she'd blacked out briefly, because it seemed like she blinked and was in a different spot.

"It's all right," Raffaele assured her, urging her away from the door.

"It's not all right," she responded dully, but stopped and turned back to him to ask, "What if they follow us to Santo Domingo? What if they—?"

"They won't follow us," he promised her quietly. "I'll make sure they don't."

"How?" she asked, not believing him, and then she added with frustration, "How are they even out there? They're vampires and it's daylight. It was daylight when they came into the room Allison and I share too. They shouldn't be able to be out now." Frowning, she added, "But it was daylight when they lured us onto their ship too. Mostly anyway. It was close to sunset then, though, and I thought—" Breaking off, she glanced to Raffaele to see the concern on his face and sighed unhappily.

Great. Now he'd think she had a screw loose. And she hadn't even told him about what happened on the ship. She'd expected to have to come up with a lie, but he and his cousins hadn't even asked . . . which was kind of odd, she decided.

Frowning, Jess narrowed her eyes and asked, "Why haven't you asked me what happened to make me jump off the pirate ship?"

Raffaele stilled briefly and then raised his eyebrows and said, "I assumed it was too traumatic for you to want to talk about, and that you'd tell me when you were ready. Women don't usually choose shark-infested waters over nice sturdy sailboats unless they feel more threatened by something on the ship than the sharks in the water."

"I suppose now you think I'm a crazy lady because of this talk of—"

"No," he interrupted firmly. "I do not think you are crazy. I think you are beautiful, and smart, and strong, and so very brave. I think you're wonderful, Jess. A wonder, and I think I was blessed to find you."

Jess stared up at him wide-eyed, his words echoing through her head. "You do?"

The small, uncertain tone of her own voice was somewhat startling. She hardly sounded like the strong brave woman he'd just described. Instead, she sounded young, unsure, and even needy. All of which she supposed she was. Jess liked to think she was strong and brave, and she had felt that way when her parents had still lived. They'd showered her with love and care and support, but when they'd died, she'd lost all of that loving support. Despite the care and concern of her aunts and uncles, she'd felt abandoned, alone. There was a difference between close family like parents or a husband, and relatives once removed like aunts and uncles and cousins.

"*Sì, bella*, I do," he assured her, and Jess was just thinking the words sounded oddly like a vow, when his mouth closed over hers.

Jess wasn't at all surprised at the passion that burst up through her at the contact. It had never really left, but had simmered under the surface from the moment she'd woken and all through their breakfast, waiting to be released again. Now it rushed up through her like a train barreling through a tunnel and she opened for him, kissing him back as eagerly as a starving woman falling on food as her arms slid around his neck.

She tried to press close to him then, but Raffaele held her back, pressing her against the wall with his hands at her waist, before releasing her to tug at the tie of the robe. It undid easily and fell away. The sides of the robe immediately slid apart a couple of inches, but it wasn't enough for Raffaele. Breaking their kiss, he glanced down. Jess followed his gaze and watched as his hands pushed the sides of the white cloth to either side, leaving her arms, shoulders, and back the only thing it covered.

"So beautiful," he murmured, one hand raising so that he could brush his knuckles lightly over one nipple. He watched it pebble under his attention, and then his other hand closed over her free breast and his gaze lifted to her face so that he could watch her expression as he began to caress her.

Jess tried to meet his gaze, but her eyes wanted to close as pleasure washed through her. Biting her lip, she forced them wider and groaned as her body arched, her shoulders pressing into the wall and the rest of her thrusting forward as he caressed her.

"So beautiful," he repeated, one hand dropping down to slide between her legs.

"Oh, God, Raffaele," Jess gasped, reaching for him as his fingers slid across her slick skin. Much to her relief, he kissed her again then, his tongue thrusting out to urge her lips apart so that it could slide inside. But it was just a quick, hard kiss before he tore his mouth away. When he released her breasts as well and clasped her waist instead, she opened her eyes and then glanced down with confusion when he was no longer standing in front of her.

He'd dropped to his knees, she saw with surprise, and watched as he pressed a kiss to her trembling stomach. But then she gasped and closed her eyes again as he urged her legs farther apart and placed the next kiss to her inner thigh before nibbling and kissing his way upward. When he suddenly tugged one leg over his shoulder, opening her to him, the light teasing kisses stopped.

Flattening one hand against the wall, and diving the other into his hair to help her maintain balance, Jess cried out, and banged her head against the wall as Raffaele began hungrily lashing and sucking at her core. The man certainly knew what he was doing. Using just the right amount of pressure, and the perfect tempo, he drove her to the edge of pleasure over and over again with his mouth and tongue, only to retreat at the last moment, his attentions becoming soothing, easing her back from that edge, once, twice, and then a third time.

Jess gasped, groaned, moaned, and begged by turn, her hands plucking and then pushing at his shoulders. She wanted him to stop doing that and kiss her. She wanted him never to stop. She wanted him inside her. She wanted *him*, and she was contemplating pushing Raffaele onto his back and mounting him to find that release he was holding hostage when he finally gave it to her. Releasing the grip he'd had on her legs to keep her in place, he added his fingers to the mix of pleasure he was giving her. She felt him push a finger inside her as he continued to torment the nub at the core of her excitement, and then it withdrew, and two pushed up the next time, and that was it. Jess threw her head back on a scream as a world of pleasure rushed at her, sending her body convulsing and shimmying until her legs couldn't hold her anymore. She felt them collapsing, but found it hard to care. She was already sliding into the waiting darkness.

It was the sound of a phone ringing that woke Jess. Sensing movement beside her, she turned her head in time to see Raffaele finish getting to his feet and dash to the end table where his phone lay.

"Hello?" Raffaele murmured, and turned to peer at her, his eyebrows rising when he saw that she was awake. Flashing a smile, he moved back to offer his hand to help her up as he said, "Yes, Zani. We're done with breakfast."

"Thank you," Jess murmured once she was on her feet, and then drew her robe closed and felt around at her sides for the ends of the sash.

"Ah, yes, well, there is a problem with that plan," he announced grimly.

Finding the ends, she quickly tied the robe closed and then glanced to Raffaele with curiosity, wondering what he was talking about. What plan?

Raffaele frowned and turned away to cross the room. That and the way his voice lowered as he spoke again told her that he'd tried to keep her from hearing in the hopes of avoiding upsetting her.

"Because the bastard's standing by the pizza shack downstairs watching our door. Or he was. Check and see if he's there on your way back . . . No. Don't scare them off. They'll just move somewhere else and we won't know where they are. Just see if they're still there."

The bastard he was talking about was Vasco, Jess knew, and recalled spotting the man as they'd set the breakfast dishes outside. She'd been terribly upset about it at the time, but a kiss from Raffaele had pushed the other man from her thoughts completely. Raffaele was better than drugs in that way, she thought wryly, and then turned her worries to Vasco.

Jess was no longer afraid of giving in to the man's seductions. She wasn't foolish enough to think she suddenly wouldn't find him attractive just because she'd had sex with Raffaele. But she was quite sure the fact that Raffaele could give her so much pleasure would give her enough backbone to resist the attraction she felt for Vasco. After all, Raffaele could show her—if not more, then at least equal—pleasure to that which Vasco had stirred in her. And he wasn't a dead, soulless, bloodsucking vampire.

"Zani and Santo are coming back and we're going to figure out how to get out of here without Vasco seeing us and following."

Jess pushed her thoughts away and smiled crookedly at Raffaele as he slid his phone into his back pocket and moved toward her.

"Then I'd better go get dressed," she said, and then wrinkled her nose as her gaze slid over him still in his jeans and T-shirt. The man hadn't even got the chance to undress when they'd had sex. They'd both been too desperate to take the time to strip him.

Shaking her head, she turned and headed through the bedroom and to the bathroom, tugging the T-shirt and her underwear and shorts from the pockets of the robe as she went. They were a little wrinkled, but she would just have to live with that, Jess decided as she pushed the bathroom door closed. She started to turn away, but came up short when she caught a glimpse of herself in the bathroom mirror.

Mouth dropping open, Jess gaped at herself. Her face was flushed, her eyes were sparkling, but it was her hair that had her staring at herself with dismay. Medusa had nothing on her. Jess's hair was a tangled mess, standing up in every direction. She didn't recall Raffaele even touching her hair, so assumed this was a result of something she'd done. Rolling her head back and forth against the wall as he'd pleasured her perhaps, or the unfortunate result of her passing out while it was still wet and it drying in a dark cloud around her head.

Good Lord, how had the man not looked at her and squawked in horror? Or laughed his head off? Instead, he'd smiled gently. The man was obviously a saint, she thought. The polar opposite to Vasco's evil. She was so lucky to have met him, Jess thought on a little sigh, and then grabbed Raffaele's brush off the sink counter and began to drag it through her hair, trying to tame the wild mass. She had to dress and get back out there. Zani and Santo were returning and they were going to come up with a plan for her to escape the evil pirate and his lusty ways.

"Vasco and Cristo are still there," Zanipolo announced grimly as he led Santo into the room. "You should have let us handle them."

"Handle them how?" Raffaele asked dryly. "We have no rights down here, Zani. The Council that governs this area has to handle them."

"But they aren't," Zanipolo pointed out with irritation.

"No, they aren't," Raffaele agreed. "But they might decide to take care of us if we break their laws and kill a couple of immortals. We aren't hunters down here."

Zani grimaced at the words, but then nodded, and said, "Still, we could have at least scared them off."

"If you managed to scare them, which I highly doubt you could, they—"

"What do you mean you highly doubt we could?" Zanipolo demanded, going stiff with outrage.

"They're pirates, Zani," Raffaele pointed out patiently. "I suspect they were real pirates back in the day. That means they aren't the sort to scare easily. But if you had managed to scare, or even just harass, them away from the pizza shack, they would have simply moved somewhere else, somewhere less visible, and then they'd see us leave and follow. That's the last thing I want. I need to get Jess a safe distance away from them."

Zani frowned, but then nodded and sighed. "Right. So . . . what do you want to do?"

Raffaele was silent for a minute and then turned to cross to the sliding glass doors. Stepping out onto the balcony, he peered around. There was a palm tree to one side of the balcony, blocking part of the view of the pools and the lounge chairs around them. Which meant the balcony was blocked from view too.

"You're thinking of getting her out this way?" Santo asked, his gaze sliding around the crowded area in the center of the buildings as he joined him.

"Yes." Turning, Raffaele strode back inside and moved to the pull-out couch. "Jess can't leave through the door so long as the pirates are standing out there watching. They'll follow us, and I promised I wouldn't let that happen."

"So, she has to leave another way," Zanipolo reasoned and, not having heard the exchange between Raffaele and Santo on the deck, asked, "What are you thinking?"

"The balcony." Raffaele tugged the blanket off the bed, tossed it over the chair, and then pulled the top sheet off and straightened. "I'll lower her down to the next balcony, climb down and lower her to the ground floor. Once we're safely away, you can grab our bags and follow. They won't follow you if Jess isn't with you. You can meet us in front of the hotel. I'll arrange a car while we wait for you."

"You don't think the suitcases might make them suspicious enough to have one of them follow us?" Santo asked dryly.

Raffaele frowned at the suggestion.

"And lowering Jess down from the third floor tied up in a sheet is likely to attract a hell of a lot of attention from the people sunbathing around the pool," Zanipolo pointed out.

"I know," Raffaele growled with frustration. "But she can't go out the door."

Pacing to the windows, he peered out and propped his hands on his hips. Raffaele considered the few options he had and then relaxed a bit and nodded. "We'll wait until dark and do it then and all of us will leave the same way."

"That means a later start for Santo Domingo," Zanipolo pointed out.

Raffaele shrugged. "It can't be helped. We weren't going to get there in time to go to the embassy anyway."

"Jess might be upset," Santo said quietly.

"I'll let her make the decision. Wait until dark and slip away, or leave now and risk Vasto following us."

"Vasco," Zanipolo corrected.

"Whatever," Raffaele muttered, and glanced toward the open French doors and the bedroom beyond as the sound of the bathroom door opening reached them.

Jess walked out to join them, a troubled expression on her face. Pausing in the doorway to the bedroom, she glanced from man to man and asked, "What are we going to do?"

"That's up to you," Raffaele said solemnly.

Eleven

Jess peered unhappily over the balcony at the empty pool area in the center of the buildings. The paths and pools became a ghost land at night. She wasn't sure why. She would have enjoyed a night swim, and there was no reason the guests shouldn't use those paths to make their way to the restaurants situated at both the top and bottom of the resort. Yet, for some reason, most of them used the outer paths on the edges of the resort.

Perhaps because that was the side where the elevators spat them out and the stairs exits were, Jess thought, but had no real idea. And she was just as guilty as the rest of the guests at avoiding the pool paths at night. She found the solid sidewalks easier to walk on in heels than the small pebbled paths around the pools on the way to dinner, and wouldn't risk tumbling into one of the pools on the way back should she slip on the wet pebbles and fall.

"Hmm," she muttered. She'd just figured out why the pool area was so dead at night. Go figure.

"What?" Raffaele asked, stopping to peer at her face. "Is something wrong?"

"No," she said with a frown, and then just as quickly said, "Yes. Are you sure this is going to work?"

"Positive," Raffaele said firmly, turning his attention back to the end of the blanket he was wrapping around her waist. "You will be perfectly safe, I promise. I am going down to the second-floor balcony first. Santo will lower you down to me. I will catch you and pull you in and then he will climb down and we will do it again to lower you to the ground floor. Once we're all down, we will call Zanipolo and he will toss the suitcases and then climb down to join us."

"Yeah, that doesn't sound too safe either," she told him with disgruntlement as he tied off the blanket and tugged to test it. His knot held. "I mean, suitcases are heavy. What if one of us gets hit?"

"No one will get hit," he assured her, and started to climb over the balcony rail.

"But—" Her words died as he paused on the other side of the balcony railing and pressed a quick kiss to her lips.

"Everything will be fine. I promise," he said firmly, and then dropped out of sight.

Gasping, Jess grabbed the rail and peered down, relieved to see Raffaele climbing over the railing of the balcony below.

"Wow. I thought he fell," Jess muttered as he disappeared from sight. Probably to reassure the people in that room that all was well and he wasn't there to rob them.

"Nay. Raffaele is like a cat. He always lands on his feet," Santo assured her as they watched. When Raffaele leaned out and gave them the thumbs-up, Santo straightened and turned to her.

"I don't think—" she began nervously, and then grunted in surprise when the huge man picked her up and lifted her over the railing to stand on the lip on the other side.

"I'm going to lower you to him," Santo said solemnly, as if she hadn't already known what the plan was.

Jess merely nodded, afraid to open her mouth for fear a tiny terrified shriek might come out. Heights never used to bother her, but after hanging from and nearly falling from her own balcony earlier, she was a bit nervous about being dangled over the edge like a baby hanging from a stork's mouth.

Grasping the blanket, Santo wrapped his end around one wrist, and then he grabbed the end closer to her body with his free hand and lifted her up off the railing. Biting her lip to keep from screaming, Jess clung to the material and closed her eyes. She so didn't want to see the ground coming up to meet her if Santo's grip on the blanket slipped.

Jess didn't open her eyes again until she felt hands clasp her waist, and then it was just in time to watch the world whirl around her as Raffaele turned her and lifted her over the railing. The moment he set her down next to him on the solid concrete floor of the second-floor balcony, she threw her arms around him in a tight hug.

"See, that wasn't so bad, was it?" he asked lightly, patting her back soothingly.

Sighing, Jess forced herself to step back so that he could lean out and look up to where Santo was. Another hand gesture had the blanket released. Raffaele caught it and stepped back as Santo swung down and dropped onto the balcony beside them.

"One more," Raffaele said encouragingly as he moved to the railing.

This time Jess watched silently as he climbed over it and dropped out of sight. They were only on the second floor now. Even if she fell, she wasn't likely to get badly hurt. At least, she didn't think so.

"Ready?" Santo asked, turning to her.

Jess walked to the railing and peered over. Raffaele was standing in the grass in front of the ground-floor balcony, looking up. Glancing to Santo, she said, "I can probably climb down too."

"Why bother when I am here and you are already trussed up like a turkey?" he asked with amusement, and picked her up to set her down to stand on the outside of the railing. It seemed to be little more than a moment later that she was standing on terra firma.

"So far so good," Raffaele murmured, pulling out his phone to call Zanipolo.

Jess merely nodded and glanced at the dark windows of the room they stood in front of. It was either unrented at the moment, or its present occupants were at dinner, she supposed as she turned her attention to the area around the pools. The lights were on, and the pools looked lovely. Any other time she might have liked to go for a swim, but that wasn't an option just now. She was too nervous that Vasco would somehow sense she was escaping and come around the building to catch her.

"Right," Raffaele said a moment later as he put his phone away. "Zani says Vasco and Cristo are still by the pizza shack. He's going to lower the luggage to Santo on the second-floor balcony, and he'll drop them to me, and then Zanipolo and Santo will climb down and we can go. Sound good?"

Jess nodded. She even managed a smile this time as she told herself it would just be a couple more minutes.

Those minutes felt like hours and Jess spent the entire time glancing nervously around and then up and then around again as the luggage was passed down to Santo, and then dropped to Raffaele. There were three suitcases. One for each man. The bags of clothing that Zanipolo and Santo had brought back for her had been put in Raffaele's suitcase rather than being left to be dragged around.

"Let's go."

Jess gave a start and glanced around, surprised to find Santo and Zanipolo standing next to them. Raffaele had just caught the last suitcase. How had the other two men got down so quickly? She didn't get the chance to wonder over that long. Taking his suitcase in one hand, Raffaele clasped her elbow with his other and began to urge her quickly through the pool area to the steps leading up to the lobby and reception area.

"You don't think they'll be able to see us on the stairs, do you?" she asked nervously as they started up.

"No," Raffaele said reassuringly, and pointed out, "The buildings with the rooms are taller than the main building."

"Oh. Right," she murmured, but couldn't shake the feeling someone was watching them as they mounted the steps. The feeling made her move a little quicker and then quicker still until she was nearly running up the steps. The men didn't say anything. They merely kept pace with her and followed her inside.

"Stay with Santo. I'll be right back."

Jess glanced around at that, and watched Raffaele approach the reception desk.

"Why don't we wait closer to the front doors?" Zanipolo said, peering around the lobby with a frown. It was a large cavernous room full of couches and chairs arranged in conversation groups, and there were a lot of people present at the moment. Some were checking out to catch late flights, others simply waiting for whatever that night's entertainment would be in the open area at the back of the lobby.

Jess glanced around nervously, half-afraid one of her relatives, or another guest from the wedding party, might spot her and approach to find out what was going on. She didn't know what she'd say if they did. She'd called Krista and told her she'd run into some old friends and was joining them for a short trip to La Romana. She hadn't wanted to mention Santo Domingo in case Vasco or one of his men realized she was no longer in Raffaele's hotel room, and read Krista's mind in an effort to figure out where she'd gone. At least this way, they'd be looking in the wrong place if that happened.

"The car's already waiting out front," Raffaele announced, catching up to them as they headed for the front doors. Taking Jess's arm again, he urged them to move a little more quickly as they approached the front doors. "They gave me the keys."

"The keys?" she asked with surprise. "I thought we were taking a hotel car into town and getting a rental there?"

"While you were napping, I arranged for a rental over the phone, and had it brought out here," he explained as he ushered her out of the lobby with Santo and Zanipolo following close behind. "We were already leaving much later than expected. I didn't want it to be midnight before we got to the hotel."

"Oh." Jess nodded and supposed it was good they could head right out without delay. It wasn't going to get them to the embassy today or anything; it was already closed. But she'd known they wouldn't be able to go there today when she'd decided they should wait for dark to leave. It had seemed to her that waiting and slipping away under the cover of darkness was safer than leaving during daylight and risking Vasco following and somehow stopping her from getting to the embassy and getting a replacement passport.

"Nice car," Zanipolo commented as Raffaele led them toward a luxury SUV.

"The windows are treated with SPF protection," Raffaele said as if that should mean something. Apparently, it did to Zanipolo and Santo. Both of them grunted with approval. It seemed they were worried about skin cancer.

Jess expected Raffaele to drive since he'd rented the car. Instead, he handed the keys to Zanipolo and got in the back with her. When he smiled at her, she smiled tensely back and then turned to peer out the window toward the hotel doors. There were people milling everywhere, coming and going, some with luggage, some without. She didn't spot anyone she recognized, and there were no pirates that she could see. But she still didn't feel safe. Jess was beginning to think she wouldn't feel safe again until she was out of the Dominican, and wasn't absolutely sure she would even then.

She *was* sure that she would be sorry to leave Raffaele, though. The man was something special, and it wasn't just the mind-blowing sex. That was just gravy on top of a very tasty meal to her mind. Jess liked Raffaele. She thought he was smart, and funny, and she liked that he was so considerate and caring. He was also a rock, like her father had been, calm and steadfast in the face of a crisis. She really would have liked to get to know him better. But it looked like that just wasn't meant to be and all they were going to be was a holiday romance. If things went as planned, she'd be at the embassy first thing tomorrow morning, and hopefully at the airport by dinner with a replacement passport. Meanwhile, Raff and his cousins would continue on with their vacation and then fly home to Italy. Her living in the U.S. and him being in Italy kind of made dating impossible. It wasn't like he'd leave his job and family and move to Montana to date a woman he'd only known a couple of days. And she certainly couldn't leave Montana until she finished her education. Nope. They'd both go home and she'd just become a memory of "that chick they once helped out in Punta Cana."

Finding the thought terribly depressing, Jess leaned her head against the window and closed her eyes on a sigh.

"Here we are."

Jess nodded mildly at Raffaele's words as he ushered her through the door Santo had just unlocked and opened. A glance back showed Zanipolo and Santo following with the luggage. Reassured by that, she turned her attention to the room as Raffaele led her out of the entry hall and into their suite. She'd thought the hotel room at the resort was nice, but this was several steps up from nice, she noted as her gaze slid over the huge living room/kitchen that was at the center of the three-bedroom suite.

The wall in front of her was all glass, high sliding glass doors in the middle, with equally tall windows running floor to ceiling on either side of them. The curtains were open to reveal a stunning view of the ocean and the starry night sky above it.

Jess's breath left her on a soft sigh as she took it in, and then she turned her attention to the room itself. A living-room-type area took up the left side of the large open room. It held a cream-colored couch and two matching chairs along with end tables, coffee tables, and a large television. The other side of the room was taken up by a dining table and a small kitchenette with a bar fridge, microwave, coffeepot, teapot, and cupboards, which she guessed probably held coffee cups and whatnot.

There was a small hallway off the left of the living room side with three doors off of it that Santo and Zanipolo were now checking out. She caught a glimpse of a bathroom through the middle door when Santo opened it, and then he turned to open the door on the right, revealing a bedroom even as Zanipolo opened the door on the left to another bedroom. Jess was just frowning at the fact that their three-bedroom suite apparently only had two bedrooms when Raffaele moved to a door on the right-hand side of the room, just past the dining table. When he opened that door, she saw that it too led to a bedroom. A huge one from the looks of it.

"You can have this room," Raffaele announced, returning to grab his suitcase. Carrying it into the room, he set it on a suitcase holder, and then headed for the door again. "Go ahead and unpack and shower or bathe if you like. I'm going to take a look at the room service menu and see if they're still serving."

Jess watched the door close behind him and then turned back to the room and simply stared around. It was a lovely room with a large bed, white side tables, and a white shelving unit across from the bed holding drawers on the bottom and then a television, and small colorful vases and artworks in the shelves above. Like the living room/dining area, the outer wall here was made up of a sliding glass door and large windows that looked out over the ocean too, and there was a table and two chairs in front of it.

Jess turned to the door on the opposite wall and opened it to find a bathroom that was almost as big as her living room at home. Eyes wide she peered at the huge Jacuzzi tub, the shower big enough to hold five people comfortably, the two-sink counter, and the open door to a walk-in closet and then shook her head and tried the only closed door in the room. Relief slid through her when she saw it led to a smaller room, almost a closet, with a toilet and bidet inside.

Stepping inside, she flicked the light switch on and used the facilities. It had been a long trip and she'd spent the last half of it wishing for a bathroom. After finishing, Jess stepped into the bathroom proper and washed her hands. She then turned to consider the tub and the shower. Which did she want? A quick invigorating shower? Or a nice long relaxing bath to ease away the tension that had been clenching her muscles almost nonstop since her cousin had dragged her onto what turned out to be a ship of vampires?

Deciding on a bath, she moved to the tub and started it running. Jess was back in the bedroom, removing her bags from Raffaele's suitcase while the water ran, when a light tap at the door made her pause and turn toward it. "Yes?"

Raffaele opened the door and stuck his head in. "Are you hungry?"

Jess nodded, and asked, "Is room service still on?"

Raffaele grimaced. "Yes. But the menu is pretty restricted at this hour. Santo and Zanipolo were thinking of going out to eat."

Jess bit her lip and glanced to the bathroom door.

"You're running a bath," he guessed, and smiled faintly. "It's all right. They can bring us back something."

Jess shook her head. Now that food had been brought up, she was hungry. "I'll just turn off the tub and change quickly . . . if they don't mind waiting a minute?"

"No, that's fine." He hesitated, and then slid into the room and paused next to her. "I'd like to change too if you—"

"Oh, yes!" She removed the last bag from the suitcase and stepped back as he quickly closed and flipped the latch to secure it.

"Is fifteen minutes enough time?" he asked as he headed for the door.

"Fine," she assured him, but thought she would probably be ready in five as she watched him leave. She moved to the bathroom then to turn off the taps, surprised to find the huge tub already full. The water pressure here was something to be envied, she decided. It took forever to fill her bath back home, and it was just a normal-sized tub.

She bent, intending to push the button that would drain the tub, and then paused, feeling bad about the waste of water. After a brief hesitation, Jess quickly stripped and stepped into it. He'd given her fifteen minutes. That was enough time for her to take a quick bath and dress.

Raffaele carried his suitcase into the room he would share with Zanipolo and raised his eyebrows when he saw the man had his laptop open and was turning it on.

"I'm going to find out our options for someplace to eat around here," Zanipolo murmured, concentrating on getting onto the hotel's internet.

"Wouldn't it be easier just to ask the concierge when we get downstairs?" Raffaele asked as he set his suitcase on the end of one of the beds and opened it to consider what clean clothes he had. He settled on a pair of dress pants and a short-sleeved, button-up white linen shirt.

"I'll do that too, but this way I get to see what kind of ambience they have."

"Ambience, huh?" he asked with amusement.

"And whether they're close to a dance club," Zanipolo added, ignoring his teasing.

Raffaele raised his eyebrows at the last claim, and considered it briefly. He then carried his clothes with him into the bathroom. He'd told Jess fifteen minutes. That was more than enough time for a quick shower.

"Mmm, this sea bass is delicious. You guys should have tried it."

Raffaele glanced up from his tenderloin at Zanipolo's comment. He was in time to see Jess wrinkle her nose with distaste and shake her head.

"Sorry, not a fish person. Never have been," she announced, and then added, "Although I don't mind shrimp with lots of that hot red sauce. But everything else from the sea should just stay there as far as I'm concerned."

"Yeah?" Zanipolo asked with interest and then glanced to him. "It seems to me you once mentioned never caring for seafood either, Raffaele. Didn't you?"

Raffaele raised an eyebrow. What he'd said was he couldn't bear the smell of seafood when Zani was eating it, and he'd refused to accompany him if he was having it for his meal. But he had never cared much for seafood when he had eaten either, so he nodded now. "I'm with Jess. Seafood should stay in the sea."

"And she's studying to teach history, while you used to teach it," Zani commented. "It's like you were meant to be."

Raffaele's eyes widened with alarm at the words. Zani was telling the truth. He had taught history in the past. Like three hundred years ago. He could hardly—

"Did you?" Jess asked, her eyes wide with surprise as she peered at him.

"Sì," Zanipolo answered for him when Raffaele turned a glare his way. "He taught Early History at the University of Urbino."

"And you gave it up to be an architect?" Jess asked now with a frown. "Did you not like it?"

"I loved it," Raffaele assured her, offering her a forced smile. He *had* loved it, but the academic community was a small one and his not aging had become a problem. Eventually, he'd had to leave to do something else. He'd become a hunter for a while, and then a concert pianist with some modest success, which had been a problem. Too much fame was not a good thing for someone trying *not* to attract attention, so he'd moved on to studying law, and done that for decades, before allowing his creative side reign again and studying and then working as an architect. Little of which he could tell Jess. She thought he was only in his late twenties or early thirties.

"If you loved it, why did you quit and become an architect?" Jess asked now.

Raffaele opened his mouth, closed it again, and then shrugged helplessly. He didn't have a clue what excuse to give for switching careers. He certainly couldn't tell her the truth. Fortunately, Zanipolo saved him again.

"The women."

"What?" Jess gasped even as Raffaele did and they both turned to Zani with amazement. Fortunately, Jess was apparently so shocked she didn't appear to notice his.

"Well, look at him," Zanipolo said with a shrug. "He might not have your typical *GQ*-type looks, but he has an animal magnetism the girls just couldn't resist."

Raffaele snapped his gaping mouth closed and sat up straight when Jess turned back to look at him. He had no idea what *GQ* was, but Jess was nodding with agreement, hopefully about the animal magnetism part at least.

"The female students were always hanging all over him and trying to seduce him," Zanipolo continued. "Raffaele quickly grew tired of having to fend them off and decided to switch to architecture."

That was utter bollocks. Women hadn't been allowed in university yet when he'd taught there, but Raffaele supposed Zani's excuse was as good as any. At least Jess was relaxing and smiling crookedly with understanding rather than looking horrified that he'd trained to be a professor and then just dumped it.

"Yeah. I can see how the girls would have been attracted to you," Jess said now, smiling faintly. "And from some of the nonsense I've seen on campus, I suppose they could be pretty aggressive about it." Expression turning teasing, she added, "Still, it's a shame you had to quit teaching to protect your manly virtue."

Raffaele just shook his head and shoveled food into his mouth to discourage further questions on the subject. But he was thinking it was damned inconvenient that she didn't know about their being immortal and what it meant. It made discussing his past hard. He was having to keep a lot of himself back, things he would have liked to share with her.

"Actually, I'm surprised a quality guy like you hasn't already been snapped up," Jess said now. "What's wrong with the girls in Italy? No taste?"

"Raff's always been particular. He doesn't just date women for dating's sake," Zanipolo said now. "I was beginning to think he'd never find the right woman, so I was glad when he found you."

Raffaele noted the way Jess's eyes widened at that, and then the uncertainty that crossed her face as she glanced from Zani to him, and suspected she'd been thinking this just a vacation romance. He was guessing that Zani had read that from her thoughts and was trying to give him an opening to let her know he planned for their relationship to continue beyond Punta Cana. Before he could do so, though, Jess quickly changed the subject.

"Wow! Well, this is really good. But it's also filling. I was kind of eyeing that tiramisu with Amaretto sauce on the menu, but I don't think I'll have the room," she said with a good cheer that was obviously forced.

"We could always get it to go and have it in the room as a midnight snack," Raffaele said quietly, letting her off the hook. He'd have to make his intentions clear later. Either tonight, or in the morning. Definitely before she flew home.

"Or we could stop in later on the way back to the hotel if they're still open. You don't want to be dragging a doggie bag around with you when we go dancing," Zanipolo protested with a frown.

"Dancing?" Jess asked with confusion.

"*Sì.* There is supposed to be a great dance club not too far from here. I thought we could go dancing and work off some of this meal," Zanipolo explained, smiling cheerfully.

"Oh." Jess frowned, and then shook her head. "I think you guys will have to go without me. It's been a stressful couple of days and I'd just rather go back to the hotel."

"What?" Zani asked with alarm. "But—"

"I'm afraid you will have to go without me too," Raffaele said firmly, interrupting Zani's protest. "A nice quiet night in the hotel, maybe watching a movie and eating tiramisu, sounds much nicer to me than fighting my way through a dark, crowded, and noisy club."

"Exactly," Jess said with obvious relief.

Zani relaxed and nodded then, but couldn't resist adding, "See. Perfect for each other. Aren't you glad I picked Punta Cana for our vacation?"

Raffaele just shook his head and looked around for their waiter. He spotted the man, even as the server noted him looking, and headed their way. Raffaele put in the order for two of the tiramisu desserts to go, and then turned his attention back to his food. By the time they were done eating, the desserts were waiting.

"Did you want a coffee or cappuccino before we head back?" Raffaele asked when Jess set her napkin over the remains of her meal and sat back in her seat with a little sigh. When Jess hesitated, Raffaele added, "Or we could pick one up to go on the way out if they have them. Or grab one somewhere else as we're heading back to the hotel."

"One to go," she decided, appearing relieved at the offer.

Nodding, Raffaele gestured to their waiter again and asked about the coffees when he hurried to the table. The man assured him that was possible and he'd get them at once. Their waiter was true to his word and, within minutes, Raffaele had settled the bill and was escorting Jess out of the restaurant, leaving Santo to watch Zani eat his dessert. The big man hadn't eaten anything himself, but he had ordered the sea bass like Zanipolo and had slid his fish and the rice side dish to Zanipolo a little at a time when Jess was looking the other way.

Much to Raffaele's amusement, that hadn't been enough to fill the young immortal and he'd ordered two desserts and two cappuccinos before Raff had settled the bill. He'd acted like he was ordering them for him and Santo, but Raffaele knew Santo wouldn't eat any of the delicious-looking dessert either. Nor would he touch the cappuccino. Santo hadn't eaten mortal food in centuries.

"I hope you didn't bypass dancing just because you were worried about me. I would have been fine going back to the hotel alone."

Raffaele glanced to Jess with surprise when she murmured that as they stepped out of the restaurant. "No," he assured her firmly as he took her arm to start up the street. "I'm not one for dance clubs. I don't mind playing in them with the band, but . . ." He shrugged and then admitted, "Watching from the stage when we're playing, it seems to me that they're just places where drunk and lonely people go to hook up with other drunk and lonely people."

"I know, right?" Jess said. "It's the same deal when I work at the bar. I see all these drunk girls leaving with guys they met like five minutes ago and I know they're just doing it because they're lonely and desperate for someone to like them. *And* that they're going to regret it in the morning." She shook her head. "I like to dance, but it hardly seems worth having to put up with the noise and crowds and drunk idiots hitting on me while I'm trying to dance." Sighing, she shook her head. "I guess working in the bar and dealing with people at the clinic and in class all the time has made me something of a homebody. When I get time off, I just want to go home, putter in the garden, and then put my feet up and read a book, do crosswords, or watch a movie."

Raffaele smiled faintly and nodded. "I am much the same way. Well, except for the working in the garden. I have a gardener who takes care of that, but I read, play the piano, and watch movies. And I love doing crosswords," he admitted with a grin. "I find them addictive."

"Me too," Jess said happily. "I even brought a crossword book with me so I could do them on the beach here." Grimacing, she added, "It was in the side pocket of my suitcase still, so I guess Vasco has that now." Sighing, she shook her head to remove the pirate from her mind, and asked him with curiosity, "What do you do for exercise if you don't garden?"

"You consider gardening exercise?" he said with amusement as he urged her to the curb and drew her to a halt. They were across from the hotel now. He waited until the way was clear and then ushered her quickly across the street.

Jess was silent until they reached the sidewalk in front of the hotel and then turned to glance at him, one eyebrow arched. "Trust me, gardening is hard work. Pulling weeds, raking, climbing trees to remove tent caterpillar webs . . . And my parents' backyard is huge. It takes a lot of work. I get a workout."

"Ah," he said with a solemn nod, noting that she still thought of it as her parents' home. She probably always would, he thought as they entered the hotel lobby. He waited until they were at the elevators before answering her original question. "I have a pool and swim in it most nights for exercise."

"Lucky you," Jess said with obvious envy as the elevator doors opened. "I love swimming. I'm no marathoner, but I enjoy splashing around in the water and stuff."

"Then you shall have to come to Italy and try my pool," Raffaele said lightly as he followed her into the elevator and hit the button for their floor.

"You don't have to say stuff like that," Jess said softly.

Raffaele glanced at her in confusion. "Like what?"

"You don't have to pretend this is more than it is," she explained gently. "I mean . . ." She shook her head. "You're from Italy, I'm from Montana, and once I fly out we'll probably never see each other again. You don't have to pretend this is more than a holiday romance. I—"

"Jess," he said solemnly, turning to face her and taking her hand with his free one. "I'd like more than just a vacation romance with you. I'd like this to continue beyond Punta Cana. I know it might be a little difficult with our living so far apart, but I think it will be worth it."

"You do?" Jess asked, her eyes wide.

"*Sì.*" He frowned slightly, unsure if her expression was stunned because she hadn't expected this, or because she hadn't wanted it. Just because they had mind-blowing sex, it didn't guarantee she'd want a relationship with him to be more permanent. Taking a deep breath, he said, "I know we have not known each other long. Even so, I think what we have could be the start of something special. Not only do we have a lot of sexual chemistry, but we seem to have quite a few things in common too, important things."

"Yes, we do," she agreed solemnly.

Raffaele nodded and glanced at the panel above the elevator door to be sure he had time before turning back and saying. "So, while I have to finish out my vacation here for Santo's sake, I would like very much to come visit you in America afterward, and have you come to Italy and Canada as well. If that would be all right with you?"

"I'd like that," she admitted sincerely.

Raffaele grinned with relief, and started to lower his head, intending to kiss her, but the elevator dinged then. Stiffening, he glanced toward it just as the doors slid open. Smiling wryly then, he simply said, "So would I," and urged her out into the hall.

It was probably for the best that their arrival prevented his kissing her, he told himself as they walked to the suite. These things rarely stopped with a kiss between life mates and the elevator wasn't a good place to end up half-naked and unconscious. Shaking his head wryly at the thought, he slipped his key card out of his pocket and unlocked the door, then pushed it open for Jess to lead the way inside.

Twelve

Jess woke up slowly, dragged to consciousness by a need to relieve herself. It was an annoying intrusion, and one she tried to ignore at first, but then simply couldn't. Sighing, she gave up the effort, rolled over, opened her eyes, and then blinked in surprise when she saw Raffaele sitting up in bed next to her.

It wasn't the fact that he was there in bed with her that caused her surprise. Their ending up sharing the room had seemed almost inevitable with the chemistry they had between them. In fact, she'd wondered earlier why he'd said she could have this room and had taken his suitcase to one of the other ones. After the crazy hot sex they'd had at the resort, she'd known they wouldn't be able to resist each other here. Especially after his telling her that he wanted the relationship to continue beyond this vacation.

The memory made her smile. He wanted to see her again. The thought made her want to hug herself with happiness. Or maybe hug him. Damn! Life was weird. Throwing an amorous vampire at her with one hand, and then a dream man like Raffaele with the other. They were polar opposites. Vasco was a walking nightmare, a bloodthirsty vampire eager to turn her into soulless demon spawn, while Raffaele was a knight in shining armor who had pulled her from the ocean and done all in his power to keep her safe since then. He was smart, and sexy, and so very kind and considerate. He was also a homebody like her, and he used to be a professor teaching history, which is what she hoped to do. Honestly, it *was* like they were made for each other. She could imagine a life with this man. In fact, she found the idea of life without him rather painful.

The thought made her grimace as she realized she was really jumping the gun here. They hadn't known each other long. Thinking about a future with Raffaele was just a bit presumptuous and premature at this point. They needed to get to know each other better, and see how they dealt with each other in normal everyday-type situations. Their whole experience so far was miles outside of normal. She'd been in a state of crisis when they met and still was, and he'd been and still was in rescue mode. They needed to see if they worked well together under normal, everyday circumstances.

The problem was, Jess didn't think she'd much care if they did or didn't. The crazy monkey sex they had together was enough to make almost anything bearable. Her body was still tingling from the pleasure he'd given her once they'd got back to the suite. They'd started out behaving themselves. The walk back had helped dinner settle enough that they'd decided to have their dessert right away. They'd put an action movie on the television in the living room, which they'd discovered was a favorite for both of them, and then had started to eat. But Jess had dropped some tiramisu on her chest. Before she could clean it up with her napkin, Raffaele had done it for her . . . with his tongue, and that was it.

Jess had woken up some time later to find herself in Raffaele's arms as he carried her to this bedroom. He'd set her on her feet next to the bed, undid her dress for her, and kissed her as he pushed it off her shoulders and POW! They'd been lost in a maelstrom of need and passion again. The man was a powerhouse when it came to sex, and the two of them together were like a forest fire. But this business of her fainting afterward each time was a bit disconcerting. Actually, it was almost embarrassing, really, she thought, her gaze sliding to the scene on the television that was holding Raffaele's attention so thoroughly. Her eyes widened when she recognized the characters on the screen.

"*Supernatural?*" she asked, sitting up with surprise.

Raffaele gave a guilty start and quickly turned off the television, muttering, "I was just channel surfing."

Jess smiled with amusement. His chagrinned expression gave him away. Besides, she'd been awake for a few minutes now and he hadn't turned the channel that she'd noticed. He'd been watching it, but was just too embarrassed to admit it for some reason. Shaking her head, she said lightly, "That's a shame. I thought that was something else we had in common. I love *Supernatural*."

"Really?" Eyes brightening, he grinned and admitted, "Zanipolo and I got hooked on the show when we first visited our cousins in Toronto. Aunt Marguerite likes it and watches it weekly. We watched it with her and then had to go back and find the first gazillion seasons."

"Are you a Sammy fan, or Dean?" Jess asked, her eyes narrowing. This was a serious question. If he was a Sammy fan . . . Well, that wouldn't bode well.

"Dean, of course," he said as if there was no question. "He is tough, smart, and has a good sense of humor. He would make a good hunter."

"He *is* a hunter," she pointed out with amusement.

"Yes, but I meant—"

When Raffaele cut himself off abruptly, she raised her eyebrows. "You meant what?"

"It does not matter," he muttered, and then his gaze slid over her and his dark eyes seemed to brighten and turn more silver. It was something she'd noticed before. When he got sexually excited, his eyes turned more silver than black. It was beautiful, but a little unusual. She'd heard of people having eyes that could twinkle and such, but she'd never met anyone whose eyes could change color with emotion like mood rings, and for a moment she just stared, but then Jess realized he was leaning toward her as if about to kiss her. She immediately leaned back and then quickly slid out of bed.

"Hold that thought," she said lightly as she dashed to the bathroom.

Jess had intended only to go to the bathroom and then rush back to bed and Raffaele, but her glance fell on the shower as she entered the room. By the time she'd taken care of the business she'd entered for,

Jess had decided a quick shower to freshen up before returning to bed and Raffaele might be a good thing.

Raffaele must have heard the shower running, because she'd just stepped under the spray once it warmed up when the shower door opened behind her. Before Jess could turn around, Raffaele slid his arms around her from behind.

"I heard the water and thought a shower sounded good," he murmured, pressing a kiss to her shoulder. "Can we share?"

"Yes," Jess murmured on a sigh, and leaned back against his chest.

"Good." Raffaele growled the word as his hands left their position around her waist and slid up to cover and caress her wet breasts under the spray. "Then I can wash your back, and you can wash mine."

Releasing a breathless chuckle, Jess arched into the caress and pointed out, "That's not my back."

"No, but then I studied history and architecture, not anatomy. I guess I'll have to explore to find your back," he teased.

Jess chuckled at the claim until one of his hands left her breast to drift down and slide between her legs.

"Exploring could be fun," he decided on a groan as his talented fingers made her moan and shift against him.

"Sì," Jess gasped, pushing back into him with her hips and feeling the hardness waiting for her. Dear God, Penisocchio was already fully erect and she hadn't even touched him yet. That thought in mind, she reached back to try to find him, but the hand between her legs suddenly slid out to catch hers. Using his hold to spin her out of the water, he urged her back up against the wall and then kissed her quickly before stepping back to look around and find the bar of soap she'd opened and put on the shelf before turning on the water.

Jess watched him grab it and begin to work up a lather, thinking that she was going to end up fainting in the shower. Despite that worry, she took the opportunity to reach for him again. Distracted as he was, she managed to actually touch him this time. Raffaele gasped as her hand closed over him, and then quickly dropped to his knees and buried his face between her legs just as she gasped with her own excitement and pleasure.

Confusion claimed Jess for a moment as she tried to figure out how she could respond to his mouth on her even before it was actually *on* her, but then what he was doing distracted her and she found it hard to think about anything else but the pleasure building inside of her.

Jess did faint in the shower, but she woke up in bed spooning with Raffaele. Jess lay still for a moment, just enjoying having him wrapped around her like a blanket, and then her gaze found the clock/radio on the bedside table, and she stiffened. It was nine o'clock. She hadn't remembered to set the alarm clock or ask for a wake-up call and they'd slept in. Actually, considering they'd spent most of the night making love, passing out and making love again with a two-hour break where they'd watched a movie, and finished the dessert they'd left in the living room, Jess supposed she was lucky to be awake this early. It was that thought that made her decide to let Raffaele sleep and head to the embassy by herself.

Moving slowly and carefully, she eased out from under his arm and slid from the bed, then grabbed the dress she'd worn the night before and popped into the bathroom to dress and run a brush through her hair. Jess then returned to the bedroom and tiptoed to the bed to grab her key card off the bedside table. She wanted to kiss Raffaele before going, but was afraid of waking him. Spotting a hotel notepad and pen on the bedside table on his side, she quickly wrote a note explaining that she hadn't wanted to wake him so was going to the embassy alone but would, hopefully, be back soon with a new passport. She signed it with kisses and hugs, and then left the room and eased the door silently closed.

It was as she sighed and turned away from the door that she spotted Zanipolo. The man was seated on the couch with his legs crossed at the ankles and propped on the coffee table. His arms were crossed over his chest, and his head was resting on the back of the couch. His eyes were closed and his mouth hanging open. Apparently, he'd fallen asleep watching TV. At least that was her guess since the TV was on, quietly giving the day's news.

A snore coming long and loud from the man's open mouth made Jess smile with amusement as she tiptoed through the large open room to the hall to the small entry. She managed to make it there without waking the man, and then was careful about opening the door, trying to do so soundlessly. She then stepped out, and paused with surprise when she nearly plowed into a man hurrying up the hall, pulling a dolly with a mini-fridge on it.

"Oh, lo siento," the man muttered, glancing up from the paper he'd been reading, and then relaxing as he noticed the number on the door still half-open behind her. "Notte?"

"*Sí.* You have the right room," Jess whispered, glancing worriedly toward the open door and letting it close a bit so they wouldn't wake the man inside as she added, "The men are all sleeping, though." Her gaze shifted to the refrigerator and, assuming the one in the suite wasn't working and the men had called down to have it replaced, said, "We have to be quiet."

"*Sí, señorita.* I will be quiet."

Nodding, Jess eased the door open again and then held it for the man to wheel the fridge in. Much to her relief, the dolly moved soundlessly. Easing the door silently closed, Jess turned to follow the man, and then moved around him to lead the way to the little kitchenette when he wheeled the dolly to the mouth of the entry, and then paused to glance toward her in question.

The man followed her to the kitchenette, eyed the other refrigerator dubiously, but then shrugged and quickly lifted the new one off the dolly, set it on the floor, and plugged it in. Jess expected him to collect the apparently broken one then, but it seemed that was someone else's job, because he simply gestured for her to follow and led the way back to the door, dragging his dolly behind him. Jess followed him out of the room, eased the door silently closed, and then turned to find the man holding out the paperwork he'd been looking at when he'd nearly run into her.

"You need to sign for it," he explained in very good English.

"Oh, yes," Jess muttered, and took the papers and pen, wishing Zanipolo had been awake to handle this. She really wanted to get to the embassy.

"Is my fault," the man said apologetically as she signed her name to the delivery form. "I was supposed to be here four hours ago, but I was in an accident. Some drunken mortal plowed into me as I started across town."

Jess glanced to him with concern as she handed back the papers and pen. "Was anyone hurt?"

"No," he said on a sigh as he ripped off the top sheet and handed it to her. "But my truck was demolished and several of the refrigerators were crushed. There was blood everywhere. Unfortunately, the refrigerator with blood meant for you Nottes was one of them and I had to call in for someone to collect me and then get another truck, load it up, and start out again. It delayed me greatly."

"Blood?" Jess breathed with confusion, but the man had already turned and was rushing away. His words ran through her mind as she watched him go. Some drunken *mortal* had hit him? She considered that briefly, and then it occurred to her that he'd apologized and explained his being late as if she'd spoken aloud the thought that she wished Zanipolo was still awake so he could have handled the delivery. Or as if he'd read her mind. *And* he'd been delivering—

She peered down at the sheet he'd made her sign and then had given her and saw that the delivery wasn't listed as a refrigerator, but as twenty-four pints of pure O positive mortal blood. For a moment, Jess just stood there, but then she shook her head and turned to the door. It was a mistake obviously. Why would Zanipolo order blood?

Opening the door again, she slid back inside, intending to go open the refrigerator and look inside, but the sound of voices reached her ear as she eased the door closed.

"So, the delivery came," she heard Santo say as she started across the entry. "What time did he finally show?"

"I don't know," Zanipolo answered. "I fell asleep on the couch around 6 A.M. and just woke up. Raff must have taken the delivery."

Jess heard Santo grunt in response just before she stepped out of the entry and glanced toward the kitchenette. She was just in time to see Zanipolo hand the larger man a bag of blood and then open his mouth and slap a second bag to his own mouth as his canines extended.

Jess didn't really recall stepping back into the entry and pressing her back up against the wall. But she did and stood there for a moment, her heart thundering in her chest and panic claiming her mind until she heard Zanipolo ask, "Another?"

"*Sì,*" Santo answered. "Two more, please."

"Yeah, I'm probably going to have three myself. We've been going pretty light on the blood since Jess popped up," Zanipolo commented. "It's hard to find a chance to feed when she's around all the time."

"It's worse for Raffaele," Santo responded. "I don't think he's managed to get more than one bag down since her appearance."

"Yeah," Zanipolo agreed. "And she must have interrupted him again before he could have any after the delivery because there were no bags missing."

"Speaking of Jess . . ." Santo said, and didn't bother to finish.

It was Zani who said, "Yeah. I suppose we'd better move the blood to your room or mine so she doesn't find it when she wakes up. The last thing we need is her finding out what we are and freaking out."

Santo grunted what might have been an agreement and then said, "Here. Hold these bags for me and I'll move it now. We should probably be feeding in there anyway."

That was when Jess finally managed to shake off the horror that had held her still and turned to stumble to the door. She needed to get out of there before the men passed in front of the entry and saw her.

Men? Vampires, she corrected herself grimly as she eased the door open, slipped out, and eased it silently closed.

Jess didn't head for the elevator. Unwilling to risk being found in the hall before the elevator could arrive to take her away, she took the stairs instead. But it was something of a wonder that she managed to walk down them without falling and breaking her neck. She wasn't exactly in top form at that moment. Her mind was spinning with horror at what she'd learned. Raffaele and his cousins were vampires too. She couldn't get the image of Zanipolo slapping that bag of blood to his fangs out of her head. And she couldn't even hope it was just Raffaele's two cousins. Zanipolo had said Raffaele hadn't had more than a bag of blood since she'd "popped up." They were all just like Vasco. All vampires. Dear God, was that why the sex was so crazy good? Was it some kind of vampire thing? Would sex with Zanipolo or Santo have knocked her socks off just as much?

And she'd thought Raffaele the polar opposite of Vasco, Jess thought with dismay. She'd been thinking of the man as her savior, painting him almost a saint in her mind, and all the time—

Jess stopped abruptly on the steps as another thought struck her. These vampires could read minds and control humans. Ildaria had done that on the ship—taken control of her and sent her to kiss Vasco. Had Raffaele controlled her and made her want to have sex with him? Had he made her just think she'd enjoyed the sex so much? Maybe it was just okay, but he'd put it in her thoughts that she'd enjoyed it, like the pirates had made everyone think they'd had a blast on the shark feeding tour. Dear God, she thought with dismay, and then an even more awful thought struck her. Had he been biting her too? Had she been fainting after the sex because it was so amazing as she'd believed? Or was she fainting because he was somehow biting her without her knowledge and "feeding" off of her until she lost consciousness?

That possibility screaming in her head, Jess glanced down at herself and quickly examined what she could see, which was just her arms and legs. She then pulled the neckline of her dress away and peered down at her chest, but the lighting in the stairwell wasn't that great and with the dress material blocking what light there was, she couldn't see much. Letting the neckline fall back into place, she started moving again, taking the steps down much more quickly than she had been. There were bathrooms off the lobby and she wanted to get to them and look herself over properly. Although she supposed she wasn't likely to find anything. He'd probably bit her places she couldn't easily see.

He *had* spent a good deal of time between her legs, Jess thought grimly and suspected she now knew why. The thought brought an image of Tyler to mind, his mouth open on a silent scream of pain and horror, and Ildaria on her knees in front of him, blood dripping obscenely down her chin. Feeling sick, Jess pressed a hand to her stomach, and finished the rest of her descent at a run.

Raffaele thought Jess must be in the bathroom when he woke up to find the bed empty beside him and the bathroom door closed. It wasn't until several moments passed without her reappearing and with no sound from the room that he got up with the intention of checking on her. That was when he saw the note on the bedside table; pausing, he picked it up and then frowned when he read it. She'd headed to the embassy without him.

It was nearly ten now. What time had she left? How long had she been gone? He wondered over that as he quickly began to drag on clothes. She shouldn't be out and about without him. What if Vasco or one of his men had followed them?

Concern eating at him now, Raffaele finished doing up his jeans and grabbed a shirt, pulling it on as he hurried for the door.

"Morning, sleeping beauty. We were beginning to think you two would sleep the day away," Zanipolo greeted him from the couch as he stepped out of the bedroom.

Raffaele grunted in response and did up his buttons as he crossed the room, heading for the entry.

"Yo, *cugino*. Where are you going?" Zanipolo asked with amusement as he turned into the entry. "If you planned on running out to grab everyone coffees, you might want to put shoes on first."

Raffaele paused halfway across the entry and glanced down at his bare feet. He then turned back with a curse. His shoes were in the bedroom. By the time he found and donned them and returned to the living room, Zanipolo was standing near the entry. When he saw that he was alone, Zani pulled his hands from behind his back and held them up. Each hand held two bags of blood.

"Get these down while you have the chance," he suggested as Raffaele crossed the room toward him. "You're looking pale, and once Jess wakes up—"

"Jess is already awake and gone," Raffaele growled, pausing to take one of the bags from him. Just seeing them in the man's hand had made him almost faint with hunger. Now he slapped the bag to his fangs and waited impatiently for it to empty.

"What do you mean she's gone?" Zanipolo asked with a frown.

Raffaele scowled at him over the bag at his mouth, and thought the answer at him. Fortunately, despite his being older than Zanipolo, his cousin had no problem reading the answer.

"She left by herself rather than wake you?" he asked with dismay.

"Not good," Santo announced, appearing from his room.

"Yeah," Zanipolo agreed grimly. "What if Vasco or one of his men followed us and are out there looking for her?"

Much to Raffaele's relief, the bag at his mouth was empty by then and he was able to tear it away and say, "That was my first worry."

Deciding one bag would have to do until he knew Jess was all right, Raffaele waved away the other bags when Zanipolo held them up in offering, and turned to hurry to the door.

"Hang on," Zani snapped, and dashed for his room. Probably to put the unused bags of blood away, Raffaele thought, but didn't wait. He rushed out of the suite and straight for the door to the stairwell. It would be faster than waiting for the elevator, he thought. As he pushed through it, he heard the door to the suite open again behind him and knew the other two men were following him.

"Your appointment confirmation and documents?"

Jess blinked at the armed guard in confusion. After quickly examining herself in the public washroom off the hotel lobby, she'd rushed here to the embassy. She hadn't found any signs of bite marks, but it wasn't like she had a mirror to check between her legs, so that hadn't made her feel much better. Jess was still feeling off-kilter and slightly stunned by the knowledge that she'd run from one vampire into the arms of another. Perhaps that was why she felt like the man was speaking Dutch to her.

"Lady? You need to show your confirmation before I can let you into the building," the guard said impatiently when she continued to stare at him blankly.

Giving her head a shake, Jess forced an uncertain smile. "I'm sorry. My what?"

"I need your proof you have an appointment. You should have printed up your appointment confirmation when you booked it online," the man said impatiently, and then his eyes narrowed. "You did make an appointment online before coming here, didn't you?"

"I—No. I didn't know . . ." Jess began weakly.

"Then go make one. You can't get in without an appointment," he said with exasperation. "If you're lucky, you might still get in today, but it's more likely you won't get an appointment until Monday."

"What?" she gasped with dismay. "No, I can't—This is an emergency. I drove all the way here from Punta Cana. I need—"

"Punta Cana?" the man interrupted, his eyebrows rising. "You should have just gone to our consular agency there. You probably would have got in right away. The lines are always shorter there."

Of course. There was a consular agency in Punta Cana she could have gone to. Jess closed her eyes briefly and then shook her head and opened them again. "I can't book an appointment. I don't have a computer. But I really need to see someone. My passport was—"

"Everyone who comes here really needs to see someone," the man said unmoved. "If you don't have a computer, you can make the appointment by phone. But you can't get in without an appointment. Go call and make one."

Jess stared at him, not believing this. Or believing it too well. This was how her morning was going, after all.

"Lady, there are others waiting and you're holding up the line. Go find a phone and book an appointment. Or don't, but get out of the way so the next person can approach."

Jess opened her mouth, closed it again, and then simply turned and moved away past the others waiting in line to get through security. What else could she do? She wasn't getting past the guard. It seemed she would have to call and book an appointment. Why hadn't she known that?

Because she hadn't looked into any of this, she reminded herself. She'd let Raffaele and his cousins take care of it. They'd taken care of everything since pulling her from the ocean. From dressing her, feeding her, even housing her in their room, and then looking up the information about the embassy. Had they known she wouldn't get in without an appointment? Had they known there was a consular agency in Punta Cana she could have gone to? And if they had, why hadn't they told her?

Because they were vampires like Vasco, a little voice in her head answered. *They're probably in cahoots with Vasco and deliberately keeping me from getting a replacement passport so I can't leave the Dominican*, she thought. *They're ensuring Vasco can claim me for his vampire bride.*

Jess frowned at the thought almost as soon as she had it. That didn't quite make sense. Vasco wanted her for himself, and if they were working with him, surely Raffaele wouldn't have slept with her? Vasco probably wouldn't be pleased to learn he had. What was happening here? And just how many vampires were out there?

A lot apparently. At least, she seemed to be running into them at every turn here. A ship full of them, and now Raffaele and his cousins. Lord knew how many more there were. How had she not known they even existed? Did they all live in the tropics? Was that why? Jess wasn't exactly rolling in money. Visiting tropical destinations like Punta Cana wasn't something she'd ever even done before. Were they all here, or were there vampires in America too? Living in her town? Perhaps even next door. The thought made her shudder with horror.

Dear God, she just wanted to go home. She wanted never to have come here and to be safe and blessedly ignorant of all of this back in the home she'd shared with parents who had been loving and kind. What was she going to do?

That last thought was full of so much panic it sort of scared Jess into calming herself. Losing it was not going to get her out of this mess. What she was going to do was find a phone and call the embassy to make an appointment. Surely if she explained that her passport had been stolen and she needed an immediate replacement to catch her flight home on Sunday, she would be given an appointment quickly? This *was* an emergency situation, after all.

Feeling a little better at this reasoning, Jess glanced around and considered where she could find a phone. She didn't have any money for a pay phone. If there even were pay phones anymore. There seemed precious few of them back home, and she hadn't really noticed pay phones anywhere since arriving here. She could go back to the hotel and ask to use the phone at the reception desk. She'd be risking Raffaele or one of the men spotting her, but that couldn't be helped. Besides, they couldn't do anything in the busy lobby with all those witnesses, right? Except maybe take control of her and make her return to the room with them, she realized, and was frowning at the thought when she noticed she was getting into a vehicle.

Confused, she glanced around sharply, her eyes widening as she found herself staring at the woman seated on her left in the back of what appeared to be a taxi.

Ildaria.

The female pirate smiled at her with amusement. "You seemed so wrapped up in your thoughts I didn't want to interrupt you."

So, she'd just taken control of her and made her get into the vehicle, Jess realized. She'd probably even made her walk to it. Jess had no idea. She'd thought she was walking aimlessly away from the embassy and hadn't been thinking about where she was going. She'd been too busy panicking about her situation at first, and then trying to figure a way to resolve it. Now she felt the blood rush from her face, and turned sharply back toward the door she'd got into the vehicle through, only to freeze again as she saw that Cristo was getting in next to her. She was trapped.

Thirteen

"I see— Shit," Zanipolo finished with dismay.

Raffaele turned on him sharply. They were just approaching the embassy and he had been scanning the people they were passing when Zani spoke. Eyeing his dismay with concern, he asked, "What?"

"She just got into that taxi," Zani said, his voice grim, and Raffaele followed his pointing finger to see the taxi in question. His eyes widened with alarm when he saw Cristo lean out to pull the door closed.

"They've got her," Santo growled with displeasure.

Not responding, Raffaele glanced sharply around until he spotted a taxi disgorging its riders nearby. Spying the driver through the front windshield, he slipped into the man's mind and took control, making him remain where he was and wait for their arrival.

"Follow that taxi," he instructed as he slid into the front seat a moment later. Zani and Santo barely managed to jump in the back before the car started to move.

"She never should have come alone," Zani said fretfully as the taxi moved into traffic behind the one holding Jess and Cristo, and it looked like a third person, although Raffaele couldn't tell who the third person was. They looked too small to be Vasco, he thought as Zani added, "I hope she didn't look in the refrigerator before she went."

Raffaele frowned at the possibility, and glanced back at the other man to ask, "What time did it finally come?"

They'd ordered the blood before leaving the resort. It was supposed to have been delivered at 4 A.M. when they'd been sure Jess would be asleep but Zanipolo and Santo would be awake to accept the delivery.

"What do you mean what time did it come? Didn't you accept it?" Zani asked now with surprise.

"No," he said sharply, and then glanced to Santo, who shook his head solemnly. When Raffaele cursed, Zanipolo pulled out his phone.

"I'll call and see what happened. I'm sure everything's fine. Even if it was Jess who answered the door, the courier would have taken control of her and put it in her mind not to look in it after he left. The couriers are usually pretty good about that kind of thing."

"Sì," Raffaele agreed, and then took a moment to reinforce his control of their taxi driver to be sure he wasn't catching any of this conversation before adding, "They are in Canada and Italy. But this is the Dominican. Who can say how professional the couriers are here."

Zanipolo frowned at the comment, but then turned his attention to the phone and began to speak in swift Spanish, asking about their delivery. Who had brought it around? Who had accepted it? What had happened?

Raffaele listened silently to Zanipolo's side of the conversation as he watched the taxi ahead of them in traffic, so wasn't surprised when the other man hung up and explained worriedly, "Our courier was in an accident. He was okay, but it put him way behind on his deliveries and he was in a rush. When Jess answered the door and said yes when he asked if she was a Notte, he didn't bother to read her mind—he just made the delivery and left."

"Not good," Santo rumbled.

"Maybe we got lucky and she didn't look inside the fridge," Zanipolo said hopefully.

Raffaele snorted at the suggestion. He doubted they'd be that lucky.

"She didn't look inside," Santo announced, and Raffaele glanced to his cousin to see that he was sitting forward in the back seat, watching the taxi ahead of them with a concentrated expression. He was reading Jess, Raffaele realized. As long as he could see her, he could read her.

"See, it's all right. She doesn't know what we are, then," Zanipolo said with relief and slapped Raffaele's shoulder encouragingly.

"Yes, she does," Santo countered, his words slow and almost lumbering as he struggled to keep a connection with Jess in the car in front of them. "She read that the delivery was blood on the slip and came back in to look and saw us feeding. She then slipped away before we could catch her."

"Oh, damn," Zanipolo muttered.

Raffaele felt his shoulders sag briefly, but then shook his head. Okay. So, she knew they fed on blood. That was a problem, but not the main one here, he reminded himself. The real problem now was that she was back in the hands of the pirates. They had to get her away from them. Mouth tightening, he growled, "If he hurts her . . ."

"He will not hurt her," Zanipolo said soothingly. "She is a possible life mate for him. Every immortal would rather kill themselves than harm their life mate."

"Maybe normal immortals, but he is rogue," Raffaele pointed out, and then ground his teeth at the thought that Jess might be a life mate for this particular rogue. The idea infuriated him. She was his, not Vasco's. The pirate couldn't have her, he thought, but knew the choice wasn't his. It was up to Jess. And he was very aware that as a possible life mate for the man, Jess would be as attracted to the pirate as she was to him. That Vasco's touch would inspire the same mad passion as his own. A passion that was almost impossible to fight, he knew.

"She's experienced it with you now," Zanipolo said soothingly. "That will help her fight the attraction."

Raffaele merely grunted, but he was silently worrying that rather than helping her fight the attraction, it might hinder her ability to do so. The first time she'd experienced life mate passion, it had probably scared her silly. It was rather overwhelming, and thinking herself on a ship full of vampires would have doubled her fear. But now she'd experienced that passion in full with him. That would have made it less scary. And she now knew she'd slept with one vampire without being harmed. Maybe she'd think they were all the same. Maybe she'd even prefer Vasco to him because Vasco had been honest with her from the start, while he'd hidden what he was from her.

"We're immortals not vampires," Zani reminded him quietly, apparently reading his thoughts.

Raffaele merely grunted at that. He normally detested the name vampires, and didn't think of himself as one. But he was quite sure Jess probably saw him as one now and that was what was important. He should have told her what he was and explained to her about immortals after the first time they'd slept together. God, he'd really fucked this up. Glancing around, he noted where they were headed and closed his eyes briefly. They were heading to port. If Vasco's ship was waiting there and they took her on board and set sail—

"Conference call Julius and Lucian and let them know what's going on," he barked furiously. "Tell them that Vasco has kidnapped my life mate and we're in pursuit . . . And that I will not hesitate to kill the man to get her back," he growled coldly, and then scowled as he noticed that traffic was getting worse the closer they got to the harbor. Cars were darting out of the side streets and cutting in front of the vehicles in front of them, forcing them to hit the brakes. The distance between their taxi and the one Jess was in was growing.

Concerned they'd lose her, Raffaele looked for a way to make the driver maneuver the taxi closer to hers, but there was nowhere to maneuver to. Traffic was already pretty much bumper to bumper. The cars that were cutting in were nosing into the slowly moving lane and basically forcing drivers to stop and let them in. His only option was to take control of the other drivers and make them pull out of the way. Raffaele was about to do that when Santo spoke.

"There's the ship," the big man rumbled behind him, and Raffaele glanced to where he was pointing. He spotted the pirate ship at the far end of the harbor almost at once. It had laid anchor next to a huge cruise ship that completely dwarfed the sloop. It cast the ship in shade and prevented the sun from reaching its occupants.

Handy for an immortal, he thought grimly. But it meant they must have taken rowboats ashore to search the mainland for Jess. He began searching for where they could have put ashore as Zanipolo spoke into the phone.

"*Sì*, but he will not like it . . . Fine. I will tell him." Zanipolo's stressed voice drew Raffaele's attention as the man covered his phone and said, "Lucian and Julius said we are to wait for the local hunters. They will meet us at the docks and join us to deal with Vasco."

Raffaele snorted at the very suggestion. "The local hunters had their chance to deal with him when we first reported him. They did nothing. I'm not risking Jess and letting—" He paused and scowled when Zani suddenly held his phone out. He glared at it briefly like it was a snake about to strike, but then straightened his shoulders and took the phone.

The moment Lucian started talking with Julius murmuring agreement in the background, Raffaele knew taking the phone had been the mistake he'd feared.

"I'll stay with her until Vasco arrives and make sure she doesn't escape again."

Jess stopped walking in the middle of the captain's cabin and turned to see Cristo nodding in response to Ildaria's words as he headed out of the room. She watched him pull the door closed behind him, and then shifted her gaze to Ildaria, watching with disinterest as the woman's relaxed pose disappeared and she suddenly moved to the desk in the corner. When the vampire retrieved a bottle of whiskey from a drawer and began to pour it into a glass, she turned away and glanced around the room. Jess wasn't really seeing it. She was just . . .

Well, frankly, she didn't know what she was doing. It was as if her mind was full of cobwebs just then, sticky, clingy cobwebs that were making it hard to think and obscuring everything around her. Really, it had felt like that since she'd fled the hotel suite. It was why she'd been slow to understand the guard at the embassy. Why she hadn't reacted more swiftly to finding herself trapped in the taxi with Ildaria and Cristo. Why she didn't now know what to do.

"Here. Drink this."

Jess stared blankly at the glass of amber liquid suddenly in front of her face, and simply turned away, muttering, "I'm not thirsty."

"This isn't for thirst. It's for shock," Ildaria said in a voice that was oddly dry and gentle at the same time. Moving in front of her, Ildaria took her arm to keep her from moving away and raised the glass to her lips. "Drink it, or I'll make you drink it. You know I can."

Jess met the woman's gaze briefly, but then shrugged and opened her mouth as Ildaria tipped the glass. Fire immediately poured into her mouth, searing her tongue and gums so that she swallowed just to get relief from it. The moment the liquid hit the back of her throat, though, it stole her breath. Eyes widening, Jess drew in a wheezing gasp, struggling to breathe, and the next moment found herself bent over, coughing violently while Ildaria patted her back and said with satisfaction, "Good! There we are. That'll clear out the cobwebs."

By the time the coughing fit ended and she was able to breathe again, Jess found herself sitting on the foot of the bed. Ildaria sat beside her, eyeing her closely.

"How do you feel now?" she asked once Jess's breathing returned to normal. "Better?"

Jess nodded and then shook her head. She could breathe again, and the whiskey had indeed helped to clear the cobwebs from her mind, but that left her having to think. Of course, the first thing her mind chose to consider was Raffaele, and the fact that she'd slept with him, and even maybe fallen a little bit in love with him, when he was a horrible, dead vampire just like Vasco and the soulless vampire bitch beside her.

"Okay, enough with the whole soulless vampire bitch thing," Ildaria snapped suddenly. "I'm neither soulless nor a vampire." She paused, and tilted her head thoughtfully before admitting, "I can be a bitch, though."

Jess blinked at the confession, but the woman quickly continued.

"However, that's got nothing to do with what I am, and I am not a vampire." Shifting impatiently, she added, "They don't even exist. Vampires are just so much paranormal nonsense. They aren't real," she assured her, and then said firmly, "I'm immortal. As are Vasco, and this Raffaele fellow who keeps floating naked through your thoughts."

Jess opened her mouth on a denial, but then closed it again. She couldn't deny it. She kept thinking of Raffaele . . . naked . . . laughing . . . making love to her. It didn't seem to matter to at least one part of her mind that he was a vampire. That part was just shrugging and spouting platitudes like, *Well, no one's perfect* and *That explains how he managed to hold you up against the wall in the shower while the two of you were getting busy. The guy is superstrong. Think of all the new positions you can try with him.*

Groaning, Jess closed her eyes and lowered her head, muttering, "What am I going to do?"

"Try those new positions with Vasco instead?" Ildaria suggested with amusement, drawing a scowl from Jess.

"This is serious!" she snapped, turning her fear and frustration on the female vampirate. "You may be fine being a soulless vampire bitch, but I—" Jess's rant died on a shocked gasp when Ildaria slapped her across the face.

"That was my inner bitch coming out," Ildaria said with a shrug when Jess gaped at her, and then added, "Besides, you seemed to be getting hysterical."

"I was not getting hyster—" Jess began between her teeth, only to be interrupted again.

"You must have been, because you called me a soulless vampire bitch again, when I know I've already explained to you that I'm not a vampire," she said dryly, and then clucked with exasperation. "Come on! You seem like a smart enough girl. Surely you realize that none of the monsters you read about as a kid are real?"

"You have fangs and drink blood," Jess pointed out with some exasperation of her own. "That sounds like one of those monsters from my childhood."

"But we're not soulless," Ildaria assured her. "We don't crawl out of graves and feed off the living. Well, I suppose we do feed a bit, but that's just—I mean, not all of us do. Some stick to bagged blood like your friends were consuming in your memory, and . . ." She paused and frowned briefly, and then said, "It might help for you to think of us as hemophiliacs with fangs."

"Hemophiliacs?" Jess asked with surprise.

"Yeah. Only instead of our blood not coagulating and there being the risk of our bleeding out, our bodies simply don't produce enough blood for us to survive healthily, so we have to get it elsewhere."

"Is it a disease?" she asked with a frown.

"No. Science," Ildaria answered at once.

"Science?" Jess peered at her with surprise.

Ildaria hesitated, and then shook her head. "Look, we don't have time for those kinds of explanations. Just keep in mind that we aren't monsters. We're just people with a few health issues. Okay?" She didn't wait for Jess to agree or disagree, but continued. "Right now I'm more interested in helping you figure out your feelings about the captain and your naked-Raff."

"I don't have any feelings about—" Jess began, and then paused to stare at her wide-eyed. "You want to help me?" That was the last thing she would have expected from this woman. In fact, it made no sense at all to her. "You put your mind-whammy thing on me to get me into the taxi and drag me here against my will, but now expect me to believe you want to *help* me?"

"It was my job to find and bring you to my captain," she said patiently. "I did that. But it won't bring him any joy as long as you're so confused about your feelings. You're a possible life mate for both men, and while you obviously love naked-Raff, I'm thinking if you got to know Vasco—"

"I'm not in love with naked-R—" Jess caught herself halfway through using the woman's nickname for Raffaele and scowled. "Stop calling him that."

"It's better than your nickname for him," Ildaria assured her, and then arched an eyebrow. "Penisocchio?"

Groaning, Jess closed her eyes. Was that nickname still floating around in her head? Maybe. She thought of the name every time he got an erection, and he seemed to get them a lot.

"Yeah, that's a life mate thing," Ildaria informed her. "Life mates are insatiable for each other. It's also why you fell so hard and fast for naked-Raff. Love comes fast for life mates. The—"

"I don't love him," Jess interrupted shortly, and not very honestly. "I hardly know him."

"Hello?" Ildaria knocked on her forehead. "I can read your mind, remember? And if how you're feeling and thinking isn't love, I'm a man in drag."

"Are you? How interesting," Jess snapped, refusing to admit her feelings even to herself.

Ildaria just shook her head. "Look, kiddo, there's no sense fighting your feelings. The nanos know what they're doing and made the two of you life mates for a reason."

"Nanos?" Jess asked, stiffening. "What nanos?"

Ildaria waved her question away. "Worry about that later. My point is, you love him, and not Vasco. But you're a life mate to Vasco too and could also love him if you gave yourself half the chance, and . . ." Noting her expression, Ildaria let her voice trail away, and then asked, "What?"

Agitated, Jess stood abruptly and paced across the cabin before swinging back to point out, "You're saying these nanos—whatever they are—know what they're doing and made me a possible life mate for Raff, who I admit is smart, and funny, and whom I actually do have a lot in common with. But then in the next breath you say I'm a possible life mate for Vasco too, which is . . ." She wanted to say *ridiculous*, but just shook her head and said, "I have nothing in common with him. In fact, we're polar opposites. First of all, he lives on the sea, and I get seasick, for heaven's sake."

"What?" Ildaria asked with surprise, and then narrowed her eyes and pointed out, "You didn't seem seasick the last time you were here. And you seem fine now."

"The boat isn't moving yet," she pointed out dryly. "And the last time I was on board I'd taken motion sickness pills because I was going on the Seaquarium trip."

"Oh." Ildaria frowned, but then rallied. "Well, he doesn't actually live on the ship anymore anyway. We just use it for the tours. He has a house on land."

Jess was shaking her head before she'd finished. "I don't care if he has a mansion. The man is crude, rude, vulgar, and unwashed. You could fry chips in the grease from his hair," she said coldly, and then, because she felt she had to be honest, reluctantly admitted, "Although I do like his taste in decorating," as she glanced around the spacious room in earth tones.

"There!" Ildaria said, brightening. "That's something. Maybe there are other things. Check out his bookshelf and see if you like the same books."

Jess scowled, but did turn to look over the books on the shelf behind her. She started out just quickly scanning them, but then slowed, her eyes widening with surprise as she noted several classics, and many titles she had herself. "These are just decoration, aren't they? Surely he doesn't read these?"

"Space is too tight on a ship to waste it on decorations. Those are his favorite books," Ildaria said with glee, the source of which Jess understood when the woman added, "And your favorites too."

She was in her head again, Jess realized with irritation, and wondered if Raffaele had tiptoed through her thoughts too at any time. Jeez, he was a vampire too. He probably had wandered through her mind a couple times. Had he controlled her too? Whirling on Ildaria, she asked, "Is there any way for you to know if Raffaele has been controlling me?"

"What?" Ildaria blinked at her in surprise, and then shook her head and said, "Never mind. I can guarantee he hasn't been controlling you."

"Really?" she asked hopefully. "How can you guarantee it?"

"Because life mates can neither read, nor control, each other. It's what makes them so special."

"Oh," Jess breathed, relaxing a little, and thinking that at least she hadn't been made to do anything she hadn't wanted. Her mistakes were her own. That was something anyway. Actually, it was more than something. She would have been completely crushed to learn that Raffaele had been controlling her and using her that way. Now she just had to deal with the fact that she'd been a willing participant in sex with a vampire, Jess thought, and sighed.

"Look, I know the captain seems to have a lot of rough edges, but most of that is just for show. Really, he's a diamond in the rough," Ildaria said quietly. When Jess met her gaze, she added, "He's a good man. A fair man. He's dragged every person on this ship from one scrape or another and takes care of us. He's a fine man, worthy of being loved."

"Why are you telling me this?" Jess asked with bewilderment.

"Because you need to know it to make an informed choice between the two men."

"No, I don't," Jess growled, turning away from her.

"Yes, you do. Look, right now you think you love naked-Raff, but that's just because you don't know Vasco. I'm sure that if you'd spent some time with him, you would have seen past his bluster, and coarseness, to the gem beneath and fallen for him. But you didn't get that chance. You jumped ship, and dropped right into naked-Raff's arms and fell for him instead. But this is a big decision. I want to help you make the right one, and you need to get to know both men to choose between them."

Jess stared at Ildaria silently, her thoughts actually on the woman rather than what she was saying. The first time she'd seen her—Jess shuddered at the memory of Tyler's horror, and Ildaria with blood dripping down her face. Shaking her head to remove the memory, she asked, "Why do you want to help me?"

"I don't. I want to help Vasco," Ildaria said at once. "He's old, and before you popped up he was showing signs of tiring of life. He needs a life mate."

Jess raised her eyebrows at that. Vasco didn't look old to her, but she simply said, "Maybe you are trying to help Vasco more than me, but I wouldn't have even expected that much from you after what you did to Tyler."

"Who?" Ildaria asked with confusion, and then her expression cleared and turned grim with recollection. Waving one hand impatiently, she said, "Oh, him. I didn't do anything he didn't deserve."

Jess eyed her dubiously. "He deserved having his family jewels chewed on?"

"He deserved to have them chewed *off*," Ildaria countered harshly. "As does any man who thinks to use them as a weapon against a woman."

"Tyler did that?" Jess asked with disbelief. "But he seems such a nice, quiet type."

Ildaria snorted at the words. "What's that old saying? Still waters run deep?"

"Yeaahhhh." She drew the word out, unsure what that had to do with anything.

"Well, those still deep waters also hide bottom feeders," Ildaria assured her, and when Jess continued to stare at her blankly, she sighed and explained, "Certain sharks are bottom feeders too."

"Really?" she asked with surprise.

"Oh, yeah, the saw shark, the horn shark, the zebra shark." Ildaria shrugged. "They're all bottom feeders."

"Oh," Jess said, and then grimaced. "It's hard to see Tyler as a shark, though."

"Well, he is," Ildaria said firmly, her expression icing over and eyes going distant as if she were recalling the incident. "He seemed nice when he first got on board. Polite and friendly, but after we were under way, he asked me to show him where the bathroom was. I was a little distracted with my chores at the time. There's a lot to do when we set sail, and I didn't think to read his mind, but quickly finished what I was doing and then told him to follow me and headed below to show him where the bathroom was. I was still thinking about what I had to do before we hit international waters when he suddenly grabbed me from behind and pushed me up against the wall, then ground against me. He was gripping me so tight that if I'd been some poor mortal girl, I would have come away with terrible bruises. I also would not have been able to escape his attentions."

"But you aren't mortal," Jess said solemnly.

"No, I'm not," she agreed. "So, I just asked what he thought he was doing. As I recall, he said, *'Come on, bitch, don't play hard to get. You know you want it. All you Dominican girls are little sluts, sucking every dick out there. Well, now you can suck mine.'*"

"No way!" Jess cried with dismay. She never would have believed it of Tyler.

"Yes way," Ildaria assured her, and then smiled grimly. "I said fine, but we'd have to move out of the hall in case someone came. He immediately grabbed my hand and dragged me down to the galley. I was reading his thoughts by then, and he was imagining what he'd do if I tried to run. He's a pretty sadistic little prick under all that preppy clothing," she added grimly.

Jess gave her head a slow shake, hardly able to credit it.

"His thoughts alone made me feel unclean," Ildaria said with remembered disgust, and then sighed. "Anyway, I wasn't running. I had my own plans for him. I wanted to make him sorry, and I wanted to scare him. When I got him to the galley, I immediately turned, caught him by the throat, and lifted him up against the wall. I wanted to choke him to death, but I just held him there and opened my mouth so he could see my fangs drop. He was so shocked and terrified at that point that I had to slip into his mind and control him to be sure he didn't piss himself. That would have ruined everything. Then I . . . Well, you saw what I did. I gave him what he wanted. I went down on him . . . in my own way. But he didn't get any pleasure from it. I made it as painful and horrifying for him as I could." Her mouth compressed and then she added, "I don't usually enjoy feeding off the hoof. But I surely did that time."

"Off the hoof?" Jess asked uncertainly.

"Biting a mortal," Ildaria explained. "I'd rather feed from bagged blood."

"Then why don't you?" she asked at once.

"Because blood doesn't come cheap," Ildaria said grimly. "The immortal blood banks here are run by a very corrupt family who has doubled and then tripled the price of blood just the last couple of years alone. Only the richest immortals can afford bagged blood now. Vasco can, and usually does, but a lot of us can't. That's why he started the shark feeding tours, to feed those of us who can't afford to feed ourselves."

Jess was listening wide-eyed. They had blood banks for vampires? Wow. Trying to understand, she asked, "But why would they charge so much if feeding . . . er . . . off the hoof is free? I mean, won't it just ensure the poorer vampires have to feed that way?"

"Because most can't feed off the hoof. It's not allowed here," Ildaria explained. "The only reason we get away with it is because Vasco takes us out into international waters before we feed. We aren't bound by the laws of the South American Council there."

"The South American . . ." Jess shook her head. First blood banks, now a council? How many of them were there, for God's sake?

"The South American Council is like our government. At least here in South America. There are other Councils in the other areas too," Ildaria said quietly. "They make our laws and have Enforcers or Hunters, like immortal police, to enforce those laws."

"Oh," Jess said faintly, and then frowned and pointed out, "But we weren't in international waters yet when I saw you biting Tyler."

"Yeah," she said on a sigh. "And I got in trouble for that. I could have been executed for it if the Council had got wind, but fortunately Vasco heard me out and just gave me a warning. But there will be no more warnings after this one," she said unhappily, and then raised her chin and shrugged. "Even so, I don't regret it. He deserved it."

Jess couldn't disagree. If Tyler had acted that way, he'd deserved what she'd done to him. It was just a shame he didn't remember it afterward, she thought. Instead, he'd come away thinking he'd had a great time.

Ildaria grimaced. "Unfortunately, Vasco wouldn't let me leave him the memory of his lesson." Shrugging, she added, "But I have some hope that maybe somewhere in a corner of his mind there is a little nugget of memory that will give him nightmares, or perhaps temper his behavior. If not, perhaps he will do the females of the world a favor and kill himself. I am hoping getting involved with your cousin will help push him in that direction. It is why I put it into their minds that they should like each other."

Jess blinked in surprise at her claim, and then burst out laughing. "Oh, that explains their behavior when they got back from the ship," she said with amusement. "And it's priceless. I can't think of two people who deserve each other more. She's as horrible in her own way as he is."

"Hmm." Ildaria nodded. "I read her thoughts. The woman is pure venom. She hates herself and enjoys nothing more than making everyone around her as miserable as she is."

Jess had no problem believing Ildaria's assessment. It was something she'd suspected herself for some time. But her thoughts now turned to the woman before her. Her first impression of Ildaria had been a very bad one, and misleading. The woman wasn't at all the monster Jess had believed she was. And yet that first impression of the woman had colored her impressions of everything else that had followed on this ship. It made her wonder if Ildaria wasn't right, if perhaps, had she not been so horrified by what she'd seen Ildaria doing, and frightened into escaping, she might have seen things differently.

Jess suspected she certainly would have ended up in bed with Vasco had she not seen Ildaria's fangs and realized everyone on board ship was a vampire. Well, if the man had managed to keep his mouth shut long enough for it to happen. Really, the attraction between her and Vasco had been off the charts crazy hot, just as it was with Raffaele. Even knowing he was a vampire, she hadn't been able to resist Vasco's kisses and caresses. Jess doubted she would have been able to avoid sleeping with him if she'd stayed on board. And she certainly wouldn't have jumped ship to swim miles to shore through shark infested waters if she hadn't been desperate to escape a ship full of vampires. So . . . would she have come to see under Vasco's roughness to the diamond Ildaria claimed lay beneath?

"I was afraid of that," Ildaria said wearily.

"Of what?" Jess asked uncertainly.

"That I was the reason you jumped ship," Ildaria explained on a sigh. "I gave the game away, and scared you enough that you jumped ship and fled right into the arms of naked-Raff." She shook her head unhappily. "If not for me, you might have stayed on board and fallen for Vasco instead." Regret covering her face, she breathed, "I messed up Vasco's getting his life mate."

"No," Jess said at once.

"Sí," Ildaria insisted. "And after all he's done for me too. God, I should be flogged."

"No," Jess said firmly. "If you want to blame someone, blame Tyler. If he hadn't attacked you, you wouldn't have set out to teach him a lesson, and so on. But none of that matters anyway," she added, and then hesitated, trying to think of a way to say it without being insulting. "Ildaria, I'm starting to kind of like you. I mean, at least I'm not scared of you anymore, and I understand why you did what you did to Tyler. And I even think your tough exterior hides a really nice person. But that doesn't mean I want to be—or even engage in a relationship with—a vampire."

"An immortal," Ildaria insisted.

Jess sighed with exasperation. "If it walks like a duck, and quacks like a duck, it's a duck."

Ildaria scowled at her with irritation. "But we don't walk and quack like ducks. We aren't soulless. We can go out in sunlight, and into churches.

Garlic has no effect on us at all except to give us bad breath like everyone else. We are just humans with a medical issue who need extra blood because our bodies don't produce enough. And many of us get that blood through donors and blood banks. I and the others under Vasco are only doing it this way because we can't afford to do it the legal way and we don't want to lose it and attack some poor mortal because we are starving. We are not vampires."

Jess considered her for a minute, and then asked abruptly, "Where did the fangs come from?"

Ildaria waved one hand impatiently. "Apparently, they evolved millennia ago to allow us to get the blood we needed before blood banks existed. And that is another way we differ from these mythological vampires," she added firmly. "We do not kill or turn everyone we bite. In fact, we never kill our hosts. That would be foolish, like killing a cow you want milk from. And we are only allowed to turn one mortal into an immortal in our life. That is so that we may turn our life mate. We aren't the monsters you think we are," she finished.

Jess stared at her silently, her words running through her mind. Ildaria was actually making her think that her kind, these immortals, truly weren't the horrors she'd first thought. Maybe they *were* different than the mythological vampires she'd been thinking them.

Except they drank blood, and could read minds and control humans, some part of her brain reminded her grimly. That still sounded like a vampire.

"We are human too," Ildaria said firmly, still reading her mind. "And we—" She paused and snapped her mouth closed when the cabin door opened.

Turning, Jess watched warily as Vasco entered the cabin. His gaze found Ildaria first, before moving around the room and settling on her. A smile immediately began to bloom on his face.

"There ye are, me lovely! Finally decided to stop playing hard to get, did ye? Well, I'm a happy man to hear it, I can tell ye," he said, starting toward her. "I've done nothing but dream about yer tuzzy-muzzy and jugs since last I enjoyed them. Come give me a kiss, lass."

Fourteen

"Where the hell are they?" Raffaele snapped, pacing the dock in front of Zanipolo and Santo.

"I am sure they will be here soon," Zanipolo said for the sixth time in little more than thirty minutes. "Lucian said the South American Council was sending Enforcers over at once to help clear up the situation."

"Well, how the hell long is 'at once'?" Raffaele snapped impatiently. It seemed to him that "at once" meant *eventually* or *in a while* here in Santo Domingo. Although the truth was he suspected it really meant *never.* The local enforcers hadn't done anything about Vasco after their earlier calls reporting on how he and his crew were luring tourists onto their ship and feeding off of them. Why would they do anything now? Jess was merely one more mortal tourist to them. Her being his life mate probably wouldn't matter much either. He wasn't from here. He too was just a tourist.

Raffaele growled under his breath, very much afraid that they were waiting for backup that would never come. He needed to get to Jess, but had promised Lucian and his uncle Julius that he would not drag Santo and Zani into a situation where it was the three of them against an entire pirate crew. Rogues didn't fight fair. They also generally played for keeps, and while he had great faith in his own and his cousins' abilities to take care of themselves, three against thirty or fifty rogue immortals was . . . well, those weren't good odds. Still, the only reason he'd agreed to wait at the time was because Santo had managed to read from the younger female immortal's mind that Vasco wasn't waiting on board his ship, and would be a while returning. Things had changed, though.

Whirling impatiently, he stared out at the sloop, and the small rowboat next to it. The captain had returned just moments ago, paddled across the water by a couple of his men who had brought the boat in to get him. He was back . . . and Raffaele could no more leave Jess to the rogue's tender mercies than he could drag Santo and Zani into this mess.

He'd go alone, Raffaele decided grimly. He'd have his cousins ride out to the ship with him, but leave them in the boat while he snuck on board. He'd then find Jess, throw her overboard for his cousins to collect, and then follow if they managed that first part without being discovered, or stay to fight to give Jess and his cousins a chance to escape if they were discovered.

"Now that Vasco has returned, they could sail away with her," Santo said quietly. As if Raffaele hadn't already thought of that himself. That was what worried him the most. Now that the captain was aboard, the boat could leave at any moment. Of course, Vasco's return meant other things might happen now as well. Things Raffaele didn't even want to think about. Jess was his, but if Vasco too was a possible life mate, she would be helpless in the face of life mate passion.

Growling under his breath, he turned back toward the harbor and quickly scanned the nearby boats.

"Where are you going?" Zanipolo asked with alarm when he started to stride off the dock.

"To get us a boat," he growled.

Jess stared at Vasco like a deer caught in the headlights of an approaching vehicle. Then panic managed to kick her out of her frozen state, and she began backing quickly away, squawking, "No."

Much to her amazement, Vasco actually stopped. Eyes wide, and head tilted to the side like a dog that didn't quite understand a command, he frowned and then asked, "No?" as if he'd never heard the word before.

Pausing, Jess breathed out a sigh of relief, and then said firmly, "No. I know you think I'm some kind of life mate or something to you," she began, and then squawked and started backpedaling again when he continued forward once more.

"Aye, lass. You're me life mate," he said, following her around the bed. "The yin to me yang. The light o' me life. We're going to have a grand time, you and me. Sailing the seas, shagging our way around the world."

"No, we're not," she assured him, coming up against the bed and then leaping onto it and quickly running across to the other side and hopping off when he lunged after her. Jess started toward the end of the bed, but then saw that rather than follow her over the bed, he was walking toward the end of it as well. Frustration rising up within her, she stopped and begged, "Please just stop and listen to me."

Much to her surprise, he did. Pausing at the other corner, Vasco peered at her quizzically. "What is it, lass? What has ye all a'twitter?"

"A'twitter?" she asked with disgust, and then shook that away to get to the point and said, "I don't want to be a vampire, and if I did," she added quickly when he started to open his mouth, "I'd choose Raffaele as my mate."

That made his mouth snap shut, she noted, and watched him stare at her with a growing frown.

"Raffaele is one of those immortals ye've been traveling with," he said with displeasure.

"It turns out she's a possible life mate to him too," Ildaria said quietly, reminding them of her presence.

"What?" Vasco bellowed, turning on the woman with dismay.

Ildaria nodded apologetically. "And she's fallen in love with him."

"I don't love him," Jess said on a sigh. "I can't. He's a vampire. And I don't want to be a vampire, or a vampire's girlfriend, or a vampire's life mate, or any of those things. I just want—" Jess cut herself off because what she wanted was impossible. But then she found herself just saying it anyway. "I want Raffaele not to be a vampire. I want to be able to continue our relationship. I want to visit him in Italy like we planned, and go with him to visit his relatives in Canada, and I want him to come to Montana and see where I live. I want him to eat tiramisu off my body, and to have mind-blowing sex on tabletops. I want to watch *Supernatural* with him, and action movies. I want to see the buildings he's designed. I want to spend the next forty or fifty years enjoying his company, talking about history, doing crosswords with him, and maybe even someday having children, who could give us grandchildren to spoil and . . ."

She fell silent and shook her head, because she couldn't have any of that. The chance for any of it happening had died when she'd seen Zanipolo's fangs as he and Santo had fed on the bags of blood in the hotel and she'd realized from their conversation that not only were they vampires, but Raffaele was one too.

For a moment, the silence in the cabin was so complete you could have heard a pin drop. Then Vasco stood abruptly and strode to the door, barking, "Stay with her, Ildaria. And make sure she stays put."

"Aye-aye, Capitan," Ildaria said solemnly as the door closed on the man.

Sighing, Jess dropped to sit on the side of the bed. She was completely exhausted, and utterly depressed. So much so that she didn't even care where Vasco had gone, or what would happen next. She really just wanted to curl up into a ball and sleep. She hadn't got much rest the night before. She'd caught short naps each time she'd fainted, but she didn't think those had lasted long before she'd woken again. Jess was sure that if she could just nap for a bit, she'd be better able to deal with the mess her life was in.

"Close your eyes and try to rest, then," Ildaria said quietly.

Jess felt a stirring of resentment that the woman kept reading her thoughts, but was too exhausted to sustain the feeling, and simply crawled up the bed to lay her head on the pillow and close her eyes.

"The rowboat's heading for shore!"

Raffaele barely heard Zanipolo's shout over the roar of the boat engine, but it didn't matter. He'd spotted the small vessel himself the moment they'd ridden around the large cruise ship and approached the sloop. It hadn't moved far from the pirate ship yet. Just a rowboat's length, but it was headed toward shore, he noted, and quickly scanned the occupants, surprised to see Vasco among them. He'd been convinced that the moment the pirate captain returned to his ship he would head to his cabin to try to seduce Jess. The fact that he wasn't, but was already leaving, was curious. Raffaele would have been doing his damnedest to seduce Jess had their positions been reversed.

"He's seen us," Zanipolo said when Vasco suddenly stood in the rowboat and stared straight at them.

Raffaele merely nodded and watched as Vasco waved at them, then sat back down again. The men immediately began to row in the opposite direction, moving back toward the sloop now.

"What do you think that means?" Santo asked behind him.

"I have no idea," Raffaele admitted, and slipped back into the thoughts of their pilot to direct him to take their craft up next to the pirate ship. Moments later, they were coming to a stop next to the sloop, just behind the smaller boat. It was empty. Vasco and his men hadn't waited for them. They'd already tied off the rowboat and started climbing up the rope netting that hung down the side of the sloop.

"Ahoy!"

Raffaele glanced up at that call to see that Vasco and his men had paused halfway up and were looking down at them. Even as he noted that, the pirate captain called out, "You can release yer boat captain, there. We'll take ye to shore when ye're ready."

Vasco didn't wait for a response, but then turned and continued climbing.

"What do you think?" Zanipolo asked quietly.

"I think we start climbing and send our driver on his way," Raffaele said grimly, and then glanced to his cousins and added, "You don't have to come with me. You can have the pilot take you back to shore and wait there for me if you want."

"And leave you to handle a boatload of pirates on your own?" Zanipolo asked with disbelief, and then snorted. "I do not think so, *cugino.* You don't get to have *all* the fun on this trip."

"What he said," Santo said firmly, and leaned out of the boat to grasp the netting.

Nodding, Raffaele turned to the man they'd hijacked. He quickly rearranged his memories to make him think he'd agreed to bring them out for a fee. He then handed him some money and murmured a thank-you before grabbing the netting and starting to climb up. It wasn't a hard climb, but it was awkward. Climbing netting wasn't quite like climbing a ladder, but he managed it and was soon grasping the railing and peering around at the situation he was leading his cousins into as he hefted himself up and over it.

Raffaele wouldn't have been surprised to find the crew all present with swords drawn, ready to make him walk the plank. But the only people nearby were Vasco and the man Jess had called Cristo. Neither man had their swords out. In fact, the moment Raffaele's feet landed on the deck, Vasco stepped forward and held his hand out in greeting instead.

"Welcome aboard," he said stiffly, and then added, "We were just coming to fetch ye back to the boat when ye came around the cruise ship."

Raffaele took the hand and shook it, but eyed the man suspiciously as he asked, "Why?"

"So ye could come talk some sense into the lass," he announced as Zanipolo and Santo came over the rail and joined them. Expression turning solemn, Vasco added, "One of us should end up with a life mate here. And ye're the one she says she wants."

Raffaele released the breath he hadn't realized he'd been holding and nodded. "Thank you."

"Don't thank me. She's the one who picked ye," he said wryly.

"But you didn't sail off with her and try to change her mind," Raffaele pointed out.

"I considered it," Vasco admitted with a grin, slapping him on the shoulder and urging him to move away from the rail as he added, "In truth, I considered killing ye and claiming her too."

When Raffaele glanced at him sharply, he offered a shark's smile and shrugged. "Wouldn't you?"

"*Sì*, I would," Raffaele admitted, aware that Santo and Zanipolo had stiffened at his back, and that Cristo was behind his cousins. It didn't worry him over much, though. Raffaele was sure Zani and Santo could handle the man. He was equally sure he could handle Vasco. Of course, the rest of the crew might be a problem, but hopefully they wouldn't attack once their captain was dead. Or would be kind enough to attack in small groups, he thought, and offered the pirate a toothy smile of his own now. "So, is that your plan? To try to kill us?"

"No. It would hurt her too much," Vasco said seriously. "So, fool that I am, I'm giving her what will make her happy instead. You."

"Big of you," Raffaele said quietly, his muscles relaxing. He meant what he said. It was big of the pirate. He didn't think he could have given her up. He might very well have killed Vasco to have Jess.

The pirate shrugged. "They say an immortal will die for their life mate. This isn't dying," he pointed out, and turned away to continue walking, but muttered what Raffaele thought sounded like, "It just feels like it," under his breath.

Raffaele didn't respond to the comment. He was quite sure the man hadn't meant him to hear it, and wouldn't appreciate anything he might say at that point. Instead, he eyed the pirate with curiosity as they continued across the deck. While feeding on mortals was rogue behavior, Vasco didn't seem like a rogue to him in that moment. Rogues were usually madmen, immortals pushed past the point of sanity by their loneliness as well as all they'd seen in their long lives. A life mate could save an immortal from that, if they found them in time. Had having Jess nearby, even briefly, cleared his thoughts enough to push the insanity away? Raffaele wondered about that, but quickly cleared his thoughts when Vasco stopped at a door leading below deck and turned to face him.

The pirate's eyes narrowed on him, but if he caught a wisp of what Raffaele had been thinking, he didn't address it, but simply said, "Ye're going to have some talking to do. She wants ye, but she thinks we're vampires and is horrified by it. In truth, I'm not sure she can be talked around, but . . ." He shrugged and turned to open the door.

It seemed to Jess that she'd just drifted off to sleep when a hand on her cheek startled her awake. Gasping in surprise, she sat up abruptly, ready to fight off Vasco if he'd returned to try to seduce her. But it was Ildaria she saw straightening from waking her.

"Sorry. I didn't mean to startle you. I didn't think you'd drifted off already, and we've got company."

The woman stepped aside, and Jess's eyes widened incredulously when she saw that the room was now full of men. Vasco, Cristo, Raffaele, Zanipolo, and Santo were all in the room. Every one of them was peering at her with a similar expression on their faces, one that was somewhere between a grimace and a smile. As if they weren't sure if they were welcome.

Jess suspected she probably had a similar expression as she peered over them. She wasn't sure how welcome they were either. She was too confused at that point to understand much of anything.

It was Vasco who finally broke the silence. Shifting impatiently, he glanced from Jess to Raffaele and said, "Well, here ye are, then. Start talking, Notte. I'm not going to do it for ye."

Irritation flashed across Raffaele's face, and he turned to glare at the pirate. "Perhaps if you gave us some privacy?" he began, but paused when Vasco snorted and shook his head.

"Not bloody likely. This is my cabin, and my ship," he pointed out, and then added on a grin, "Besides, I might yet have a chance if ye muck this up."

Raffaele scowled at the man, but then turned to Jess and sighed, his expression morphing into a pained smile before he opened his mouth to speak. But nothing came out and he closed it again, and then frowned uncertainly.

When he opened his mouth again, only to close it once more without speaking, Vasco rolled his eyes and said, "Oh, rot it!"

Jess shifted wide eyes to the man and shrank back slightly as he moved up beside the bed, but he didn't touch or even really get close to her. He stopped next to the bed, but a good foot away, and said, "After what ye said, I went to fetch the man back to ye. But as it turned out, I didn't have far to go. He was already making his way out to the ship."

Jess frowned, her gaze shifting from Vasco to Raffaele to see him nod almost stiffly. She presumed he was verifying what Vasco had said, but turned her gaze back to the pirate and asked, "Why were you bringing him back?"

"So the two o' ye could talk, o' course," he said with exasperation, and then his expression sobered and he added, "We need to sort ye out, lass, before ye make the biggest mistake o' yer life."

Jess's eyebrows rose in surprise. "What mistake?"

"For some unknown reason, ye've gone and fallen in love with the Notte here," he said between clenched teeth, as if just saying it left a bitter taste in his mouth.

Jess noted that absently as her gaze automatically followed his gesture toward Raffaele. It slid over his impassive expression to the encouraging smile on Zanipolo's face before she glanced back to Vasco and opened her mouth on an automatic protest that she didn't, *couldn't*, love him. But she let it close again without uttering the lie when Vasco held up a hand to silence her.

"I know," he said dryly. "Ye're telling yourself it's too soon, and it can't possibly be love and all that mortal rot. But that doesn't change the fact that ye *do* love him. Unfortunately, being mortal, ye're also horrified at the idea of loving what ye think is a vampire. Or, at least, something that to you seems so close to one as to be indistinguishable." Frowning, he shook his head. "But, lass, ye're laboring under the influence o' years o' horror stories in books, movies, and such, and they all don't mean a fig here. This is yer life, yer *future*. Ye need to know what ye'd be giving up, and ye need to know the facts to make a proper choice."

"What choice?" Jess asked warily.

"Yer heart's chosen the Notte, that means ye've now got two more choices," he said solemnly. "Either ye accept that ye love the man and agree to be his life mate, or ye reject both him and what he is."

Jess swallowed, but didn't comment. Her mind was busy running around in circles arguing over what she felt, wanted, and knew. She was still having trouble accepting that there were even vampires out there. The knowledge had rocked her world when she'd first seen Ildaria with her fangs and her face covered in blood, and was still rocking it now. Her feelings for Raffaele on top of that . . . well, that was just more turmoil in the tornado of her mind.

"Now, if ye accept and agree to be the Notte's life mate," Vasco continued, and then paused and blew out a long breath, before saying, "If ye do that, the two o' ye will be among the lucky ones. Ye'll have a mate who would never stray. Who values ye above everything and everyone in his life. Ye'll be his light in the dark, his heart, and his reason for being and he'll treat ye accordingly," he assured her. "He'll give his life for ye if need be, lass. Because that's what a life mate is worth to an immortal, his very life."

Jess stared at Vasco through a sudden glaze of tears that blurred his image, and then lowered her head to hide those tears. She'd heard more than his words as he spoke. She'd heard his heart. The pirate wasn't just speaking of Raffaele here. She was quite sure he was speaking of himself too. He'd give his life for her, but he'd also give her up.

"Now doesn't that sound grand?" Vasco asked abruptly when she remained silent.

Jess smiled wryly, and blinked her unshed tears away as she thought that it did sound wonderful. But there was always a catch, she thought next, and raised her head to say, "But he'd also turn me into a vampire too."

"An immortal," Vasco corrected firmly. "But yes, he'd—"

"Not necessarily," Raffaele interrupted, moving up on the other side of the bed across from Vasco as he finally joined the conversation. "Not if you do not wish it. That would be up to you," he assured her.

Vasco scowled at him, and then turned to Jess to add, "But ye should know that if ye do agree to be his life mate, but refuse the turn, ye're damning him to watching ye age and die, and then having to continue without ye. And that's crueler than ye can imagine to an immortal."

"But worth it," Raffaele inserted.

Vasco shook his head. "Ye think that now, Notte, but I can tell ye it's soul destroying. Ye spend the entire time fretting over their well-being, fearing every minute they're away from ye. Worrying even when they're with ye that some accident might befall them that will steal them away before their time. And then by the time they are old and dying, ye almost wish that accident had happened and spared ye what feels like dying a bit every day as ye watch them struggle for life in a failing body." His mouth tightened. "By the time they take their last breath, ye want nothing more than to lie down next to them and set the bed on fire so ye can go with them."

Raffaele had turned to scowl at Vasco with irritation at the interruption when he'd first started speaking, but slowly that expression had turned solemn, and full of respect. When the pirate fell silent, Raffaele said, "You have already had a life mate. One who chose not to turn."

It wasn't a question, but Vasco nodded and told him, "It's a rough road to travel."

Raffaele nodded with respect, and then said, "But so is surviving over two thousand years without one. I won't turn her if she does not wish it, and will be grateful for what little time I—"

"Hang on," Jess snapped sharply, glaring now as her brain processed what he'd said. "Two thousand years? Are you fricking kidding me? You aren't saying you're that old?"

Raffaele turned a startled expression to her, but admitted, "I was born in 120 B.C."

When Jess stared at him in horror, Vasco grinned and said, "Hmm. I could tell he was old when I first saw him, but even I am surprised at just how ancient he is."

Jess just gaped at the pair of them, unable to believe it. Turning her focus on Raffaele, she pointed out, "But that makes you two thousand, one hundred and—" She stopped and shook her head, her mind boggling. She'd been having crazy monkey sex with someone older than . . . well, anything she could think of. Good Lord! She was lucky parts of him hadn't snapped off while they were doing it.

A snicker from Ildaria and the men at the foot of the bed drew her attention, and she could see the way they were eyeing her forehead. They'd obviously heard her thoughts. Jess scowled at them for their rudeness, and then turned to glance between Raffaele and Vasco. "How is that possible? You don't age and die?"

Raffaele shook his head almost apologetically, but Vasco's eyebrows rose and he asked with amusement, "Well, why did ye think we're called immortals, lovey?"

Jess just stared at him. Why indeed? she wondered, but looked them each over more closely. Neither of them looked a day over twenty-five or so. Actually, she realized as her gaze slid over the others, none of them did. But Raffaele was over two thousand years old? Then how old were the rest of them? Her gaze slid around the group again and then settled on Vasco and she asked, "How old are you?"

"I'm not sure," he said with a shrug. "I don't keep track. It's just a number," he said with unconcern. But when thunderclouds immediately started gathering on her forehead, he quickly added, "However, I was born in 1519."

The thunderclouds dissipated at once, blown away by horror as Jess did the math. "So, you're nearly five hundred years old?" she asked in disbelief.

"Aye. A mere pup compared with the Notte here," Vasco pointed out with a grin, as if he thought that might give him a leg up.

Jess just shook her head and glanced around at the others. When her gaze settled on Ildaria, the woman sighed and said, "I was born in 1812."

At least the woman was younger than the U.S.A., Jess thought, relaxing a little. Her gaze skated to Cristo, but he remained silent and stiff lipped. Shrugging, she shifted her gaze to Raffaele's cousin Santo.

"I was born in 965," the big man rumbled, and then added, "B.C."

While Jess was blinking over that, Zanipolo spoke up, offering cheerfully, "Well, I was only born in 1928, so I guess that makes me the youngest."

"Dear God," Jess breathed, and closed her eyes, letting herself fall back on the bed.

Fifteen

"Are ye all right, lass? Ye've gone a might pale and don't appear to be handling this as well as I'd hoped."

Jess opened her eyes to find Vasco's concerned face over her. Apparently, he'd feared she'd fainted when she'd dropped back and closed her eyes. Raffaele had too, she guessed when his head appeared as well, his expression also full of concern.

"Of course she's not all right. Look at her, she's white as a sheet," Raffaele growled, and then offered Jess a pained smile and suggested, "Try to take slow and steady breaths, my love. Deep breaths, give your brain a chance to process."

She was processing. And what she was coming up with was that these people were all really freaking old! Good Lord, Santo was nearly three thousand years old! Raffaele wasn't much better at more than twenty-one hundred years old, but even Zanipolo, who was the youngest of them, was almost one hundred. Well, a decade or thereabouts short of it, but still . . .

Shaking her head, she breathed, "Dear God, you must all see me as little more than a baby."

"Oh, lovey, no," Vasco said at once. "Why no red-blooded man could look at those lovely jugs o' yers and think ye a baby."

Jess closed her eyes on a groan at that, but opened them again when Raffaele actually growled. Seriously, he growled under his breath like a dog, and then snapped, "Stop looking at her jugs."

"I can look all I want," Vasco snapped back. "This is my ship. So as long as she doesn't mind, I'll be looking."

"Well, she obviously *minds*," Raffaele snarled, and then added, "And I certainly mind."

"I don't care what *you* mind or *don't* mind," Vasco assured him grimly.

Jess closed her eyes on their bickering, thinking that for all they were supposed to be so ancient, they still sounded like children fighting over a toy. Three thousand years old, her mind screamed silently. How was that even possible? Ildaria had said—

She sat up abruptly, forcing the men to stop arguing and straighten to avoid banging heads with her, and then glared accusingly at Ildaria. "You said you were immortal not a vampire, and that it was because of science not some paranormal nonsense."

"Sí." Ildaria nodded, and moved closer to the foot of the bed.

"But Santo is nearly three thousand years old," Jess pointed out, and glanced to him to see him nod solemnly, confirming his age. Turning back to Ildaria, she arched her eyebrows. "What the hell kind of science was around three thousand years ago? They didn't even have toilet paper back then, for God's sake."

"They did in Atlantis," Zanipolo put in, stepping to the foot of the bed too.

"Atlantis?" Jess asked, staring at him blankly.

"Actually, Atlantis did not have toilet paper," Santo rumbled, moving forward as well.

"Then how did they wipe their arses?" Cristo asked with surprise, joining the others so that Jess found herself alone on the bed but almost surrounded by the group.

"I gather they had a system not dissimilar to the bidet seats that are now being developed and sold," Santo said with a shrug.

"Bidet seats?" Ildaria asked uncertainly.

"Oh! Yeah, yeah," Zanipolo said suddenly, and nodded. "I know what you mean. Those seats they've brought out with the washing and drying thingies in them."

"*Sì,*" Santo rumbled. "I was told that they would have considered toilet paper to be barbaric and—"

"Hello," Jess growled, not interested in the toiletry habits of Atlanteans. Or anyone else, really. Glaring at Ildaria, she pointed out, "You still haven't answered my question."

"Zanipolo did," Santo said solemnly.

Jess peered at him uncertainly. "All Zanipolo said was that Atlantis had toilet paper."

"*Sì*, which is wrong," he informed her, just adding to her frustration. She really didn't want another go-round on potty talk.

"What Santo means," Raffaele said, appearing to recognize her mounting irritation, "is that it was Zanipolo's way of saying that Atlantis had the advanced technology to create immortals, and did," he explained quietly, and when she turned to him, he added, "Although it was not wholly on purpose. Originally, they were just trying to develop a noninvasive way to heal injuries and fight disease."

"Noninvasive," Jess murmured, and then her eyes widened. "The nanos!"

"*Sì,*" Raffaele said with surprise. "How did you—?"

"Ildaria mentioned them earlier. She said nanos decided we were life mates, but didn't explain what exactly the nanos are."

"Ah." Raffaele nodded. "Well, they are tiny bioengineered robots that are injected into the bloodstream. They use blood for . . . well, everything," he said wryly. "To travel through the body, to propel themselves, to effect repairs, and even to create new nanos if more are necessary to tend to matters."

"Aye," Vasco said now. "The scientists of Atlantis were brilliant. Unfortunately—or fortunately, depending on how ye look at it—after developing the nanos and getting them to work with the body, the bastards didn't bother to program them right."

"What do you mean?" Jess asked with surprise, but it was Raffaele who answered.

"He means that rather than program nanos for each individual possible wound or sickness that might occur, the scientists made one program with a map of both a healthy male and a healthy female body at their peak condition, and instructed the nanos to keep their host at that peak condition."

"It was only once they started poking them into people that they realized what they'd inadvertently done," Vasco said dryly, and when she peered at him in question, he explained. "The human body is at its peak at between twenty-five and thirty years old. After that, it's all downhill."

"So, if one of the people they tested it on was older . . ." Jess said slowly.

"The nanos repaired the damage aging had caused and they became young again," Raffaele finished.

"But that wasn't the only surprise they encountered," Zanipolo said now. "The nanos were supposed to deactivate, break down, and be flushed from the body when they finished their work. But between air pollution, pollens in the air, and the traces of viruses on every surface . . ." He shrugged. "They just never deactivate."

Jess bit her lip, putting together everything she'd learned, and then said, "I suppose they need a lot of blood to do their work?"

"More than a human body can produce," Raffaele said quietly. "In Atlantis, they dealt with that issue through transfusions. But when Atlantis fell—"

"How did it fall?" Jess interrupted with curiosity. A society as advanced as that shouldn't have fallen easily. At least, she didn't think it should.

"Earthquakes or some such thing," Vasco said with a frown. "Apparently, Atlantis slid into the ocean. Everyone was lost except for those who had been experimented on with the nanos."

Jess smiled wryly. One point to Mother Nature, then. No technology could beat her.

"The survivors," Raffaele continued, "found themselves crawling out of the ruins to join a world that wasn't nearly as advanced as theirs."

Eyes narrowing, Jess tilted her head and asked, "How is that possible? I mean, how could the Atlanteans have been so advanced when everyone around them was still living in huts and huddling around fires?"

"Apparently, Atlantis was isolated from the rest of the world by mountains and ocean. It discouraged anyone from approaching them and left them to develop at their own speed, which was obviously faster than everyone else."

"Okaaayyy." Jess drew the word out with disbelief. "But what about the Atlanteans? If they were messing with nanos, they must have had modern forms of transportation that could have got around those mountains and the ocean. So, again, why were they so isolated? Why didn't they go looking outside of Atlantis?"

She watched the others peer blankly at each other, and then Raffaele admitted, "I don't know. My grandparents never explained that and I didn't think to ask. I guess I shall have to do that when next I see them."

"Your grandparents?" Jess squeaked.

"Sì," Raffaele smiled faintly. "They were among the people the nanos were tested on in Atlantis."

Jess remained silent for a moment, but her mind *wasn't* silent. It was squawking up a storm. Dear God, the man was over two thousand years old and still had grandparents who lived! Most people she knew started losing them under twenty, in grade school even. One grandma or grandpa would have a heart attack or something and pass here, and another would follow a few years later, maybe of cancer. And from what she could tell, most people had lost them all by the time they were fifty. Yet, Raffaele still had his. And they'd been alive since before the fall of Atlantis, whenever that had happened. Obviously, before Christ since Raffaele was older than that.

Unbelievable, she thought. As unbelievable as everything else she'd been told, she supposed. And yet Jess believed it all. It was just too nuts to be made up. Besides, she doubted they'd all got together to come up with such a fantastical story.

Sighing, she shook her head and thought that if they lived that long, they definitely deserved the name *immortals*. The thought made her frown.

"So, you can't die," she said now. "These nanos will just repair any injury, and fight off any disease?"

"We can die," Vasco said even as Raffaele opened his mouth to respond. "We don't age, we don't even get sick, and killing us is hard to do, but can be done."

Jess narrowed her eyes and guessed, “Beheading?” That was how zombies were killed, she thought, and noted the winces from the others around the bed.

“We are not zombies,” Ildaria said stiffly.

“And beheading won’t necessarily kill us if ye stick the head back on the neck quick enough,” Vasco informed her, and then added, “The nanos heal it up. I had it happen once.”

“What?” Jess asked with dismay, and he nodded his head, which didn’t fall off his neck, despite having once been removed.

“Aye. I was executed for piracy around about 1535,” he explained. “I was just a lad of sixteen at the time. Considered a man then, but really, too stupid to be out on me own. I hooked up with a bad lot o’ pirates. We got caught and boarded on my first voyage with them, and were all executed. But me brothers took me body away right fast and put me back together. The nanos did the rest.” Grinning at her horrified expression, he lifted his chin to show her his neck. “Not even a scar.”

Jess shifted to her knees and moved to the edge of the bed to get a closer look at his neck. But there was nothing to see, not even the hint of a scar. His skin was as smooth as a baby’s bottom, she noted with wonder.

“Obviously, you did not learn your lesson,” Raffaele said stiffly, drawing Jess’s gaze his way. “You still sail a pirate ship and act the rogue.”

When Vasco lowered his head to eye Raffaele narrowly, Jess dropped back to sit on the bed with a sigh. Hoping to prevent the two men from arguing again, she asked the first question that came to mind. “So, if beheading doesn’t do it, how can you be killed?”

The men continued to glare at each other over her head and it was Ildaria who said, “Beheading can kill us if the head isn’t returned to the body quickly enough. But the surest way to kill us is fire.”

Jess glanced to her with surprise. “The nanos don’t protect you against that?”

“The nanos will heal us if we survive a fire,” Zanipolo assured her. “But their one flaw is that they’re highly flammable. And they make us highly flammable too. Fire is death to us.”

“Oh.” Jess considered that and then said, “So, the nanos weren’t programmed to give you fangs and . . . stuff," she finished, waving one hand vaguely.

"No," Raffaele assured her, withdrawing from his war of glares with Vasco to smile at her faintly. "That evolved after the fall. The world the survivors found themselves in after Atlantis . . . Well, they obviously didn't have blood banks and intravenous gear. There was no way to get the blood they needed except from the people the Atlanteans found themselves living among."

"Surely a couple of your scientists survived and could cobble together something?" she protested.

Santo shook his head. "None of the individuals given the nanos were scientists, or even doctors."

"Of course they weren't," Jess said dryly, thinking that the people who had got the nanos had been little better than lab rats to these scientists who wouldn't have risked trying them out themselves until they had them perfect. Their loss, she supposed. Only those lab rats had survived.

"So?" she said now, and prompted, "The Atlanteans were suddenly in a new, much less advanced world, and . . . ?"

"Well . . ." Raffaele frowned, seeming to need a moment to regather his thoughts, and then said, "The nanos had been programmed to keep their hosts at their peak condition. They needed blood to do that. So, they took it upon themselves to ensure their hosts could get the blood they needed. To do that, they forced a sort of evolution on their hosts."

"Like the fangs to get the blood they needed," Jess suggested.

"Aye," Vasco said. "And increased strength, and speed to be better hunters."

"Better hearing and sight," Ildaria put in.

"Plus, amazing night vision too," Zanipolo added. "And the ability to read the minds of, and even control, their quarry so that they could get what they needed to survive."

"That was before blood banks, though," Raffaele said, taking up the thread again. "When we didn't have a choice. Now that society has progressed to having blood banks and such, most of us are socially evolved enough not to want to bite mortals to get the blood we need. We prefer to get it through bagged blood from our blood banks, supplied by voluntary donors. In fact, North America and South America have both outlawed feeding any other way except via bagged blood," he announced, and then added, "Except in an emergency or cases of consent between an immortal and a mortal lover."

Jess frowned at Raffaele's words, knowing how they would affect Vasco and Ildaria. It seemed obvious Raffaele had no idea why Vasco did what he did and that he did it in international waters, so wasn't actually rogue. It was equally obvious that he didn't think much of the man because of that, and was poking him. Deciding it was high time he knew, Jess said, "Raffaele, Vasco isn't—"

She paused and glanced sharply at Vasco when he touched her arm to get her attention. The contact had sent a shaft of awareness and excitement shooting through her arm. They were both silent for a moment, staring at each other, and then Vasco cleared his throat, and smiled at her gently.

"Ye needn't defend me, lass. I don't give a rat's arse what he thinks o' me." Turning his gaze to Raffaele then, his voice grew chilly as he added, "And ye're not wholly correct, Notte. Biting under any situation is considered rogue behavior here now. The emergency and lover provisos were redacted by our Council."

Raffaele stiffened and frowned. "Really?"

"*Sí*. So, I hope ye've not bitten our beautiful lass, here. If so, and an Enforcer or someone from the Council reads it from her mind, you might find yourself on a pyre o' burning wood."

It didn't sound as if Vasco thought that would be too much of a tragedy, Jess noticed, but was more concerned with Raffaele's answer to the question. It had, after all, been one of her first concerns after seeing Zanipolo's fangs and the two men feeding on the bagged blood. Had Raffaele bitten her? Was that why she'd fainted after sex each time?

"Of course I haven't bitten her," Raffaele snapped, scowling at the pirate. "She had no idea what we were, so couldn't give consent, and—unlike you—I am not a—"

"The fainting was because you are possible life mates," Ildaria announced, apparently having read the questions in Jess's mind, and no doubt more than happy to use answering it for her as a way to prevent a fight between her captain and Raffaele. When the two men fell silent, and Jess glanced to her in question, the woman nodded. "It is common between life mates to faint after—"

Ildaria stopped abruptly, and Jess followed her gaze to Vasco just in time to glimpse the pain on his face. But then his expression closed, hiding it.

Sighing, Jess lowered her head. The things Ildaria had told her about him suggested Vasco was a good man. There was much more to him than the bluff, laughing pirate he presented to the world. In fact, she'd noted more than once that when he got distracted, his speech lost much of its colorful-sounding piratiness. Which she knew wasn't a word, but felt should be. There was no other way to describe the man when he was in full-on pirate mode.

"So," Vasco said abruptly, drawing her attention again. "Knowing what we are now, can ye see yer way clear to being a life mate and spending the rest o' yer days enjoying the bliss of shared pleasure with your life mate, and—"

"Whoa, back it up," Jess interrupted sharply. Arching an eyebrow, she asked, "Shared pleasure?"

Vasco peered at her nonplussed for a moment and then glanced from her to Raffaele and back. "I assumed from the things ye've said, that the two o' ye had . . ." He glanced back to Raffaele. "Did ye not show her the benefits o' shared pleasure?"

Raffaele glared at him resentfully for a moment, but then sighed and admitted, "No. I couldn't explain what she was experiencing, so didn't let her touch me. Or tried not to at least."

Jess eyed him silently, recalling the few times she'd managed to touch him. She remembered feeling a wave of excitement and pleasure roll through her. It had seemed to come out of nowhere, and couldn't be explained by what Raffaele had been doing at the time. Was that the shared pleasure they were talking about?

"Oh, lass," Vasco breathed, turning on her with wonder. "Ye've so much yet to experience. The Notte's barely scratched the surface. Ye've no idea o' what ye can do. How pleasuring yer partner can bring ye pleasure too, intensifying it for ye." Shaking his head, he muttered, "And ye thought what ye experienced was mind-blowing. Wait until ye experience that."

Jess glanced at Raffaele uncertainly. "You mean it gets even better than what we . . . ?" The thought was almost frightening. Jess was quite sure that any more pleasure than he'd already shown her would kill her. Her heart wouldn't be able to take it.

"Not better," Raffaele said, glaring at Vasco, and then shifting his full attention to her, he explained, "Just different. The pleasure is shared between life mates. You experience your own pleasure, plus your partner's. So that when you are . . . performing acts on them," he said delicately, "you experience their pleasure as well."

"He's talking about gamahuche," Vasco said with disgust, and when Jess stared at him blankly, he frowned and admitted, "Well, that's an old term. Ye maybe never heard it. How about pearl diving? No?" He frowned when her expression remained blank, and then said, "Clam-lapping? Fish-licking? Eating the peach? No?" he said again, and frowned. "Damn me, this is—What about fanny-noshing? No? Dinner beneath the bridge? Mumbling in the moss? Tipping the velvet."

"Oral sex," Ildaria said with exasperation before the man could continue.

"Oh," Jess said with understanding, but the way Ildaria's mouth twitched as her eyes narrowed on her told Jess the woman knew she'd just been pretending not to understand to see how many outrageous ways the man had to describe going down on a woman. He had a lot of them, she noted, and wondered if that meant he was as good at it as Raffaele.

"Right," Vasco said with apparent relief. "That oral business."

"I see," Jess said primly, and then bit her lip to keep from laughing at his kerfuffled expression. Honestly, it was nice to not feel like the bewildered one for a change. Half of what he said went right over her head.

"Anyway," he said now on a sigh, "as ye know, yer choice is either to accept the Notte as a life mate. Or me," he added, glaring at Raffaele as if daring him to protest his including himself. "Or to refuse and reject us both and go on with yer life."

Jess nodded, but then noticed Zanipolo's troubled expression and the way everyone else was suddenly avoiding her eyes, and asked suspiciously, "Why do I have the feeling that means more than just my saying, 'No thank you,' and flying home?"

"Because ye're no son of a biscuit, lass," Vasco said quietly.

Hoping that meant she wasn't stupid, Jess raised her eyebrows. "So, what else does saying no mean?"

"It means that your memory would be wiped of everything having to do with me," Raffaele said quietly, and then corrected it to, "Us, really," as he gestured at the people around her.

Jess stilled. "Wiped? What is that?"

"What it sounds like," Raffaele said solemnly. "You would leave Punta Cana with some vague memory that you had a lovely time, but with no recall of myself, Zani, Santo, or any of the other immortals you've met here."

"Or immortals at all," Ildaria added quietly. "You wouldn't remember that we exist in the world. You could go back to feeling safe in your ignorance."

The way she said it told Jess that Ildaria had been poking in her mind again, because that was exactly what she'd been wishing for earlier. And Jess had meant it at the time. Or had thought she did. But, oddly enough, now that she knew that was possible, it wasn't looking so attractive. Not remembering having met Raffaele? Never remembering how good and kind and caring he'd been? Or how incredible sex with him had been? The very idea felt like someone was trying to wrench her heart out of her chest.

"Well, lass?" Vasco asked solemnly. "What'll it be?"

Panic claiming her, Jess stalled with questions. "Ildaria said that life mates can't read or control each other. Is that true?"

"Aye," Vasco answered.

"Yes," Raffaele assured her at the same time, and then smiled wryly, and added, "That's what makes life mates so special. Each one can be their own person. We can relax with each other, let our guard down, without fearing that someone will be poking in our thoughts. And, of course, not being able to control each other is a benefit as well."

"Why?" she asked.

"Because if the ability is there, so is the temptation to use it," he explained, and then seeming to realize that she didn't really understand, he continued. "Think of it. What if you were arguing with someone, and you were sure you were right, but they were stubbornly refusing to acknowledge that? Now imagine that same argument, but while you have the ability to just change their mind and make them see things your way? Could you resist doing it?"

Jess wanted to say yes, of course, but there were some pretty stupid people in the world, and she wasn't at all sure she *would* be able to just not take control and make them see things her way, which—right or wrong—she obviously believed was the right one.

"Having a mate you could control means winning every argument, because you can make them agree with you," Raffaele said quietly. "But it's as good as living alone, or with a blow-up doll. They would do what you want, when you want, because you make it so." He shook his head. "It's just better and healthier to have a real partner, one with thoughts and ideas of their own, and whom you can't control. It makes them special."

"Of course, life mate passion is a hell of a benefit too," Vasco reminded her, obviously feeling left out.

Jess smiled at him faintly, but asked, "Is it awful having to drink blood?"

"We don't exactly drink it," Raffaele said at once. "At least, not normally. Usually we feed from bagged blood, which is popped onto our fangs. They do all the work, without our ever having to taste it if we don't want to."

"Really?" she asked with relief, and thought the not-tasting-it part sounded good. Jess definitely didn't think she could ingest the blood if she had to drink it like tomato juice. Realizing the path her thoughts were taking, Jess shook her head and sat up straight. Was she really considering agreeing to be Raffaele's life mate and allowing him to turn her? Jess was pretty sure she was. At least, she couldn't seem to accept the idea of refusing him and having him wiped from her memory as if he'd never been in her life. And now that they had explained their origins, and convinced her that they weren't some evil, cursed demon race of beings who would steal her soul . . . But—

Raising her head, she asked Raffaele, "What if they're wrong?"

"Who?" he asked with confusion.

"The nanos," she explained. "What if I agree to be your life mate and it turns out we don't get along, or—"

"That won't happen," Raffaele assured her firmly, settling himself on the bed next to her and meeting her gaze solemnly. "I've lived a long time, and seen many, many life mate pairings, and not one of those pairings has been a mistake. I don't know how they do it, or if it's even really the nanos that do it, but once an immortal finds their life mate, it's never wrong. My own parents have been together for longer than I've been alive and are still very happy together, and my grandparents have been together since Atlantis."

"And you're sure that's what I am? That I'm a life mate for you?"

"Sì," he said solemnly.

"But how can you be sure?"

"Because I can't read or control you. Because we enjoy the shared pleasure. And because my appetite for food and sex has returned. All of those things together tell me that you are my life mate."

Jess wondered about the bit about his appetite for sex and food returning, but left it for now, and asked, "But then how can I be a possible life mate to Vasco too?"

Raffaele shifted his gaze to Vasco and then sighed. "It does not happen often, but sometimes a situation occurs where one person could be a life mate to two different immortals. It is always a difficult situation, and painful for the one not chosen. But a choice must be made."

"Or we could share her," Vasco said suddenly.

Jess glanced around with amazement at the suggestion. She hadn't even considered that. But didn't think she wanted to either. She'd come to like Vasco a bit now that she'd seen more of him than his delight with her tuzzy-muzzy and jugs. She even respected him for how he was trying to help the poorer immortals who couldn't afford the blood they needed, but not enough to spend a lifetime hearing him spout things like "*Let me grope for trout in your river, and gnaw on your jugs.*" She just couldn't do it.

"Or I could kill you," Raffaele said silkily.

Vasco raised an eyebrow. "Does that mean that sharing is out?"

When Raffaele glowered at him, he rolled his eyes and muttered, "No sense o' humor at all." Turning to Jess, he asked, "So, are ye agreeing to be this landlubber's life mate, or no?"

Jess bit her lip and tried to imagine it, and then her eyes closed as the possibilities slid over her. She could have all those things she'd told Ildaria and Vasco that she wanted with Raffaele. She could go to Italy with him, swim in his pool, see the buildings he'd designed, meet his family, both there and in Canada. And she could show him her home in Montana. They could watch action movies, and *Supernatural* and do crosswords, have crazy hot sex on tabletops, and against the wall . . . and dammit, she wanted that life, Jess admitted to herself, and opened her eyes to stare at Raffaele.

For a moment, that was all she did. She stared at him. Imagining seeing his face every morning when she opened her eyes, and every night before she closed them. And imagining the beautiful children he could give her, and then she smiled at him. That was all, just a smile. But it was enough.

"I'm guessing that's a yes," Vasco growled when Raffaele smiled back. But when she leaned toward Raffaele, Vasco barked, "Do not even think o' it, lass. In fact, get off me bed. Off, off, off."

"I was just going to give him a kiss," Jess said defensively as Raffaele stood and offered her his hand to help her up.

"Aye, and we all know where that would have led. I'd rather savor me memories o' you and me in that bed, without clouding them with this big ugly mug beside ye, thank ye very much," Vasco said dryly.

Jess felt the blush that heated her face, but she also felt Raffaele stiffen next to her, so she wasn't surprised when she turned to find him eyeing the pirate like he was something that he wanted to squish under his shoe. Or at least punch. Fortunately, they were all distracted when the phone chose that moment to ring.

The sound was so unexpected that Jess actually gave a start of surprise. Glancing around then, she saw Zanipolo pull a cell phone from his pocket and frown as he looked at the number showing.

"It's a local number," he said with bewilderment.

"Probably the Enforcers who were supposed to meet us," Raffaele said with disgust.

"You called the local Enforcers?" Jess asked with worry as she saw the glances exchanged between Vasco, Cristo, and Ildaria.

"Sì." Raffaele smiled wryly, his arm sliding around her shoulders as Zanipolo answered the phone. "Not that we needed them in the end. A good thing since they didn't bother coming out. They are probably calling to say they can't come."

Everyone stood silent and still as Zanipolo told whoever was on the other end of the line that everything was fine and their assistance was no longer needed. Noting his frown as he listened to the caller's response to that, Jess wasn't surprised when he ended the call and said with concern, "They were calling to see where we were. They're here in the harbor. I told them it was fine, and everything was resolved, but they're coming out to the boat anyway. They said there are things they need to take care of."

"Who said that?" Vasco asked, his voice hard.

"The Enforcers Lucian got the South American Council to send out," Zanipolo said, looking uncomfortable. "Miguel something."

"Villaverde," Ildaria breathed, paling.

"That's it, yeah. And a something-or-other Cardoso."

"Dieguito," Cristo muttered.

"That's it." Zanipolo nodded. "Dieguito. I've never heard the name before."

Cristo wasn't listening; he'd turned to Vasco. "Capitan—"

"I know," Vasco growled, and then sighed and ran a hand around the back of his neck before turning to Jess, Raffaele, and his cousins to bark, "Stay here. It will be safer for you not to get involved."

On that cryptic note, Vasco headed for the door. But when Ildaria and Cristo started to follow, he paused and blocked the woman's path. "Ye're not going, Ildaria. Stay here and out of sight," he ordered firmly. "I'll not see ye beheaded and burned today."

He waited just long enough for Ildaria to give a reluctant nod, and then led Cristo out of the cabin.

Sixteen

Jess watched the cabin door close behind Vasco and Cristo and then slipped out from under Raffaele's arm and crossed the room to Ildaria. The other woman was just standing in front of the door staring at it. Reaching her, she took her hands, concerned when she noted how cold they were. Beginning to chafe them, she asked quietly, "What did he mean he won't see you beheaded and burned today, Ildaria?"

Sighing wearily, Ildaria stared down at their hands and murmured, "I told you if the Council caught wind of my feeding on that *lamecharcos* Tyler before we were in international waters they'd execute me," she reminded her, and then shrugged unhappily. "Miguel and Dieguito are Enforcers. They basically do what the Council tells them."

"Yes, but I didn't tell the Council," Jess assured her, relaxing a little. "I didn't even tell Raffaele and his cousins."

Ildaria tugged her hands free and paced toward the desk, apparently too agitated to stand still. "The cousins would have read it from your memories."

Jess glanced toward the men, and knew at once from the guilty expressions on Zanipolo's and Santo's faces that Ildaria was right. The two men *had* read her mind. She scowled at them for it, and then moved toward Ildaria as the woman continued, unhappily. "And no doubt they mentioned what they learned to whoever they called at the Council. Otherwise Dieguito and Miguel wouldn't be here," she assured her.

"No," Zanipolo said at once when Jess glanced toward the men again. Grimacing, he admitted reluctantly, "We didn't tell the South American Council. We told Lucian, the head of the North American Council, and he probably told whoever he talked to at the South American Council."

Jess sighed with disappointment, knowing that meant that this Miguel and Dieguito probably *were* here to execute Ildaria. She scowled at the men for blabbing.

Santo and Zanipolo appeared uncomfortable, even guilty, under the look, but Raffaele frowned and moved to join her and Ildaria by the desk. Zanipolo and Santo immediately followed. She knew they weren't moving closer to hear better. With their nano-hearing, they'd heard fine from where they were. They were offering their support, and perhaps even help if they could. Jess nodded silently in acknowledgment, but then turned to Ildaria as the woman continued.

"Miguel, especially, wouldn't bother coming out unless he thought he had something that could be used to force Vasco back into the family fold. He is Vasco's brother," she told her grimly, but then moaned and muttered, "They'll threaten to execute me as a rogue unless he gets back in line and does what his father wants."

Jess shook her head with confusion. "I don't understand. Why would the Council send Vasco's brother out here to make him get back in line? Why would they care? Is his father on the Council or something?"

"His father *is* the Council," Ildaria said grimly. "There are others on it, but they're all in Juan Villaverde's pocket and vote whichever way he wants."

"I see," Jess murmured, and then asked, "And what does his father want Vasco to do?"

"Obey him, get out of his way, and stop raising a stink about the fact that he's charging such exorbitant fees for blood. But ultimately to make him stop helping the poorer immortals get blood with the shark feeding tours, so that they have to buy it, can't pay their rent or mortgages, and can be forced out of the area he wants to develop."

"Ah, jeez," Jess muttered with disgust. It always came down to money. It seemed immortals could be just as greedy and selfish as mortals.

"I do not understand," Raffaele said now. "Vasco thinks he is *helping* poorer immortals by going rogue and making them go rogue too?"

"He isn't rogue," Jess said patiently. "They only feed once they are in international waters. I guess Council laws don't reach that far?" she asked.

"No, it does not," Raffaele agreed, and then said, "So, he is taking poorer immortals out to international waters to feed because they cannot afford the blood because his father is—"

"Because his father is a corrupt *hijo di una hyena*," Ildaria snapped, slipping into Spanish in her upset.

Jess wasn't sure, but it sounded like she was calling the man a hyena or something. She didn't ask her to clarify, though. It didn't seem to be the moment. Jess didn't explain anything to Raffaele either. He seemed to have a grasp on the situation. Instead, she said, "We have to do something, Raffaele. It's our fault those men are here."

"Not entirely," he pointed out gently. "Ildaria was feeding on your friend Tyler before the ship was in international waters."

Jess glared at him. "I never told you that. It was plucked from my mind. What wasn't plucked, because I didn't know it at the time, is that Tyler deserved it."

"What?" Raffaele asked with disbelief, and she nodded firmly.

"He sexually assaulted Ildaria. She was just teaching him a lesson. One he didn't even remember afterward," she pointed out grimly. "Essentially, he got off scot-free, and she could be killed because he's a jackass pervert." Mouth tightening, she added, "That or Vasco will be forced to stop helping people to save her and then all those people, every crew member on this ship, will lose their homes and not be able to get the blood they need. All because his father is a selfish prick who wants to build something where they live." She fell silent then, her heart pounding and fury rushing through her veins, and then narrowed her eyes when she noticed the way Raffaele was looking at her. He was staring at her as if he'd never seen her before, she thought, and asked warily, "What?"

"I am just amazed at your fire, *cara*," he said with a smile. "You are beautiful when you are impassioned."

"Oh." Jess smiled crookedly, and then patted his arm. "That's sweet," she said, and turned to head for the door.

"Where are you going?" Raffaele asked with concern, but it was Ildaria who got to her first and grabbed her arm.

"Vasco said to stay here," the woman reminded her, trying to steer her away from the door.

"Vasco can't order me around," Jess told her calmly, and then spotting the determined expression on Raffaele's face as he approached, added, "And neither can Raffaele. I'm going to go see what I can do to fix this."

"Still glad she isn't a doll for you to control?" Zanipolo asked dryly as Jess headed for the door.

Jess glared over her shoulder at the man, but then glanced to Ildaria when she caught her arm, drawing her to a halt again.

"You can't fix this," Ildaria said firmly.

"Of course I can. I'll deny that I saw you feeding on anyone, or say it was in international waters," she assured her, tugging on her arm.

"Thank you," Ildaria said sincerely. "It is kind of you to want to help me, but that will not work. They can read your mind, little dove," she reminded her gently. "They'll know you are lying."

Jess stopped struggling and frowned, but couldn't just do nothing. She knew intellectually that it wasn't her fault if Zanipolo or Santo had read the memory from her mind and told someone. But emotionally she felt responsible. Besides, she was starting to like the woman, and she *had* been snooping when she'd walked into the galley. If she'd minded her own business, Ildaria wouldn't be in danger of being burned to death. Mouth firming determinedly, she asked, "Is there a way to stop them from reading my mind?"

Ildaria hesitated, and then said, "Repeating nursery rhymes in your head sometimes prevents their reading you, but you have to really concentrate on the words . . . And they can't read you if they can't see you."

"So, if I stand behind someone or something like that?" she asked.

"*Sí*. They wouldn't be able to read you then," she said, and Jess thought there was a touch of hope in her face now. It was enough to make her determined to do something.

Nodding, Jess patted Ildaria's hand gently, and then pried it off her arm. "Wait here. I'll see what I can do."

She headed for the door again, but was aware that Raffaele and his cousins were following. She was grateful to have them with her, but was very aware that they were leaving Ildaria alone to worry.

Raffaele moved up to Jess's side the moment they stepped out on deck. Clasping her elbow lightly, he glanced around as they paused to survey the situation. It looked as if every member of the crew was topside, except for Ildaria. The crew, men and women both, filled the deck, looking tense and troubled.

Vasco and Cristo were standing at the rail on the side of the ship, looking down at the water below, so that was the direction he steered Jess in. Although there wasn't really any steering necessary. She appeared determined to save both Vasco and Ildaria from the results of the woman's actions. Raffaele could sympathize. Normally, he would have left the matter for the local Council to deal with, but it was starting to sound like the Council here was corrupt, and a fair judgment wasn't guaranteed.

Since Jess was upset by the situation, and he felt somewhat responsible for instigating the call to the Council when Jess had been taken, he felt he should do something to help.

"What are you doing here?" Vasco's sharp voice drew his attention and Raffaele glanced to the man as they reached his side. He didn't bother to answer, however, but peered over the side of the ship to see that a sleek-looking motorboat with two men on board was just coasting to a stop next to the pirate ship.

"You should go below until we handle this, lass. This could be a bit tetchy," Vasco said grimly when Raffaele ignored him.

"I know. But we want to help," Jess said anxiously, trying to move up beside Raffaele to look over the side. He immediately caught her arm, and drew her back as he turned to face Vasco.

"Are either of these men older than you?" Raffaele asked, keeping Jess by his side.

Vasco grimaced. "Both are."

Raffaele nodded, and then urged Jess toward him. "Keep her back from the rail. They can't read her if they can't see her."

Nodding, Vasco took Jess by the arm. Careful, Raffaele noted, to grasp it on the sleeve rather than the bare skin. It was a small thing, but told Raffaele a lot. The man wouldn't try anything while she was in his care.

"If the men start to board the ship, take Jess below to your cabin, and stay there with her so you can't be read. You'd better go too, Zanipolo," he added, glancing at his cousin. "You're young enough to be easily read and you saw what was in her memory." He wasn't worried about Santo. He was old as hell and would not be easily read.

When his cousin nodded, he glanced to Vasco and added, "You'll want to make anyone younger than the two Enforcers, who know what happened with Ildaria and Tyler leave the deck too and stay out of sight."

"No one but Cristo knows besides Ildaria, myself, and Jess," Vasco said solemnly.

"But I'm older than both men," Cristo announced now. "They won't be able to read me."

"Good. Then if they come on board, tell them that Vasco is in his cabin trying to convince Jess to be his life mate and won't appreciate being interrupted."

"That won't stop them," Vasco said solemnly.

"Then I'll have to make sure they don't come on board," Raffaele said grimly, and turned to the rail.

"Raffaele?" Jess caught his arm, and he paused and turned back to glance down at her. Smiling crookedly, she said, "Thank you. Please be careful."

Raffaele smiled faintly back and bent to press a quick kiss to her forehead before turning back to the rail and swinging a leg over it.

"Don't worry about him," he heard Zanipolo say as he swung his other leg over and started to climb down. "Raffaele can kick ass with the best of them. He's spent half his life as a warrior of one description or another."

"What? Really?" he heard Jess ask with interest. She sounded impressed, he thought with a smile, and decided he couldn't wait to be able to actually tell her about himself and the adventures he'd had. More than what he'd been doing just the last decade or so. He suspected she'd enjoy the tale. He also suspected they'd have a lot more interesting adventures together in the future. He was looking forward to it.

"There was no need to climb down. We are boarding the ship."

Raffaele heard that announcement behind him as he drew level with the smaller boat, and ignored it as he turned and stepped on board. Nodding a silent greeting, he looked the two men over. He knew at once which one was Vasco's brother. The two men could have been twins. But while Miguel was older than Vasco, he was younger than Raffaele, who had no problem reading that the man really didn't want to be here. In fact, Miguel Villaverde would rather be working with his brother than against him. He abhorred what his father was doing, but felt he couldn't rebel like Vasco. It would leave their sister alone to deal with the old man. Until he could get her away from him, Miguel Villaverde was forced to act as an Enforcer for the corrupt old bastard. A job he hated, and one that made him feared by people who should be able to look to him for protection.

Deciding he wouldn't be a problem, Raffaele withdrew from his thoughts and turned to the other man. The moment he slipped into his mind, Raffaele loathed Dieguito Cardoso. Darkness and a sly intelligence pervaded his mind like a cancer. But there was also cowardice in there, Raffaele noted, and felt himself relax.

Withdrawing from the man's mind, he smiled widely and finally responded to the comment.

"I felt bad for dragging you out here for nothing," he said with a shrug. "So, I thought I'd save you further trouble and come down to you."

Miguel looked relieved, but Dieguito eyed him suspiciously and Raffaele felt a nudge in his mind. Ignoring it, he continued silently reciting "Old Mother Hubbard" in his head. It was a necessity to keep the younger immortal from reading anything he didn't want from his mind. Normally, Raffaele's advanced age would ensure that wasn't an issue. But all immortals were easily read after first meeting their life mates. Even ones as old as him.

"We were told Vasco had kidnapped an immortal's life mate," Dieguito said finally.

"Mine," Raffaele said with a wide smile that he couldn't have held back if he'd wanted. Jess had chosen him. He savored that for a minute and then turned his attention to the situation at hand, and said, "Unfortunately, I was mistaken. It seems she could be a life mate to Vasco too, and she came willingly. As I learned when I and my cousins gave up waiting for you and came out to the ship to get her ourselves."

"Vasco has met his life mate?" Miguel asked with surprise.

"No," Raffaele assured him. "He met a possible life mate, who is also my possible life mate and who I intend to claim and make my actual life mate."

"Oh," Miguel said, and frowned with concern.

"That's fine, but we were also told that Vasco's people were biting mortal tourists," Dieguito said now.

"Yes. They are," Raffaele agreed easily. "My cousin read that from my life mate's mind. Unfortunately, until we got here, he did not read further to learn that they do it in international waters. None of them are rogue."

"Well, then I suppose this was a wasted—" Miguel began almost eagerly, but was cut off by Dieguito.

"We'll need the girl to tell us that," Cardoso said firmly.

"No," Raffaele said mildly.

"What?" Dieguito asked sharply.

"I said, no," he repeated, dropping the smile as he added coldly, "Because that's not going to happen. I am not having my life mate interrogated. I have already passed on all relevant information. Unfortunately, Vasco is not a rogue, nor is anyone on his ship. I wish I could claim otherwise and have him burned alive to get him out of my hair. However, it would be a lie, and my life mate would not approve. So, I am stuck with the truth, and letting the bastard live." Pausing, he raised an eyebrow. "So? Are we done here?"

"No. I want to speak to—" Dieguito began.

"*Sí.* We are done," Vasco's brother said firmly, overriding Cardoso. The two men glared at each other briefly, and then Miguel turned to Raffaele and nodded. "Give my brother my regards."

Raffaele turned to climb back up the netting without responding. Agreeing to do that didn't seem like something he would have done after blustering about wishing the man dead.

He felt the men's eyes following him but didn't look back. He also continued to recite nursery rhymes until he heard the boat engine start and then fade away as the small motorboat moved off.

"You did it!" Jess cried, hugging him with relief the minute his feet landed on deck. "What did you say? How did you get them to leave?"

"He said I wasn't rogue, but he wished I was because then they could execute me and get me out of his hair," Vasco announced with amusement as Raffaele slid his arms around Jess to hug her back.

"You didn't!" she gasped, pulling back to look up at him with dismay.

"He did," Vasco assured her before Raffaele could respond. "And it worked. So, I am grateful. Thank you, Notte."

Nodding, Raffaele accepted the man's hand and shook firmly.

"But what about Ildaria?" Jess asked once they'd finished and stepped back.

"I told them the bite was in international waters and that Zanipolo just didn't read that part until we got out here on the ship," Raffaele explained quietly.

"So, you lied," Zanipolo said dryly. "And now I'm going to have to lie to back up *your* lie if Lucian or Uncle Julius ask me about it."

"And you will lie if necessary," Jess said firmly. "Otherwise, Ildaria could be executed and she only bit him because he attacked her. It wouldn't be fair if she ended up being punished because he wanted to rape her."

"Fine." Zanipolo held up his hands in defeat. "I'll lie," he assured her, and then turned to Vasco and said, "But you have to keep the perverts away from her. Next time she might not be lucky enough to get away with it."

"There won't be a next time," Ildaria announced, crossing the deck to join them. "I'm thinking it might be a good idea if I leave Punta Cana."

Vasco turned sharply at that news, and frowned. "That's not necessary, Ildaria."

"It is," she said solemnly. "That was the second time I retaliated when a tourist attacked me. I seem to be a trouble magnet. I don't want to risk there being a third and having it used against you. You've been too good to me, Vasco."

He frowned slightly, but asked, "Where will you go?"

She shrugged. "I don't know. America, or Canada, maybe."

"You should come to Montana," Jess said excitedly. "You could come stay with me while you look for a job and stuff. Or if you want to go to school, we could work something out."

"Really? You wouldn't mind?" Ildaria asked uncertainly.

"No, of course not. I inherited my parents' place and it's way too big for one person. Three of the bedrooms are empty. You can have your pick."

Raffaele was eyeing the two women with alarm when Vasco burst out laughing.

"Have fun, Notte," he said with amusement as the two women moved away, chattering excitedly. "Ildaria has a good heart, but she *is* a trouble magnet. And she doesn't have it in her not to retaliate if someone wrongs her."

Raffaele cursed under his breath and then glanced at the man. "Can we get that ride to shore now?"

"Of course," Vasco said, sobering. His gaze slid back to Jess, and then he sighed and glanced toward Cristo.

"I'll take them myself," Cristo said solemnly without waiting for him to ask. "There isn't enough room for all of them and two men to row."

When Vasco nodded, the man started over the rail to climb down to the rowboat.

"I think you're leaving."

Jess glanced around with surprise at Ildaria's comment, and saw that Santo and Zanipolo were disappearing out of sight over the side of the ship, and Vasco was moving toward them while Raffaele waited by the railing.

"I better go get your things," Ildaria said, slipping away as Vasco reached them.

"Oh, right," Jess said wryly as she recalled that Vasco had taken everything she had brought with her on this trip. Recalling that she'd also had a few choice words she'd wanted to give him on the subject, she turned to meet him now with a sour look.

Vasco raised his eyebrows at the sight of it. "What's got ye all a'twitter, lass?"

"You stole my stuff," she reminded him grimly.

"No," he assured her. "I was bringing them along so you wouldn't have to. I would never steal."

"You're a pirate, Vasco," Jess pointed out with sudden amusement at the claim. "It's kind of what you do, isn't it?"

He merely shrugged at that, and then grinned and said, "Ye're a fine one to talk. Ye're a better thief than me."

"Me?" she asked with amazement. "What did I steal?"

"The Notte's heart for one," he said lightly, and then added solemnly, "And mine."

When Jess simply stared at him, not sure what to say to that, a crooked smile curved his lips and he reached out to caress her cheek gently. "We could have been good together, lass. I'd have treated ye like a princess." His hand dropped away, as did the crooked smile. "Go on. There's no use waiting on your things. There isn't room in the rowboat for your luggage and all o' you too. I'll have one o' the men row it over and deliver it to the hotel later."

Jess nodded, but then hesitated, feeling like she should say something, but unsure how to apologize for not loving him, not even sure if she should.

Sighing, she simply reached out and squeezed his arm, then moved past him and toward Raffaele.

Epilogue

"Oh! I love this! Look, Jess."

Jess smiled at Caro's excitement. The woman was the wife of Raff's cousin Christian, and she was a doll, Jess thought as she leaned to the side and peered at the magazine page Caro was pointing to. Jess's eyes widened when she saw the dress that had excited the woman. A muted rose color, long, flowing, sleeveless, and with a V-neck, it was a beautiful gown that could be used by the bridesmaids for special occasions even after the wedding.

"Oh, yeah," she said with a smile, handing her the sticky pad. "Definitely mark that one as a finalist."

"I can't believe how pretty bridesmaids dresses have gotten," Lissianna said, shaking her head as she flipped through her own magazine. When Jess glanced to the blonde, who was a cousin to Raff by virtue of her mother, Marguerite, marrying his uncle Julius, the woman continued, "Jeez, I remember when they used to be these horrible poofy things in nasty colors that just screamed, *The bride is determined we all look ugly next to her in the wedding pictures.*"

"Oh, those are definitely still out there," Rachel, Lissianna's sister-in-law and another of Raff's new cousins, assured her. "Jess and I saw some in the bridal store. It's why she decided to look through magazines instead and order them."

"Will we be able to get them in time?" Jeanne Louise, yet another cousin through marriage, asked with concern. "I mean, the wedding is only three months away."

Jess grimaced. Jeanne Louise said that like it was just around the corner, but it seemed miles away to Jess. Which was kind of ironic when she'd squawked so much three months ago when Raffaele had insisted on marrying a year to the day from when they'd met. Knowing from helping with Krista's wedding that there was scads to get done for a wedding, the thought of managing one in six months had put her in a panic. But with all the help she was getting from his aunt Marguerite and his other relatives in Canada, as well as Ildaria in Montana, who had become a dear friend, her to-do list for the wedding was clearing up shockingly fast. The only reason the bridesmaids' dresses were even on the table still was that with everyone so busy it had been hard to get them all together at the same time, and there were several not here, including Ildaria who'd had to stay in Montana to work on a project for her Business course.

"We'll find something we can get here in time for the wedding," Lissianna said reassuringly. "Or we'll hire someone to make them. Mom knows a really great seamstress."

Jess smiled and glanced around at the women at the table. Her new family. Well, the Canadian branch of it. They were wonderful women. But then everyone she'd met so far through Raffaele was wonderful. It didn't make up for eventually having to give up her old family, but that was a ways off yet. She had a while before the fact that she wasn't aging would start to become obvious and she'd have to disappear. Ten years, Raffaele had said. Well, nine years and three months now, she supposed. The thought made her sad, but then she reminded herself that at least there wasn't a single Allison among these people.

"Jess!"

Everyone at the table paused and glanced at each other at that shout from Raffaele.

"Jessica!"

"Uh-oh," Rachel teased. "Sounds like there's trouble in paradise."

"Bet he just found out that you invited Vasco to the wedding," Lissianna said with amusement.

"No," Jess said with surprise. "How would he find out?"

"One of the guys," Caro said with a slow nod of certainty. "They just can't keep secrets."

"No, they can't," Jeanne Louise agreed on a sigh. "Honestly, they gossip worse than old women."

"Hmm." Jess frowned slightly, but just shook her head and picked up her tea as she waited for Raffaele to find her. It had been nine months since she'd agreed to be Raffaele's life mate, and they'd been together ever since. Literally together. They hadn't been apart for more than an hour or two since that day. Jess hadn't expected that. She'd thought they'd do the normal long-distance dating thing, and then move on to possibly one of them moving to live in the same country, and then moving in together, and marriage in whichever order it had come. But she hadn't been factoring in the shared pleasure life mates enjoyed. It was as addictive as heroin was purported to be, and neither of them had been able to tear themselves away from the other. Heck, they'd found it difficult to drag themselves out of bed for most of the first three months and they'd only got out then so that Raffaele could turn her. Or, at least, Raffaele had got out of the bed then.

The turning had been an experience she'd like to say she wouldn't soon forget, but she mostly had. While Jess had been told afterward that she'd screamed and thrashed in agony for three days during the turn, she didn't recall that. Whatever the drugs were that Rachel had given her had been amazing. The only thing Jess recalled of the turning were terrible nightmares and feeling hot. She hadn't told Raffaele that, though . . . something that came in handy at times like this. Guilt could be handy in an argument.

"Jessica."

Turning her head, she smiled sweetly at Raffaele's scowling face as he stormed into the kitchen. He really was upset. The man was seething with emotion, she noted with a slight frown, and watched him open his mouth, close it again, and then shake his head.

"What is it, love?" she asked, getting up to cross the room to him.

The moment she got close enough, he caught her hand and turned to head out of the kitchen, tugging her behind him.

"See you later," Caro called on a laugh.

"Have fun," Jeanne Louise added.

"Don't do anything I wouldn't do," Rachel teased.

"Take it to your room so we aren't tripping over you later," Lissianna shouted as Raffaele dragged her up the hall.

Jess heard Raffaele growl under his breath at the teasing, and bit her lip to keep from laughing as he dragged her upstairs and straight to the room they were occupying while here visiting his Aunt Marguerite and Uncle Julius.

Leading her inside, he pushed the door closed and then turned on her. He glared for a full minute, and then finally growled, "You did *not* invite Vasco to our wedding. You didn't. You just would not do that."

Jess hesitated, and then reached up to toy with the buttons of his shirt as she admitted soothingly, "Of course I did." When he opened his mouth to no doubt shout at her for it, she added quickly, "He was there at the beginning. He has to be at the wedding."

"He was there at the beginning, trying to bed you," he snapped.

Ignoring that, Jess added, "And he's the reason we met."

"Because I had to drag you out of a shark-infested ocean after you jumped ship to get away from him," he growled.

"And he fetched you back to the ship so you could explain about immortals."

"I was already at the ship," he said succinctly. "He probably saw me coming, and just set out in the boat so he could claim he was going to fetch me and look like a good guy."

"He helped you explain about immortals," she reminded him gently.

"And slammed me every chance he got, still trying to seduce you to agree to be his life mate, rather than mine," he ground out.

"And I want your aunt Marguerite to meet him and maybe find him a life mate so I don't have to feel guilty about being so happy with you," Jess said solemnly.

Raffaele opened his mouth, closed it, and then groaned and leaned his forehead on hers. "You're going to kill me, woman."

"Never," she assured him. "I love you too much."

A smile tugging at the corners of his mouth, he murmured, "I love you too."

Pulling back, Jess beamed at him. "Does that mean you're not angry anymore that I invited Vasco to the wedding?"

"Not quite," he said dryly.

"Hmm." Leaning into him, she let her lips hover by his as her hand drifted down to his groin, and then murmured against his mouth, "Perhaps if I showed you how much I love you?"

A groan sliding from his mouth, Raffaele claimed her lips, kissing her with a passion that hadn't waned a drop in nine months. Then he broke the kiss, and scooped her up into his arms.

"One of these times, that isn't going to work at easing my temper," he warned as he carried her to the bed.

"Impossible," she said with confidence.

"Yeah," he agreed on a sigh.

"You know he probably won't come anyway," she said as he laid her in the bed.

Raffaele froze, bent over her and arched an eyebrow before saying, "Yes, he will."

"Do you think so?" she asked dubiously.

"I know so," he assured her, easing onto the bed next to her before saying dryly, "He'll come just to get to look at you." Grimacing, he added, "Driving me crazy will be a bonus."

Jess laughed at the words, and cupped his face. Meeting his gaze, she said, "You shouldn't let him bother you. Just remember that you're the one I love and chose to be with, not him."

"And I am grateful for it every day," he told her solemnly before kissing her.

Do you love Lynsay's vampires?
If so, you do not want to miss her Highlanders!

Look for her next sexy
Scottish Highlander romance . . .

THE WRONG HIGHLANDER

Coming February 2019